Win a case of wine

courtesy of

Wines Direct in association with Poolbeg Press
have 2 cases of wine to give away to 2 lucky readers.

To celebrate the publication of *Behind Every Cloud*,
in which four strangers' lives are changed out of all recognition after meeting
at a wine course, we are giving away two cases of wine.

To be in with a chance of winning one of these cases of delicious wine
answer the question below, fill in your contact details
and send this page in an envelope to: *Behind Every Cloud* competition,
Poolbeg Press, 123 Grange Hill, Baldoyle, Dublin 13.

Q. Name one of Pauline Lawless's previous novels.

Answer: _____

Name: _____

Contact number: _____

Address: _____

E-mail: _____

Behind
Every Cloud
Pauline Lawless

POOLBEG

This novel is entirely a work of fiction. The names,
characters and incidents portrayed in it are the work of the
author's imagination. Any resemblance to actual persons,
living or dead, events or localities is entirely coincidental.

Published 2012
by Poolbeg Press Ltd.
123 Grange Hill, Baldoyle,
Dublin 13, Ireland
Email: poolbeg@poolbeg.com

A catalogue record for this book is available from the British Library.

ISBN 978-1-84223-506-5

Typeset by Patricia Hope in Sabon 10.5/14.1

Printed and bound by CPI Group (UK) Ltd, Croydon, CR0 4YY

www.poolbeg.com

About the Author

Pauline Lawless was born and reared in Dublin but spent her adult years in the midlands. This is her fourth book in as many years. Her previous three have all been bestsellers.

She has a Diploma in wine studies from the British Wine & Spirit Education Trust and lectured and ran courses for them in the midlands for many years. This is the background of her latest novel *Behind Every Cloud*.

She now lives between Belgium and Florida and enjoys playing golf and bridge and drinking wine with good friends.

Her previous novels, *Because We're Worth It*, *If the Shoes Fit* and *A Year Like No Other*, were also published by Poolbeg.

Also by Pauline Lawless

Because We're Worth It,
If the Shoes Fit
A Year Like No Other

Published by Poolbeg

Acknowledgements

To all those who helped me get this book on the road, a big thank-you. That includes the good people at Poolbeg Press: Paula, Kieran, Sara, Ailbhe and David, and also my editor, Gaye Shortland.

Thank you to Ciara, once again, for your proofreading, critique, sound advice and support. I couldn't do it without you.

To all the friends who have shared many a bottle of wine with me in the name of research for this book (that's my excuse and I'm sticking to it!), I look forward to sharing many more with you in the future. Foremost of these and special mention must go to the Alexanders of Gloster and of course, my beloved JM. A big thank-you also to my lovely friend, Annie Parham, for the great book party she threw for me in Florida. What a fun night we had!

To my fellow writers who give such constant help and encouragement, in particular Shirley Benton, Mary Malone, Elizabeth Jackson and Sheryl Browne.

I'm very grateful to Paddy Keogh of Wines Direct, Mullingar, Co. Westmeath for his generous donation of wine for the promotion of this book. I know whoever wins the competition will get great enjoyment from his wines.

Many thanks to Garda Damien Hogan of the Garda Press Office who so kindly and patiently answered the questions I had re Garda procedures.

Last, but not least, thanks to you the readers. I appreciate that you made my last novel *A Year Like No Other* a top bestseller. I hope you enjoy this book equally well and I look forward to hearing from you at **www.paulinelawless.com**.

For three dear friends who sadly passed
away in 2011 and are very much missed.

Bob Marsh

Mona Gay

Brigitte Risselin

1

Ellie Moran loved weddings despite the fact that she cried through most of them. She sat beside her mother now, tears rolling down her cheeks as she watched Kate Middleton walk down the aisle on her prince's arm. The new Duchess of Cambridge looked radiant and was positively glowing with happiness. Ellie dabbed at her eyes as she watched them come out of Westminster Abbey and wave to the cheering crowds. Ellie had taken the day off work from the beauty salon to watch the wedding on TV and she was loving every minute of it. Kate's dress was fabulous and, as for Pippa's – there were just no words to describe it. It was all so romantic and perfect. She sighed, reaching for another Kleenex.

Ellie had dreamed of being a bride ever since she was a little girl. Her favourite game back then had been 'getting married', when she would cajole her friends into taking turns to stand in as the groom. Ellie was always the bride, walking down the garden path, a bunch of daisies in her hand and her mother's discarded net curtains trailing behind her. She still dreamed of being a bride and had expected that she would by now have met her prince. Not a real prince like William, of course – but a dashing, handsome man who would sweep her off her feet and down the aisle for the most wonderful wedding imaginable. However, this was beginning to look more and more unlikely. She was twenty-three now and the only man in her life was David – not exactly the sweep-you-off-your-feet type!

He was an accountant and ten years older than Ellie. She'd met him in Gibneys pub in Malahide where she and her girlfriends went for a drink every Friday night. She'd noticed him there before – all the girls had. He was hard to miss with his height and dark George Clooney looks. Initially, she'd refused to go out with him thinking he was too old and mature for her, but eventually on her twentieth birthday, after far too much champagne, she'd caved in and agreed to go on a date with him.

To her surprise they got on well, although unfortunately he had none of the actor's famous sense of humour. However, he *was* very gallant and protective of her and treated her like a princess. Somehow he had grown on her and she felt comfortable with him. However, there was none of the *va-va-voom* that she had expected would happen when Mr Right came along.

She'd made it clear from the start that she did not want an exclusive relationship and that they would both be free to date others. David agreed to this and, although Ellie did go out from time to time with other guys, David stayed faithful to her alone. He was such a workaholic that she couldn't imagine how he'd find the time to date other women in any case. Most of the men she met in pubs and clubs were interested only in beer, football and sex, not necessarily in that order. Not exactly prince material! Eventually she'd given up on them and now she and David were considered a couple. She'd begun to accept that *va-va-voom* was the stuff of romantic novels and films. They'd settled into a comfortable relationship. She did, however, continue to go drinking and clubbing with the girls on a Friday night, but more for the *craic* than in the hope of meeting 'the one'.

"I do hope they'll be happy," Ellie's mother, Marie-Noelle, said to her in French, as they watched the royal couple drive along the Mall in the magnificent carriage.

Marie-Noelle had been born to French parents who had both sadly died in an accident shortly before her marriage. They'd left France as a result of a family feud and moved to Ireland where she'd been born. She'd been raised speaking French and she in turn had always spoken French to her two daughters, wanting them to know of their heritage. She had sent them to a school run by an order of French nuns and as a result both Ellie and her sister, Sandrine, were now bi-lingual.

"Of course they'll be happy. It's all so romantic," Ellie replied, as she watched the newly married couple wave to the crowds.

Marie-Noelle looked at her youngest daughter with concern. Ellie was so trusting and soft-hearted that people often took advantage of her. She tried to please everyone and was a sucker for lost causes. As a child she'd constantly arrived home with stray kittens, dogs and even a couple of birds with broken wings. She couldn't pass a beggar or collection box without helping out. She was so naïve and such a hopeless romantic that Marie-Noelle worried about her.

The same couldn't be said of her older daughter,

Sandrine, now an accountant, who had bossed poor Ellie mercilessly all her life. A hard-nosed career woman, intent on making her way in the world of finance, Sandrine had no time for such nonsense as romance and love. Marie-Noelle had no fears that anyone would try to take advantage of Sandrine. Let them just try, she often chuckled to herself. No, Ellie was the one she worried about most.

"It takes more than romance and a fairytale wedding to make a marriage work, you know," she said now.

Ellie had never thought much further than the wedding. She was in love with the *idea* of getting married. She'd never much considered what came after the ceremony. She hoped fervently that the royal couple would live happily ever after, as they always did in fairytales, if not necessarily in real life.

"David has booked a table in Bon Appetit for this evening, to celebrate," Ellie told her mother. She'd been surprised and delighted when he'd suggested it as he'd shown absolutely no interest in the wedding up to that point.

"That's very nice of him. He'll make some girl a wonderful husband someday," Marie-Noelle remarked, looking slyly at her daughter.

"*Mmmm*," Ellie replied nonchalantly. "How about a cup of tea?" She jumped up, not wanting to continue with this conversation.

"Lovely," Marie-Noelle replied, aware that she'd hit on a touchy subject. "I have some chocolate éclairs in the fridge. Let's have them now."

When they arrived at the restaurant that evening, Ellie was surprised to find that David had ordered a bottle of champagne.

4

"How fabulous!" she exclaimed, pleased with this romantic gesture.

The wine waiter poured it and handed her a glass. He was grinning like a Cheshire cat and she noticed that David was beaming inanely too. As they clinked glasses she spotted something in the bottom of hers.

"I think there's something in my glass," she said, peering into it, afraid it might be a piece of broken glass.

"There is indeed," David replied, seemingly not too worried.

Ellie looked more closely and gasped aloud. She couldn't believe her eyes. There at the bottom of the glass was a glittering diamond ring. She fished it out and looked up at David enquiringly.

"Will you marry me, Ellie?"

She looked at him disbelievingly.

"As today was such a special day for you, I thought it might be a good time to ask you to be my wife. Please say yes."

Ellie was a great believer in fate and if this wasn't fate – being proposed to on the day of the Royal Wedding – then she didn't know what was.

She was deeply touched and her heart went out to him. He hadn't exactly swept her off her feet but she did love him, and this was so romantic. It was the most romantic thing that had ever happened to her. She burst into tears.

"Please say yes," he begged, taking her hand in his, a worried look in his dark eyes.

"Oh yes, David, yes," she answered him, smiling through her tears.

Reaching across the table, he put the ring on her finger and kissed her as the other diners in the restaurant, aware of what was happening, broke into a round of applause.

She smiled back at them. She held her hand out in front of her to admire the ring. It was the biggest diamond she'd ever seen. Obviously she'd seen photographs of massive knuckledusters on celebrities like Maria Sharapova and Kim Kardashian but never one as big as this in real life. It was fabulous!

"David, it's beautiful. Exactly what I would have chosen myself," she told him, her eyes shining as she moved her hand this way and that.

"I'm glad you like it, darling."

"I can't believe it. It feels like a dream."

"It's not a dream," David replied. "Any time you doubt it, just look at your ring." He smiled at her fondly.

"It's beautiful. Thank you, David." She kissed him again, thinking how handsome he was. She knew she was a lucky girl.

David was happy that Ellie had agreed to be his wife. They'd been together three years and he reckoned it was time they named the day. For a moment there, when she'd burst into tears, he'd been afraid that she was about to say no.

He'd been with his brother in Gibneys the first night he'd set eyes on her. She had the face of an angel and was, without doubt, the most enchanting woman he'd ever seen. She had luminous, almost translucent, skin, which glowed with freshness. Her eyes were a very unusual violet blue under long dark curly lashes and her mouth was a perfect cupid's bow which gave her a very sweet smile. Her long, dark, glossy hair swung as she spoke animatedly and he was instantly smitten and longed to get to know her.

He found himself back in Gibneys every Friday night after that and to his delight she was always there, with the same two friends. For a couple of weeks he watched her surreptitiously, wondering how best to approach her. She had an innocent and vulnerable air about her that made him long to take care of her and protect her. When eventually he screwed up the courage to ask her out, she'd turned him down. He was gutted but he persevered and finally won her over. Now this beautiful girl had agreed to marry him, making him a very happy man indeed.

Ellie was on cloud nine all the following day. Her parents were delighted for her and everyone in the beauty salon where she worked congratulated her on hearing the news. She received many envious glances from both staff and clients when they saw the stunning ring she was sporting. They all tried it on, *ooh-ing* and *aah-ing* as it sparkled in the lights. Ellie was on a high and unprepared for the avalanche of cards and engagement presents that flooded in during the following weeks. She felt like a real princess. It was all so exciting.

She couldn't wait to be a bride!

2

Wednesday was 'Pamper Rachel Day'. This was the one day of the week that Rachel Dunne kept solely for herself. Every other day was manic, a whirlwind of committee meetings, charity lunches, formal dinners and all the other functions that the glamorous wife of a successful politician had to perform. But she tried hard to keep Wednesdays free. She needed this day for herself. This was the day when she recharged her batteries and chilled out. She also needed it to maintain the glossy appearance that was the envy of all the women she encountered. She, more than anyone, knew the effort it took to look good all the time, so this one day per week was essential to her well-being.

She dropped the children – Jacob who was almost eight and Becky who was six – to school in her BMW X6 before heading into Dublin city. She hummed to herself as she pulled away from the private school, waving to the other mothers who looked enviously after her.

Even though things had taken a terrible downturn in Ireland, they luckily hadn't affected her or her family. Her husband, Carl, had been very savvy with his money, unlike many of their friends who had lost everything in the Celtic Tiger crash. Now he was riding high as a newly elected TD – or 'Member of Parliament' as Rachel jokingly called it – and everyone predicted that he was destined for higher things.

Rachel parked the car in the RAC car park and strolled down Dawson Street to the beauty salon on South Anne Street where she was a favoured client. The owner greeted her effusively and the other clients in the waiting room, recognising her, smiled warmly at her.

Now that Carl was a public figure, her photograph featured constantly in the newspapers and society magazines. She and Carl were *the* new glamorous young couple in Irish politics and she was still trying to come to terms with this new-found fame and the attention that went with it. It was ridiculous really but people treated her differently now that she was a recognisable face. She was still the same person after all.

She was whisked immediately into the luxurious inner sanctum where she succumbed to the tender ministrations of Chantal, the masseuse.

Utterly relaxed as she lay on the bed, lulled by the soft music and candlelight, she felt the stress drain away. She was constantly being told how lucky she was to have such a wonderful life and she *was* grateful for her blessings, but it wasn't all quite the plain sailing people thought it was.

Rachel was the only child of wealthy parents and had indeed sailed through her early years, admired and petted, lacking for nothing. Nothing, that is, except siblings, which she had wanted very badly, but the idea of which her parents had refused to contemplate. She had worried that it was because she was a disappointment to them that they didn't want another baby. She had a lonely childhood and envied her friends who had sisters and brothers.

She was very beautiful and no one was surprised when, shortly after she left college, she attracted the attention of the successful, debonair, ambitious Carl Dunne. He came from a middle-class family and had worked his way up from nothing to become a big player in the lucrative property market of the Celtic Tiger years. He had made a lot of money during the boom times and was one of the few clever enough not to overstretch himself and to get out before things started to disintegrate. As a result he was financially sound and that, coupled with her father's money, meant that Rachel would never want for anything in the future. As a wedding present her father had built her a beautiful house on Howth Hill, overlooking Dublin Bay.

Their wedding had been *the* social event of the year. Rachel first saw him as he was running with windblown hair along the beach in Marbella, where her parents owned a villa. It was love at first sight. He was tall and broad-shouldered with shoulder-length dark-blond hair and twinkling blue eyes. His body was tanned and athletic and he exuded an energy and charisma that was irresistible. With his good looks and easy charm Carl seduced everyone he met, and Rachel was no exception. And she easily ensnared him. She had long honey-blonde hair which shimmered like silk and, together with her olive skin and soft dark-brown eyes, made for a stunningly attractive woman.

Rachel had always been on the skinny side of slim but the birth of her two children, in quick succession, had given her new curves. Carl said it made her more voluptuous and she wondered if he was just being kind.

Of course she would need to be extra careful with her diet now – what with all the functions they had to attend. She had no intention of letting herself go like so many of the women in public life had done.

Together she and Carl made a very handsome couple and were much in demand at all the smartest parties and now that he had become involved in politics, well, the world was their oyster. They had moved onto the national stage and Carl was in his element, enjoying every moment of it. Rachel was not enjoying it quite as much. She felt they had become public property and he was hardly ever home, now that he had so many demands on his time.

Of course, her life before politics had not all been plain sailing. When a man was as good-looking, sexy and charismatic as Carl, it was inevitable that there would be women throwing themselves at him. And Rachel knew her husband was no saint. He had a voracious sexual appetite and she'd suspected for some time after Becky was born that he was not being faithful to her. However, she'd turned a blind eye in the hope that she was wrong but, when she'd accidently caught him out (thanks to Tiger-Woods-type texts on his phone), she could no longer ignore it and the shit had hit the fan. What had hurt most was the fact that the woman in question was a neighbour whom Rachel had considered to be her best friend.

She'd thrown him out of the house and threatened to divorce him and take the children with her. An abject and penitent Carl had begged and pleaded with her to reconsider and had sworn that it would never happen again. Rachel still loved him madly and wanted more than anything for her marriage to work, so eventually she'd forgiven him. Needless to say she'd never spoken to the other woman again.

Carl loved the cut and thrust of politics and she hoped that this new interest would keep him fully occupied with no time for dalliances. Rachel knew that he knew it would hurt his new career if he were to be caught up in any scandal. She figured that this would keep him on the straight and narrow.

Rachel left the salon three hours later, feeling alive and rejuvenated. She tripped lightly along towards her favourite restaurant, One Pico. The owner welcomed her warmly and she was aware of the looks and whisperings of other diners who recognised her. She ordered a Caesar Salad – no croutons, and dressing on the side – and a half bottle of wine, relying on the wine waiter to suggest a good one. She wished she was more knowledgeable about wine but, even though she loved it, she found it all a bit confusing and intimidating. She decided to buy a book on the subject that very afternoon.

After lunch she made her way to her hair salon in South William Street for her weekly hairdo. With her hair newly washed, conditioned and straightened, she headed to Brown Thomas to check out the latest collections. Now that she had to accompany Carl to so many functions she seriously needed to update her wardrobe. It annoyed her that people expected her never to wear the same outfit twice. Who could possibly afford that? Even Kate Middleton was to be seen reprising her dresses. Still, Rachel knew she did need to invest in some new clothes. She bought a beautiful royal-blue Diane Von Furstenberg wrap-over dress and a Michael Kors leather jacket, which fitted her like a glove.

On her way back to the car she stopped by Sheridan's cheese shop and bought a selection of their fabulous cheeses. On the spur of the moment, she popped into

Hodges Figgis bookshop and headed to the wine section. She was flabbergasted at the sheer number of books on the subject and in the end settled for one by Oz Clarke. She'd seen him on television and he'd seemed to be passionate about his wine but not too stuffy and serious.

Driving home, she looked forward to the evening ahead with pleasure. Every Wednesday afternoon Rachel's mother collected Jacob and Becky from school and they stayed with her and their grandfather in Kinsealy overnight. This suited everyone. Her parents got to spend time with their grandchildren whom they spoiled rotten. The kids loved it and it gave Rachel and Carl at least one night alone together every week – well, it *had*, until he'd been elected a TD. Now he held clinics for his electorate every Wednesday in Baldoyle, Sutton and Howth. However, he'd promised to be home by ten thirty every week and he hadn't let her down yet.

Although she adored the kids, she had to admit she loved the freedom that came with just her and Carl in the house for the night. The nanny, Paloma, also had Wednesdays off and wouldn't return until lunchtime on Thursday so they had the whole house to themselves. Often they made love on the floor in front of the fire, in the shower, or even, Rachel blushed at the thought, on the dining-room table. With no chance of a little one or a nanny interrupting things, they could be as uninhibited as they pleased.

Arriving home, Rachel changed into her red silk pyjamas and took some slivers of the delicious cheese and a bottle of Merlot into the den. Curling up on the sofa, she opened Oz Clarke's book and started to read. She became so engrossed in it that the hours flew by and it was Carl's key turning in the lock that brought her back to reality. Goodness gracious, she thought, could it be that time already? Guiltily, she realised that she had almost finished the bottle of wine completely. Closing the book, she got up to greet her husband.

"Someone's been drinking, I see," he said, kissing her wine-stained lips. "None left for me?"

"Sorry, darling. I bought a wine book and just got lost in it." She twined her arms around his neck.

"Oh, so you're just following their instructions, is that it?" he teased. "Well, let me open another bottle and you can educate me." He released her and headed for the wine rack.

"Seriously, it's fascinating," she told him, pouring the little left in the bottle into her glass and draining it in one gulp. "I never realised that wine could be so interesting."

"Oh, I've no doubt it is. They actually run wine courses now." He began to open another bottle of Merlot. "I saw a poster tonight for one starting in Clontarf soon. Maybe you should consider joining?" He poured a glass of wine for himself.

"Gosh, that sounds super. Where and when?" she asked, holding out her empty glass to him so that he could refill it.

"I don't remember. You'd better ring Graingers in Baldoyle to find out." He refilled her glass. "That's where I saw it. They'll give you the details."

"I'll ring them tomorrow," she promised, taking a sip and moving closer to him.

He chatted about the people he'd met that evening, entertaining her with his usual witty observations. She told him about her day and what she'd read in Oz Clarke's book. Draining his glass, he nuzzled her neck then slipped his hand inside her top. All thoughts of wine disappeared as she enjoyed the sensation of his hand caressing her nipples. She felt quite uninhibited and more than a little drunk. The bottle of Merlot was left unfinished as they made love on the sofa and then wound their way up the stairs where they started all over again.

The following morning Rachel rang Graingers and got the number for the wine course, which she then dialled. She crossed her fingers, hoping that the course would not be on a Wednesday. She was in luck. A very nice guy, who said his name was Sam, told her that they would be starting the first week in June and it would be held on Monday nights. That suited her perfectly as Carl held his clinic for the other part of his constituency on a Monday. Great! She got the details from Sam and enrolled on the spot, promising to send a cheque in the post.

Satisfied, she prepared to go to the charity luncheon for the Rape Crisis Centre. Things were really tough now for charities in Dublin and Rachel tried to support them whenever she could, but she had to be selective and prioritise or otherwise she'd have had to go to at least three luncheons not to mention dinners every single day. People didn't realise how difficult life could be for a politician's wife. Everybody wanted a piece of her husband and sometimes she feared that there would be nothing left for her. She saw less and less of him since he'd taken office and lived life constantly in his shadow. She hadn't been prepared for the multiple demands on her time either, but she took her responsibilities very seriously. Luckily she had Paloma and Olga, the housekeeper, who came in every morning to keep things on the home front running smoothly. Otherwise she couldn't imagine how she would have coped. She knew that she led a privileged life in comparison to the hardships many other women suffered. She appreciated that, but it brought with it its own problems.

She posted the cheque to Sam, for the wine course, on her way to the lunch.

3

Ronan McIntyre was searching in the wardrobe of the spare room for his old running shoes. He thought that he might take up running again now that the evenings were so much brighter. He didn't find them but what he did find shocked him to the core. He pulled out at least ten bags with the names Brown Thomas, A Wear, Next, Gap and Coast artfully scrawled across them. His heart sank and he dropped on to the bed, his head in his hands. His wife, Louise, had promised him that she'd cut back on her shopping. She knew the company he worked for was in a perilous state and that his job might be on the line very soon, but she was still spending with no thought of the future. He emptied the bags on the bed. Shoes, handbags, jeans, dresses, tops, all came tumbling out. He looked at them in despair. She must have had at least a hundred pairs of shoes, some she'd never even worn, not to mention about fifty bags, but still she bought, bought, bought. He knew without a doubt that it was an addiction. When it had first started she'd tried to explain to him that it was the thrill of acquiring something new that she loved – not whether she needed it or indeed would ever even wear it. He didn't understand it but he'd been as generous as he could afford to be with her, hoping it would help with her depression. Now, years later, she was still shopping but the problem had escalated rather than gone away.

For a long time he'd never discussed it with anyone, feeling that it was just between them and that it would be disloyal to Louise to reveal it to an outsider. Last year, however, he'd finally confided in his brother, Conor, who had three children and was happily married to Betty, an exemplary wife, not given to spending her husband's wages on one shopping spree. Conor was at a loss to understand Louise's problem and could offer him no advice. There was no one else Ronan could discuss it with.

Things were so bad in this post-Celtic-Tiger Ireland, that they'd already taken a pay-cut and lived every day in fear of losing their jobs. There was not much call for draughtsmen these days with building sites standing idle all over the country. What would happen to him if the firm closed down? Ronan couldn't even begin to contemplate the possibility. His mortgage was so high that the chances were they would lose their house, which was already well into negative equity.

Ronan was feeling desperate. He could feel the blood pounding in his temples. This couldn't go on. Her spending would have to stop, but how could he get this through to his shopaholic wife?

Louise knew the moment she saw his face that he had found her secret stash. She geared herself for a confrontation.

"Louise, when did you buy this stuff?" he asked her, throwing one of the dresses on the table.

"Oh, ages ago," she replied nonchalantly. "They were

17

reduced to nothing in the sale. They were practically giving them away." She continued grilling the steaks, not looking at him.

He turned on his heel and went into the living-room for his laptop. Going online he accessed his credit-card account and sure enough there it was. A list of purchases, all made the previous Friday in Dublin city. He blanched when he saw the final figure. How on earth would they pay this?

Returning to the kitchen, he walked to the cooker and turned Louise around to face him. He was shaking with fury.

"Giving them away?" he cried, grabbing her arms. "You spent over five hundred euro in one day! Where do you think the money will come from to pay this bill? We're already up to our eyes in debt, thanks to you!"

"Don't get your knickers in a knot." She wrenched away from him, her green eyes flashing. "It's on the credit card. We won't have to pay for ages."

"You really don't get it, do you?" he cried, white with anger. "*We – just – cannot – afford – it!*" He realised he was shouting and tried to calm down. He wanted to shake her to get this into her head but he let her go. He had never raised a hand to her in all their fifteen years of marriage and he wasn't going to start now. His own fury shocked him. He was normally a quiet, gentle man.

"Louise, this can't go on," he said, slumping down in a chair. "I just can't take it any more."

"Oh, for God's sake, you're overreacting," she snapped, putting his dinner on the table. "Everyone says that the recession is over and things are on the up again."

"Not in our business, they're not. Besides, even if I don't lose my job – which I possibly will – I still cannot afford to have you spending like this."

"You're a cheapskate!" she cried, rushing from the room, her long auburn hair flying behind her.

He looked down at the plate of steak and onions in front of him and suddenly he had no appetite for it. He pushed it away. She was being very unfair. He'd always been very generous with her. How could he get her to realise the seriousness of the situation?

Now her addiction was in danger of wrecking their marriage beyond repair. Not that their marriage had been in great shape for quite some time. The love and joy had gone out of it and they were constantly bickering. It was very difficult to be loving and joyous when you were constantly worrying about money. He was at the end of his tether now and he knew it was affecting his health. The doctor had warned him to avoid stress but it was all very well for *him* to say that. *He* wasn't in debt or in danger of losing his job and perhaps even his house, or to top it off – married to a shopaholic!

Ronan sighed. He would have to try and find someone who could help Louise. But where could he turn for it? He decided to have another chat with Conor at the weekend. Maybe this time he'd confide in Betty. She might know someone who could help.

The following Saturday was Ronan's thirty-ninth birthday and they'd been invited to Conor and Betty's for dinner. He'd warned Louise that he didn't want a birthday present. God knows how much she would have splurged on that! She had been giving him the silent treatment since the row but he'd thought that as it was his birthday she'd relent and at least wish him a happy birthday. No such luck! It was going to be very embarrassing at Conor's if they were still not talking.

After a silent cold-war breakfast, Ronan decided that he might as well go and play a round of golf. When he came home that afternoon, Louise was out.

Please God, let her not be out shopping, he prayed.

She arrived in after six, no bags in sight, thank God.

"You do know we're expected at Conor's for dinner at seven," he reminded her.

"I'm not going," she replied, the first words she'd spoken for three nights.

"We can't cancel at the last minute just like that." He could feel his blood pressure rising yet again.

"It's okay. I rang Betty and told her I didn't feel well," she said sullenly. "I said you'd be going alone. She understood."

He looked at her sadly, shaking his head. She'd obviously made up her mind.

"Fine, if that's how you want it."

At least he'd get a chance to talk to his sister-in-law about his problems now.

"Happy birthday, old boy!" Conor greeted him with a hug. "Next year's the biggie, eh? My God, forty! That's seriously old!" Grinning broadly, he clapped him on the back.

He was one year younger than Ronan and never let him forget it. They were so alike that people had often taken them for twins. Both were very tall and slim with similar dark hair, although Ronan's was a tad longer. Their grey eyes held a warmth and gentleness that was reflected in both their characters. However, more than anything else it was the graceful way they moved that confirmed, even to those who did not know them, that they were brothers.

"Yeah, that'll be you in two years' time!" Ronan punched him playfully.

"Happy birthday, love!" Betty joined them in the hall, kissing her brother-in-law warmly. She was small and a little plump – unlike the tall, slim Louise – with a kind happy face that was always smiling. It was obvious Conor adored her.

Their three children came bounding down the stairs. "Happy birthday, Uncle Ronan!" they chorused, almost strangling him with hugs.

He laughed at their enthusiasm. "Mercy, mercy!" he cried, untangling himself. He proffered the bag of goodies that he always brought for them and they pounced on it greedily.

"Now, kids, no chocolate before dinner," Betty said sternly, whipping the bag away before they could protest.

"Back upstairs while I give poor Uncle Ronan a drink to revive him," Conor said, ruffling the hair of his youngest son, Myles.

They scampered away and Ronan looked after them fondly. How he wished he'd had kids of his own. He envied Conor his lovely family more than anything. How different this house was to his own! He tried not to dwell on it too much.

Conor opened a bottle of champagne and poured them each a glass.

"Happy birthday again, big bro!" he said as they clinked glasses. "We're sorry Louise couldn't make it. What's the matter with her?"

Ronan pursed his lips. "Nothing physical. We've had a dreadful row. I'll explain all after dinner. Let's not spoil the evening so early on."

Conor and Betty glanced at each other knowingly and then at Ronan, sympathy in their eyes. They'd guessed it was something like that when Louise had cried off. They'd known for quite some time that things were not going well in that marriage. It made them appreciate all the more how

21

very lucky they were. Conor patted Betty's hand before getting up and taking an envelope off the mantelpiece.

"Your birthday present," he smiled, as he handed it to his older brother.

Ronan opened it, wondering what it could be. He slid out a gilt-edged card, which read:

CHÂTEAU WINES
GIFT VOUCHER
Eight-week Wine Course

"Wow, that's fantastic! Thank you both so much!" He beamed at them, kissing Betty and hugging Conor. "Something I've always wanted to do." He read the rest of the details on the card.

"You just have to ring them and they'll tell you when and where," Conor explained, pleased with Ronan's reaction.

"Just what I need right now," Ronan said with a grimace. "Escapism!"

Conor didn't say more, knowing that Ronan would elaborate in his own good time.

Betty went off to dish up the dinner, calling for the children to wash their hands and come down to the table.

Betty was a good cook and the meal was delicious but it was the loving warmth around the table that pleased Ronan the most. Amid the banter he could feel the love that enveloped them all. When they'd finished, the three kids asked to be excused and the adults were left alone.

"That was wonderful, thanks, Betty," Ronan said as she cleared his dessert plate away.

When she went to fetch the coffee Conor couldn't contain his curiosity any longer. "Well, do you want to tell me what's wrong with Louise now?" he asked gently.

Ronan leaned back in his chair. "Same old problem – her shopping! She's spending like there's no tomorrow and if she doesn't stop she'll bankrupt me."

Betty came in with the coffee and caught the end of that remark.

"Oh, dear! Is she still shopping as much as ever?" she asked. Then seeing Ronan's expression, she blushed. "Sorry, but Conor did tell me last year about your problem."

"Sorry, Ronan," Conor said, "you know I can't keep anything from Betty. We have no secrets. I told her in confidence and she would never have repeated it, so no one else knows."

"It's okay. I wanted to ask your advice anyway, Betty. Do you know if there's a Shopaholics Anonymous anywhere here in Dublin. I tried to Google it but with no success."

He looked so downhearted that Betty wanted to take him in her arms. What a dreadful problem. That Louise was a silly thing. Betty had never had very much time for her.

"I don't know of any such thing myself but I'll certainly make enquiries of my friends." Then, seeing the look of panic on his face, she added, "Don't worry. I won't mention who it's for."

"Please don't. I don't want everyone in Raheny to know and be talking about it."

"Don't worry, dear, I'm the soul of discretion." She patted his hand. He relaxed, knowing that he could trust her to keep her word.

"How bad is the problem? I've never come across it myself but I have read about it," Betty said sympathetically. "It's an addiction, I think, a bit like gambling."

"Yes, once she starts she can't seem to stop. She buys things that she never even wears. It's the act of buying that she craves." Ronan ran his fingers through his hair. "I don't understand it at all but then I don't understand gamblers either. All I know is that it has to stop before she ruins us financially." He shook his head in bewilderment.

"Oh dear! How often does she go on a spree and how much does she spend at a time?"

"It's been escalating. It can be as often as every week and can be as much as €500."

"Holy God!" Betty exclaimed in a shocked voice, putting her hand to her chest. "That's dreadful!"

"You can't sustain that," Conor chipped in angrily.

"Don't I know it! I'm really at the end of my tether."

"Have you actually sat down and talked to her about it?" Betty asked.

"In the beginning, I did, and she promised she'd try and curb it but she can't help herself. Now she won't discuss it at all and we end up arguing all the time."

"You poor thing," Betty commiserated. "Leave it with me. I'll try and find out if there's any help out there. There must be."

"I'd appreciate that. And please, not a word to Louise. She'd be mortified if she thought I'd told you." Ronan smiled wanly.

"Of course not." Poor man, Betty thought, looking at him closely. He's aged a lot in the past two years. I'm not surprised. She looked at her husband. They no longer looked like there was only a year between them. Conor now looked five or six years younger than Ronan – *and* he had three growing boys to contend with. She smiled fondly at him, thinking as she always did, how very lucky she was.

4

Ellie's new fiancé had recently been head-hunted by the most important accountancy firm in Dublin and he was over the moon about it. But he was quite nervous when, after their engagement, he and Ellie were invited to dinner at his new boss's house.

As she got ready for the dinner Ellie was excited but also a little apprehensive. She didn't want to let David down. She cast a critical eye over her reflection in the mirror. She was wearing her new hyacinth-blue Karen Millen lace dress which she had bought the previous Sunday, especially for the occasion, and she prayed that it would pass muster. It matched her blue eyes perfectly, making them look almost violet.

Ellie was a fashionista of the highest order but most of her clothes would have been too short, too revealing or just too trendy for the evening ahead. She did a last-minute check. Her teeth were a dazzling white thanks to the whitening treatment they'd undergone the previous Monday. She hoped her fake tan was not too much. Her friend and colleague, Chloe, had stayed back late last night to do it, and had been given dire warnings not to make it too bronze. Chloe was great and had understood exactly how important this night was for Ellie. She'd also applied fabulous gel nails with tiny diamond stars painted on them. They complemented her engagement ring which she now waved in front of her for the umpteenth time, admiring the way the large diamond caught the light. David had really chosen well. He had such good taste. The ring was perfection and she loved it.

Ready at last, she exited the messy room, her sleek dark hair swinging behind her. It had been carefully blow-dried to look like silk, during her lunch-hour, by her friend Keisha who worked two doors up from the beauty salon. Keisha wasn't her real name – it was Marian – but she'd decided that Keisha sounded so much more glamorous and Ellie agreed with her absolutely.

"Do I look okay?" she asked her mother nervously as she came into the kitchen.

"You look lovely, dear. That dress really suits you."

"You don't think it's too short?" Ellie asked, tugging it down at the hem.

"No, it's fine," her mother replied, thinking that it was longer than what her daughter usually wore.

Her father whistled in appreciation as he came into the kitchen to say that David had arrived to pick her up. "You look gorgeous, sweetheart. I'm sure you'll be the prettiest girl there."

"Thanks, Dad," she said, giving him a hug and feeling a bit more confident.

"Just relax and be yourself," her mother advised as she kissed her goodnight.

"I'll try. Thanks, Mum," she replied, throwing her cream leather jacket over her shoulders as she sashayed out the door on her five-inch nude-patent platform pumps.

"Hey, you look great!" were David's confidence-boosting words as Ellie slid into the passenger seat of the BMW. "You look different."

Poor David! He hadn't a clue how women ticked and she wasn't about to enlighten him about all the effort she'd put into looking 'different'. She was even surprised that he'd noticed. Honestly, for a man of thirty-three he was very naïve about the female species.

"Thank you," she smiled, reaching over and pecking him on the cheek, as the luxurious car purred into action.

As they drove across the Liffey on their way to Killiney, David was warning her yet again that she had to be on her best behaviour tonight. He'd already told her this about ten times. She wasn't stupid!

"What exactly are you trying to say, darling?"

"Just that this is a very important dinner for me," he stressed yet again, "so please go easy on the wine."

She was about to make an angry retort but changed her mind. She could see from the way he was clenching the steering wheel, his knuckles white, that he was even more nervous than she was. He would be starting his new job the following Monday and this dinner party was being hosted by his new boss so that David could meet the other directors and some of his new colleagues. She reached over and patted his knee, feeling sorry for him all of a sudden.

"I promise," she relented.

She could see where he was coming from. She did get awfully tipsy on wine, although strangely she could drink beer and cider all night without falling down. However, she doubted there would be either of those on offer tonight as David had said it would be a very up-market do. More likely it would be fancy cocktails or champagne – both of which were lethal for her – and no doubt there would be fabulous wine on offer too. She liked wine but she normally slugged it back like it was orange juice which was why it made her so drunk. Yeah, she'd have to be very, very careful about what she drank tonight.

Her friends always said she was hilarious when she got drunk but somehow she didn't think that David's new boss and his wife would find her quite so funny. For starters, they lived on the south side of Dublin and Ellie always felt intimidated as soon as she crossed the Liffey from her home ground on the north side. She knew it was stupid but she couldn't help it. It was well known that south-siders looked down on those who hailed from north of the river. Those awful jokes that were always going around didn't help either. The latest one doing the rounds was: *'Why do birds fly upside down when they fly over the north side?' 'Because it's not worth shitting on.'* Ellie snorted. Was it any wonder that she was suspicious of south-siders when they coined cruel jokes like that?

She was gobsmacked when they arrived at the gates of a house that would not have been out of place in Beverly Hills.

"Wow!" she exclaimed as David pressed the bell on the gate.

"Yes, sir?" a stiff voice came over the intercom.

"It's David Murphy," David replied, a slight shake in his voice.

"Good evening, Mr Murphy. Please drive right on in."

The gates opened slowly as a myriad of security cameras watched their every move. They drove slowly up the long drive which was lit with lanterns all the way up to the house. There, a uniformed man came out and offered to take the car and park it. David handed over the keys of his precious BMW without as much as a murmur – something he'd never done for her, Ellie couldn't help thinking.

Entering through the large marble columns into a sumptuous foyer, Ellie's eyes were out on sticks. Imagine that such houses existed in Dublin and less than ten miles from the city centre! She knew of course that Bono and some other stars had mansions in this area, but she'd never imagined that she'd ever be actually standing in one of them. A butler took her jacket as an attractive grey-haired man came forward to greet them.

"David, so glad you could make it," he said, pumping David's hand.

"Thank you for inviting us, Mr –" David started, a slight quiver in his voice but the man cut him short.

"Please, call me Frank. We're all on first-name terms in this company." He winked at them. "And this is . . .?" He looked towards Ellie with a glint in his eye.

"Sorry, Mr – er – Frank, this is my – eh – fiancée, Ellie."

Ellie blushed prettily. David still hadn't got used to calling her his fiancée. Well, it was only natural, wasn't it? They'd been engaged such a short time. She, on the other hand had said the words, 'my fiancé, David,' a dozen times a day – if only to herself – as she flashed her hand with its large diamond ring in front of her. She still marvelled at the fact that she *was* actually engaged to be married.

Ellie smiled at the older man, her dimples enhancing her attractive, pretty features. "Pleased to meet you, Frank," she said breathlessly, offering her hand.

He took it and put it to his lips. "Well, David, you certainly know how to pick them," he said, his eyes never leaving Ellie's.

I don't believe it! This old geezer is flirting with me. She couldn't help herself and pealed with laughter. Frank laughed too and winked at her lasciviously. David joined in although he didn't have any idea what he was laughing at. He guessed he'd missed something, somewhere.

"Frank, darling," a plummy posh voice rang out and Ellie turned to see a woman teetering towards them on five-inch heels. Ellie reckoned that she was in her mid-fifties although she could have passed for forty-five. Ellie's eagle eye, honed from five years of working in a beauty salon, appraised the woman's face and in a jiffy pinpointed the botox, cheek fillers and without doubt a face-lift too. The boobs certainly defied gravity and were unnaturally high and firm for a woman her age – and what about those lips? She'd obviously asked for the Angelina Special!

Ellie baulked at the thought of anyone filling their face and body with toxic chemicals. She was of the 'less-is-more' school of thought which was losing out to the 'more-is-still-not-enough' practices of today's plastic surgeons. For the life of her she could never understand why women continued to do this to themselves. There was enough help out there now, such as was offered in the beauty salon, without the need for all these invasive practices. She swore that she would never do anything like that to her face. Never!

"Darling, I've been searching for you," the woman said haughtily to Frank, irritation in her voice and eyes. Even though she was obviously angry, not a facial muscle moved.

"Judith, darling, do come and meet the newest addition

to Buckley Steadman. This is David Murphy and his gorgeous fiancée, Ellie."

"Nice to meet you," Judith remarked coldly. She looked Ellie over from head to toe in a patronising manner. David was rewarded with a smile which never quite reached her eyes.

Thank God I bought this new Karen Millen dress, Ellie thought. She could just imagine the older woman's sneer if she'd turned up in something from Penneys! Judith was wearing a beautiful emerald-green dress which screamed 'money' and 'designer', although Ellie had no idea which designer it might be. Emeralds flashed from her neck and ears – genuine, no doubt.

"Can we get you something to drink?" Frank asked, beckoning a passing waiter.

"A white wine would be lovely," Ellie murmured.

"What kind?" Judith asked archly.

"Chardonnay would be fine," Ellie said, smiling, in the hope of melting this ice queen.

"Sorry, we don't *do* chardonnay," Judith snapped. "We can offer you Pinot Gris, Gewürztraminer or Riesling."

"Oh, any will be fine," Ellie replied, not knowing what any of them tasted like. Although her mother was French, she was a teetotaller, and her father was a beer man so there never was wine at home. She sometimes drank white wine at parties and it was mostly chardonnay, though to be honest it could have been anything.

"A whiskey for me, please," David said, seeing that that was what Frank was drinking.

"A man after my own heart," Frank said, clapping him on the back.

Judith gave the order to a passing waiter and moved off to speak to some other guests.

"Don't mind her," Frank winked at Ellie. "Chardonnay seems to be out of fashion at the moment and my wife is nothing if not fashionable."

Ellie thought she detected a harsh note in his voice.

The waiter returned with their drinks and Frank took her elbow. "Come, you lovely young people, let me introduce you to some of our other guests."

Ellie was trying not to gape but she couldn't help it. He led them into a magnificent room where about twenty people were gathered. The women were all beautifully groomed and expensively dressed. They were also all a good bit older than Ellie. Even older than her parents, she thought, looking around. She felt completely out of place and intimidated as Frank introduced them to everyone. She held onto David's hand for dear life as she plastered a smile on her face. The women were appraising her silently while their husbands were ogling her appreciatively. The men all had a prosperous air about them. Some of them were handsome and fit while others had definite paunches and less hair on their heads.

There was only one other youngish couple there and their welcome was obviously genuine. The girl, Anna, who Ellie guessed was in her early thirties, was smiling and friendly. Her husband, Mike, was a little older and greeted them warmly as Frank introduced them and then moved off to welcome some new guests.

Anna took Ellie's arm. "Come look at the fabulous view," she said, steering Ellie out the open French doors onto a terrace, away from the crowd.

It was indeed a fabulous view. It was a beautiful bright evening and she could see right across Dublin Bay to Sutton, where she worked.

"Wow!" she exclaimed as she took it all in.

"I know it's your first time here and I remember how terrified I was on my first visit." Anna lowered her voice, looking around to make sure no one could overhear. "It can be overwhelming."

"Yeah," Ellie whispered back, "they are pretty intimidating, especially the women."

"They're always like this with newcomers, especially with younger, prettier women. They can be very bitchy but don't let them get to you."

"Some of them are pretty scary," Ellie grinned. "The way they looked me up and down! *Phew*!"

"I know what you mean," Anna laughed. "I felt like that when I first came here but I soon realised that they're sad really. They spend their time trying to reverse the aging process – they're terrified that they'll lose their husbands to younger women. I just grin and bear it every time I come here. I have to, for the sake of Mike's career."

Ellie was horrified. "I hope this won't be a regular thing – these dinner parties," she said, turning to look anxiously at the other girl.

"I'm afraid it probably will. Judith likes to show off at least four times a year. The only respite is summer when all the women decamp to Marbella. That's when the men have their little flings." Anna grinned wickedly.

Ellie thought she was hearing things but, before she could reply, Mike and David came out on the terrace to join them.

"Get a load of this view," Mike said to David. "Isn't it something?"

"Fabulous," David agreed, beaming from ear to ear. "This is a beautiful place, isn't it, Ellie?" He put his arm around her shoulders. "And Frank and Judith are both terrific," he added enthusiastically.

She looked at him to see if he was joking and, when she saw that he wasn't, her heart dropped. My God, he's serious, she thought with dread. She caught the sympathetic look Anna gave her as they were called in to dinner.

5

To Ellie's consternation Frank appeared out of nowhere and put his arm proprietorially around her waist.

He whispered in her ear, "I wanted to change the settings and have you next to me, my dear, but unfortunately Judith wouldn't hear of it. However, you are seated towards the head of the table where I will be presiding."

Then he patted her bum twice, and if he'd been anyone but David's boss she would have slapped him.

He led her to her seat, Anna trailing behind them.

"I believe your place is on the other side," he said to Anna. "Let me escort you."

"No, no," Anna said firmly. "I can find it myself, thank you."

Frank moved off with a smile and a shrug, and Anna threw Ellie a discreet ironic glance.

Ellie was horrified to see David moving to the other end of the table. He turned to look at her and she shot him a look of panic but he just shrugged his shoulders helplessly.

"Who's sitting beside you?" Anna asked, seeing the still-empty spaces beside Ellie. She picked up the place-card on Ellie's left side. "James," she read out. "Poor you!" she whispered, throwing her eyes to heaven. "He's a crashing bore. Who's on your other side?"

Ellie leaned down and read the name. "Sam," she replied.

"That's better! He's a real sweetie. You'll like him."

Anna moved to the opposite side of the table and took her place. She too was separated from her partner who was at the other end of the table, near David. Obviously she was used to this, thought Ellie.

As people trickled in, a portly, bald man came to the table and stood on Ellie's left side. This must be James.

"Good evening, my dear," he said to Ellie. He spoke exactly like Prince Charles.

When everybody had arrived at the table, with the exception of the man to Ellie's right, they all sat down.

"Sam will be a little late," Frank said from the head of the table.

"What's new?" James commented and Frank laughed.

Just then Ellie spied an attractive young guy come into the dining-room and for a moment she thought that it was the actor Jonathan Rhys Meyers, who had played Henry VIII in the TV series. But when he came and sat down in the empty chair beside her, she realised this must be Sam. He was uncannily like the actor but up close his dark-blue eyes were laughing eyes, unlike the actor's broody gaze.

"Sorry I'm late. A crisis at work, I'm afraid," he said to the company as he took his place next to Ellie. "Hi, Anna, nice to see you again," he said, blowing her a kiss.

Ellie was surprised to see Anna blush.

Next he turned to her. "Hello. We haven't met before. I'm Sam." He offered his hand and took Ellie's in a firm handshake.

"Ellie," she introduced herself. She had no time to say

any more to him as James, the 'crashing bore' on her other side, launched into a monologue which she guessed was about the state of the stock-market but which was in fact incomprehensible to her. Anna had not been exaggerating about him either. He *was* the most awful bore. He finally took a breath and asked her where she was from.

"Clontarf," she replied.

"Oh, the north side!" he remarked and she heard the disdain in his plummy voice.

She felt herself blush. Luckily the first course was served at that moment so she was saved from saying anything. She turned her attention to the lobster salad in front of her and wished the evening would end. At least the boring old fart had lost interest in her, thank God. She sipped the white wine that had been poured for her. It was delicious. She wondered what wine it was. Something wildly expensive, no doubt!

Sam turned to her just then and whispered, "If you need rescuing from James anytime in the future, just nudge me. I know how dreadfully boring he can be."

"Thank you. I'll remember that but I think he lost interest in me when he heard where I'm from."

"And where's that, Ellie?"

"Mars," popped out of her mouth before she could stop herself.

"Mars?" he repeated, raising an eyebrow, wondering if he'd heard right.

"Well, I might as well be," she retorted. "People on the south side seem to think that the north side is on another planet."

His eyes crinkled with merriment as he let out a low husky laugh. "That's a good one. If that's the case, then I'm a Martian too."

She looked at him quizzically. "What do you mean?"

"Well, I live in Clontarf so I must also be an alien."

"Are you serious?" She looked at him, her blue eyes wide and full of doubt. She was afraid that he was teasing her.

"Absolutely! Castle Avenue."

"You're joking me! I'm from Clontarf too. Kincora Road," she grinned.

"Howdy, neighbour." He shook her hand again.

They stopped talking as the waiters removed the plates from the first course.

"I see you're engaged," Sam said, nodding at her engagement ring. "Where's the lucky guy?"

"My fiancé is David, sitting at the other end of the table, beside Judith."

"Ah, yes, David is the newest addition to Buckley Steadman, I hear."

"Do you work for the company too?" Ellie asked him.

"Good Lord, no! Heaven forbid! Do I look like an accountant?" he said with a grimace.

She couldn't quite figure him out but he was a refreshing change from boring James. There was something very mysterious about him. She wondered what he was doing at the dinner at all if he didn't work for the company.

As the main course of Beef Wellington was served, he asked her what she worked at. She told him about the salon and kept him amused with some of the funnier antics of the clients. He seemed genuinely interested and laughed a deep husky laugh, throwing his head back as he did so.

The red wine which was served with the beef was wonderful. "I've never tasted such heavenly wine!" Ellie sighed with pleasure as she sipped.

Frank, who overheard this remark, spoke. "You have

Sam here to thank for that. He supplies all my wines. He has a wine business."

"Really?" Ellie was surprised. "Is that what you do?" Now she understood why he'd been invited to the dinner. "I know nothing about wine whatsoever except that I love the wine we're drinking tonight."

"You should take one of Sam's wine courses," Anna said, from across the table. "I took one last year. He's brilliant!" She beamed at him and he seemed embarrassed at the compliment.

"Where do you have them?" Ellie asked Sam.

"In Clontarf. I've actually got one starting quite soon."

"Gosh! That would be handy." This was fate again. "Can you tell me about it?"

"Sure. Better still, I'll give you my card and you can check the courses out on my website." He fished a card out of his pocket and handed it to her.

"Thank you, I will," she said, putting his card in her bag. "Actually, I made a major faux-pas tonight," she whispered to him. "I asked Judith for a glass of chardonnay and she informed me that she doesn't *do* chardonnay. I nearly died."

"Don't mind her! Poor Judith doesn't know the first thing about wine." Ellie detected a note of disdain in his voice. "In fact, the white wine we had with the lobster was Chablis which is actually made from chardonnay grapes, but of course she doesn't realise that."

"I didn't know that either," Ellie admitted.

"I think you really should join my course so," Sam said teasingly.

"Maybe I will," she replied, rising to the challenge. "Tell me more."

Sam then started to talk about wine and she could see

how passionate he was about it. His face was animated and his eyes aglow as he explained how wines were made and what made them different from one another. Ellie was fascinated. She'd never realised that it was such an interesting subject. She decided then and there that she would definitely join Sam's wine course. After all, if she was going to have to attend more of these parties in the future, she'd need to educate herself about such things. She smiled happily, thinking how pleased David would be with her when she told him.

6

Zita Williams looked on as Rachel Dunne was being interviewed for the television news. What an airhead, she thought disgustedly, listening to Rachel enthuse about the work of the Rape Crisis Centre. What the hell does she know about it? She was sick of seeing photos of Little-Miss-Perfect and her oh-so-handsome husband plastered all over the papers every weekend. What had Rachel Dunne ever done but look beautiful and snap up a gorgeous husband?

Following the TV interview, Rachel was now giving an interview to a popular women's magazine. Zita snorted as she listened to Rachel going on about her busy days and how chock-a-block her diary was.

"But I do try and make time for myself," she added, smiling graciously at the interviewer. "Last year I did a Fine Arts course and I've enrolled on a wine course this year as it's a subject I'm really interested in."

"How lovely," the interviewer said. "And where are you doing this course?"

"At Château Wines in Clontarf – I'm *so* looking forward to it," Rachel enthused.

The interview finished and just then Rachel's husband, Carl, appeared at her side and kissed her on the cheek.

"Hello, darling, I had a meeting nearby and thought I'd drop in and say hello."

Zita saw Rachel's eyes light up.

"Carl, what a lovely surprise!" Rachel said, giving him a lingering kiss on the lips.

"*Yeuch*!" Zita said under her breath as the television crew came running back to start filming the new golden boy of politics. She was sure the accidental meeting had been engineered by the Dunnes to gain publicity. She watched Carl smiling and charming everyone in sight. He exuded energy and sexuality and Zita could feel the charisma, even from a distance. I wonder what he's like in bed, she thought, surprised at herself for thinking that. She doubted that the prissy Rachel would be able to satisfy him in that department. Zita couldn't help but admire his broad-shouldered physique and, as she did so, Carl looked her way and a flash of chemistry passed between them. They locked eyes for a moment and Zita knew she was not imagining the sexual message he was sending her.

Zita had no illusions as to her looks. She was not pretty or glamorous like Rachel Dunne. She'd often been called interesting – but never beautiful. She was tall and rangy with small perky breasts and a slim waist and hips. She generally wore unisex clothes: jeans, biker jackets, biker boots and dungarees, which she felt suited her boyish figure. Her hair was jet-black and cut short in a pixie style. She had high cheekbones and a long patrician nose but it was her eyes that were her most arresting feature. They were an unusual gold colour and gave her a distinctive feline look. Despite her masculine clothing and demeanour, men found her intriguing and it was obvious from Carl's glance that he was not immune to her attractions either. Well, well, she thought, so this show of affection with his wife is maybe not all it seems to be. *Hmmm . . .*

Zita was ambitious and ruthless and as she watched Carl she sensed that he and she were very alike – both opportunists! The idea formed in her head that he could be very useful to her. There was no doubt that he was the new darling of the political scene and word had it that his star was in the ascendant. Yes, he could be very useful indeed.

Zita worked as a production assistant for a national television station and knew that she was brighter and more intelligent than many of those higher up the ladder than she. It was a known fact that political interference had been the reason many lesser beings had been promoted to the positions of producer and director. This was what Zita wanted. Perhaps she'd just found the political clout that would catapult her up that ladder and perhaps enjoy a sexual liaison at the same time. But how could she get to Carl? She'd have to find a way.

Zita lived in a small apartment on the very top floor of a beautiful Georgian house on Stephen's Green in Dublin city centre. She took the four flights of stairs at a run a couple of times a day to the dismay of her neighbour and friend, Marcus, who was forever complaining about the climb. She also cycled everywhere and was a familiar figure pedalling through the city-centre streets at weekends. She did most of her thinking while cycling to and from work and now as she cycled home she thought about how she could wangle her way into Carl Dunne's life.

Then it hit her! Brilliant! Of course! I'll join that wine course and cultivate his wife and, through her, get to meet him socially. She grinned at the idea. Kill three birds with one stone! Hook Carl, take the smug smile off his wife's face and learn something about wine at the same time. *Yeeeessss!*

Zita had no illusions where men were concerned. She'd been abused from the age of ten by a priest who was a family friend and when, aged fifteen, she'd finally found the courage to tell her parents, they hadn't believed her. She'd run away to London then and from there made her way to Australia. It had taken her a long time after that to trust any man but, aged just twenty-one, while working for a TV company in Australia, she'd met and fallen hard for a much older man. Too late, she'd discovered what an evil bastard he was. He introduced her to drugs and then put her to work, prostituting herself to pay for her habit and for his profit. She spent three miserable years with him before finally finding the courage to walk away. With great difficulty, she got clean of the drugs. However, she was no innocent little girl any more but a hardened, bitter woman and she'd extracted her revenge. And how! She still remembered the satisfaction she'd felt at what she'd done.

She returned to Ireland immediately after that and since then she'd steered clear of the opposite sex, never allowing herself to become emotionally involved. She knew some of her colleagues suspected that she was a lesbian. No doubt her boyish look and clothes gave fuel to this idea and she laughed to herself to think how absurd it was. Women didn't interest her in that way. She had sex with men from time to time but always with strangers and always on her terms. No man would ever dominate her again. She now used men in exactly the same way she'd been used by them and got great satisfaction from doing so. It was more about power than pleasure. She often wondered if she was missing out but she reckoned that the way she operated was the only way possible for her. The only way she could avoid getting hurt.

"Watch out, Carl!" she said quietly as she locked her bike away. She now had him in her sights and was very much looking forward to the challenge.

7

Louise heard Ronan leave for Mass on Sunday morning and snuggled down even more in the guest-room bed. She'd moved in there the night that he'd had a go at her for that shopping spree, as he called it, and she had no notion of going back into his bed until he apologised. In fact, she would not talk to him until he did, even though it was now four days since they'd spoken. She knew Ronan – he'd come around sooner or later. He was a softie but, honestly, he was becoming so mean it was ridiculous. He should be married to her friend Melissa who spent far more than Louise on clothes and you didn't hear *her* husband complaining. Okay, so she worked as a solicitor and was earning good money, but still . . . !

Melissa was calling for her at eleven so she had another half-hour in bed. They were travelling down to Kildare to the Outlet Centre which Louise had heard was fabulous. Melissa was a regular customer there but it was Louise's first visit and she was really excited about it.

She had told her friend about how Ronan was behaving.

"I'm afraid, Mel, that I won't be able to buy very much. Thanks to my husband's stinginess I'll have a miserable day." Her green eyes were glistening with tears.

"Don't worry, Lou, things are dirt cheap there and anyway you can always pay by credit card."

Louise brightened up. "Well, if things are that cheap maybe I can buy a couple of things." Things were looking up. After all, she hadn't bought a thing, well hardly anything, since the big row they'd had.

Melissa was full of sympathy. She was a plain woman and quite a bit overweight and she admired and envied Louise her fabulous figure and looks.

"You're so lucky, Lou," she sighed. "Everything looks great on you. You could wear a sack and still look a million dollars, unlike me."

"Yeah, I'm lucky," Louise agreed with her, pulling down the mirror on the sunshade to check her make-up. She applied some gloss to her lips and smoothed her hair while admiring her reflection. "You'd think Ronan would appreciate that, wouldn't you?"

"Absolutely! He should be delighted that you always look so great. You could have any man you wanted," Melissa said enviously. "Even my Jeremy fancies you."

Louise didn't think that was much of a compliment. Jeremy must be seventy if he was a day. There was a huge age-gap between him and Mel though she seemed to be genuinely fond of him. He was filthy rich of course and very generous too. Maybe I should have married a rich sugar-daddy, Louise thought bitterly, though she didn't say this to her friend.

Louise couldn't believe her eyes. The Kildare Village retail outlet centre was a revelation. They went into the information office where they picked up a booklet with a plan of the centre. Louise glanced at it but stuffed it in her bag, impatient to get started. With Melissa trying to keep up, she veered wildly from shop to shop, her heart racing madly. She felt like she'd died and gone to heaven. And the prices! Even Ronan – the cheapskate – couldn't complain if she bought one or two things here. It was unbelievable!

Melissa laughed at her enthusiasm. "I told you they're practically giving stuff away."

"They surely are."

"Now we must make a plan," Melissa said, but Louise had already disappeared into the Coast shop. Melissa shook her head, and followed her. What have I let myself in for, she wondered.

Louise was trawling through the racks, *oohing* and *aahing* as she grabbed one dress after another and threw them across her arm. Her eyes were sparkling with excitement. She felt so alive.

"Oh, Mel, this is fantastic! Look at the prices. It's crazy! I'll never buy anything in Dublin again!" She sailed into the dressing room on cloud nine, her arms weighed down with beautiful dresses.

An hour later, they emerged from the shop. Louise had four bags on her arm, Melissa had none.

"I can't believe how much I'm saving," Louise cried gleefully, her green eyes aglow.

Melissa did not relish traipsing around after Louise all day. Everything looked so good on her friend that it made her feel even more frumpy than usual. Besides, she had some birthday and wedding presents that she needed to buy, so she suggested that they split up and meet again for lunch.

"Look, I'll give you the spare key to the car and you can go and put your bags in it – to save you carrying them around – and we'll meet up . . ." she looked at her watch, "at, say, three for lunch in L'Officina. Okay?"

"Perfect. Happy hunting!" Louise beamed at her as she took the key. Just then she spotted the shop 7 For All Mankind. "Oh my God! My favourite jeans in the whole world," she cried, sprinting away from Melissa, her hair and bags flying.

Melissa laughed at her enthusiasm. She'd never met anyone who could shop quite like Louise.

Three pairs of jeans later, Louise deposited her bags back in the boot of Melissa's car and set off again. She ran into Melissa on her way.

"I won't have enough time," she moaned. "I want to see everything."

"That won't be possible," Melissa said primly. "Look, let's grab a coffee in Starbucks and you can mark off the shops you absolutely *must* see, and then the ones that you'd *like* to see."

"That's a great idea," Louise agreed, following her to the coffee shop.

They ordered two cappuccinos and sipped them while Louise marked the most important shops she wanted to visit. The centre closed at seven. She hoped she'd have enough time to do them all. She wasn't sure how much she'd spent but what the hell, she'd saved so much it was worth it.

By the time she met up with Melissa for lunch, she'd been back to the car once more to deposit more purchases there. By now she'd decided that she might as well be hung for a sheep as a lamb and, anyway, Ronan couldn't be much angrier with her than he already was.

After a delicious lunch, which she insisted on paying for – after all, Mel had done the driving – she bought some lovely lingerie in Wolfords. She badly needed these as she'd put a red blouse in the wash last week with her white undies and now they were all pink. *Yeuch!* The manageress, Sharon, was so sweet and so helpful that she bought much more than she'd intended. She could not resist the gorgeous gold shoes in LK Bennett and just as she was leaving saw a pair of denim platforms for €10. Just incredible! They'd cost at least €80, if not more, in Dublin. My God, this was fantastic!

After another trip to the car to dump her bags, Louise noticed that there were only *her* bags in the boot. Had Mel bought nothing at all? How was that possible? She looked with dismay at all the bags. She hadn't realised that she'd bought quite so much. Better not think about it. She didn't want to spoil the day.

She walked slowly back to the centre from the car park and, feeling exhausted all of a sudden, she decided to take a break and went for another coffee in Starbucks. She was poring over the plan again, wondering should she perhaps check out the sunglasses shop, when she became conscious that someone was studying her. It was an older man who was sitting at the next table. He had the kind of tan that one didn't get in Portmarnock or Brittas Bay and everything about him screamed money: the expensive suit, the perfect shirt, the silk tie, the Rolex watch and gold jewellery. Louise took it all in at a glance.

"Excuse me for staring, but are you Louise Redmond?" he asked.

She was shocked. Redmond was her maiden name. "How do you know me?" she asked, flustered now.

"Don't you remember me? I'm Alan Brown. I used to come into Elegant Modes when you worked there."

Louise racked her brain but for the life of her could not remember him. She'd had dreams of becoming a model when she'd left school but even back then it had been a difficult world to break into and the best she'd managed was a job as a house model with the clothing company. She'd only been there a short while when she'd met Ronan and, as they say, that was that. He had been infatuated with the beautiful red-haired, green-eyed girl and she had fallen pretty hard too.

At nineteen – and four months pregnant – she'd left to marry the bright young draughtsman, both of them dreaming of a promising future. That first pregnancy had ended in a miscarriage and was followed by three more over the next six years. Suffering from depression, Louise could not even consider returning to work and, by the time she could, she was too old for the modelling scene. She'd had to give up her dream of becoming a model and also, as it turned out, her dream of becoming a mother. She wouldn't hear of adopting and the only thing she found that helped lift her spirits was shopping. That was when their problems had begun.

Now this man was catapulting her back in time.

She tried to remember the buyers who frequented the wholesale company back then as he asked if he could join her. Surely she would have noticed this glamorous, obviously charming man. No matter how hard she tried, she couldn't place him.

"I'm sorry but it's been so long ago . . ." She smiled at him.

"All the guys were mad about you then," he told her as he got up and came to sit down opposite her. "I'm not

51

surprised you didn't notice me. I came in once a month to buy for the company I worked for back then. I think I probably bought everything you ever modelled!"

A faint glimmer of recognition surfaced in her memory as he smiled at her. "Yes, I do remember you – but you look completely different," she said, surprise in her voice.

He threw back his head and laughed aloud. "Yes, well, I rather hope so. I like to think I've improved and matured somewhat since then."

She vaguely recalled a plain dowdy guy who dressed badly, his eyes following her every move. How had he evolved into this handsome, gorgeous man?

"*You* haven't changed," he said smoothly. "If anything you're even more beautiful."

Louise blushed. This was like music to her ears. He *was* a charmer!

"What are you doing here?" she asked.

"I'm here on business," he replied. "I've come quite a long way since I used to admire you in Elegant Modes."

I'll say, Louise thought.

"I now have a manufacturing company and a chain of fashion shops and I also franchise a lot of international clothing companies, both here and in the UK and Europe."

"Wow!" She couldn't believe her ears. He *had* come a long way.

"What are you doing here?" he asked.

"Just shopping."

"Well, this is your lucky day, Louise," he replied. "I have big discounts in most of the shops here. Come with me and I'll save you loads."

"Even more than I can save already?" she asked dubiously.

"Most certainly." He stood up, offering her his arm.

She spent the rest of the afternoon with him, not able to believe how the salesgirls reacted when he entered the store. She chose a pair of tan leather trousers in DKNY and tried on a matching jacket which was simply fabulous. Alan said she absolutely had to have them both. She agreed with him but when she proffered her credit card, the salesgirl told her that he had already settled it.

"Oh, I couldn't possibly accept this," she protested to him.

"Please, indulge an old man. It gives me great pleasure to see you enjoy yourself," he smiled, his blue eyes twinkling.

"Well, if you insist," she said.

She'd never had so much fun. She bought a pair of fabulous blue Le Creuset bowls that were reduced from €70 to €10. What a steal! They would be perfect for salad or pasta. Ronan could hardly complain about that! They visited Samsonite where Alan bought a new briefcase. He chose a lovely tan calfskin one and, if Ronan had been talking to her, she would have loved to buy one for him for his birthday – but he'd said he didn't want a present anyway. His loss!

Finally, exhilarated and shopped-out, she texted Melissa to meet her in Starbucks. She couldn't wait to tell her what a fab time she'd had.

Melissa couldn't believe her ears. "God, Lou, you're something else! I leave you for ten minutes and you pick up a gorgeous man," she said admiringly.

"I did not pick him up," Louise retorted. "*He* picked me up."

"Are you going to see him again?"

"I think so. He said he'd call me."

"They all say that."

"No," Louise said dreamily. "I think he meant it. In fact, I'm sure he did."

Melissa was shocked when she got back to the car and saw the amount of stuff Louise had bought.

"Lou, you can't be serious! How much did you spend?"

"Not that much really. It was all so cheap and then Alan . . ." She broke off sheepishly.

"Ronan will have a fit." Melissa couldn't believe that Louise would risk his anger like this.

"Well, I was going to ask you if you would take care of this stuff till later," she asked her friend.

"Of course, but I don't know how you'll manage to avoid Ronan finding out."

"Don't worry about that. I'll sort it," Louise replied, speaking with more confidence than she felt.

She changed into some of her new clothes in the ladies' before they set off for Dublin. She made sure to pull off all the labels first. Ronan would never notice that they were new. He never noticed what she wore. Tired and happy, she arrived home with just the Le Creuset bowls, to find that Ronan was out, thank God. He'd left a note to say he was going out for a pint with his friend Jim.

"Blast!" Louise cursed aloud. She could have taken all her new clothes home with her after all! Now she'd have to wait till later in the week to retrieve them from Mel. To be on the safe side she even hid the Le Creuset bowls under the bed in the spare room. Better wait until things were resolved with Ronan before bringing them out! He'd never believe her that they'd cost so little.

8

Ellie was searching for Sam's card. She was trying to remember which bag she'd been using the night she'd met him. Having trawled through the top eight bags in her bag closet, she eventually found it. That's the problem with changing my bag to match my outfit every day, she thought, frustrated at the time she'd lost looking for it. *Château Wines*, she read. "Of course, how stupid of me! I should have remembered that."

She dialled Sam's number. "Hi, Sam, I don't know if you remember me. It's Ellie. I was sitting beside you at the Buckleys' dinner party last week."

"Ah, Ellie from Mars! I was wondering if you'd gone back there in your spaceship," he laughed.

Ellie was glad that he couldn't see her blushing. She was embarrassed that he'd remembered what she'd said.

"I wanted to ask about your wine course. When is it starting?"

"Next Monday actually."

"Oh, right. Good! Would you have space for me on it?" she asked tentatively.

55

"Even if I didn't, I'd make space," he replied gallantly.

She found herself blushing again. "Well, I'd like to enrol, if it's okay with you."

"Of course. You're very welcome."

"Can you tell me where and when and how much it costs?"

He gave her the address and time it would start. "It's €300, payable before the course starts, I'm afraid," he added. "So many people used to book and not turn up that I now have to ask for it upfront." He sounded apologetic.

She had been hoping it would be less, while not really knowing what such a course would cost. But, never mind the price – she was determined to do it. "Of course, I understand. I don't have a cheque-book but I could drop the cash around to you, if you like."

"That's fine."

"I can come around straight away, if that's okay with you."

"No problem. I'm here all evening. See you soon, Ellie."

"How did she think I wouldn't remember her?" Sam spoke aloud, scratching his head. She was exceptionally pretty and Sam always had an eye for a pretty girl. She was also funny and had made him laugh. She'll add some spice to my course, he thought, grinning to himself.

He was looking forward to the course very much. He was a born teacher and loved imparting his passion for wine to his pupils. It was wonderful to see a student become enchanted with the subject, as always happened to at least one or two out of every class. He wondered who it might be on this course.

Ten minutes later Ellie arrived at the address he'd given

her. It was a massive house with steps going up to an impressive front door. The house was so huge that she assumed it was let in apartments but she couldn't see any bells with names on them, just one brass bell, which she rang. As she waited, she noticed that the drapes in all the windows were the same. It looked like a private dwelling. Sam could hardly live in this massive house all alone, could he? Maybe he lived with his parents or else he'd married an heiress. Stranger things have happened, she thought. She rang the bell a second time, wondering if he'd had to go out. Looking over the railing, she noticed that there were steps down to a basement as well. Just then a breathless Sam flung open the door. He had a phone under his chin.

"Sorry for taking so long," he whispered, his hand covering the phone speaker, "but I was in the basement, working."

He ushered her in as he continued speaking on the phone – in French, she noticed. It surprised her that his French was so good. He was looking really cool in a pair of torn jeans and a denim shirt. He could have stepped out of a Levi's ad. She couldn't help but admire his butt as he led her into a massive room. It had high ceilings and beautiful big windows that let in lots of light. It was breathtaking.

"Make yourself at home here, I'll just be a few minutes," he said, loping away.

Ellie caught her breath as she took in the beautiful room. It looked like something out of *House Beautiful* or *Homes and Gardens*. She noticed both magazines lying on a coffee table. As she looked around she knew instinctively that the décor had a woman's touch. There must be a Mrs Buckley lurking around somewhere. Obviously no children, as the place was immaculate.

Sam interrupted her thoughts as he returned brandishing a bottle of wine and two wineglasses. "Sorry about that but I was on to a producer in Bordeaux about a delivery. Well, how are you?"

"I'm fine!"

"You look lovely," he remarked as he opened the bottle.

Ellie blushed at the compliment. What was it about this man that made her blush? "I love your house. It's so elegant. Do you live here alone?" What a dumb thing to say, she thought as soon as the words were out of her mouth. He'll probably think I want to know if he's married or not.

"I'm afraid so. My last girlfriend departed about four months ago – luckily, or else we would have killed one another." He grinned as he said this and handed her a glass of white wine. "I remember you liked the Chablis Frank served at the dinner."

"How thoughtful of you," she said, smiling, and raised her glass to him. "*Sláinte*!"

"*Santé*!" he replied, smiling back.

"Well, how about you? Do you live with your fiancé?"

She laughed. "Oh, no, I still haven't flown the nest. David's place is far too small for us both. Anyway, I like living with my family. Of course, once we're married that will change. We're looking for a house at the moment."

"Well, it's a good time to buy. When are you getting married?"

"We haven't set a date yet. I'm just enjoying being engaged at the moment." She held out her left hand and looked at her ring.

Sam hid a smile. She was so transparent. The words 'an innocent abroad' came to his mind.

"Enjoy it while you can," he advised. "Getting married is no joke."

"Yes, everyone tells me it's nerve-wracking, planning a wedding," she said, biting her lip. "How about you? Did you find it so bad?"

"Oh, I wouldn't know. I've never been married but I think I'd elope if I were you."

"Oh, no!" she squealed. "I adore weddings. They always make me cry."

"You're a romantic. Do you know how many weddings end in divorce?"

"Don't say that!" She felt her voice quiver.

"I'm sorry. I'm an old cynic. Of course there are many happy marriages out there and I'm sure yours will be one of them." He could have kicked himself. Here was this sweet young girl, newly engaged and dewy-eyed, and he behaves like an insensitive lout. Just because he didn't believe in marriage or romance didn't mean he had to throw cold water on her dreams.

"Your house really is beautiful," she said, wanting to change the subject. "Was it your girlfriend who did the décor?"

"God, no, I wouldn't have let her near it! She'd have had everything black and white and stainless steel. An interior designer friend of mine did it."

"Well, whoever it was, they did a great job."

"Thank you. I'm very happy with it. Would you like to see around?"

"I'd love to. I've never been in a house as nice as this – well, except maybe Frank and Judith's, where I met you."

"Yes, I suppose for Mars this is considered a nice house," he teased.

He smiled as he saw that she was blushing again. He

showed her around the house, pleased that she was so impressed with everything. They ended up in the basement.

"This is where I have my office and in this next room I hold my wine courses," he said, opening the door for her.

"Do you hold many every year?" she enquired as she looked around the airy bright room. There were large French windows looking onto the back garden.

"Well, I lecture for the Wine Board and prepare students for the Certificate exams. On top of that I bring my employees here on a regular basis to update their knowledge and for wine tastings."

"Employees? How many do you have?"

"Fifty, last count."

"My goodness! Fifty!" she exclaimed, amazed. "What do they all do?"

"Well, I have ten wine shops and an import business and I'm about to start an online business as well."

Ellie was gobsmacked. No wonder he could afford this house! She guessed he was still in his twenties. She turned to him, her blue eyes widening.

"Goodness gracious, what a success you've made of your life – and you're still only what . . . twenty-nine . . . thirty?"

"Do I look that old?" He pretended to be offended. "Actually, I'm twenty-eight," he laughed, seeing her stricken look.

"Gosh, you must have been a genius at school."

"No way! I dropped out before my Leaving and went to France to work in a vineyard. My parents were horrified. They wanted me to go to university but I hated school and I knew I wanted to be in the wine business so off I went. I spent five years there and made lots of contacts before coming home to open my first wine-shop."

Ellie was impressed. "I hated school too and was useless at studying."

"Yes, but you like what you do now, don't you?" He cocked his head to the side and looked at her with interest. "I remember you told me some funny stories about the beauty salon the first night I met you." He was grinning as he recalled it.

"I like the clients and the two girls I work with but the job itself is pretty boring. What I really would have liked was to have become a vet. But with my Leaving results that was out of the question. I'm not that smart."

"Being smart has nothing to do with passing exams," he said gently. "It's important to love what you do. I do. I love working with wine. Hey, I see your glass is empty. Let's go back upstairs."

She followed him up to the living-room again, admiring the lovely paintings lining the walls. This really was an exquisite house. She sighed, thinking of the poky little houses she and David had been looking at on the Internet and could barely afford.

Over another glass of wine they chatted on, until Ellie realised that it was getting on for ten o'clock.

"Oh goodness, look at the time! I'm sorry, I do go on sometimes. I'd better go," she said, standing up.

"I've really enjoyed talking to you. You livened up my evening. I look forward to seeing you next Monday night."

"Oh God, I'm sorry, I almost forgot to pay you and that's the reason I called around," she said, embarrassed, as she reached into her bag for her purse. She handed him the €300 for the course.

"Thanks. Hold on a jiffy, I have to go downstairs to get you a receipt."

He turned to go but Ellie stopped him. "Don't worry about it. You can give it to me next Monday."

"Fine, I look forward to seeing you then," he smiled as he shook her hand. He showed her out and Ellie walked home, swinging her bag, thinking that with Sam as the lecturer the course was going to be very interesting. She was really glad that she'd decided to do it.

9

Ronan was tired of the stand-off with Louise. The strain of living in a house with someone who hadn't spoken to him in a week, along with the uncertainty at work and his dire financial situation, was all taking its toll on him. He was feeling completely stressed out. At least Louise seemed to be making an effort. She hadn't been out of the house since Sunday, or so she said, so at least she hadn't been shopping. On Wednesday he went to the doctor who prescribed some medication for him and warned him to chill out. When Conor rang and asked him to meet him that night for a pint he jumped at the chance to escape another night of silence. At the least a few pints would help him relax.

Louise was relieved to hear Ronan say he was going out for a few pints as it meant she could at last retrieve the stuff she'd bought in Kildare the previous Sunday from Melissa's house. The moment he'd left the house she rang her friend.

"Hi, Mel, it's me. Ronan's gone out for a few hours

and I'd like to come around and collect my stuff straight away."

"Hi, Lou. I'm sorry, but I'm just about to go out actually. I'm meeting my sister in Wong's for a Chinese."

"Oh Mel, I have to have it now. Couldn't you drop if off on your way? I'm dying to have it and I may not be alone again another evening this week. Puhleease?" she begged. "It won't take that long. Can't you ring your sister and explain you'll be ten minutes late?"

Melissa sighed. Louise had been bossing her around ever since they'd been at national school together and she was still at it. "Okay, I'll be around in ten."

She dropped the bags off shortly after and was greeted by an excited Louise.

"You're an angel! I can't wait to see everything again. I've almost forgotten what I bought." Her eyes were sparkling and her face aglow.

"Did that guy Alan ring you?" Melissa asked her.

"No, not yet," Louise replied as she took the bags into her bedroom, "but he will. I know he will."

How great to be so sure of yourself, Melissa thought enviously, as she drove away.

Louise emptied all the bags on the bed and looked with excitement at the mound of clothes. She had to work quickly. First she cut off all the labels and price-tags and then burned them, along with all the bags, in the incinerator in the garden. Ronan would not be out there till the weekend at least. She had already burnt all the receipts the previous Monday when Ronan had left for work. She couldn't risk him finding any trace of this latest spree. She had been quite shocked to see that she had spent just over €900, and that was without the leather jacket and trousers that Alan had paid for. God, it was amazing how quickly it all added up!

Caressing the beautiful clothes she carefully stored them all away. She couldn't resist changing into her new lingerie, a DKNY top and the 7 For All Mankind jeans. Wow! The jeans fitted her like a glove. She felt fantastic!

When all the evidence had been secreted away she was in such a good mood that she opened the last bottle of wine that they had in the house. By the time Ronan came wearily in, she was in great form and ready to forgive him.

"How was Conor?" she asked him, taking him by surprise. "Did you have a nice evening?"

His shoulders visibly relaxed. The cold war was obviously over! She looked very attractive, curled up as she was on the sofa.

"Great. Conor says hello." He'd said no such thing but a little lie wouldn't hurt.

"Would you like a glass of wine?" she asked, getting up to get him a glass.

He didn't really want one but he wasn't going to upset the apple-cart now. "Yes, just a small one," he replied, noticing that there wasn't much more than that left in the bottle.

"You look very nice," he remarked. "Are they new jeans?"

"Course not! I've had them for years. I just haven't worn them in yonks," she said, taking him at his word and handing him a miniscule glass of wine. She poured the remainder of the bottle into her own.

Ronan didn't think he'd ever seen the jeans before but then she had so many pairs that he could have been mistaken. He wasn't very observant of what women wore at any time. So he let it go.

Going up to bed he was pleasantly surprised to discover that she'd obviously decided to move back in with him. He considered initiating sex but, after the few drinks and with all the stress he was feeling, he didn't think he'd be able to get it up. Instead, he kissed her chastely as he turned out the light and turned over.

Louise fell asleep immediately, dreaming of racks and racks of designer clothes. Ronan tossed and turned for ages before he eventually drifted off.

Louise knew that she was not out of the woods. There was still the question of the €905 she had put on the credit card. Ronan probably wouldn't discover it until the end of the month so she still had time to do something about it. Then she had a brilliant idea. She rang Mr Mahony, the bank manager, and asked for an appointment. He agreed to meet her the following day.

She dressed with great care as she prepared to go to meet him. He was a bit of a ladies' man and she wanted to look as attractive as possible.

"Louise, you look charming, my dear," he said, ushering her into his office. "And what can I do for you?"

She had it all prepared – a big rigmarole about an opportunity to start a small business from home, making eclectic jewellery, if only she could get the €1200 she needed to get started. She was ever so convincing as she leaned towards him, aware that her top was giving him a nice view of her cleavage. The poor man never stood a chance! When he agreed to give her the loan, she came around the desk and hugged him.

"Oh, you're a terror," he said, obviously enjoying the encounter. "You have all us men wrapped around your little finger!" He even patted her bum as she left his office €1200 richer.

She punched the air once she'd left the bank. "*Yyeeees!*"

She drove to another bank where she lodged €905 to their credit-card account. She had a good story prepared for Ronan when he would finally discover the transactions. Meanwhile, she still had €295 in her pocket to spend! She took the DART into Dublin where she blew all of it, in less than an hour, in the fabulous Jervis Street Centre.

She had all her latest purchases put away in her wardrobe by the time Ronan came home that evening. She felt exceedingly clever as she dished up his dinner of Marks and Spencer's lasagne. She'd even bought a bottle of red wine to go with it.

Ronan didn't know what had come over her. She was in an exuberant mood but it was a hell of a lot more pleasant than the silent treatment he'd suffered the week before. He was grateful for small mercies.

10

The following Monday Zita came out of the meeting positively fuming. What were they thinking? Here they were, about to make a documentary about 'The Women Behind Our Successful Men', and they'd chosen the biggest chauvinist they could find to produce it. Not only that but he was a skirt-chaser and had sexually harassed most of the women at the station and got away with it. Luckily, he knew better than to try it on with her. She wouldn't have taken it lying down. Despite her anger she laughed aloud at the unintentional pun.

She was still furious. If she didn't love her job so much, she'd pack it in, in protest. But what would she do then? She decided to forego lunch and go for a cycle instead in the hope that she could cool down.

"Honestly – men!" she said aloud as she pedalled her way along the seafront at Sandymount.

This prick had been promoted only months ago, by another male of course and with a push from someone in the last government just before they were voted out. It was so unfair. Zita had been up for the same position but had lost out, despite the fact that she was much more qualified to produce this programme than that idiot. But such was life. She really would have to get some political backing, and fast.

People thought that Irish politics had cleaned up their act in the aftermath of all the corruption that had come to light, but in reality nothing had changed. Things were as corrupt as ever. It was a case of 'you scratch my back, I'll scratch yours'. She guessed it would never change. Anyway, she might get her chance very soon. Tonight she was starting her wine course and would begin her assault on Mr Perfect Politician, Carl Dunne, and his unsuspecting Stepford Wife. She grinned to herself at the thought.

Rachel was feeling very hassled. Poor Paloma had been down with the flu for the past five days and it couldn't have come at a worse time. She'd had to cancel two lunches and an interview with *VIP* magazine so that she could look after Paloma and take care of the children. Olga was a great housekeeper and kept the house really clean but she would not have been able to manage it all on her own. Rachel had to cancel a parent-teacher meeting but luckily the school principal understood her problem and had re-arranged a private consultation for her with the teachers. Thank God for the perks that went with being the wife of a politician.

Her wine course was starting that evening and she needed to have her hair blow-dried. She'd been to visit the local day-care centre that morning but she had overrun on time. As a result she had to cancel her hair appointment with her usual salon in Dublin city. She'd never have made it there and back in time to collect the children from school at two thirty. Luckily, she'd been able to secure an appointment with the local hair salon in Sutton.

As she sat with her eyes half-closed she saw the very pretty girl who came in to talk to Keisha, her stylist. Oh, to be so young and pretty again, she thought, as she watched the young girl laugh and smile, admiring her exquisite face. While having her head massaged, her thoughts moved to the evening ahead. She was very much looking forward to the wine course, though for a while it looked like she would have to miss it. Luckily, Paloma had recovered quickly and was on the mend and her neighbour's daughter, Tiffany, had agreed to baby-sit for the evening.

Sam, the guy who was running the course had sounded lovely on the phone. She'd told him that she knew nothing about wine and hoped that the other students were not experts. He'd assured her that they weren't, which made her less apprehensive. It wouldn't do to make a show of herself in front of the others. She'd hinted at this to Sam but he was lovely and understood where she was coming from. She just knew she was going to like him.

Sam prepared for the course that evening firstly by putting a big notice outside, directing everyone down the steps to the basement. He didn't want strangers traipsing through his lovely home. He wondered what his students would be like. They would be eight in total and, as he placed their name-cards and course literature on the tables, he thought about what his first impression of each of them had been. Ellie, of course, he'd met, and also the two apprentices that he'd taken on in his Malahide wine shop for the summer. The two young men were both enthusiastic and eager to learn, in the hope, he suspected, that he would offer them a permanent job at the end of the holidays. This course would sort them out. He made all of his staff follow the course and some had even gone on to study further. It paid back dividends big-time for Sam. His staff were knowledgeable and interested and his customers appreciated that. This in turn led to increased sales which made everyone happy.

As Sam placed Rachel's name-card down beside Ellie's, he wondered if she would last the pace. He'd recognised her name of course, the minute she'd called. It was hard to escape Carl Dunne and his wife these days. They were the new media darlings – both young and handsome. He suspected Rachel was a chatterbox. She'd certainly kept him long enough on the phone looking for reassurance that she wouldn't be the only greenhorn on the course. Despite her looks and wealth she was obviously very insecure. Sam wondered if that had anything to do with her successful, handsome husband. More than likely it had.

Zita Williams was a complete dark horse and had enrolled and paid for the course online so Sam knew nothing about her. He'd been surprised that she hadn't phoned him for directions. Hopefully, she'd find the place okay.

Ronan McIntyre had phoned for directions. He sounded like a lovely chap – quiet and well-spoken. He'd been given a gift voucher for the course for his birthday and he did appear to be very interested in wine. Sam was glad to have another male student there to balance out the women.

He decided to put the two young girls who had been sent along by the supermarket chain sitting at the table with his two young employees. He didn't hold out much hope for these two young ones. He'd found on previous courses that they had little or no interest in the subject. They were there because the supermarket paid for them and insisted that they attend. They would probably rather be almost anywhere else than listening to him expound on wine. Well, we'll see, he thought. Maybe I'm wrong and one of them will turn out to be a model student. Anyway, he'd know soon enough. The first arrival was already ringing at the door.

Ellie was the first to arrive. She had her hair up in a ponytail and was wearing pale-blue torn jeans and a denim jacket over a white T-shirt. Sam thought she looked rather like a schoolgirl let out for the night and would have demanded to see her ID if she'd attempted to buy liquor in any of his shops. He greeted her warmly and when she took off her jacket he looked at the logo on her T-shirt with interest.

"*Anything But Chardonnay*," he read aloud. "What's all this about? What's wrong with chardonnay?"

"Isn't it cute? I saw it in a shop last week and it reminded me of that snooty woman, Judith, telling me she 'didn't *do* chardonnay'," Ellie replied, grinning. "I couldn't resist buying it."

Sam roared laughing. "I remember that now," he said. "And then I told you that the Chablis she was serving was in fact made from chardonnay grapes."

Now it was Ellie's turn to peal with laughter. "Yes, I remember."

"Actually, I think maybe you should know . . ." Sam hesitated, not knowing quite how to say it. "I have to tell you that Judith is in fact my mother."

Ellie looked at him in horror, her face going pale. "Oh my God! Why didn't you tell me that first night when I was going on about her?" she cried, mortified.

"I was enjoying it too much. And anyway you're right – my mother can be very snooty indeed."

"I'm so embarrassed," Ellie said, putting her hands to her face which was now turning a bright red.

"Don't worry, I promise I won't tell a soul," he laughed, his eyes full of merriment.

Of course! Sam *Buckley* – I should have guessed, Ellie thought. Buckley Steadman. Why didn't I put two and two together? She felt really stupid! But, in fairness to her, he had been referring to them as Frank and Judith.

Rachel bustled in looking as if she were going to a first-night theatre-opening. She was wearing a red silk suit and outrageously high heels and her hair and make-up were perfect. Ellie was relieved at the distraction.

"Hi, I'm Rachel Dunne," she introduced herself, shaking Sam's hand and giving him a 100-mega-watt smile. She hadn't been prepared for him to be this young or this attractive. He certainly didn't look like a wine expert with his unkempt hair and casual denim shirt and jeans. She'd always thought that wine types were stuffy old men. What a nice surprise!

"Welcome, Rachel – I'm Sam," he replied, thinking that she looked even lovelier than her photos portrayed her. And what a figure! "And this is Ellie."

"Hi," Rachel said, turning her attention to the young girl. Gosh, it was the beautiful young girl who'd come into the hair salon earlier that day.

"Didn't I see you in Rainbows hair salon in Sutton today?" she asked.

"Why, yes," Ellie replied, surprised that someone as well-known as Carl Dunne's wife would have recognised her. Ellie had even voted for him in the election. He was divine! "Keisha is a friend of mine. I work in the beauty salon two doors down."

"Really! That must be very interesting." Rachel smiled at her.

Ellie didn't have the heart to tell her that it wasn't really all that hot.

Sam showed them to their places and Ellie avoided his eyes, still embarrassed by his revelation. She was pleased to see she was sitting beside Rachel who was obviously very friendly. She sneaked another look at the older woman. God, she was perfect – so glamorous and not a hair out of place! Ellie felt scruffy beside her in her torn jeans and wearing no make-up except for mascara and lip gloss. She had to wear a lot of it at work so she preferred to let her skin breathe when not working. Now she regretted she hadn't made more of an effort.

There was a flurry at the door and Sam's two young workers arrived along with the two girls from the supermarket chain.

Gosh, they're all kids, Rachel thought with dismay. She was only thirty-six but she was old enough to be their mother – and probably Ellie's too for God's sake! Then, as Sam was showing the young ones to the other table, Zita arrived. Rachel breathed a sigh of relief. Thank God, she thought, someone my own age. She gave Zita a dazzling smile as the other woman sat down beside her. Rachel had a feeling that she knew her from somewhere but couldn't quite place her. She sighed. She was normally very good at remembering names and faces but she met so many people these days that it was getting harder all the time. She introduced herself to Zita.

What luck, Zita thought – I'm sitting beside Mrs Prim-and-Proper Dunne. Let the assault begin!

Ellie thought Zita was very unusual-looking. She was wearing Doc Martens and a black leather biker jacket over a denim waistcoat and dungarees. But it was her eyes that were scary and sent a shiver up Ellie's spine. They were watchful, like a cat's, and Ellie had the strangest feeling that this woman could read her thoughts. Zita smiled at her as they shook hands but the smile never reached her eyes. Ellie was instinctively wary of her but Rachel didn't seem to notice as she rattled on.

Ronan was the last to arrive. The women admired the elegant quiet-spoken guy as he joined their table. *Hmmm . . .* he's good-looking, Rachel thought, smiling at him. She'd always gone for quiet shy guys like this – until she'd met Carl, that is. No one could call Carl quiet or shy. Extrovert and gregarious more like! It looked like they were all present as there were no more chairs in the room and Sam had closed the door.

The wine course was about to begin.

11

"Hi everyone, and welcome," Sam began. "Firstly, I'd like to tell you a little about myself. I fell in love with wine when I was fourteen years old and went on a student exchange to France for a month where I stayed with a family in Bordeaux who owned a vineyard. I was fascinated by the whole business, not least because they allowed me a glass of wine every night with dinner which would have been enough for my parents to drag me home had they known about it."

Everybody laughed at this. They could very well imagine it.

"Anyway, I went back every year after that," Sam continued, "and before long knew that this was what I wanted to do with my life. To my parents horror, I left school in fifth year – I wasn't exactly academic – and headed back to Bordeaux to work in the wine business. Five years and a lot of knowledge and contacts later, I came back to Ireland and opened my first wine shop. I now have ten shops, with two more opening shortly along with an online business."

They all looked at him in amazement.

"My goodness!" Rachel exclaimed.

"How did you get into running courses?" Ronan asked him.

"Well, when I got back here I studied for two years for my wine diploma which allows me to lecture for the British Wine & Spirit Education Trust – or the WSET as we call it."

"I thought you said you weren't academic," Ellie joined in.

"Believe me I'm not, but when you're studying something you love, it becomes more like a hobby than hard work."

"*Mmmm* . . ." Ellie said, not convinced.

"So about this course: it runs over eight weeks and at the end of it you should have a comprehensive knowledge of the world of wine and how it's made. Each session consists of an hour of tuition followed by an hour of tasting. I hope that at the end of it you will all have a deeper understanding of this wonderful beverage we call wine. You all have a pack in front of you." He picked up Ellie's one to show them. "It contains a manual, which covers what we'll be doing, as well as a tasting notebook and some other info. You'll also receive a box of six tasting glasses which are yours to keep. You'll take them home with you this evening and please don't forget to bring them next week." He smiled around the room at them all.

"Now, before we start, could I ask each of you to write your name, phone number and email address on this sheet of paper and I'll make copies for everyone." He handed the paper to Ronan. "Now I'd like you to introduce yourselves and tell me what it was that persuaded you to join this course? Can we start with you, Rachel?"

Rachel nodded at Sam and smiled at the others as she rose to her feet. "Yes, well, my name is Rachel Dunne and I have two children: Jacob who's almost eight and Rebecca – we call her Becky – who's six. My husband has recently been elected to the Dáil." She looked around to see if the others had already recognised her. To her satisfaction it seemed they had. "I'm here because I now have a lot of functions to attend and also entertaining to do and I know absolutely nothing about wine, except that I love to drink it."

The others smiled as she sat down with the exception of Zita who thought she might puke.

Ronan was next. "My name is Ronan McIntyre and I'm a draughtsman with a small firm of architects. Like Rachel, I love wine but know nothing about it so I was thrilled when my brother gave me a gift of this course for my birthday. Mind you, I also love my pint of Guinness."

He sat down to the laughter of the group.

Zita was next. "Hi, I'm Zita Williams and I work in television. I'm interested in learning more about wine." She sat down. Nobody laughed. There was something intimidating about her which was felt by all.

"I take it you like drinking wine too, Zita," Sam said. "Looks like I'm going to need more bottles than I'd bargained for tonight!"

Everyone laughed again which lightened the atmosphere somewhat.

Ellie was next. "Hi," she began, beaming at Sam. "My name is Ellie Moran. I work in a beauty salon and I recently got engaged. My fiancé David is an accountant. We were at a dinner in his new boss's house lately and I felt embarrassed not knowing anything about the wine. I met Sam there," she said, smiling at him, her dimples making her even prettier, "and he told me about this course. So, *voilá*, here I am!" She lifted her arms up dramatically. "Oh, and yes, I love wine too except that it makes me very tipsy so it's safer if I stick to beer and cider!"

Everybody in the room laughed and smiled back at her, even Zita. She had that effect on people.

Sam's two young employees from his Malahide shop introduced themselves as Dave and Keith and it was obvious that they were enthusiastic and willing to learn.

Lastly, the two young women from Cash Value Supermarkets spoke. They were called Karen and Hayley. Karen spoke first.

"I'd like to learn more about wine because I work in the wine department of Cash Value and want to be able to help customers choose the right wine." She smiled shyly as she sat down.

Hayley was the last to introduce herself and it was obvious to everyone that she wasn't particularly happy to be there. She had been texting all the time that the others had been speaking. Now, her phone still in her hand, she told the assembled group that her boss had said she had to do the course. Her look told them that she'd rather be anywhere else tonight but here.

The course began.

Sam started by telling them about the different grape varieties and how they were grown. He explained it all so clearly and with such passion that he had his audience hooked. It was fascinating. The hour flew by and with the exception of Hayley who was texting under cover of the table, they all listened intently. Sam felt it was going to be a good group.

"Right, we'll take a fifteen-minute break now while I get the wines ready for tasting. If anyone needs to smoke, they can go outside, but I should warn you that smoking will interfere with your taste buds and therefore affect how you taste the wines."

Hayley didn't seem to care and got up to go out, a pack of ciggies in hand.

"C'mon," she said to Karen who smiled apologetically at Sam.

"We'll just go out for a breath of fresh air," Keith told him. "We won't smoke."

Sam grinned at him. It was already obvious that Keith was interested in Karen.

The other four sat and chatted as Sam opened bottles of wine.

"Can I help, Sam?" Ronan asked him.

"Thanks, Ronan. If you could take these boxes of glasses and put one in front of each place – that would be great." Ronan did as he asked.

"He's fabulous, isn't he?" Rachel whispered, nodding towards Sam. "He reminds me of Jonathan Rhys Meyers – you know, the actor guy?"

"I thought that the first time I met him," Ellie agreed with her. "Sam really knows his stuff. He makes it so interesting." She was leafing through the literature he'd given them. "I can't believe that there are thousands of grape varieties. I've only heard of four or five."

"Well, I know a few more but I could count them all on two hands." Zita concurred.

"He's so passionate about wine, it's catching." Rachel observed. "I can't wait to learn more."

"Yeah, I'm really glad I decided to come," Ellie said as the four young ones came back in the room, Keith and Karen chatting animatedly together. Hayley looked as sullen as before.

The second part of the evening was about to begin.

"This next hour will probably change the way you look at wine forever," was how Sam introduced the tasting session. They all looked at him expectantly, wondering what he meant. "You will never again be able to drink a wine without tasting it professionally and then analysing it."

He told them to take out their tasting glasses and line them up. When this was done he went around and poured two different white wines for each of them.

"This is the part I'm looking forward to," Rachel told them. "I'd like to learn to taste professionally, the way I've seen them doing on TV. I've no idea what to look for."

"Me neither, I haven't a clue," Ellie chimed in.

Sam was familiar with this reaction. Most people, he found, had no confidence in their ability to taste.

"You'll be surprised," he told them. "I want you to taste both wines and then tell me which you think is the best."

They did as he asked. "Now, who thought the first one was the best wine?"

No hands went up. Hayley was about to raise hers but, when she saw nobody else doing so she changed her mind.

"And who thought the second one was the best?"

Eight hands shot up.

"You see, you can already tell the difference between a poor quality wine and a good one. Well done, everybody."

They grinned at one another, pleased that they'd got it right. Ellie gave a little laugh and didn't feel so stupid any more. Rachel sighed with relief, knowing that she hadn't made a complete fool of herself. For all her outward confidence and poise she was insecure underneath it and cared a lot about what others thought of her.

"Tasting is a technique that I'm going to teach you," Sam informed them.

He then demonstrated how to do it, spitting into what looked like an ice-bucket when he had finished.

"Now it's your turn," he told them. "We'll start with the first wine. Take a sip – not too much – suck in air through it, roll it around your mouth and finally spit it out into the spittoon on your table – or swallow it if you prefer."

They did as he instructed, some of them almost choking at the effort. Then, as they spat, it came out in a dribble rather than in the expert way Sam had done it. Everybody laughed.

"Don't worry! This happens to everyone in the beginning. You'll get the hang of it soon enough." Sam smiled at them.

He explained that wine was a very subjective thing and learning to recognise quality was the key.

"There are a lot of bull-shitters – excuse the language – out there, who purport to be wine buffs and all they do is turn people off. The important thing is what *you* find in the wine and my aim is to teach you what to look for."

After that the mood in the room took on a party atmosphere as they tasted, swirled, mostly swallowed, and listened to Sam as he directed them. By the time they'd tasted the six wines – three white and three red – they were entering into the spirit of it and offering their opinions.

"It tasted like cherries," Ellie said of the last wine.

"It has a bitter taste at the end," was Zita's contribution.

"Terrific! You're really getting it!" Sam glowed at them. "That perfectly describes it. It's quite characteristic of Italian wines."

Ellie grinned at Zita who smiled back, both of them extremely pleased with themselves.

By now they were all offering freely of their opinions. Rachel was so extravagant that when she mentioned "sweaty saddles" Sam suspected she'd been reading Oz Clarke. He tried to hide a smile.

When the tasting was over he thanked them for coming, reminding them not to forget their glasses and book packs.

"By the way, I'm looking for some temporary part-time staff for evenings and weekends at three of my shops," he said, as he handed out copies of the list with everyone's phone number and email address. "If any of you know anyone who might be suitable, then I'd like to hear from them. I always prefer to recruit my staff on recommendations."

"I don't really know anyone," Rachel murmured, shaking her head.

"I have a friend who might be interested," Karen said.

"Good. Ask her to give me a call and mention your name, Karen," Sam said, smiling at the young girl.

"Let me think about it," Ronan said, as Ellie frowned, trying hard to think of anyone she knew who might be interested.

"Well, I'm heading to the Castle for a pint, if anyone would like to join me?" Sam said as he tidied up his desk.

"Sure," Ronan said. "I could murder a pint right now."

"Sorry, I can't," Rachel apologised. "I'm driving tonight and I have a baby-sitter, but next week I'll join you if you're going and take a taxi."

"How about you girls?" Ronan asked Zita and Ellie.

"Sorry, I can't either," Ellie replied. "But next week, I'll come too."

Zita decided that if Rachel wasn't going, then she wouldn't bother either.

"Sorry, I'd better not, I'm on my bike."

"Well, we wouldn't want you wobbling home," Sam joked and they all laughed at the image, even Zita herself.

"I'll stay next week," she told him, and was rewarded with a big smile from Rachel.

Cycling home with just the merest wobble, Zita reflected that she'd actually had a great time. Much to her surprise she'd found the course very interesting although she would not be deflected from her real reason for being there. She still had Rachel in her sights.

Ronan helped Sam to tidy up and after Sam had locked up they headed for their pint.

"That was really interesting," Ronan said. "You're a born teacher."

"Thank you," Sam said modestly. "I get a great kick out of sharing my passion for wine. It's a challenge for me to fire someone's interest in it. I really enjoy running these courses."

"Well, you certainly fired some of us up tonight. It's a fascinating subject."

Sam smiled happily and they made small talk until they arrived at the bar.

"I'll get this," Ronan insisted, grateful to Sam for the evening.

"You said you work for a firm of architects," Sam queried him as they took the first sips of their Guinness. "How are things in the business? I guess it must be pretty dire at the moment with the state of things in the property market."

"Dire isn't the word. I'm afraid I'll be out of a job soon." Ronan looked dejected as he spoke. "There's just nothing coming in and I fear the company I work for is about to close down."

"God, I'm sorry," Sam commiserated with him. He'd heard of professionals taking jobs in McDonald's to help pay the mortgage. "Do you have a family?"

"Just a wife."

Sam saw the way Ronan's mouth turned downwards at the mention of her. Things were obviously not good between them. There but for the grace of God go I, Sam thought, thinking of the narrow escape he'd had with Amy, his ex-partner.

"I was actually wondering . . ." Ronan continued, looking away in embarrassment, "the part-time staff you were looking for in your shops . . ." He hesitated. "Well, I was wondering if you would consider me for the job?"

Sam was taken aback but when he saw the look in Ronan's eyes he realised that he was deadly serious. What had things come to in this country when a qualified draughtsman had to plead for a job in a wine shop? Sam had taken a liking to the elegant, well-spoken man. He didn't too often come across people as genuine as Ronan appeared to be.

"Of course – I'd be delighted to have you!" Sam smiled reassuringly at him. "Why don't you call around to my house tomorrow night at – say – eight thirty and we'll discuss it?"

Ronan smiled in relief. "Thank you, Sam, I'd appreciate that."

They shook hands on it.

12

Ellie had promised her mother that she would colour her hair for her after the wine course, which was why she'd declined to go for a drink with the guys. She arrived home to find Marie-Noelle waiting and ready with the colour already mixed.

Ellie pulled on the rubber gloves and, as she parted the hair and started to apply the cream, she excitedly told her mother all about the evening.

"It was brilliant! I learnt so much. It's really a fascinating subject," she exclaimed breathlessly. "And Sam is a brilliant lecturer. I never felt the two hours go by."

Marie-Noelle was delighted with this new-found interest. As she listened to Ellie gabbling on, she smiled to herself. Ellie had been hopeless at school, not because she was stupid but because her mind was so active, darting here and there. She was easily distracted so couldn't concentrate on any one thing for very long. This had frustrated her teachers who had found it hard to hold the child's interest for any length of time. But they told Marie-Noelle, who had known it already, that Ellie was exceptionally bright and that once she found her niche, she would be very successful. Sadly, it just wasn't to be found in school. Her exam results had been dismal but her mother had hoped that as Ellie matured she would find her métier. She got the job as receptionist and odd-job girl in the beauty salon just a week after leaving school. Marie-Noelle had hoped she would find something else more challenging eventually but, five years down the road, Ellie was still there.

She was too easy-going and happy-go-lucky. Marie-Noelle often wished that Ellie had inherited some of Sandrine's ambition. Her older daughter certainly had enough of it to go round and would benefit if she could exchange it for some of Ellie's happy nature. Marie-Noelle sighed. They were as they were and she had to accept it but, hearing her daughter's enthusiasm for this wine course, she dared to think that maybe things were about to change.

As they waited for the colour to take, Ellie recounted the tasting and had her mother in stitches as she described how they'd all spluttered trying to master it. She then described the other students in such detail that Marie-Noelle felt as if she'd been at the course herself. Ellie had missed nothing and left out no detail. Marie-Noelle thought she would make a terrific journalist.

"Carl Dunne's wife was there – you know, the good-looking politician – and holy moly, you should see her! She is just *per*-fect! Fabulous skin and hair and her shoes were to die for. I felt so scruffy beside her."

"Well, I suppose she has to look good all the time with the paparazzi always on the prowl. I see her photo in the paper every second day. What's she like?"

"That's just it – she's lovely. She's very friendly and really interested in everyone."

Laughing at her daughter's enthusiasm, her mother finally went to shampoo the colour out.

"Sam is brilliant. He knows so much about wine," Ellie remarked as she blow-dried her mother's hair.

"How did he get interested in it?"

"He went on a student exchange to Bordeaux and the family he stayed with owned a winery. He loved it there and later dropped out of school and went back there to work with them. He says it's a fabulous place."

"Oh, it is. I have fond memories of the one time Mother took me there as a child to visit my grandmother who was ill. She died shortly afterwards."

"I'd love to go there. Does that cousin of yours still keep in touch?"

"Yes indeed. Josette writes every Christmas."

"Wouldn't it be fun to take a trip there? We could visit some wine places and you could meet up with her," Ellie said excitedly.

"Maybe we will. That would be nice. I'll write to Josette tomorrow."

After hugging her daughter goodnight Marie-Noelle sat thinking about the possibility of returning to Bordeaux with Ellie. It would be so wonderful. Maybe Sandrine would come too. Yes, she'd definitely have to look into it.

Rachel arrived home from the wine course to discover that Carl was still not home. She checked on the children and then, kicking off her shoes, she changed into her dressing-gown. She opened a bottle of wine and curled up on the sofa to read the literature that Sam had given them. She had thoroughly enjoyed the evening. She'd never imagined that so much went into the making of wine and was thrilled that she'd decided to join the course. Sam was so knowledgeable and made it all so interesting. Yes, she was going to enjoy the next eight weeks. The others at her table were very nice people too. Ellie was a darling and Ronan a thorough gentleman. She didn't quite know what to make of Zita but she'd been very friendly and Rachel found her intriguing. She looked forward to getting to know her better.

When Carl arrived home he raised his eyebrows to see his wife with an almost empty bottle of wine in front of her.

"Well, how was the wine course?" he asked, throwing off his jacket.

"Fabulous! I loved it," she said as she reached up for a kiss.

"Doing your homework, I see," he said, lifting the wine bottle. "This is becoming a bit of a habit."

"Absolutely! Sam said we're to taste as much as possible during the week."

Carl heard the slight slur in her voice and poured the rest of the wine into a glass for himself, figuring that Rachel had had enough. He drank it quickly and then stood up.

"I'm wrecked. Time for bed. You coming?"

Reluctantly Rachel left her wine and joined him.

Zita climbed the four flights of stairs to her apartment, anticipating an early night, but as she put her key in the lock her friend Marcus stuck his head out of the next-door apartment and waved a bottle of wine.

"Well, how's the new wine expert?" he asked, grinning. "Want to come in and tell me which end of the vineyard this comes from?"

"Oh, shut it!" she replied, laughing at him but resigning

herself to joining him. If Marcus wanted to chat she might as well do it comfortably over a glass of wine.

"Well, tell me, tell me – what's the gossip?" he asked as he poured the wine for them.

Marcus was the biggest gossip in the land. He was also as gay as Christmas and he was probably the only true friend she had. He had managed to worm all of her secrets out of her – well, not all, but most of them. He knew things about her that nobody else did and yet still he accepted her as she was. Of course, Marcus had more than a few shady secrets in his own past.

"And how was Lady Dunne tonight? Have you persuaded her to be your BFF?"

Zita laughed. She had shared her plans with Marcus about how she was going to use Carl Dunne to forward her career. He thought it was a brilliant idea. He loved intrigue almost as much as gossip.

"Best Friends Forever? Actually, I was surprised. She's quite nice and very friendly. A total airhead, of course, but it's hard not to like her." She got up to read the label of the wine bottle. "*Mmmm* . . . I thought so. Bordeaux."

"You see, one lecture and she thinks she's an expert! God, you're not going to become one of those awful wine bores, are you?" He threw his hands up in mock-horror.

"Of course not, you idiot!" she cried, punching him playfully.

Ronan went home with a light heart. He had found the course riveting and Sam a great guy. To top it all it looked like Sam would give him some part-time work which would mean that he could clear off some of their debts. Things were looking up.

Louise was in a foul mood when he got home and he

feared that it might be the start of another bout of depression. That meant that she would seek retail therapy and their finances just couldn't take any more. He'd better keep an eye on their credit-card account – just to be sure.

He told her about the course but she didn't seem interested. She didn't even pass any comment when he told her about the part-time job Sam had offered him. She just kept staring listlessly at the TV.

Behind Every Cloud

13

Ronan was aware of an air of despondency in the office the following day. After lunch the managing director called a conference and announced that, if business did not improve immediately, they would have no option but to wind up the company. Everyone was fearful and all eight of the staff went for a drink after finishing work. Ronan stayed for just two pints as he had his appointment with Sam to think about. Anyway, the drink didn't lift anyone's spirits – it only made everyone even more downcast.

The meeting with Sam went even better than Ronan could have hoped. Sam asked him to work Wednesday nights, Thursday nights and all day Saturday in the Raheny shop. This suited Ronan perfectly as it was only a walk away from home. It meant that his weekly Saturday golf game would have to go by the board but, well, that was a sacrifice he'd have to make. He could always try and get a game in on Sundays. The way things were going he wouldn't be able to afford to renew his membership next year anyway.

"You'll be standing in for Fiona, who's worked here for three years and lives in the flat above the shop. She's unfortunately having problems with her pregnancy and has been ordered bed-rest by her doctor until the baby arrives," Sam explained. "I'm not sure when she'll be ready to come back to work. Until she does, I'm juggling people around from other shops to fill in for her – but I'm having difficulty covering these hours I am offering you. And so, if you can work these times, the job is yours. It's primarily a wine shop but of course we sell beer and liquor too. No business can survive selling wine alone. I have a great manager there, Dermot, who'll show you the ropes."

Sam was being very generous and the pay he offered was €13 an hour – well above the basic rate.

"That's very generous," Ronan remarked, delighted.

"I find it pays me to pay my staff well," Sam told him. "You know what they say – *pay peanuts, get monkeys.*"

Ronan laughed and Sam laughed along with him.

They shook hands on it and Ronan agreed to start the following Saturday. Sam would be there to introduce him and show him round. He was a lifesaver, although he didn't know it, and Ronan was extremely grateful to him.

Ronan stopped off for a pint at his local on the way home. He couldn't face Louise just yet. He wanted to enjoy the moment. The wine job wouldn't clear his debts of course but he reckoned that he'd be working eighteen hours a week which would mean another €234 weekly, minus deductions, in his pocket. It was a start and every little helped. If only Louise would stop spending then he could manage it. He felt like a weight had been lifted off his shoulders. The pint tasted better than any he'd had in a long time.

14

Ellie was on her lunch hour on Friday and flicking through some copies of *Brides* magazines that a newly married client had given her. She and David had finally decided on a winter wedding and Ellie was getting very excited about the whole thing. She had not been prepared for the large number of engagement presents that she'd received. Truly astonishing! No one had told her it would be like this.

There was so much to arrange and only seven months to do it all. Most important of all was the wedding venue. She wanted a beautiful big wedding with all her friends and family there and she wanted to have it in Clontarf Castle which was only a stone's throw from her home. David had said he was quite happy to let Ellie take care of all the wedding arrangements as he was so busy at work. Earlier that week she had booked the Castle provisionally for the first Saturday in January. She explained to David how lucky they were to get a date at all. The banqueting manager had told her that Saturdays were fully booked out for two years but that they'd had a cancellation. Imagine! Two years in advance! She wondered why the couple in question had cancelled.

The reception was only a small part of the whole wedding of course. The hotel would take care of all that and they seemed to be very professional. Ellie had made a list of all the things that needed to be done. She would have to decide on what she wanted for the table settings, the menu, the wines, the champagne, the flowers, the cake, the goodie bags, the music, what to serve to the evening crowd and last but not least who to invite. God, the list was endless!

Then there was the church and the flowers for there, the service, the music, the vows, the photographer, the cars . . . it went on and on. She had never imagined that there would be so much to do.

Very important, of course, was her dress and all the paraphernalia that went with it: flowers – again! – shoes, veil, headdress. The make-up, fake tan, nails and hairdresser would not be a problem – Chloe and Keisha would take care of all that. She had asked them to be her bridesmaids along with her sister Sandrine. Then there was all of the above for them and the flower-girl and her mother too, of course. It was overwhelming.

She'd have to decide on her hen weekend too and last but not least the honeymoon. She was thinking of either Mauritius or Cuba. She'd never realised that weddings were so much work. No wonder people hired wedding-planners! Well, it would already be expensive enough without having to pay one of those. No matter, Ellie wanted to plan her own wedding and it would be just perfect. David would take care of himself and his best man and groomsmen. She sighed. She understood now why people said that it was a very stressful time. Still, it would be worth it in the end.

Friday nights were not the same any more and Ellie was annoyed with her two friends, Chloe and Keisha. They had started going steady lately with two brothers who now tagged along to the disco every Friday night with them. Ellie felt like a gooseberry and this Friday night was even worse than usual. While her friends smooched on the dance floor she was left fending off numerous drunks who wanted her to dance.

"Dance, huh!" she snorted to the girls when they joined her again. "More like a free feel is what they're after." She was having a miserable time. *She* hadn't pulled out of their Fridays when she'd met David, not even when she'd become engaged. Now it was no fun any more with the two boys hogging her friends' attention. She had no intention of getting up to dance with the four of them.

She decided to leave. She went into the hallway and had just called a taxi when she felt a tap on her arm and a masculine voice say, "Hello there."

She turned around, scowling, to see who was annoying her now, about to snap his head off. Her eyes opened wide with surprise when she saw it was Sam. She saw the cheeky grin as he threw back his head and laughed.

"Sam! What are you doing here?" she asked.

"About to have my head bitten off, I gather, by the look on your face."

"Sorry," she said sheepishly. "I've been pestered by drunks all night and I can't stand it a minute longer. I'm just waiting for my taxi."

"And where's Sir Galahad – your fiancé, I mean? Is he not protecting you?"

"Oh no, it's not David's kind of thing." She gave a little laugh, shaking her head at the idea. "I come here with the girls every Friday but now they've met two guys and I feel like a right gooseberry."

"Poor Ellie," he said, trying to suppress a smile. She looked so forlorn and fed-up.

"What about you? I wouldn't have thought this was your scene either."

"It's not. I was dragged here by some friends." He made a face. "Wish I could leave now too, to be honest with you."

She could see every girl who passed eyeing him and trying to catch his attention. Just then Chloe and Keisha came into the hallway, on their way to the ladies'.

"Hey, Ellie, we've been looking for you!" Chloe cried, looking Sam up and down.

"Fine, well, I'll see you Monday, Sam," Ellie said.

"See you!" Sam said, giving a little wave to all three girls and grinning broadly. He knew Ellie would be in for the third degree from the inquisitive looks on her friends' faces.

"Yummy . . . wouldn't charge him a penny," Chloe drawled as Sam started to walk away, winking as he looked over his shoulder at them.

"Hey, who's the gorgeous hunk?" Keisha wanted to know.

"Naughty, naughty!" Chloe wagged her finger at Ellie.

"Don't be silly. That's Sam, the wine lecturer. I just bumped into him."

"Well, aren't you the dark horse!" Keisha cried. "You never told us he was so sexy."

"If you had, *I* would even have joined the wine course," Chloe said, pouting.

"Don't be ridiculous. Listen, I'm leaving now," Ellie told them as she spotted a taxi pulling up.

How unfortunate that they'd spotted Sam. Now they'd tease her unmercifully about him.

15

Things were so strained at home that Ronan was glad to have the excuse of going to work on Saturday to get away from Louise. He was looking forward to starting work for Sam but also a little apprehensive that he wouldn't be able to cope.

He was amazed at the size of the shop inside. "I didn't realise the shop was so big!" he remarked. "It looks quite small from the outside."

"Yes, it's deceptive. I extended it back, last spring, but it's still not large enough for all the wines I want to stock," Sam explained as he showed him around.

"Oh, gosh, I hope I'll be able for this."

"Of course you will," Sam assured him. "Look, it's all quite simple. Come!"

He walked Ronan around, showing him where everything was stocked. Ronan observed that it was divided in sections by country and then subdivided by grape variety.

"It's well organised," he said, admiring the clearly marked layout.

"That's thanks to Dermot here," Sam said, as a young man appeared beside him, a big smile on his face.

"Nice to meet you," Dermot said to Ronan, giving him a strong handshake. "I'm really glad you're here. Don't worry about a thing. You'll quickly get the hang of it."

He was charming and Ronan warmed to him immediately. By now his fears had calmed somewhat. What have I got to lose, he asked himself. If he didn't like it he could always quit, but he was determined to give it a damn good try. Sam showed him where everything was and how to work the register and card machine. He stressed to him the importance of watching out for underage drinkers. Under no circumstances could alcohol be served to anyone under eighteen or Sam could lose his licence. Ronan was to look for ID if he was in any doubt whatsoever.

"It's not always easy to tell, especially with young girls who are all dolled up, so we have to be ever-vigilant," he stressed.

"Gosh, there's more to this than I thought," Ronan said, trying to remember everything he'd been told. This was different to anything he'd ever done before.

"Don't worry about it," Sam assured him. "Dermot will be here all day and on Wednesday and Thursday evenings, initially. Just ask him if you need any help. You'll be fine."

Ronan hoped he was right.

Sam left and Ronan walked around, trying to familiarise himself with where everything was until the first customer, a little old lady, walked through the door.

"Hello, sonny. You're new here. Where's Fiona?"

"I'm afraid the doctor's ordered her to rest for a few weeks so I'm helping out till she's back."

"That's a shame. What's your name, dearie?"

"Ronan." He smiled at the little woman.

"That's nice. It must be hard for poor Fiona, pregnant

and with no husband to help her. I don't know what the world's coming to – all these young ones having babies with no man on the scene!" She shook her head sadly.

This was news to Ronan. Sam had said that Fiona lived in the apartment above the shop but he hadn't realised that she was a single mother. He'd assumed there was a partner involved somewhere.

"It must be very hard for her alright," he replied. "And what can I get you, Mrs . . . ?"

"Delaney. The usual, sonny. A baby Power."

Ronan got the whiskey for her, checked the price and wrapped it in a paper bag. Mrs Delaney had exactly the right change ready so it was all quite straightforward.

"Well, Ronan, you tell Fiona I was asking for her when you see her," she said, before putting the whiskey in her bag. "Bye, dearie. It's been nice meeting you."

With a little wave, she left.

"My first customer! Well, that wasn't too bad," Ronan grinned at Dermot who was hovering around. He was grinning broadly too and Ronan gave him the thumbs-up sign.

"You'll be fine," observed Dermot. "We have a lot of regular customers like Mrs Delaney who know exactly what they want. Daytime business is generally quiet. Thank your lucky stars that you don't have to work Friday or Saturday nights. Then all hell can break loose."

Ronan settled in quickly and the day flew by. He couldn't wait now to learn more about this fascinating subject of wine and was looking forward to the Monday-night course with great anticipation.

He got to meet Fiona that afternoon. She came into the shop, her pregnancy very obvious, and introduced herself to Ronan. He passed on the message from Mrs Delaney.

"Ah, the old dear," Fiona smiled. "She doesn't really approve of my being a single mother. She's a bit of a nosy parker but she has a kind heart."

Ronan liked Fiona straight away. She was pretty – although not in the same league as Louise – and had a bright sunny nature. She looked very young, twenty-two or three he guessed, yet here she was about to become a single mother. Sam had said that she was a great worker and obviously thought very highly of her.

"Do you mind if I sit and chat for a while?" she asked. "It's usually quiet at this time. I get so bored sitting in the flat with my feet up all day."

"Be my guest," Ronan replied, bringing out a stool for her from behind the counter. She hoisted herself up on it.

She was very easy company and Ronan found himself warming to her. She seemed to know the few customers who came in to the shop very well and it was obvious they were all pleased to see her.

"Well, I enjoyed meeting you," she said, smiling at Ronan, as climbed down off the stool.

"Me too," he assured her. "Drop down any time. I'm here Wednesday and Thursday nights and all day Saturday."

"Yeah, Sam told me. I hope you enjoy working here. He's a great boss. The best."

Ronan didn't doubt it.

Ellie and David had a huge row that Saturday night. There was no doubt he had changed greatly since he'd started this job with Buckley Steadman. For starters, she now saw him only at weekends and then all he could talk about was work, work, work. Whenever she tried to talk about the wedding, he brushed it aside. It was very upsetting. He didn't seem at all interested in it.

Then, over a Chinese takeaway in his flat, he dropped a bombshell.

"I think that we should maybe look for a house on the south side," he remarked casually.

"What?" Ellie gasped, hoping he wasn't serious. He'd been talking for some time about selling his apartment in Malahide and buying something bigger close by and, now that they'd decided on a winter wedding, it was becoming urgent. Ellie often stayed over with him on a Saturday night but the apartment was awfully tiny and really only suitable for one person. Once they were married they would definitely need something bigger and Ellie wanted to have a house with a garden. Until then Ellie insisted on living with her parents as she'd always done. She and David had looked at some houses in Malahide and Sutton, which would be very handy for Ellie's work.

"Yes. Frank was saying the other day that it would be a much better investment and, of course, a better address," David remarked, unaware of the shock he'd just administered to his fiancée.

She looked at him, appalled at the idea. "You can't be serious?" she cried, barely able to get the words out. He couldn't be suggesting that they would leave the north side where they'd both lived all their lives and where all their friends and family lived, could he?

"Yes, think about it, Ellie," he continued, completely oblivious to her distress.

"I work in Ballsbridge now and I would be much closer to the office, not to mention all my colleagues who live south side too. Our social life will be there once we're married."

"You *are* serious," she whispered, tears filling her eyes.

David finally realised that something was wrong.

"Come here, pet," he said pulling her close. "It's not that far and you could get the DART to work. That wouldn't be a problem."

"But I've lived in Clontarf all my life. All my friends are here, not to mention Mum and Dad and all your family and friends too. I know no one there. I really would much rather find a house on the north side."

"We're only talking about a couple of miles, Ellie," he said irritably, trying not to lose his temper with her. "We could check out Sandymount or maybe even Ballsbridge . . ."

She cut him off. "We couldn't afford Ballsbridge or Sandymount. And besides what's wrong with Malahide? You've always said you love it there. You love its village atmosphere."

"Dalkey has a lovely village atmosphere too."

"You know we can't afford Dalkey, David. The houses there cost mega bucks and it's a lot further away than even Ballsbridge."

He let it drop. He knew better than to insist but he hoped that she would come round eventually.

Then, not realising how upset she was, he foolishly added fuel to the fire.

"Anyway, Frank was saying that we really should have our wedding reception in Fitzpatrick Castle Hotel Killiney. His daughter got married there and they did a super job."

"*What?* I'm sure his daughter's wedding was great but I know where I want to have *our* wedding and it's not Killiney Castle, where I've never set foot in my life, but Clontarf Castle which is like a home from home to me and my family!"

With that, to his surprise, Ellie burst into tears and stormed out of the room.

Since when is Frank making all the decisions for us?

Ellie asked herself as she paced as much as she could in the tiny bedroom. David thinks every word he utters is gospel.

She wiped her tears. David had told her that the wedding plans were in her hands and now all of a sudden *he* wanted to make the decisions.

There was a knock on the door and David came in.

It took him over an hour to calm her down but he still didn't commit to anything. He was sure she'd see things his way before long.

16

By Sunday Rachel was exhausted. She'd had a hectic week what with charity lunches and book launches and a political dinner. Carl had even insisted that she accompany him to two funerals that he had to attend. Mind you, they'd turned out to be the most fun. What was it about Irish people and funerals? They were like one big piss-up. She'd thoroughly enjoyed them and Carl had been a bit annoyed at her when she'd got tipsy but while he was busy – networking, as he called it – people were buying her drinks, left right and centre. At one stage she'd had three gin and tonics lined up in front of her.

She wasn't so stupid as to think these people were interested in her for herself. She knew that they were using her as a way to get to Carl. They saw her only as the other half of an up-and-coming politician. She was slowly coming to the realisation that there were very few genuine people in politics. They were all phonies.

And honestly, the things people expected of their politicians! It was as if Carl was now public property and Rachel was beginning to think that they had no private life any more. Carl and she were like two ships that pass in the night, these days. She hadn't expected that it would be quite as demanding as this.

To top it all, here she was spending the afternoon listening to about a hundred screaming children. It was Jacob's eighth birthday and he'd wanted to hold it in this newest play centre which was the 'in' place at the moment. What happened to good old-fashioned birthday parties at home? Nowadays one had to take them to an adventure park or paintballing or something, and each year it was becoming more exotic. Still, it was better to have had it at this venue than to have had them all careening around the house in Howth. She shuddered at the thought.

She'd told Jacob that he could invite ten friends but her son, a chip off the old block, was gregarious and popular like his father and had gone and invited his whole class of twenty-two. What could she do about it? She couldn't have uninvited them. And it would have broken Jacob's heart. Said father, of course, was nowhere in sight but was off playing golf in Royal Dublin with some high-powered financiers. Even on the golf course he was networking!

Sighing she popped two Ibuprofen in her mouth. She wished that she could have a drink to calm her down but that was obviously out of the question with all these kids to supervise.

Hassled and exhausted, Rachel got the children home and while Jacob rushed off to play with his new PlayStation game, Becky retired to her bedroom and her dolls to tell them all about the party. Today was Paloma's day off.

Rachel kicked off her shoes and poured herself a large – make that very large – gin and tonic. As she felt the cool liquid hit her throat, she started to relax. What a day! But it had been worth it to see Jacob's happy little face as he blew out his candles. He'd hugged her then and had said it was the best birthday party ever. That had made it all worthwhile.

She finished her drink in double-quick time and then, as there was no sign of Carl, she poured herself another. By the time he arrived home she was totally relaxed and even a little tipsy. It was obvious that he'd had a few too after his round of golf. They ordered a take-away and, as Rachel was tucking the kids up in bed, Carl opened a lovely bottle of Rioja to go with it. Afterwards she could barely drag herself up the stairs to bed. It cheered her up to think that tomorrow night she would have her wine course. She fell asleep dreaming of rivers of wine flowing down a mountainside.

17

Zita was in foul humour on Monday morning at work. The old, bad nightmares had returned and she'd woken up several times last night, bathed in sweat and shivering violently. She'd had to drag herself out of bed in case she fell back into the dream and as a result she was cranky from lack of sleep. There was nothing she could do about it.

To make matters worse, she had gone down to Westmeath on Sunday to visit her aging mother, which was always guaranteed to upset her. Her father had died shortly after she'd got back to Ireland and she'd been persuaded, against her better judgement, to go to his funeral. She and her mother had come to a sort of truce although there was no love lost between them. She would never forgive her parents for not believing her when she'd told them of the terrible sexual abuse she'd suffered but something inside her drew her back to the only family she had.

She visited her mother about twice a year. She was one of those moan-a-minute mothers who complained constantly and always managed to make you feel it was your fault that she was miserable. No matter that Zita's aunt told her that her mother had always been a miserable sod, Zita always managed to come away feeling guilty. This last visit was worse than usual and she had been relieved to escape from the depressing and oppressive atmosphere of the house where she grew up.

Work wasn't going well either and Zita was more determined than ever to do something about it. Tonight was her wine course and she planned to make a concentrated effort to cultivate Rachel Dunne as a friend.

When Ronan got home from work on Monday evening, Louise was humming to herself and in great form altogether. She was all dressed up, obviously ready to go out. He could hardly believe it. What a turnaround! However, anything was better than seeing her sitting listlessly in front of the telly. He breathed a sigh of relief.

"Your dinner's in the fridge. You just need to reheat it," she told him as she applied the final touch of lip gloss to her lips.

"You look lovely. Where are you off too?" he asked her.

"Just out for a drink with the girls," she replied, flashing him a dazzling smile.

"Please don't drink and drive," he said. "Take a taxi home."

She stuck her tongue out at him.

"Is that a new leather suit?" he asked. "I haven't seen that on you before."

"No, it's an old one of Melissa's but it doesn't fit her any more." She avoided his eyes as she sprayed Chanel Allure on her neck and wrists.

Ronan didn't believe that for a minute. He'd known Melissa for almost seventeen years and she'd been as chubby then as she was now. No, there was something fishy going on here. He felt the muscles in his stomach contract with fear. Please, Lord, don't let her have been shopping again! With a feeling of dread he went into the study to check his credit-card account online. He couldn't believe his eyes. There was a list of purchases, made . . . let's see . . . two Sundays ago . . . which totalled €905 and there was also a lodgment made to the account the following Friday of €905. What was going on? He was mystified. He could hardly believe that even Louise could have spent that much money in one afternoon. But as for the lodgment of €905, well, that was a complete mystery.

Perplexed, he went back into the living-room.

"Louise, what are all these debits on the credit card that you made last Sunday week? And where did this €905 lodgment come from?"

"Oh, that," she said blithely. "Melissa forgot her credit card when we were down in Kildare Village that day and I paid for her things. Then she paid me back last Friday and I lodged it to the account." She beamed at him, almost believing the story herself.

"Oh, I see," he said, not really seeing at all. He knew Melissa was not a big spender so it surprised him that she had spent so much in one afternoon. Still, he felt a great sense of relief that it was not Louise who had spent that €905.

She came to kiss him goodbye before swirling out the door in a cloud of Chanel Allure.

"Women – I'll never understand them!" he remarked to the empty room.

He reheated his dinner and when he'd finished he set

off for the wine course. He was really looking forward to it.

Louise was in an exuberant mood because Alan Brown, the guy she'd met in Kildare Village, had phoned her that day. He'd had to go out of town unexpectedly, he'd said, which was why he hadn't called before now. He asked her to meet him some evening for a drink. He would be out of town on Wednesday and Thursday so they settled on the following Monday, when Ronan would be at his wine course.

"I can't wait to see you," he told her. "You've been on my mind non-stop since I saw you again."

She felt a little flutter in her stomach. His voice sounded so sexy on the phone. It was thrilling and, although she hadn't told him so, he'd been on her mind a lot too. Now she felt exhilarated and dying to see him again. She rang Melissa with the good news and asked her to meet up for a few drinks. She felt like celebrating. She also rang Deirdre and Kate who agreed to join them. She could hardly contain her excitement.

"I told you he'd call," she said smugly to Melissa when they met although secretly when he hadn't called after a week she'd thought he'd forgotten her. Her friend just sighed enviously. Louise had all the luck!

18

The second week of the course began. Sam watched as his students took their place, smiling at the fact that they all made for the same seats that they had sat in the previous week. People always did this. It was interesting to observe that humans were such creatures of habit. It never ceased to amaze him.

Ellie was looking very pretty in a short denim dress and red shoes so high that Sam thought they must give her vertigo. Zita had on the same dungarees and waistcoat that she'd worn the week before. Ronan was wearing a well-cut blazer over a crisp white shirt and looked very elegant indeed. Sam suspected that it was Rachel who had raised the bar style-wise the previous week and this week was no different. She was looking very chic in a cream blazer over a navy shirt and trousers.

They were chatting together and it was obvious that they were all happy to be there. Even the four younger ones seemed animated and Sam hoped not to disappoint them tonight.

He didn't! They all listened fascinated as he explained

what happened to the grapes once they left the vineyard and entered the winery. He spoke with such passion that even Hayley seemed caught up in it and asked him a question about something she didn't understand.

The tasting session went a little better than the week before and Sam was pleased to see that they were getting the hang of it. There was less spluttering and choking than there had been the first week. Ronan appeared to have a very good palate and Ellie was pretty good at discerning the flavours in the wine too.

All in all it was another successful evening and Sam, Ronan, Ellie, Rachel and Zita left in a happy group for a drink in the Castle Bar. The four young ones declined to join them but Rachel overheard them planning to go to The Yacht together.

"They probably don't want to be seen with old fogies like us," she exclaimed laughingly to the others as they walked to the pub.

Sam insisted on buying the first drink. "Then we can all put a few euro in the kitty for the next drink. That okay with everyone?"

They all agreed that that was a good idea. Ronan was relieved. A round would be quite expensive with five people there! Drink prices in Irish pubs were scandalous, he thought, especially now that he knew how much the drinks actually cost in the off-licence. Sam asked them what they wanted.

"Gin and Slimline Tonic for me, please," Rachel said.

A pint of Guinness was what both Zita and Ronan wanted and Ellie asked for a glass of white wine.

"Anything but chardonnay," Sam remarked, grinning mischievously at her.

She blushed, swatting him playfully. He roared with laughter as he went to the bar to order.

"What's all this 'no chardonnay' about?" Rachel wanted to know.

"Well, I was at this very upmarket dinner with my fiancé – it was in his new boss's house – and his wife, who was frightfully snooty, told me she didn't *do* chardonnay when I asked for one."

Rachel looked at her sympathetically.

"Well, I felt like an ass, I needn't tell you, but then Sam – who is their wine merchant – told me that the white Chablis she was serving was actually made from the chardonnay grape. That made me feel better, as you can imagine!"

The others laughed with her and Zita suggested that she should have put the snooty bitch in her place.

"I wish I could have but it was David's boss's wife, so I couldn't very well, could I?" She couldn't bring herself to tell them that the lady in question was Sam's mother.

"No, I suppose not," Rachel agreed with her. "Still, I bet you felt one up on her."

"I sure did but I suppose I owe her. It was because of her that I decided to do this wine course."

"Well, we should be grateful to her so," Ronan said gallantly.

"Yes, her loss is our gain," Rachel smiled.

"I never imagined it would be so interesting," Ellie remarked, wanting to change the subject as she spotted Sam coming back to the table.

He gave Rachel and Ellie their drinks and went back for the pints. He returned shortly afterwards and joined in the lively discussion they were having about what they'd learnt that evening.

Sam noticed that Rachel was drinking very fast and that the gin was having an effect already. He'd also noticed that she was the only one who never spat the wine out at the tasting session but swallowed it every time. Methinks the lady likes her liquor, he thought as they all put €7 on the table for the next drinks.

They had a great time and Zita and Rachel were obviously getting on great as they nattered away to each other. This surprised Ellie as they were so different. She still couldn't make Zita out. Instinctively, she didn't trust her. There was something strange about her – but obviously Rachel didn't think so.

By the third drink Rachel was quite merry and the wine was also having its effect on Ellie. They were both giggling and Sam and Ronan smiled indulgently as much as to say 'women – they just can't hold their drink'. Zita had no problem however and was as sober a judge after three pints.

Rachel wanted to buy a fourth round for everyone but Ronan and Sam both declined, saying that they had to work the following day.

"I'm fine, thanks," Ellie giggled. "If I have another one, I'll fall down."

Rachel looked disappointed and it was obvious that she wanted another one.

"Okay, I'll have a glass of Guinness so, not a pint though," Zita told her and was rewarded with a grateful smile.

Rachel went to order. She was having a wonderful time. They were all such lovely people, she thought as she stood at the bar. They liked her for herself, not just because she was Carl Dunne's wife. That was a welcome change!

As she was drinking her fourth G&T she had a brilliant idea.

"Listen, guys," she said excitedly, "I'm having a party next Saturday night and I'd love you all to come. We've had such fun tonight. Please say yes."

"Well, I don't know. I usually spend Saturdays with David," Ellie replied dubiously.

"Oh, all your partners are invited too. It's our annual Midsummer's Eve party and there'll be music and we're having a spit-roasted pig. Please say you'll come. I'd love to have you all there."

She sounded so earnest that Ellie texted David to see if he would come. She hoped he would. Gosh, her friends would be madly jealous. The Dunnes' parties were famous!

"I'll come," Zita replied.

"Me too," Sam added. "You had me at spit-roasted pig." The others laughed.

"Brilliant!" Rachel cried, clapping her hands. "What about you, Ronan?"

"Well, I'll just check with Louise, my wife, but I don't think we have anything on next Saturday."

Ellie read David's reply: **Sure why not?**

"Great! David and I can come too," she confirmed happily.

"Splendid!" Rachel exclaimed, clapping her hands. She gave each of them her card and asked them to confirm it later with her – then she would give them directions to her house. "It will be so nice to meet all your other halves and I'm dying for you all to meet Carl," she told them, smiling happily.

Not half as much as I'm dying to meet him, Zita thought to herself.

Amid a flurry of kisses and hugs they all said goodbye. Rachel had ordered a taxi while Ronan and Zita set off to take the DART home. Sam offered to walk Ellie home which was only five minutes away.

"She couldn't possibly walk in those heels," Rachel shrieked, pointing to the five-inch stilettos. "My taxi can drop her off."

"It's not my shoes I'm worried about," Ellie admitted with a giggle. "It's all the wine I've had."

"See you all next Saturday," Rachel called happily as they entered the taxi.

"Rachel's something else, isn't she?" Sam remarked to Ronan as they parted.

"She sure is," Ronan grinned, "and she has a good heart."

"It's so great to have made such nice new friends," Rachel confided to Ellie as they entered the taxi.

"You must have lots of friends," Ellie remarked.

"Not at all," Rachel replied sadly. "I have two very good friends, Naomi and Charlotte. We go way back to our junior schooldays, but unfortunately Naomi is married in New York and Charlotte moved to Italy. I really miss them a lot."

"What about all the people you meet through Carl?"

"You can't find true friends in that circle. You never know who you can trust. You think they like you for yourself and then you find out that they want something from you or that they're talking to the media."

Rachel's voice sounded sad and Ellie felt really sorry for her. Her life was obviously not as perfect as it looked from the outside.

They had arrived at Ellie's home and as the taxi came to a standstill Ellie turned to Rachel. "Well, you can trust me, Rachel, and I'm honoured to be your friend."

"Thank you, Ellie. I appreciate that." They hugged goodnight. "See you next Saturday."

"I'm looking forward to it."

On the drive to Howth Rachel thought of the way she'd been betrayed by some friends in the past. It hadn't taken her long to realise that some women befriended her only so that they could get close to Carl. His affair with her best friend had shattered her trust in women and had made her wary ever since. For the hundredth time she wished that Naomi and Charlotte hadn't moved away. She missed them so much.

Ellie had mentioned earlier that she had a sister although it appeared they didn't get along all that well. Rachel had always envied the girls at school who'd had sisters. How wonderful to have someone with whom you could share everything! Someone you could trust. Lost in thought, she realised with a start that she was home. Paying the taxi driver, she went inside, putting these thoughts out of her head.

Zita took the DART into Pearse Station and walked the rest of the way home.

Marcus was waiting for her. "Well?" he enquired.

"*Yeeesssss!*" Zita laughed, pumping the air with her fist. "Mission accomplished!"

"Tell me, tell me!" he shrieked, following her into her apartment.

She opened a bottle of wine and, pouring two glasses, handed him one and sat down on the armchair, her legs dangling over the arm.

"We, my darling, have been invited to a party chez Dunne, next Saturday night."

"You're kidding me!" he cried. "I'm invited too?"

"Well, I can bring a partner and as you're my partner in crime . . ." She rolled the words on her tongue, her catlike eyes glistening.

"*Oh my God*!" he bellowed, unable to believe his ears. "The gorgeous Carl Dunne – up close and personal – I don't believe it!" He jumped up and did a little dance around the room. "*You* are something else, Ms Williams. How did you manage that?"

"I hav vays and means," she replied, acting mysterious.

"Oh, my God, what will I wear?" he cried. "Do you think my purple velvet suit would be okay? It's not too over the top, is it?"

"You? Over the top? Spare me! You're never anything else," she laughed.

"Now, seriously. Tell me all!" he demanded. "How did you get us invited to chez Dunne?"

Rolling a joint expertly, she inhaled deeply and then handed it to him. She told him all that had happened that evening, Marcus interrupting her every thirty seconds for more details. He could hardly believe it! They both got high and drunk as skunks as they fantasised about the following Saturday. It was going to be brill!

To Ronan's relief, Louise's good humour lasted throughout the week. She was even excited about going to the Dunnes' party on Saturday. They rarely went anywhere together these days. Eating out in Dublin was so damned expensive and as for concerts and shows – the prices for them were ridiculously exorbitant. Even a trip to the cinema could cost upwards of €40. Throw in a few drinks before or after and you were talking of €80 – even €100 if you needed to take a taxi. Crazy times, Ronan sighed.

He hoped Louise would not be looking for a new rig-out for the party as their finances would just not stretch to that. So far she hadn't mentioned anything and anyway she had three wardrobes full of clothes to choose from. It

119

was not as if any of the people there would have seen them before.

He was really enjoying the work in Sam's wine shop and was already settled in there and had got to know the ropes. The extra money he was earning was a godsend and meant he could pay a little more off their credit-card bill. There was light at the end of the tunnel. Fiona came down to the shop every time he was on duty. He had offered to go up to her at his break to save her climbing the stairs but she insisted on coming down, saying that she liked the opportunity to escape the confines of her apartment.

"It gets pretty boring looking at the four walls all day," she confided to him. He didn't doubt it so he asked her to come at his break-time so that they could chat without interruption and share tea and biscuits together in the small staff kitchen behind the shop.

He was amazed when she told him that she was actually twenty-seven years old. She looked much younger. He was growing quite fond of her and wondered how she had found herself in this predicament. He didn't know her well enough yet to ask her and she didn't venture any information. Still, she was always good-humoured and laughing and he enjoyed their little chats.

19

Rachel was in a tizzy. Carl had disappeared to meet some of his cronies when there was so much yet to be done. He really was most inconsiderate. The house was a scene of chaos. The caterers were flying all over the place, pushing past her with trays of food. She dared not go in the kitchen as she would only be in their way. They had set the roasting pig up earlier and it had been rotating on its spit in the garden for hours. The aroma coming from it was delicious. The string quartet that would play for the first part of the evening had just arrived and were setting up beside the fountain and the band who would play later were busy trying to get the amplification right. She counted at least five guys, besides the musicians, who were helping with this. It felt like an invasion had taken place. She just wished it was all done and then she could relax.

Carl's friend, who had a drinks company, was delivering the bottles of spirits but had rung to say he was running a little late. She hoped he would be here before her guests arrived. Trust him – always the last minute!

Luckily she had insisted to Carl that she order the champagne and wine from Sam, who had delivered it all the previous day unlike Carl's merchant, so at least they had plenty of that. The champagne was chilling, ready to be served to their guests as they arrived. Sam had given her a generous discount, unlike that other creep who she suspected charged them more because of who they were.

This reminded Rachel that what she badly needed was a drink, and she went to get one.

Sipping a large gin and tonic, she surveyed the scene. Because the weather had turned out to be glorious and the forecast was that it would stay that way, they had considered dispensing with the large marquee altogether. However, knowing how often the forecasters got it wrong, they had decided to erect it, just in case. They would, however, leave the sides open and the canvas drawn back as drapes. There were heaters set amongst the tables for later in the night when it could get chilly and they could always close the sides if the unthinkable happened and it rained.

The caterers were decorating the tables and chairs which were now arranged in the open marquee and Rachel had to admit it looked great. She had gone for an *Arabian Nights* theme and it did look very exotic with deep orange-and-red chiffon draping on the ceiling, making it look like a Bedouin tent. There were candles in lanterns on the tables and hanging from the ceiling and Rachel was delighted that the caterers had done such a wonderful job. She had also secured the services of a fortune-teller, Madame Farah, to add to the fun. She would be located in a tent at the bottom of the garden. Yes, even though it was still pretty chaotic it was beginning to come together very nicely, no thanks to Carl. Where the hell was he, she wondered as she angrily texted him.

They'd had quite a row on Monday night when she'd told him she'd invited some of the people from her wine course to the party.

"They'll have nothing in common with my friends," he'd whinged.

"How do you know?" she'd demanded angrily. "They're nice, genuine people which is more than can be said for some of the hangers-on you've invited."

Carl didn't reply knowing that it was useless to argue with her when she was drunk, which she clearly was. They'd been cool with each other ever since.

Finally, everything was ready. Carl was home – he'd even brought her a big bouquet of flowers which had pleased her. She knew it was meant as an apology. The spirits had been delivered – albeit only thirty minutes before the guests were due – and the scene was set. For once the weather forecasters had got it right and it was a truly beautiful Midsummer's Eve night.

Rachel and Carl had showered and changed and were both looking resplendent. She was wearing a striking two-piece in a burnt orange which accentuated her colouring. She'd had it made especially for the occasion and it was a modest version of a harem dancer's costume, with silk and chiffon harem trousers, a beaded, chiffon-sleeved top and gold jewelled sandals. She looked exotic and eastern and her bare midriff was tanned and toned. Carl was wearing a genuine Moroccan rigout which he'd bought in a Moroccan souk the previous year. It was a white linen tunic top with gold embroidery, loose white trousers and a sleeveless floor-length gold silk coat. They made a stunning glamorous couple. Carl poured them both a drink and they went out to the garden for a last-minute check.

"You look beautiful, my darling," he said, as he raised his glass to hers. "Every man in the place will be madly jealous of me."

She smiled, looking into his eyes. "You look pretty gorgeous yourself. I'll have to keep my eye on you tonight with all the beautiful women around." She said it half-jokingly.

"None will be a patch on you, my dear," he murmured, taking her hand and kissing it.

They heard the doorbell ring. The first guests had arrived. She gave the string quartet the signal to start playing.

Ellie and David didn't want to be the first to arrive so they came about twenty minutes late. The taxi was stopped at the gate where a man with a clipboard checked them off the guest list and opened the security gates to let them through. They drove down the steep drive to the house where the taxi deposited them at large entrance doors which stood open.

They passed through these and entered through huge glass double doors into a large spacious foyer where they were greeted warmly by Rachel and Carl.

"You look sensational," Ellie exclaimed, admiring Rachel's exotic outfit.

"Thank you, you look very pretty too," Rachel replied, kissing her on both cheeks. "This is my husband Carl. Carl, this is Ellie from my wine course and her fiancé . . . eh . . ."

"David," Ellie introduced him.

"Nice to meet you both." Carl took Ellie's hand to his lips and kissed it.

She blushed. What a charmer! And even better-looking than his photos!

"Beautiful *and* a wine expert," Carl said, making her blush further.

"Oh, I wouldn't quite say that," Ellie giggled.

As they were chatting Ronan arrived with Louise and Rachel made the introductions once again. Carl went through the same routine with Louise who was obviously flattered by his attention and flirted right back at him.

Rachel took an instant dislike to her although she *was* awfully pretty with that gorgeous red hair and green eyes.

"Quite a house you have here," Ronan remarked, looking up at the glass dome which was reflecting the evening sun and filling the space with light.

"Thank you, we love it," Carl replied.

"Ronan works for a firm of architects," Rachel explained.

"Oh well, you'll be interested in the design of the house so. I'll show you round later."

"Thanks. I'd appreciate that. I did read about it in the *Plan Architectural Review*."

"Yes, that was a good article," Carl replied, pleased with his interest.

"Are your children here?" Ellie asked. "I'd love to meet them."

"Good heavens, no!" Rachel cried, throwing her hands up in mock horror. "They're spending the night with my parents. I'd never get them to sleep with all this going on."

"That's a pity. I'd love to have met them but I can see your point."

"You'll meet them another time," Rachel promised.

"They're wonderful kids," Carl smiled at Ellie.

"I'm sure they are," she smiled back, unable to resist his charm.

They chatted some more and sipped on the champagne offered to them by a passing waiter. Then, when Rachel and Carl went to greet some newcomers, the two couples moved out onto a terrace at the back. Below, an uninterrupted view of Dublin Bay stretched out before them. It was stunning. They went down a long flight of steps to a lower terrace just above the garden.

"Wow!" Ellie exclaimed as she turned and gazed up at the amazing house which was set into the hillside. She saw it was built on three levels and it appeared to be made almost entirely of glass. "What an amazing house!"

"Holy moly!" David exclaimed, looking up at the fabulous structure. "That is a house and a half. Like something out of the future."

"Wow, this is something else, isn't it?" Louise remarked breathlessly.

"It sure is," Ellie replied. "This is how the other half lives." There was awe in her voice.

David and Ronan smiled at each other as if to say 'hope this doesn't give them any ideas'.

"What a house!" Louise said, waving her hand around. "It's fabulous. They must be filthy rich. Lucky buggers!"

Ronan squirmed at the inappropriate nature of her remark.

"And just look at this garden," Louise continued, unaware of his discomfort. "God, it's gigantic! We could fit our garden into it twenty times over."

Ellie heard the envy in her voice as they surveyed the scene. "It *is* stunning," she agreed.

Beneath the huge terrace where they were standing was a formal garden with a fountain beside which a string-quartet was playing. There was a sun-deck to the side of the house with luxurious white leather sun-loungers dotted around it and a hot-tub. To the other side of the house there was a state-of-the-art children's playground.

"So you're an architect?" David remarked, turning to Ronan.

"No, I'm a draughtsman. Not a very good profession to be in, in this economic climate," Ronan replied ruefully.

"I can imagine. I play golf with an architect and he's always moaning about how bad it is."

"Where do you play?" Ronan asked, wishing to change the subject.

A conversation about golf ensued and Ellie was pleased to see that they were hitting it off really well. Well, it would have been impossible not to like Ronan. He was such a sweetie. Ellie wasn't so sure about his wife who she didn't much care for.

"I can't even imagine what it must be like, living in a place like this," she observed, turning to Louise.

"Some people have all the luck," Louise replied sulkily.

Ellie decided to steer the conversation away from the Dunnes' good fortune.

"What do you work at, Louise?" she asked as she sipped her champagne.

"I don't. I did work in a boutique near us but it closed down last year. It's impossible to get any kind of job nowadays with all those Eastern Europeans taking them."

Ellie heard the bitterness in her voice. "Do you have children?" she tried again.

"No. We can't have them." Louise pressed her lips together in a firm line.

"Oh, I'm sorry," Ellie said sympathetically, waiting for Louise to say more, but nothing more was forthcoming.

Ellie was at a loss for words. Every time she opened her mouth she seemed to put her foot in it. She decided to try another tack. "I really like your shoes. They're Louboutins, aren't they?"

Louise brightened up visibly as she lifted her shapely leg and twirled her foot around. "Yes, aren't they gorgeous?" She was smiling again now.

"I'd love a pair but they're dreadfully expensive, aren't they?"

Ronan happened to catch that last remark and eavesdropped on their chat.

"Yes, they are, but I know a site online where you can buy the most fabulous shoes and pay by instalments."

Ronan winced. What was she up to now? This was the first he'd heard of her shopping online. He groaned. God knows how much interest they were charging her. He'd have to tackle her about it as soon as they got home.

He turned back to David who was saying something to him.

"Sorry, David, what was that?"

"I was just observing how amazing it is that Northern Ireland has produced such terrific golfers."

Ronan agreed and they debated the merits of Rory McElroy and Graeme McDowell and what the future held for them as the two girls continued talking about fashion. Ellie was relieved that she'd found something in common with Louise.

Just then Rachel came out onto the terrace leading Zita by the hand. Zita was dressed in a fitted black tuxedo suit over a white shirt which was open low enough to show off the contours of her breasts. She also wore a loose black tie, strategically low, which drew attention to them, and topping it all off was a black fedora hat. Her Doc Martens were abandoned in favour of a vertiginous pair of black patent boots. She was accompanied by a very colourful guy who had a long ponytail and was dressed very dramatically in a purple velvet suit.

All conversation stopped.

"Oh, my God! Look at that woman with Rachel!" Louise whispered. "She's weird."

"That's Zita. She's on our course," Ellie told her.

"And I don't think she's weird," Ronan informed his wife. "She just dresses uniquely."

"You can say that again!" Louise sneered.

Ellie was amazed. She'd thought Zita didn't give a damn about how she looked but she'd certainly pulled out all the stops tonight. Men were turning their heads to look at her admiringly.

Rachel led Zita over to them. "Ronan, could I ask you to make the introductions? I have to get back inside to greet some more guests."

"Of course." Ronan proceeded to introduce Zita to David and Louise as Rachel hurried away.

"This is Marcus, my friend," Zita said, introducing him to everyone.

"Hi, guys! This place is hot, isn't it?"

"Don't tell me he's not gay," Louise whispered to her husband who glared back at her, hoping that no one had overheard her.

"It certainly is," Ronan replied to Marcus. "It's actually won some architectural prizes."

"Not surprised. It's something else!"

The place was beginning to fill up and Ellie looked around at the glamorous guests who were filing onto the terrace now in a steady stream. She recognised some faces from the television and newspapers. There were actors and TV people and lots of politicians. She even spotted an international rugby player.

"Oh my God, there's that American actor who was on the *Late Late Show* last week," she exclaimed, as she saw the famous face chatting to some people nearby. She wished that she could remember his name.

"I must go and get his autograph," Louise cried, opening her bag to find a pen and paper.

Ronan grabbed her arm and pulled her back. "You'll do no such thing," he hissed. "This is a private party and he won't want to be bothered by autograph hunters."

Louise made a face but stayed put. She thought it was most unfair as she had noticed some other famous faces from TV too.

"My goodness, half the government is here," David observed, looking around.

"Yes, we are partying in exalted circles tonight," Zita remarked in an ironic tone. Working in television, she was used to mixing with all these famous people and it always amused her to see how impressed normal folk were by them. They were no different really to everyone else but your average Joe Soap couldn't see that. Celebrity was a curse, she thought grimly, as she finished her champagne.

"I'm going for a decent drink," she announced. "One glass of this stuff is enough for me."

She headed for the bar but it was packed. She looked around and spotted Carl walking towards the sun-deck. She ambled over after him. He was standing alone at a bar in the corner.

He saw her walk towards him. God, she was sexy. There was something erotic about a woman dressed in a man's suit and she certainly knew how to wear it.

"Hello there," she said, her eyes looking him up and down.

"Well, hello," he replied, surprise in his voice. "I see someone else has discovered my secret haunt."

"Yes, I thought I'd seek out a decent drink. One glass of champagne is all I can stomach."

"Me too," he smiled at her, asking her what she'd like.

"A whiskey, please. On the rocks."

"A girl after my own heart," he smiled and nodded to the barman who took a bottle of Lagavulin single malt from under the counter.

"My private stash." He grinned like a guilty schoolboy as the barman poured it for her.

"I'm honoured," she said sarcastically.

"*Sláinte*!" Carl raised his glass to her.

She nodded and raised her glass to him, regarding him from under her half-closed eyes.

"I've seen you before," he said, the memory stirring in his mind. "In the Four Seasons, I think." He couldn't really remember the location but remembered locking eyes with her and feeling the chemistry between them.

Zita was secretly pleased that he had remembered her but feigned that she had no memory of it. "I don't think so," she remarked.

"I'm Carl Dunne. And you are?" He extended his hand to her, knowing instinctively that kissing her hand would not impress her. It irked him that she hadn't remembered seeing him. That didn't happen to him often.

"Zita Williams. I'm on the wine course with Rachel." She took his hand in a firm handshake.

He held it longer than necessary. "You look very distinguished. A nice change from all the girly frocks here tonight. I like your style." She was certainly different, he thought, as he looked into her eyes. They could have belonged to an exotic cat such as a leopard or panther.

131

They were a most unusual colour and she certainly knew how to use them. Her body also had a feline grace about it. God, but she was exciting!

She surveyed him coolly, her gold-flecked eyes half closed and her long, black lashes making her look sultry and dangerous. She was aware that she had aroused his interest. This was what she had intended of course, why she had dressed as she had. She had obviously succeeded!

"I work in television," she told him.

"Interesting," he said. "I'd better keep in your good books so." He looked at her sexily over the rim of his glass.

He really was the most outrageous flirt. She threw back her head and roared with laughter.

"I'll keep you in mind when I come to do a programme I'm planning. It's about Irish success stories."

She had appealed to his ego. She watched as he puffed his chest out and visibly preened.

"I'd like that," he said, flashing that devastating smile of his.

God, but he was sexy. Once again she found herself wondering what he would be like in bed. She had no doubt that he knew how to please a woman. Well, she hoped she'd get to find out soon.

"Do you have a card?" she asked.

"Not on me but I'll get one for you. Give me an excuse to talk to you again."

"Never off duty, I see," she observed, raising her eyebrows and giving him a mocking smile.

He laughed. "You're something else! I like you. Don't you have your card on you?"

"Of course," she replied, taking one out of her pocket and handing it to him.

"*Mmmm* . . . more than just a pretty face, I see." He smiled lazily at her after reading the card.

She laughed and raised her glass to him.

Turning her back on him she went back to the table, adrenalin coursing through her body. Carl Dunne would be a piece of cake. She would play him like a cat with a mouse. Yes, sir! It would be a thrilling game. She was looking forward to it.

20

Zita rejoined the group. There was still no sign of Sam although the place was heaving. There must have been close on eighty or ninety people there.

"Does anyone know if Sam's coming?" she asked the assembled group.

"He said he'd be here," Ellie said as she looked to the others for confirmation.

"I spoke to him today," Ronan told them, "and he said he might be a little late."

"I hope he makes it before supper or he'll miss that delicious pork," Ellie remarked, as she watched people start to move down into the marquee.

David sniffed the air. "That smells so good. I can't wait to taste it."

"I love spit-roast pork. That crackling . . . yummy . . ." said Ellie.

"Speak of the devil – here comes Sam now," Zita said and they all looked towards the upper terrace of the house where Sam had appeared.

Rachel was leading him down the steps towards them, a pretty dark-haired girl following.

"Look who's here," she cried, smiling happily around the group.

"Hi, guys," said Sam.

Rachel then introduced him to those he hadn't met yet and he shook hands with them.

"This is Orla," he said, bringing the girl forward to meet them.

Ellie was surprised. Sam had told her that he'd just recently broken up with his long-term girlfriend. He certainly hadn't wasted any time replacing her. Unless, of course, this was her and they had made up again.

A ringing cry came from behind him. "Sam, I don't believe it!"

They all looked to see who the owner of this husky American drawl might be.

Ellie gasped. My God, it was Jade Keating, the famous Irish actor who had made it big in Hollywood. She was even rumoured to be dating Colin Farrell.

"*Dahhlling,* how lovely to see you again!" cried Jade, draping her long arms around Sam's neck as she kissed him full on the mouth.

"Jade, great to see you," Sam replied, untangling himself from her grasp.

Ellie felt completely insignificant beside her. It didn't help that David, Ronan and Marcus were all gaping at Jade, their mouths open. She was even more beautiful than her photos. Six-foot-two, with a tiny waist and boobs that were most certainly not the ones nature had bestowed on her. They were barely concealed in a low-cut wisp of a dress which clung to her contours like clingfilm. It barely covered her knickers and her long legs seemed to go on forever. She towered over them all. It was no wonder the men were staring with open mouths.

"It's been too long," she replied, snuggling into Sam. He looked embarrassed.

To Ellie's surprise, Orla didn't seem a bit put out and smiled as she shook Jade's hand.

Sam introduced her to the rest of the group.

"Sam is a *very* old friend of mine," Jade drawled, intimating that they were much more than just friends.

Friends with benefits, more like, ran through Ellie's mind – the new hip expression for good friends who had occasional sex with each other. Ellie could never understand that kind of relationship.

Louise was acting star-struck and Ronan was afraid she might ask for Jade's autograph. He was a bit overawed to have this famous actress here in the flesh – very much in the flesh – chatting nonchalantly with them.

"Okay, time for supper!" Rachel cried, clapping her hands.

She led them to the marquee where they saw from the table plan outside it that they were all to be seated together on Table 9. Jade stayed latched on to Sam and it was obvious she intended sitting with them.

The group was surprised and pleased to see that Rachel also was joining them.

"Don't you need to sit with Carl and all the VIPs?" Ellie asked her.

"No, I'm very happy to be sitting with you guys," she replied, giving a little grimace. "He's sitting with – I won't call them friends – but business acquaintances of his."

Ellie felt sorry for her. Despite her outward gaiety and confidence, Ellie could see that Rachel was very lonely. From what she had confided to her in the taxi, it would seem that Rachel had become disillusioned with her 'perfect' life.

They had to pull another chair up for Jade. She

plonked herself between Sam and Orla and Ellie felt sorry for the young girl. If Jade had done that to her, she'd have been furious. Rachel was quite pleased to have such a famous actress at her party and took great satisfaction from Carl's surprise when he saw Jade sitting at their table. He'd hot-footed it over and sat chatting to them all before dragging himself back to his political pals.

Take that, Carl! Rachel thought smugly. He'd be happy now that she'd invited her friends to the party!

There was a marvellous buffet set out along the back of the marquee and they all went to help themselves, loading their plates with all the lovely salads and different types of potatoes and vegetables. Then they passed by the spit where a chef sliced the pork and piled it on their plates. There was also fish and other meats on offer but everyone went for the delicious roast pig. Jade naturally didn't indulge, stating that she wasn't hungry.

"There's no secret to being that skinny," Rachel said in a low voice to Ellie as they made their way back to the table. "If I didn't eat, I'd be that skinny too." Ellie giggled. The champagne was having its effect on her.

"She's chain-smoking too," she whispered, noticing that Jade was lighting one cigarette off another. "That can't be good for her."

"No, but she probably does it to stay slim."

"*Yeuch*! I don't know how she stands it. I hate cigarettes."

Ellie made a face and Rachel laughed. She really was getting very fond of the young woman. Pity her fiancé was such a bore.

Listening to an older TD colleague of his rattling on about the latest bill proposed by the opposition, Carl longed to escape to the wine-club table, not least because the mysterious Zita and the gorgeous Jade were there. From what little he'd seen of them, he could see that they were a fun bunch. Ronan and Sam were good guys and Ellie was a cute little thing. Marcus seemed to have a quick wit and was keeping them all entertained. As they laughed uproariously at a story he was telling them, Carl looked over at them enviously and caught Zita's eye. Gosh, but she was damned exciting!

Over at their table, Rachel was hopping up and down like a hen on a hot griddle, checking on the food and making sure her guests were all being catered for. She ate little but Ronan noticed that she was never without a glass in her hand.

The group was enjoying the wonderful spit-roast pig, especially relishing the crisp crackling.

"I think I'm going for more," Ellie announced. "Anyone else coming?"

As one, they all rose, laughing aloud. Jade wrinkled her pretty little nose at this display of gluttony. While they were gone, she poured herself another glass of white wine and lit yet another cigarette. If she had to have calories, she preferred them in liquid form – alcoholic, of course.

Rachel was delighted that they were all having such a good time and delighted that she'd thought to invite them. With reluctance she left the table yet again to circulate among the other guests, most of whom Carl had invited with an ulterior motive. There were bankers and developers, not to mention hordes of politicians of course, all networking like mad. If Rachel were to be honest, she had very little in common with any of these people. She hopped from table to table saying a few words to everyone and making sure they were all enjoying themselves. Due to the endless supply of alcohol there was no problem there. Waiters kept replenishing bottles of wine on tables and many people complimented her on her choice of wines, asking her where she'd found them.

"Thank you," she replied graciously to each one. "I've started a wine course and the wines are imported by my lecturer, Sam. He's here tonight. I'll get his card for you if you like?"

She was pleased to be bringing business his way. She returned to Sam and took all the cards he had on him to distribute to those who'd asked for them. Sam was grateful to her.

"Hey, you've hardly eaten anything," Sam remarked when she finally returned to the table.

"Oh, I'm fine. I'm too worried about everything to think of eating. I'll eat later when everyone else is finished."

"Sit down here, girl, and have your supper!" Sam ordered her. "Everyone's having a great time. Just listen to the decibels of people talking."

She cocked her head and had to agree that the noise was pretty encouraging. She did as he'd ordered and with a grateful smile accepted the glass of wine he poured for her as she tucked into her food.

"*Mmmm* . . . this is good," she mumbled between mouthfuls. "Thank you, Sam."

"My pleasure," he grinned back, raising his glass to her.

Ellie noticed that he hadn't been remotely concerned that Jade had not eaten a bite.

"It really is a fabulous evening, Rachel," she told her hostess. "You've done a brilliant job planning all of this." She waved her hand around.

"Thank you," Rachel smiled with pleasure at the compliments.

"I guess this is all your doing," Zita interjected. "I don't suppose Carl did much to help?"

"Well, you know, he's frightfully busy with his Dáil work. He leaves all this kind of thing to me," Rachel replied loyally. "Besides, I really enjoy doing it."

"Well, you've done a super job. I hope Carl appreciates it."

"Oh, he does," Rachel gushed but Zita wasn't convinced.

Just then the man in question arrived at their table. "I reckon this is the most fun table in the room – I feel like I'm missing where the party's at," he told them, laughing and swigging back his whiskey. "My card, Zita," he said, handing it to her. "We met when we both went to the sun-terrace bar for a whiskey," he explained, mainly for his wife's benefit. "Zita's going to interview me for a TV programme she's involved with."

"Wonderful!" Rachel cried, clapping her hands.

"Can I get you another whiskey, Zita?" he asked.

"Thank you, that would be lovely," she purred.

"Hey, what's wrong with my wine?" Sam asked.

"I love wine with my meal but otherwise I'm a whiskey drinker," she informed him, unabashed.

"Anyone else for a drink?" Carl asked.

"I'd like a gin and tonic, please," Louise piped up.

Ronan was apprehensive. She'd been knocking back the wine like nobody's business and now she was starting on gin and tonic. God! The last thing he needed was for her to get drunk. He knew he must avoid that at all cost.

After the supper had finished with a fabulous array of desserts, the tables were pushed back to the side of the marquee leaving the centre free for dancing.

"I need to go to the ladies'. Can you tell me where it is, Rachel?" Ellie asked, standing up.

"Come, I'll show you," Rachel answered. "I need to go and circulate again anyway and see how everyone is doing."

"I'll come too," Louise said, jumping up and grabbing her bag.

Orla wandered off to talk to some people.

After they'd gone, Carl arrived over to the table and beckoned to Ronan.

"Want to see the house now, Ronan?" he asked.

"Can I come too?" Marcus asked jumping up quickly, full of anticipation.

"Sure, no problem."

"Do you mind if I join you?" Zita asked.

"Our tour will be all the more interesting if you do," Carl replied, holding her in his gaze.

She smiled at him, her eyes languid. The handsome devil was flirting with her again.

Ronan was relieved that Louise had gone to the ladies' with Ellie, otherwise she would surely have wanted to come and it would have been like a tourist tour of the White House. He hadn't missed how taken she was with Carl. He was everything she'd ever wanted. Ronan knew that he was a big disappointment to his wife. She'd thought when she'd married him that it would all be a bed of roses. It hadn't worked out like that, of course. He had opted to join a small dedicated firm which was committed to improving the structure of hospitals and schools. Not a big money-spinner unfortunately, but Ronan loved the work he did. Louise would have relished being married to someone like Carl with all the glitz and glamour it entailed, not to mention the millions that would have been at her disposal. He knew his wife was thinking this same thing. Maybe it had been a big mistake bringing her here.

Blinded by love, it had taken Ronan a while to realise just how shallow his wife was. He knew she didn't love him any more and sometimes he wondered if she ever had.

Jade had disappeared to talk to some friends and Sam was sitting alone with David at the table as they waited for the band to start up. He was trying hard to make conversation with Ellie's fiancé but was finding it increasingly difficult. It was obvious that the other man was not enjoying himself.

"Are you not having a good time?" Sam couldn't resist asking.

"I'm afraid I hate these kinds of parties." He grimaced. "It's all so . . . shallow, I guess is the word I'm looking for."

"Oh, it's not so bad," Sam replied. "Rachel and Carl are very welcoming and you have to admit they've put on a jolly good show."

"I suppose. It's just not my kind of thing. No decent conversation."

Sam gave up on him. It was a party for God's sake and David wasn't exactly the world's most interesting conversationalist. He wondered what Ellie saw in him. Sam sure as hell couldn't figure it out.

Rachel gave Ellie and Louise directions to the ladies' room where they marvelled at the opulent furnishings. There were fresh flowers and Jo Malone toiletries on the marble tops and even a chaise longue and two armchairs. It would not have been out of place in the poshest hotel in Dublin.

"Oh my God, I'd kill for a house like this," Louise moaned. "Look at these gold fittings and just look at all the beautiful towels in here!" She opened cupboards one after the other. "Rachel is a lucky bitch!"

"Yeah, well, she can't have an easy life. Being married to a politician is not exactly a piece of cake. I think she hardly ever sees him."

"That would suit me just fine," Louise said, with a grimace.

"How can you say that?" Ellie asked haltingly.

"Well, you know, marriage isn't always a bed of roses, especially when there are money problems."

Ellie heard the despair in her voice. "Well, I suppose times are tough now for everyone," she said gently, not wanting to disparage Ronan.

"Not for Rachel, obviously! I hope your David has pots of money."

Ellie was horrified by this announcement. "What's money got to do with it? What about love?"

Louise stopped applying her eyeliner and looked at Ellie as if she was mad. "Love has nothing to do with it. Trust me, it's true what they say – love flies out the window when poverty comes in the door."

Stunned into silence, Ellie applied her lip gloss, troubled by what Louise had said. Did Ronan really have such money problems and was he as unhappy as his wife appeared to be? God, it must be awful to be stuck in an unhappy marriage. Ellie shuddered.

"Let's have a nose around," Louise suggested when they'd finished and left the ladies' room.

Ellie felt very uncomfortable as the other girl opened doors and peered into rooms. She felt like an intruder and was hoping nobody would come along and catch them.

"I'm going back," she insisted when Louise wanted to go into the other wing of the house.

Annoyed, Louise had no choice but to follow her, but insisted on detouring by the sun-deck to have a look at it. Seeing the hot-tub made her even more discontented. "Honestly, some people don't know what to do with their money," she grumbled. At the same time it was obvious that she was green with envy as she tried out the luxurious leather sun-loungers.

They passed by the bar and Ellie asked for a sparkling water while Louise opted for a gin and tonic. Ellie figured she'd had enough alcohol for the moment. She didn't want to disgrace herself by getting drunk. David would never forgive her. Anyway, the night was young yet.

The band was just starting up when they got back to the table. Sam and David were sitting in obviously uncomfortable silence and Ellie wondered why they weren't chatting. The others were still on their tour of the house and Orla and Jade were nowhere to be seen.

Rachel came back to join them.

"Phew! Well, thank God supper is over and everything went well," she said, smiling around at them. "Now we can all enjoy the dancing. This band is great."

"What about your neighbours, Rachel?" David asked. "Won't they be bothered about the noise?"

"Most of them are away in Marbella for the summer and those who aren't are here tonight," she informed them with a laugh.

"Good move!" Sam raised his thumb in an okay sign.

"Do *you* not go to Marbella for the summer?" Louise wanted to know.

"Well, we have done for years. My parents have a place there but this year we're going to the south of France instead. We're spending the month of August there in a friend's villa. Unfortunately, the Dáil doesn't recess until the end of July, so we can't go till then."

"You're so lucky," Louise sighed. "I wish I'd married a man who would have given me this fabulous house and exotic holidays."

A change came over Rachel's face. "Actually, the house is mine," she said, her voice icy cold. "It was a wedding present to me from my father."

"Oh, sorry," Louise said, realising that she was being put in her place. "Well, you're still very lucky," she continued, ignoring the disgusted glances of the others.

"David, come on, let's dance," Ellie said, grabbing his hand.

"No, Ellie, I'm tired. I don't feel like dancing tonight."

"Ah, come on! The band is great."

"No, please. I have a headache. I think I have a migraine coming on."

Sam saw the disappointment in her eyes and felt sorry for her.

"I'll dance with Ellie – if that's okay with you, David," he offered, looking at the other man.

David shrugged his shoulders. "Fine, if Ellie wants to."

"Yes, please," she said, her smile dimpling as she grabbed Sam's hand.

They ran on to the dance-floor where the band was playing a medley of Abba songs.

"You're a bit young to appreciate this music," Sam joked as she gyrated around him, as if there were decades between them.

"No, I lovvve Abba!" Ellie shouted so that he could hear her over the music.

"You *are* full of surprises, Miss Ellie Moran," he teased her.

"I saw *Mama Mia* five times," she said earnestly.

"Oh, of course, that's how you know them. I was wondering, because they were way before your time."

"But not yours!" she countered.

"Hey, I'm not that old," he laughed at her and she laughed back as she swirled around him.

The night was a roaring success. The band was as good as Rachel had promised and Ellie was on the dance-floor continuously. David still refused to dance and when she came back, breathless and exhilarated from jiving with Ronan, he suggested that it was time to go home.

"Ah, David," she wailed, "I'm having a great time. It's only eleven and Rachel said there's going to be fireworks at midnight." She looked at him, eyes pleading.

"I'm exhausted. I've had a tough week at work and this headache is getting worse. I would like to go home now." He stood up.

Seeing the stricken look on Ellie's face, Sam couldn't resist interfering. "Look, David, Orla and I can drop her home if you want to go on ahead. What do you say?"

Relief flooded Ellie's face as she looked at David hopefully.

"Well, if it's not too much out of your way, Sam?"

"Not at all. It's no trouble," Sam assured him.

"Thanks, darling," Ellie said happily, giving David a kiss.

He called for a taxi and when he was gone Ellie relaxed and continued to enjoy the wonderful party. She danced with Marcus and with Sam again. Jade still hadn't returned to the table, thank God. She had a long chat with Orla who told her that she was studying political science at Trinity. Ellie liked her a lot and wondered if she and Sam were dating seriously. They seemed very comfortable in each other's company.

"You and Sam seem very well suited' she couldn't resist remarking.

"We are!" Orla replied, leaving Ellie longing to ask when they'd started going out together.

Orla didn't elaborate and Ellie didn't want to appear nosy so she stayed mum.

Louise was knocking back gin and tonics like nobody's business and Ronan was keeping a watchful eye on her. He hoped she'd last until midnight at least, because he loved fireworks.

The girls made their way to Madame Farah's tent to hear their future. They all looked on it as a great lark. The men had refused to go, much to Rachel's disappointment. Louise was thrilled when the fortune-teller predicted that she saw lots of money coming her way in the near future but Ellie thought the old woman was talking through her hat when she told *her* that she hadn't yet met her true love. Honestly, the things she'd said! She didn't believe in fortune-tellers or Tarot cards or any of that stuff but it was a bit of a laugh.

Zita didn't believe in fortune-telling either but Rachel was so anxious for her to go that she did, just to please her. Madame Farah refused to tell her what the future held for her which made Zita angry. Try as she would, she could not get the silly old woman to open up. Marcus was dying to know what Madame Farah had foretold and when Zita told him she'd refused to tell her anything, he roared with laughter.

"Ho, ho! What is it she sees that's so bad it's unspeakable?" he teased her.

"Don't be ridiculous." She lowered her voice so Rachel wouldn't hear her. "I told you, I don't believe in it. It's all utter crap! I did it just to please Rachel."

Just before midnight Carl joined them and they watched the fantastic fireworks together. Afterwards, as Rachel was seeing Ronan and a drunken Louise into a taxi, Carl asked Zita to dance.

It was a slow number. She liked the feel of his muscular body next to hers and the way he held her close. She could feel his hardness against her and it gave her a sense of power to know that he wanted her. Yes, her instinct had been right. He would make a great lover. She looked forward to a romp in the hay with him. It wouldn't take much to persuade him, she guessed.

"You're the most exciting woman I've ever met," he whispered in her ear as the dance ended and he let her go.

She gave him her most seductive look. "Till we meet again," she said coyly.

This time he did take her hand and bring it to his lips. "I can't wait," he replied, his eyes hot with desire.

The party continued into the early hours and it was a tired and happy Ellie who said goodnight to Rachel and Carl.

"It was a brilliant party. Thank you so much for inviting me," she said, hugging them both.

"Same here," Sam told them as he tried to keep a comatose Jade from falling down. She'd arrived back at the table after midnight, much the worse for wear. Seeing her unfocused eyes, Sam knew she'd been indulging in more than alcohol.

"I'm coming home with you, Sam," she announced. "That bastard can go jump!" She waved her hand vaguely at the bar.

Sam shrugged his shoulders and wondered who she was talking about. Had she come with someone or had she just met someone at the party? You never did know with Jade! He sighed deeply and told her that would be okay.

"Thanks for coming. I'm so glad you enjoyed it. See you next Monday night," Rachel said as she hugged them. She was more than a little tipsy now.

Between them they manoeuvred Jade into the taxi.

"Where do you live, Orla?" Ellie asked.

"In Dalkey, but I'm staying with Sam tonight."

"Oh!" said Ellie. Sam certainly had his hands full. They dropped her off first in Malahide and she stole into the apartment careful not to disturb David. She needn't have worried. He was snoring loudly as she slipped into bed beside him. He probably hadn't even missed her.

"What a great night. You did a brilliant job, darling," Carl said, putting his arm around his wife's shoulders. "I really liked your new friends. They're fun people."

"Yes, they are. I'm really glad they came and that they enjoyed themselves," Rachel replied with a big yawn. "Let's go to bed. I'm bushed."

21

Ellie had to drag herself out of bed on Sunday morning, exhausted from the previous night. She felt a warm glow remembering what fun it had been. Whoever would have thought that a wine group would be so much fun? She'd really warmed to Rachel who had made such an effort to ensure they were all having a good time. The more she got to know her, the more she felt sorry for her. Yes, she had the fabulous house and the gorgeous husband but Ellie felt that there was something missing in her life. She was sorry she hadn't got to meet Rachel's children.

David's headache was gone and he wanted to go for a run which was the last thing Ellie wanted but, as he'd been so good as to let her stay on at the party, she thought she'd better make the effort to join him. It was a big mistake. She hadn't gone half a mile when she started to feel ill and after a mile she was bent over throwing up, right there on the seafront in Portmarnock. She was mortified and David was furious with her.

"That's what you get for drinking so much last night and dancing your silly head off."

She glared back at him in between her retching. When she'd finished she sat down on a wall and told him to go on by himself, which he did. She was upset that he hadn't been more sympathetic. She waited for him while he ran to the end of the beach and back. She was feeling a little better by then.

He seemed to have softened a little. "Are you okay now?" he asked. "Do you want me to go and get the car?"

"No, I'll be okay. I'll follow you back."

He stopped running and walked back with her in silence.

They went back to his apartment where they showered and changed before going for brunch. Ellie wanted to go to their usual place in Malahide but David wanted to go to Kitty O'Shea's, which was across the Liffey, in Ballsbridge.

"But that's miles away," she objected.

"It's not far. It will be nice for a change. All the guys say they do a mean brunch there at weekends."

By 'all the guys' she supposed he meant his new friends at Buckley Steadman. She knew there was no point in arguing with him and she couldn't eat a bite anyway as her tummy still felt off, so she agreed to go with him.

Once inside Kitty's it was obvious that all his colleagues were there with their spouses and families. David introduced her to everyone and they all welcomed her warmly. Ellie was delighted to see Anna and Mike whom she'd met at the Buckleys' dinner party. It seemed so long ago now.

"How are you?" she asked Anna, who moved over to make room for her on the seat.

"Great! I was wondering when you'd get roped into these Sunday brunches," Anna laughed.

"You mean you meet here every Sunday?" Ellie asked, surprise in her voice.

"Like clockwork." Anna could see that Ellie didn't know that fact. Seeing the dismay on the younger girl's face, she patted her hand gently. "Don't worry, Judith never comes. Frank does sometimes, but usually it's only the younger set."

Ellie didn't know what to think. She was annoyed at David for not telling her. She looked at him now, smiling and laughing with his colleagues. He seemed like a different man. He seemed . . . she searched for a word . . . at home! It was strange to see him so at ease and in good form. All they'd seemed to do lately when they were together was argue. Ellie wondered if it was her fault.

The other women were very friendly to her and some of the small kids adorable. She took one of the babies on her knee.

"Ellie's getting married in six months," Anna informed the other women.

"Oh, God love you," Mandy, the youngest of them said. "I'm just recovering from my wedding last year. I'm sorry now I didn't elope." She rolled her eyes to heaven as the other women laughed.

"Where are you having your reception?"

"In Clontarf Castle. I live just around the corner from it."

"Well, good luck with all the organising," Mandy said. "You'll lose half a stone from all the stress."

"Don't be put off by her," Anna laughed. "We had a great day at her wedding."

"Where did you have your reception?" Ellie asked.

"Fitzpatrick's in Killiney, of course. They do a brilliant job there."

"I had my reception there too," Anna joined in.

"Me too," another girl piped up. "They're by far the best and they make it very personal with lots of nice touches other hotels don't give you."

Ellie pressed her lips firmly together. She had no doubt that what they said was true but it wasn't for her. She was beginning to feel like she had stepped into the world of the Stepford Wives. What one did, they all did. While they were all very nice, it felt like an exclusive club – one Ellie wasn't sure she wanted to join.

David sat down beside her. He had a huge plate loaded with everything an Irish breakfast could offer. Ellie felt ill just looking at it. She was bouncing the baby on her knee and the little girl was gurgling with happiness.

"You obviously have a way with babies," Joanne, the mother of the baby observed. "Do you plan to have any?"

"Oh, yes, lots," Ellie smiled at her and shook her hair at the little girl who grabbed it in her tiny fist.

David stopped eating long enough to butt in. "Not lots exactly, but one or maybe two, eventually," he said.

Ellie looked at him strangely. They'd never discussed it but he knew she loved children and she'd assumed he'd want a big family too. She felt uneasy. She'd thought they were both on the same wavelength but lately his ideas seemed to have undergone a major change. They definitely needed to sit down and have a serious talk.

Louise woke with a hangover on Sunday morning after all she'd had to drink at Rachel's party but it didn't dim her spirits as she remembered what Madame Farah had told her. She took two Nurofen, which helped, and then rang Melissa to see if she would go to Liffey Valley Shopping Centre with her that afternoon. Although Melissa had already made other plans, she cancelled them. Her sister was forever berating her for jumping whenever Louise clicked her fingers but Melissa couldn't help herself. Louise had always had that effect on her.

When Ronan heard that she was going out he decided to go to the golf club and see if he could get a game. He was surprised that Louise was in such good form. Maybe taking her to Rachel's party had been a good idea after all. It had certainly lifted her spirits.

To Melissa's surprise Louise hardly bought anything, just a bottle of perfume. All she really wanted to do was talk about her upcoming date with Alan. Melissa had never seen her best friend so exhilarated. She seemed really keen on this guy. Seemingly they'd been texting each other regularly and according to Louise he was just as keen. Melissa felt uneasy. She was worried that Louise might get hurt or, even worse, mess up her life.

Rachel was also suffering from a hangover but she'd promised her parents that she would be over to have brunch with them and collect the children. There was a bottle of champagne half-full in the fridge so she made herself a bucks-fizz as the hair of the dog. No point in wasting the champagne, she figured. She felt much better after a second one. *Mmmm* . . . champagne and orange juice was a wonderful pick-me-up. She really should have it more often.

Carl had already left for his weekly golf game and she left Olga to supervise the caterers and cleaners who were busy cleaning up in the garden.

Zita was up and about early on Sunday morning and after a bracing cycle arrived home to drag Marcus out of bed and down to the Chatham Brasserie for brunch. They sat sipping Bloody Marys as they waited for their food to arrive.

"Mission accomplished," Zita smiled as she raised her glass to him.

"Yeah? What do you mean?"

"Well, Mr Carl Dunne gave me his card last night and I naturally gave him mine. I said I'd call him this week." She was grinning broadly now.

"My God! How did you manage that?"

"Easy. I told him I wanted to interview him for a TV programme."

"Oh, you scheming bitch!" He laughed.

"He also told me, as we were dancing," she added, her eyes glittering brightly, "while his hard-on was pressed against me, that I was the most exciting woman he'd ever met."

"Well, I'll drink to that." He clinked his glass to hers. "How thrilling!" He was practically dancing in his seat now. "You sure know how to haul them in," he laughed.

They chatted over brunch about the party the previous evening.

"To be honest, I hadn't expected it to be much fun but it was great," he admitted. "They're a good bunch, your wine crowd."

"Yeah, they're not so bad. It was just the partners that were gross. That awful Louise – what a nightmare – and Ronan is so sweet."

"Yeah, I like him a lot but that David – Ellie's fiancé – what a dork! I can't imagine what she's doing with him."

"He's a pain in the arse alright. They're getting married soon," Zita told him as she speared another crab cake with her fork.

"If he doesn't bore her to death in the meantime," Marcus remarked, rolling his eyes.

Their conversation was interrupted by a text coming in on Zita's phone: **Really enjoyed meeting u last night**, it read. **Look forward to ur call.** *Cxx*

She saved the message and handed the phone to Marcus. He beamed at her.

"Poor Carl. He doesn't realise he's met his Jezebel."

"His Waterloo, more like." Zita laughed wickedly.

22

Ronan knew the moment he walked into the office on Monday morning that something was wrong. It didn't take long to find out what it was. The managing director called the staff into the conference room to tell them that the business would be closing down the following Friday.

"We're truly sorry to have to do this but we can't survive in this economic climate any longer. We have done our best to keep afloat as long as possible but it's become unsustainable. I know this is a hardship, especially to those of you with families to support and mortgages to pay, but there is unfortunately no other option open to us. I'm so sorry." He looked around the room at the stricken faces and wished he could have been anywhere else on earth at that moment. It was the most difficult thing he'd ever had to do in his whole career. "You will of course get twelve months' severance pay and the best reference possible. I do hope that you all find other employment quickly although it is a tough world out there right now. I thank you all for your service and loyalty to this company."

With that, he left the room, tears in his eyes.

They looked at each other in stunned silence. They'd known for some time that redundancy was a distinct possibility but had hoped against hope that it wouldn't come to pass. Now it had.

"Christ!" Ronan was the first to break the silence. "What are we going to do now?"

"Get a job in McDonald's," said one of the others.

They'd all sniggered when they'd heard of architects and solicitors queuing up for a job in the fast-food chain some months ago. It didn't seem so funny now.

"At least the severance pay will clear my mortgage," observed one of the older men, "but I'm too old to get another job."

"You're lucky," the youngest colleague said bitterly. "I have a huge mortgage and have no idea how I'll pay it. And the chances of my getting another job are nil at the moment. I'll have to emigrate."

"The banks are being very forgiving," another man tried to reassure him.

"I have two kids at university," the last man said. "There's no way I can keep them there if I'm unemployed."

Ronan realised that of the five of them he was probably the luckiest. He had no kids, a modest mortgage and thankfully now he had his part-time job with Sam.

The five men sat with glum faces, pondering their future. Their mood was sombre as they slowly filed back to their offices. Ronan wondered how they would survive. He supposed they were no different from many thousands of others in Ireland at the moment. What a mess the country was in! He blamed the government. They'd lost control of the banks and the property developers.

With a heavy heart he started to finalise what he'd been working on. Time to bury the Celtic Tiger!

They broke off work at five and headed to the local pub to drown their sorrows. None of them were keen to head home and break the news to their wives and partners. They needed to be together for a while longer to digest the awful news.

Ronan rang Louise to tell her he'd be late, only to be told that she was going out with some friends from the gym. He hoped it wasn't going to be an expensive night. You never knew with these girls' nights out.

Louise had been in a state of nervous excitement all day, preparing for her meeting with Alan. He was calling her every hour saying how impatient he was to meet her. She'd taken a long fragranced bath and moisturised her body afterwards with the Crème de La Mer which she'd kept hidden from Ronan. If he ever discovered how much she paid for it he'd have had a heart attack. Dressed in her new La Perla lingerie, she stepped into her leather suit. Finally, she sprayed her wrists and behind her ears with Angel by Thierry Mugler which the salesgirl yesterday had told her was *the* sexiest perfume in the world. It was quite possibly also the most expensive, but she loved it and was sure Alan would too. If so, it would be worth every cent.

It was with a heavy heart that Ronan arrived at the wine club. He had decided not to mention his problem to anyone. He didn't want to spoil the atmosphere, which was buoyant after Rachel's party.

The course was even more fascinating this week as Sam

took them on a tour of the vineyards of France. Ronan got completely lost in it, forgetting his troubles for the two hours. Afterwards, Sam, Rachel, Ronan, Ellie and Zita headed for the Castle once more, the young ones having again declined the invitation to join them. They discussed the party again in detail and Ronan was surprised when Rachel asked him if there was anything wrong.

"I'm fine," he lied. "Why do you ask?"

"You seem subdued tonight. Not your usual self."

"I thought I was always quiet," he said, smiling at her.

She looked at him probingly. "You are, but you're different tonight."

How very observant of her, he thought. There was more to Rachel than met the eye. Her intuition was bang on the button.

"I'm fine," he insisted, smiling brightly.

She patted his hand, not at all convinced by what he was saying. There was no doubt he had problems with that awful wife of his. And he was such a lovely guy. He deserved better.

Just then, Zita claimed Rachel's attention and began to regale her with talk about her job. The two of them seemed to be really hitting it off, Ellie thought as she ear-wigged on their conversation.

"I'd love to see behind the scenes of a TV studio," Rachel was saying to Zita.

"That would be no problem. Actually, we've got the go-ahead for a programme on 'The Women Behind Our Successful Men'. You'd be a fascinating subject: 'Beautiful wife of young up-and-coming politician. How she juggles her private and public life.' What do you say?"

"I don't know," Rachel replied hesitantly. "Do you really think people would be interested?" She sounded dubious.

"Hell, yes, I'll let you know after I discuss it with my producer."

"That's very kind of you, Zita, if you really think it might work." Rachel smiled at her, not at all convinced that people would be interested in her life. Ellie still couldn't get a handle on Zita. There was something unnerving about her. She seemed to be almost reeling Rachel in. Ellie wondered, not for the first time if she wasn't gay and trying to seduce Rachel. Poor Rachel wouldn't see it in a million years.

Rachel was yet again drinking faster than all the others and insisted on buying another round at the end of the evening. Again, Zita was the only one to join her. Zita had a crazy moment when she had to break off her conversation with Rachel to take a text from Carl. She smiled to herself at the irony of the situation. He certainly seemed keen and was pushing her to make a definite date to meet up. Let him wait. Playing hard-to-get was certainly the way to go with the suave Mr Dunne.

Louise had butterflies in her tummy as she walked into the bar where they'd arranged to meet. He'd chosen well. It was so dark that she could barely make him out, sitting on a banquette in the corner. God, he was handsome, she thought, her heart giving a lurch as she went to meet him. He stood up and, putting his arms around her, drew her close.

"I thought this night would never come," he whispered into her hair. She shivered with excitement. "*Mmmm . . .* You smell divine. Angel, isn't it?"

She smiled, pleased that he had recognised it.

He moved over to make room for her on the seat and held her hand tightly.

"Would you like some champagne?" he asked. "I have a feeling tonight is a night to celebrate."

"Yes, please," she whispered, feeling the force of his personality. She had a powerful feeling that this was the start of the rest of her life.

Afterwards she couldn't remember what they'd talked about. She could only remember his closeness and his eyes piercing into her being. Was it possible to fall in love in one night? She had never felt so alive. Every nerve in her body tingled. When Alan asked her if she could come away with him the following weekend, she never hesitated for a moment.

"I want our first time to be very special," he whispered.

She closed her eyes in anticipation.

She appreciated the fact that he hadn't wanted to take her to an anonymous hotel for a quick romp. This relationship was going to be more important than that. She left him, on a cloud of happiness, already thinking ahead to the weekend. He rang her while she was on her way home in the taxi.

"I think I've fallen in love with you," he said quietly.

It gave her a warm glow.

When she got home Ronan was in bed and to her relief he was asleep. She undressed in the guestroom and slipped into bed beside him, hugging her arms around herself as she relived the evening. She had never been so happy. She knew this was meant to be.

23

When Ellie got home from work on Tuesday, her sister Sandrine was sitting at the kitchen table with her mother, drinking tea.

"To what do we owe the pleasure?" Ellie asked, grabbing one of the chocolate biscuits off the plate. Sandrine normally worked till seven or eight most evenings so it was a surprise to see her so early.

"I want to talk to you about the wedding," Sandrine stated.

She was to be Ellie's chief bridesmaid – well, she only had one sister, she didn't have any choice – did she?

"What about it?" Ellie asked warily. Her sister was known to meddle and always wanted to be chief bottle-washer when it came to family occasions. She hoped she wasn't about to start in on her wedding, trying to take it over.

"Well, David rang me today and he would really much prefer if you were to hold it in Fitzpatrick's Castle in Kill–"

"Don't even go there!" Ellie shrieked, giving her mother a jolt and shocking even Sandrine to silence. "How dare David go behind my back and ring you about *my* wedding!" She was shaking with fury.

"Be reasonable, El. It's his wedding too, you know," Sandrine said primly.

"It's none of your business!" Ellie cried. "Just keep out of it. It's between David and me."

"Obviously not or he wouldn't have involved me. I think you should give it some thought."

Ellie stuck her chin out in the obstinate way her sister knew so well.

"*I* am having *my* wedding reception in Clontarf Castle or there'll be no wedding reception at all!" she said resolutely, her voice rising with each word she uttered. With that she turned on her heel and went up to her bedroom.

"Better not interfere, dear," her mother said to a dismayed Sandrine as she poured her another cup of tea.

"Well, honestly, I was only trying to help," her daughter replied with a miffed air.

Ellie lay on her bed shaking with fury. How dare David try and involve her sister behind her back and how dare Sandrine attempt to force her to change her plans! She was livid with them both. She somehow felt betrayed. When she'd calmed down a little she rang David. It went to his voicemail and she left him a message to call back urgently. He rang back ten minutes later and couldn't understand her anger.

"I just thought maybe Sandrine could change your mind . . ." He tailed off feebly not knowing how to handle this situation.

"Well, she didn't. And no doubt she'll probably be in touch to tell you what I said – if she hasn't rung you already, that is."

"She has actually," he said sheepishly.

"And what do you have to say about that?" Ellie demanded.

"It's okay. We'll have it in Clontarf Castle if it's really so important to you," he replied, resignation in his voice. He was afraid that she'd meant what she'd said about no wedding at all. He didn't know what had got into Ellie. She'd been acting very out of character lately. Maybe it was her hormones. You never knew with women. He sighed.

"That's settled then," she replied, somewhat mollified. They made small talk for a few minutes but when she'd hung up she was still feeling dejected. She hoped this arguing would not continue until their wedding day. She'd never stick it. Everyone had told her that it would be a stressful time but she hadn't expected David and herself to be fighting. It was very upsetting.

Louise had been sleeping when Ronan left for the office that morning. He was relieved to be able to put off telling her that next Friday he'd be out of a job. Tuesday was the night she went to the gym and she and her girlfriends always went for a drink afterwards, so after work Ronan decided to go over to Conor's house.

His brother was surprised to see him.

"Hey, you look like you have the weight of the world on your shoulders. What's up?" he asked, concern in his voice.

"The company is closing on Friday. I'll be joining the ranks of the unemployed." Ronan tried to smile but none was forthcoming.

"Jesus, Ronan, that's desperate. When did you hear?"

"Yesterday. We're all devastated." He ran his fingers through his hair.

"I can imagine," Connor remarked as he poured two whiskeys. "Here, drink this – you need it." He handed a glass to Ronan. "What will you do now?"

"I've no idea," Ronan answered, taking a large gulp of

the whiskey which warmed him as it went down. "I can't think straight."

"God, man, I don't blame you. This country is in a mess." Conor's voice was bitter. "Have you told Louise? How did she take it?"

"I haven't had the courage to tell her yet to be honest. I'm sure she'll go ballistic."

"Well, it's not your fault. It's happening all over the place. People are losing their jobs every day. She'll have to understand."

"You don't know Lou." Ronan laughed bitterly.

Conor didn't know what to say. He was angry. The bloody Fianna Fáil government and their buddies the banks! It made him furious to think how they had sold out the country. He ran his fingers through his hair exactly as his brother had done earlier. It was a shared habit they both indulged in when they were worried.

"Surely she'll understand," he said. "This will certainly put a stop to her gallop. No more shopping sprees for a while."

"I doubt it. It's when she's depressed that she goes crazy. You know the saying, *'might as well be hung for a sheep as a lamb'*? That's her motto."

Silly cow, Conor wanted to say but he resisted, not wanting to hurt his brother.

"At least I've got the part-time work in the wine shop. That's something but it won't pay the mortgage." Ronan looked into his glass and drained the rest of the whiskey in one gulp.

Conor poured him another large one.

"I'll have to go and talk to the bank manager about the mortgage – God, I hope we don't lose the house," he said, his voice anguished.

"Will you stay for dinner?"

"Well, I certainly can't drive after these large whiskies." He made a grimace as he went on. "Louise is not home anyway. She was out last night and again tonight with her friends so I'll stay for dinner but I'm not terribly hungry. Thankfully she's out as it means I can put off telling her for a little longer." He laughed harshly.

"Great stuff! I'll just tell Betty."

"Isn't this your card night?" Ronan asked him, suddenly remembering that his brother played cards with friends every Tuesday.

"Don't worry about that," Conor assured him, his hand on the door handle as he went out. "I can cancel that, no problem."

Conor left the room to tell Betty to put another name in the pot.

Ronan thought how lucky he was to have such a supportive brother. He could always rely on Conor, which was more than could be said for his own wife. Downing his whiskey, he went out to greet Betty.

Sitting at the table later, sipping yet another whiskey which he had to admit was dulling the pain somewhat, he marvelled that he had been able to eat a second serving of lasagne. Betty was such a great cook and his appetite had returned as he tasted the delicious dish.

After the children had been packed off to bed, the three of them had sat chatting for a while and then Conor insisted that Betty drive Ronan's car home while he and Ronan followed in theirs. Louise wasn't home and Conor took an unsteady Ronan by the arm as he opened the door for him. Ronan went straight up to bed and within seconds was asleep.

24

The next evening Ronan went straight to the wine shop from the office, feeling very despondent. He had found a way to simplify withdrawals from the bonded warehouse and Sam had asked him to implement it. He worked on it every chance he got but tonight he couldn't concentrate on it. Fiona came down when it was time for his break and they went into the staff kitchen where Ronan made a pot of tea and brought out the shortbread biscuits that she liked so much. Dermot took over in the shop for him, as usual, while he took his break.

"My mother is really pressing for me to go and stay with her now," Fiona confided as she nibbled on a biscuit. "She's terrified I'll go into labour when I'm on my own."

"That would be pretty scary, I'm sure," Ronan agreed.

"Well, I wanted to stay on here in the flat as long as possible but I suppose I'll have to go sooner or later. I've only four weeks left although first babies are usually late. Mam's a terrible fusser so the later the better." She smiled ruefully.

"I can imagine that's the last thing you need," he said sympathetically.

Fiona heard the dejected note in his voice.

"Is everything okay, Ronan?" she asked, her voice gentle.

"No," he replied, shocked to find tears coming to his eyes.

"What is it?" she asked, her face suffused with alarm.

"I've been made redundant and I haven't even got the nerve to tell Louise. She'll go ballistic."

"It's not your fault. Half the country is out of work. I'm sure she'll understand."

"You don't know Louise!"

Ronan thought it was funny that he'd had this exact conversation the night before with Conor. They all thought that Louise would understand. He knew better.

Fiona wondered, not for the first time, what kind of a battle-axe Ronan was married to. She could sense that he was deeply unhappy.

"I'm sure something will turn up," she said reassuringly.

Ronan shrugged as he got to his feet, realising that it was time to get back to work.

They said goodnight and Ronan went back into the shop where Dermot was busy with customers. Fiona put the stuff away and washed the cups then waved goodbye before she made her way back up the stairs.

The next day Fiona came down to see Sam. She found him in a foul humour because the girl who was due to replace her that day had not turned up for work that morning.

"No phone-call, no message, nothing!" Sam growled.

Fiona thought he looked even more handsome when he was angry. His navy eyes became almost black.

"These young ones are so unreliable," he grumbled. "That's the second girl who hasn't turned up this week. I'll have to find someone else and quick. I can't have people letting me down like this. I had to cancel two important meetings today." He was lifting bottles out of boxes with a vengeance. "Dermot can't manage alone and I've too much else going on to stay here."

"What about Ronan?" she suggested.

"What *about* Ronan?" He looked at her as if she was speaking double Dutch.

"Well, you say he's a great worker. He could take over my day-shifts."

"Don't be silly. He works Monday to Friday."

"Not any more he doesn't," she smirked.

Sam stopped what he was doing. "What did you say?" he asked, raising his voice.

"He's been made redundant. He finishes up tomorrow and he's distraught about it."

"Oh my God, the poor chap! Why didn't he tell me?"

"He's a bit embarrassed about it, I think. He hasn't even told his wife yet. He says she'll go ballistic." Fiona's eyes clouded over.

"Well, that's good news for me. I'll ring him immediately and ask if he can fill in till he gets another job." He beamed at her happily. "Problem sorted!"

"It's pretty unlikely he'll get another job in this economic climate," she nodded sagely. "Please don't tell him I told you."

"And who will he think told me? The fairies?" Sam shook his head disbelievingly. "He won't mind that you've told me – not if it benefits us both."

"I suppose," Fiona replied hopefully.

Ronan couldn't believe his luck. The call from Sam was like manna from heaven. At least he could face the bank manager now with some kind of hope. He must remember to buy Fiona a big bunch of flowers. If she hadn't mentioned it to Sam he might still be in a deep hole. Now at least Louise wouldn't have him under her feet all the time.

He went straight from the office to meet Sam and discuss hours and salary before starting his evening shift. He stopped off on the way to buy flowers for Fiona. Thank heaven for small miracles, he thought as he strode to the wine shop.

Once again, Sam was a lifesaver. He was happy to have Ronan take over all of Fiona's hours which meant he would have every Monday off and would have to work one Sunday in four. He would work the evening shift as before on Wednesday and Thursday and work till five the other days. The salary was more than Ronan could have hoped for. He couldn't believe his luck.

When he had left Sam he took the stairs up to Fiona's apartment two at a time. Fiona's face broke into a huge smile when he presented her with the bouquet of yellow roses.

"They're my favourite," she cried, burying her nose in them before giving Ronan a big hug. She barely got her arms around him as her tummy was in the way.

They both laughed at the incongruity of it. She put the kettle on for tea. "Now it's my turn to make you tea," she laughed as she brought out a coffee cake that her mother had made.

"*Mmmm* . . . looks great."

"It is. By the way, I've decided to stay in the flat as long as I possibly can, before going to my mam's."

"If that's what you want to do, you should," he advised. "Do you know if it's a boy or a girl?"

"It's a boy. 'Ronan' is actually one of the names I have for him on my shortlist."

"Poor kid," he laughed and then ventured to ask. "What about his father?"

Her face took on a disgusted look. "He did a runner the minute I mentioned I was pregnant," she told him, a hint of bitterness in her voice. "I don't even know where he is. Abroad, his mother told me. I don't want anything more to do with him." She stuck her chin out defiantly.

"Silly sod! Some men are fools."

"I don't need him in my life. I'm better off without him. I can see that now. He's a waster." She sounded strong and determined.

Ronan marvelled at her courage, her being willing to take sole responsibility for this little being she was about to bring into the world. He knew she would be a great mother. He ate two huge slices of the cake which was delicious and, as he took his leave, Fiona thanked him once again for the flowers. He could see that she was genuinely delighted and he was pleased that he'd thought to do it.

25

In the office the following day Ronan could sense the despair around him. He supposed he was luckier than most. It was with a heavy heart that they spent their last day working together. Ronan spent his lunchtime at the bank where he'd made an appointment to see the bank manager. Mr O'Mahony was very understanding.

"You're not the only one in this position," he'd assured Ronan. "At least you've got this wine job to tide you over. However, I do think that your credit-card spending is far too high and I suggest that you cancel the card, for the moment at least."

"Yes. I'm afraid my wife doesn't see it as spending when she uses it."

"Ah yes, Louise. Charming girl. How is her jewellery business coming along?"

"Jewellery business?" Ronan asked mystified.

"She's a wonderful girl. It's great that she's willing to help out by starting this little jewellery business. I hope it's getting off the ground okay."

"Oh, sure," Ronan replied, shocked. He knew there

was no jewellery business and suspected that Louise had conned the poor man into lending her money. He tried to keep his voice nonchalant as he asked, "How much is the interest rate on that loan? Louise couldn't remember."

"Let me see . . ." The manager turned to his computer and entered some information. "Yes, here it is. She borrowed €1200 to be paid back within twelve months at 12% interest rate."

Ronan paled as he felt the anger rise inside him. How could she have done this without telling him? Jewellery business, my arse! He felt like throttling her. Then he remembered the lodgment for €905. This explained it. All that glib lying about Melissa borrowing her card! Ronan felt sick to his stomach.

Mr O'Mahony saw by his reaction that something was not right.

"There is no jewellery business, is there?" he asked, sympathy in his voice.

Ronan couldn't trust himself to answer and just shook his head numbly.

"I'm sorry. I really do think we should cancel the card immediately – to prevent any more of this over-spending." It was obvious from the tone of his voice that he was angry at having been conned and that he understood the situation perfectly.

Ronan nodded his assent and reached into his wallet for his credit card.

"That won't be necessary," Mr O'Mahony told him gently. "But the next time someone tries to use it, it will not be accepted."

The meaning of this was left unspoken between them. With a heavy heart, Ronan left the bank and trudged back to the office for his final afternoon there. There would be some fur flying tonight when he tackled Louise about the lies she'd told and the money she'd borrowed without telling him.

At three o'clock the managing director wrapped things up and all the staff headed to the local pub for a final drink together and in truth to drown their sorrows. Ronan was looking for Dutch courage to go home and face Louise.

They finally said their last farewells and Ronan trudged home, rehearsing how he would handle things. Besides tackling her over her lies, he had also to break the news to her that he was now officially unemployed – as a draughtsman at any rate. He didn't think Louise would be too happy about the idea of him being a full-time off-licence salesman. Thank God his parents weren't alive to see it. They'd struggled financially to keep him in Bolton Street College for the four years it had taken him to qualify as an architectural draughtsman. They'd been so proud on his graduation day. He wouldn't have wanted them to see it come to this.

He knew the moment he opened the door that the house was empty. A waft of a perfume that he didn't recognise enveloped him. Where the hell was Louise? Just what did she do all day that she could never be there when he arrived home? His anger, coupled with the few drinks, had made him irritable. There was a message for him on the kitchen table:

Decided to go with Mel to visit her sister in Galway. Your dinner is in the microwave. Will be back Sunday night. Louise.

Ronan slumped down in the chair. Could she not have called him to tell him this person to person instead of leaving this cold, impersonal note? He shook his head sadly. It was time to face facts. His marriage was heading down the tubes – just like his career. A chasm had opened up in their relationship that he now felt couldn't be bridged. Apart altogether from the problem of her profligate spending and lies, they just seemed to have no life together any more. He remembered something that his dad had said to him around the time he'd met Louise: "Life is too short, son, to spend it with the wrong person." He wondered now if his father had thought that she was the wrong person. Perhaps he had, and Ronan was now beginning to think so too.

26

Zita had never been pursued with such zeal. Text and voice messages were flowing from Carl like the Niagara Falls. It amused her and the more she ignored him, the more persistent he became. On Friday, he bypassed her mobile phone and rang her in the office. She wondered idly how he'd got her number. No doubt he'd charmed it out of the receptionist. Grudgingly, she had to admire his determination. She was so taken aback that she finally gave in and agreed to meet him.

"I can meet you . . . let me check my diary . . . next Friday," she suggested.

He agreed immediately.

Carl had no idea what other engagements he may have had but he knew he wouldn't get another chance with Zita. He was exhilarated as he came off the line. She had somehow got under his skin. She was on his mind day and night. He couldn't understand it but all he knew was that he had to see her. On checking his diary he saw that he had arranged a meeting with a very important supporter for the following Friday night. Nothing for it – he rang and rearranged it for another night.

Since the party he'd been busy arranging meetings with all those who'd offered their support. He was off now to have dinner with the director and editor of a national newspaper who certainly needed to be kept on-side. He had an extra spring in his step thanks to his conversation with Zita. What a woman!

Ellie had asked David to meet her on Friday night as she really felt they would have to have a serious talk and clear the air about some misunderstandings they appeared to have – like how many children they wanted, for example. She hadn't seen David since the brunch in Kitty O'Shea's when he'd shocked her by saying they'd have one, or possibly two children – eventually. It was the 'eventually' that really threw her. She wanted to start a family right away but David obviously had other ideas. This was a very important decision for them and it needed to be thrashed out before they got married. Unfortunately, David couldn't meet her as he was getting together with the guys from the office to watch the football.

"Do you not see enough of each other all day, every day?" she asked, secretly hurt that he wouldn't make the effort when she'd stressed that it was important.

"It's all go in the office so it's nice to relax together outside of it," was his explanation.

Ellie said nothing. She didn't want to appear possessive but she felt that he could have cancelled just this once.

She had decided she was not going to the disco with Keisha and Chloe any more. She was fed up playing gooseberry. She did, however, go to meet up with them in Gibneys for a drink as the three of them had done for years. The girls could see that she was in a foul mood and listened as she complained about David and his attitude.

"This is meant to be the happiest time of your life," Chloe said, "but you've honestly been in bad form since you got engaged."

"I suppose," Ellie agreed. She looked crestfallen. "It's all the fault of this new job David's got. He's changed so much. It's given him airs and graces."

"Well, at least he's agreed to Clontarf Castle," Keisha said, hoping to cheer her up. "Did you confirm it with them?"

"Yes, it's definitely happening."

"Well, you'd better get a move on then," Chloe observed, rolling her eyes to heaven.

"Yeah. I want the three of us to meet on Tuesday night to look at some ideas for your dresses. What do you think?"

"What about Sandrine?" asked Keisha.

Neither she nor Chloe liked Ellie's bossy sister too much.

"Yeah. She's free. My house, eight o'clock. Okay?"

"Sure. Oh, I love all this wedding planning," Chloe said, rubbing her hands together.

"Yeah," Ellie replied but she didn't sound too enthusiastic.

It was close to ten when Carl finally got home to find Rachel sitting in her usual chair in the den, the customary glass of wine in her hand. There was a half-empty bottle on the coffee table. Somehow it irritated him.

"Don't you think you should go easy on that stuff?" he remarked.

"Well, that's a nice greeting, I must say," she said truculently.

He knew by her voice that she'd had much more than one glass. Wine always made her aggressive. He preferred her drinking gin and tonic.

"I just worry that you're drinking a lot these days," he replied wearily as he sat down.

"Do you blame me? I hardly see you these days. When was the last time we had dinner together?"

"We're going out with Anita and Bill tomorrow night."

"That's not what I meant. I mean sitting down to dinner here – just the two of us."

He sighed. He could hear the slight slurring of her voice. He wondered was that her first bottle of wine. Possibly not. He made a mental note to check later.

"You know how busy we are now before the Dáil recess," he said. "That's political life, my dear. We'll have the month of August together in France."

He went up to change into something comfortable and look in on the children who, as usual, looked like perfect angels when asleep. He kissed them both and pulled the covers back up on Jacob before going to the kitchen for ice for his whiskey nightcap. The empty bottle of wine sitting on the counter top seemed to be mocking him. As he'd suspected, Rachel was on her second bottle. This was worrying. She really was drinking far too much. He would have to keep an eye on her.

When he got back to the den she was fast asleep, the glass of wine tilting in her hand. He took it from her with a sigh and put a pillow behind her head. Going into his office he caught up with his emails before settling down to watch TV.

It was almost midnight when Rachel appeared.

"I'm off to bed," she mumbled, poking her head around the door of the TV room.

"I'll be with you soon," he told her, reluctant to join her in case she was feeling amorous, which she often was when drunk. That was the last thing he wanted tonight. He wondered what Zita was doing now and if she was making love to someone right at this very moment. He felt an irrational jealousy at the thought. This was crazy. Slowly, he went up to bed where he fell into a deep exhausted sleep.

27

Meanwhile Louise was in Paris, in seventh heaven. It was her first time there and she was loving every minute of it.

Alan had texted her on Thursday: **My driver will pick you up tomorrow morning at nine. Bring your passport.**

She could hardly contain her excitement and spent all that evening preparing for what she guessed would be the most exciting weekend of her life.

Then, that morning, Alan's driver had collected her in a beautiful Jaguar and driven her to the airport where he handed her a ticket.

"Mr Brown will be waiting to meet you at Charles de Gaulle airport," he'd told her, his face inscrutable.

Oh my God, Paris! She'd almost fainted with delight. Trust Alan, she smiled to herself. As she said goodbye to the driver she'd wondered briefly what he thought of her and whether he'd done this kind of thing before. It didn't matter. She was giddy with excitement as she read the ticket and saw that Alan had booked her in business class. She'd always envied the people who could afford to travel like that. Now she was one of them.

She was like a kid in a sweet shop as she sipped champagne and ate the delicious lunch served to her. Beats Ryanair, she thought with a snort as the good-looking steward refilled her glass. She'd only ever flown Ryanair with Ronan.

All too soon they'd landed and, coming through the gate, she'd seen Alan, smiling and waving at her. She could hardly breathe her heart was racing so fast. He took her in his arms and this time she almost did faint.

After the longest kiss, he said huskily, "Let's get the hell out of here."

He led her outside and into a limousine which was waiting for them. It whisked them to the Ritz where Alan had booked a suite. Louise was completely overawed. She'd never seen such opulence in all her life. The doormen seemed to know Alan and addressed him as Monsieur Brown.

"Do you stay here often?" she whispered as he led her inside.

"Goodness no," he laughed, "I usually stay in a much more modest place but I do have a lot of meetings here. However, for you, *chérie*, only the best is good enough."

After they'd checked in they were shown to their suite and Louise was dumbstruck by the beautiful furnishings and opulence of the whole place. Alan laughed at her excitement.

"Paris is the city of love so where better to start our love affair," he said gently as he took her in his arms.

Within seconds he had undressed her and carried her to the huge four-poster bed. Louise thought she was living a dream or acting in a fabulous film. Alan turned out to be the gentlest of lovers and took her to heights she'd never imagined existed. They made love all afternoon in between sipping the chilled Cristal champagne he'd ordered and talking – "catching up on our lives", as he called it. She was so blissfully happy that it was a huge effort to drag herself out of bed to prepare for dinner.

They'd had a shower together, he lathering the gorgeously scented shower gel all over her body – which of course led to another bout of lovemaking.

"Oh God, you're so beautiful," he'd exclaimed when they were finished. "I want to stay with you forever and never let you out of my sight."

Louise felt pretty much the same way.

As they were being driven along the Champs Elysées on their way to dinner at Maxim's, Louise's eyes were out on stalks, taking in all the famous landmarks she'd only ever seen in photos.

"Don't worry, my darling, tomorrow I'll show you Paris, if I can drag myself out of bed with you, that is."

He laughed and she joined in.

He couldn't keep his hands off her and she didn't want him to. He was forever stroking her skin and hair and planting little kisses on her arms and neck. He made her feel indescribably sexy. She could barely wait for the evening to be over and to be back making love again. She sighed a deep sigh of contentment. Life didn't get any better than this.

28

Ellie and her mother headed for Swords on Saturday morning where she had made an appointment with Bridal Heaven, the well-known bridal shop. Sandrine, luckily, had had to work so couldn't be there, much to Ellie's relief. She absolutely had to get going on her wedding plans and the first and most important item was her dress. She couldn't plan on flowers or anything else until that was decided. She'd made an appointment and they were welcomed warmly by the proprietor, Liz, who would give them an hour exclusively, to look through the wonderful range of dresses.

Ellie was spoilt for choice as Liz brought out one beautiful dress after another. Liz very quickly got an idea of what Ellie wanted and soon presented them with the most exquisite dress Ellie had ever seen. She gasped at its beauty. Shaking with excitement, she went into the dressing room and tried it on. Liz tied up the laces and, fixing the neckline so that it sat perfectly, she led Ellie out of the dressing-room.

Marie-Noelle gasped. She couldn't help herself but

suddenly seeing Ellie as a bride brought tears to her eyes. Her daughter looked radiant. The dress was breathtakingly beautiful and suited her perfectly.

"Oh, darling, it's exquisite!" she exclaimed emotionally, as the tears slipped down her cheeks.

Liz directed Ellie to the wall of mirrors and she too was awestruck as she stared at her reflection.

"It's beautiful," she whispered, turning this way and that to get a better view. She felt like a princess. It was the most fabulous dress she'd ever seen. It was made of gossamer white-silk taffeta and the strapless top was beautifully cut in a V and studded with seed pearls. It was pleated into the waist and the skirt flared out over a net petticoat. It was simple but exquisite. This was the dress for her. No other one would do.

Liz then added a tiara and a long veil that completed the look. It was just perfect!

Somehow, seeing herself in this beautiful bridal gown brought it home to her that she was in fact going to be a bride very soon.

Ellie was in a great mood when she met David for lunch in The Yacht.

"I've found the perfect wedding dress," she exclaimed as they kissed hello.

"That's nice," he said as they found a table and she could tell from his tone that he wasn't particularly interested.

"Well, you could show a little bit more enthusiasm," she rebuked him, expecting him to be happy for her.

"Sorry, I have a dreadful hangover. We didn't finish up till after two last night. I *am* glad you've found a nice dress."

They ordered lunch and David gradually started to feel better.

This was obviously going to be a weekly occurrence, this going out with the lads on a Friday night. Not that she begrudged him having fun but he seemed to have dropped all his old friends and his whole life was being defined now by his work and his colleagues there. His mother had even rung Ellie, complaining that David hadn't called to see her in almost three weeks which was most unlike him.

"We need to have a serious talk, David," she started, her voice full of concern. "We've got to sit down and discuss our wedding and not just that but our whole future. The weeks are flying by and we've done nothing really."

"I'm leaving all that up to you, Ellie. You know how very involved I am with this new job. I just don't have the time to organise a wedding."

"You have time to stay out drinking till 2 a.m. with your work buddies!"

She hadn't meant to sound so bitter, but she felt he was being very unfair. "It's your wedding too, you know." Her voice wobbled and she was afraid she was going to cry.

"Ah, honey, I'm sorry. You're right. I'm not being much help." He took her hands in his. "I promise I'll try and be more co-operative, okay?"

Somewhat mollified, she told him that the girls were getting together on Tuesday night to get things moving.

"That's great. Well, at least you've got your way about having the reception in Clontarf Castle. Whatever makes you happy makes me happy."

She smiled at him then, things back on an even keel.

He patted her hand. "Now what is it about our future that you want to discuss," he asked her.

"Well, I've been thinking about what you said in Kitty's last week about having one, or *maybe* two children, *eventually*. You didn't really mean that, did you?" she asked him, her eyes searching his earnestly.

David guessed that this was probably what had been bugging her all week. She'd been cool with him whenever he'd spoken to her on the phone. Now he understood. "What I really meant to say is that we have plenty of time. I want us to enjoy being a married couple first before we start a family. But of course we'll have kids, eventually."

She noticed that he'd said 'kids'. Maybe she'd misjudged him, thinking that he didn't want kids at all. She let out a huge sigh of relief and reached for his hand. "I understand, darling," she said, feeling happier.

When Fiona came down to the wine shop on Saturday afternoon, she saw instantly that Ronan was in very bad form.

"Did you tell your wife about losing your job?" she asked, thinking this was the reason he was so downcast.

"No. When I got home last night I found a message to say she'd gone away for the weekend. My marriage is in deep trouble."

Fiona thought he was joking. Surely his wife would have checked it out with him first? She shook her head. Louise sounded like a prize bitch and it was obvious that they had a pretty awful marriage. She had no doubt that it was more his wife's fault than Ronan's. He really was the kindest, gentlest soul she'd ever met and she'd grown very fond of him. Some women have all the luck, she thought. Why did I have to fall for a prick like Danny when there are nice guys out there? She sighed deeply. She'd made her bed and now she had to lie on it.

"Oh, I'm sorry to hear that. Have you tried marriage counselling?" she asked hesitantly.

"I think maybe it's too late for that."

He looked so forlorn that her heart went out to him. "They can be a great help, I'm told. Maybe you should consider it."

"Yeah. Maybe I'll suggest that to Louise when she gets back. Yeah, that's a good idea. Thanks, Fiona."

She was glad she'd been able to help.

29

Ellie was feeling much more positive the following day and agreed to go to Kitty O'Shea's again for brunch. She had to admit that David's colleagues were friendly and welcoming and she could see how relaxed and animated he was in their company. She'd heard so many jokes about boring accountants but obviously when they got together as a group they were as much fun as any bunch of people out together.

After two glasses of wine she was in particularly good humour and when David suggested that they go and look at a townhouse he'd found, she agreed to go, thinking that it couldn't do any harm to have a look. It was in Sandymount, literally ten paces off the Strand Road and Ellie wasn't prepared for how much she would like it. It was the cutest townhouse she'd ever seen.

"Oh, it's gorgeous!" she cried, as he let her go in ahead of him.

She went from room to room, exclaiming over the lovely features and the lovely wooden floors. The whole house was bright and airy and she loved it, particularly the master bedroom with its fabulous en-suite. The colour scheme was all neutral colours – but that could be changed.

"The colour scheme is a bit boring but we can repaint it in bright colours," she suggested.

David quite liked the neutral colours, he thought they were chic, but if it meant she'd agree to the house then he'd paint them purple, if that's what she wanted.

She squealed with joy when she realised that she could even see Clontarf across the bay from the window in the guest bedroom. There was a third smaller bedroom which David mentioned could be used as a study.

"Or a nursery," she suggested, smiling.

"Or a nursery," he agreed, pulling her to him. "Honestly, Ellie it's going for a song. One of the guys in the office is moving to Canada and he's selling it complete, furniture and all. I wouldn't even need to take out any more of a mortgage than I have already." His eyes were glowing as he placed his arms around her back. "Please think about it. We'll need to move fast as it will fly once he puts it on the market." He was pleading with her now.

"I don't know . . ." She could think of no reason not to buy this lovely little house except that it was not in Malahide or Portmarnock, which is where they'd agreed they would live. This was a world away from her family and friends.

He read her thoughts. "Look, let's drive straight to Clontarf right now and if it takes longer than fifteen minutes then I'll forget about it. What do you say?"

"Okay."

They locked up behind them and, getting into the car, they synchronised their watches before he drove her across the East Link Bridge to her parents' house.

"Eight minutes forty, exactly," David whooped as he stopped on Kincora Road.

"I can't believe it!" Ellie cried. "It's faster than coming from Malahide or even Sutton." She had to agree that he had a point.

"If you agree to it, Ellie, I'll even buy you a new car to celebrate so that you can come and go here as often as you want. And, if you really hate living there, then we can sell and buy somewhere else."

He obviously wanted it so much that she couldn't resist him. "Okay, let's go for it!"

He grabbed her in a bear-hug and squeezed her so hard that she thought she might deflate completely.

"It's going to be perfect, Ellie. I just know it!"

She wasn't quite as convinced as he was but at least it was another major problem solved. They would now have their own place to move into after their wedding.

Dress and house sorted in one weekend. Things were looking good!

Ronan was having a less good day. Having spent a long hard day in the wine shop on Saturday he'd met Conor later for a few pints too many. Nursing a hangover this morning, he'd played the worst golf of his life and he now sat eating a packet macaroni cheese which was doing nothing to cheer him up. He was watching the football on TV when he heard the door bang and Louise came breezing in. She looked beautiful and he could see that she was in an exhilarated mood.

"Had a good weekend then?" he asked.

"Brilliant!" she replied, going to the fridge and opening a bottle of white wine.

"Drink?" she asked, waving the bottle at him.

"Why not? I need to talk to you." He figured he might as well get it over with. He'd have to tell her about losing his job. She'd know soon enough when he didn't go to work tomorrow.

"Me too," she said brightly, pouring the wine and raising her glass to him.

"Well, I don't know how to tell you . . ."

"Me first!" she cried, looking straight at him. "I want a divorce."

If she'd said 'Pigs are flying outside' Ronan couldn't have been more gobsmacked. "A . . . divorce?" he repeated, hardly able to say it.

"Yes," she replied as she smoothed her skirt with her elegant hands.

He looked at the perfectly manicured nails, mesmerised by their stroking action.

"A divorce?" he repeated yet again, thinking that he must have misheard.

"Yes, I've met someone else and I realise now that you and I are not meant for each other." Her voice was matter-of-fact.

"Are you serious, Louise?" he asked her, standing up and pacing the room. He couldn't quite believe what he was hearing.

"Deadly. I plan on moving out tomorrow."

"Who is this guy? Did you just meet him this weekend?" Ronan couldn't believe that even she could be that stupid.

"No. It's someone I've known since I was single and I ran into him again recently. We're in love and he wants me to move in with him as quickly as possible."

Ronan was almost speechless. "How long has this been going on?" he managed to croak.

"Not long, but we know we're right for each other." She even smirked as she said it.

"Don't you think you should take the time to consider

this carefully? I thought maybe we could go for marriage counselling."

"No, it's much too late for that. I've made up my mind and so has Alan." The manner in which she said his name, lovingly with a smile playing on her lips, made him want to throw up. "I'll want a divorce of course but I won't want anything from you. Alan is very wealthy."

Not for long, with you around, Ronan thought bitterly. "Well, I take it there's nothing I can do to get you to change your mind?" he asked, knowing the answer already.

"Absolutely not. It's been decided. Now what was it you wanted to say?"

"Nothing, nothing at all," he answered sadly.

"Well, in that case, I'll go and start packing. Obviously, I'll sleep in the guest room tonight." She got up and headed for the bedroom.

Ronan sat for he'd no idea how long, listening to her opening and closing doors and drawers and clattering hangers in wardrobes. She was serious. She was leaving him.

Bolting from the house, he walked down to the local pub. There, to the surprise of his mate, Jim, he downed the best part of a bottle of whiskey before finally telling him of his problem. Jim was horrified and took an almost comatose Ronan home with him and settled him comfortably on his sofa for the night.

Louise knew that she had given Ronan a huge shock but there was no point in beating around the bush, was there? There was no way she could have sweetened the bombshell she'd dropped so it was better all round to be honest and not fudge the issue. Their marriage was over and he would come to realise that it was for the best. Life was too short and they both needed to move on.

She did feel a little guilty that he hadn't come home last night and she hoped that he was okay but, really, he wasn't her responsibility any more.

She had packed all her clothes and shoes and was shocked at just how many cases and large black plastic bags she'd filled. She looked around, wondering if she had missed anything, but there was nothing more she wanted from the house except for her CDs. In any case she had run out of bags. With a last look around the house she'd lived in for the past fifteen years, she left to start her new life with Alan.

Alan had organised a van to move her stuff and, when the guy had loaded up, she ordered him to follow her in the chauffeured car that Alan had sent to take her to her new abode. She gasped in awe as they pulled up at the beautiful big detached house on the leafy Ailesbury Road in Ballsbridge. It was simply fabulous.

Alan was standing at the front door and ran down the steps to greet her, swinging her off her feet. She gasped with pleasure, laughing up into his face with sheer joy. She was home. Everything was going to be simply wonderful from now on. Her life was truly beginning.

30

Ronan finally surfaced and felt bewildered to be in a strange room. He started to get up but the blinding pain in his head knocked him back. Then he remembered where he was and why.

"Well, you certainly did a good job on yourself last night," Jim said, coming into the room with a steaming cup of coffee.

"Oh God!" Ronan moaned, holding his head in his hands as he tried to sit up.

"Here, drink this," said Jim. "It might help you feel better."

Ronan took the coffee. "Sorry for all the trouble. I hope Sheila didn't mind my staying here last night."

"Of course not. My wife was very sympathetic when I explained about you and Louise."

Ronan moaned. "Yeah, well, what's done is done. What time is it?" He looked at his watch, surprised to see it was almost midday. "Just as well I don't work Mondays in the wine shop. I suppose I'd better get home. I'll feel better after a good shower." He started for the door.

"I'll drive you home."

"Thanks, Jim. I appreciate what you've done. Sorry if I talked the ear off you last night."

"What else are friends for?" Jim replied, his voice gruff.

He felt sorry for his pal but, really, that Louise was a bitch and Ronan would be far better off without her, though he'd never tell him that.

Ellie bounced into the wine course that evening, full of beans and smiling brightly.

"You look like the cat that got the cream," Rachel observed.

"Yeah, well, I had a good weekend. I found *the* most divine wedding dress. Honestly, it's just out of this world," Ellie's eyes were sparkling as she spoke.

"And . . . we found the cutest little house as well," she added, her big smile making her dimples more pronounced than ever.

"That would rate as a good weekend, I guess," Rachel smiled back at her, happy for the bubbly young woman.

"Where is the house?" Sam asked, on hearing the exchange.

"In Sandymount."

Sam raised his eyebrows, his eyes twinkling with merriment. "Oh, so you're deserting Mars then?"

Ellie blushed, as she did every time he mentioned Mars. Was he never going to let her forget that comment? "Well, we timed it and it is only eight minutes forty exactly, from there to here." She busied herself putting out her wine glasses, not wanting him to see her discomfiture.

Rachel looked from one to the other, not understanding this exchange, although it was obvious Ellie was embarrassed.

Luckily for Ellie, Ronan and Zita came in just then, followed immediately by the young ones, so she escaped Sam's teasing.

"Ronan looks dreadful," she whispered to Rachel.

"I hope nothing's happened," Rachel whispered back, concerned to see the grey look on his face.

She smiled at Ronan as he took his place beside her. He gave her a wan smile.

They were all a little more subdued than usual as the class began. Ellie was still smarting from Sam's remark and Rachel was concerned about Ronan who could barely focus on what Sam was saying and had to make a huge effort to concentrate and take it all in. The tasting session went a little better as they all became engrossed, surprised at how good the Italian wines Sam gave them were.

"There are some stupendous wines coming out of Italy, as well as a lot of crap, of course," he explained.

There was certainly no crap on offer here as they tasted one delicious wine after another. They all agreed that the final wine, an Amarone from the Veneto, was the best wine they'd ever tasted.

"I must order a case of this," Rachel exclaimed, draining her glass.

Ronan sighed. Rachel's life was so trouble-free. Did she realise how lucky she was?

They headed for the Castle again after the class.

Sam had noticed that Ronan wasn't his usual self and fell into step beside him.

"Is everything okay with you, Ronan? You seem very quiet tonight," he enquired as they walked to the pub.

"Had a bad weekend," Ronan replied in a low voice. "I don't want the others to know but my wife's left me."

"Oh God, man, I'm so sorry," Sam said, putting his arm around Ronan's shoulders. "That's a shit thing to happen."

"Yeah, well, things haven't been good for a while but now she's met someone else."

Sam didn't know what to say. Anything he could say would sound like a platitude. "God, I'm sorry. You're really having it all thrown at you at the moment," was all he could manage. "Listen, if you want to take a couple of days off, we'll manage in the shop somehow."

"No, no," Ronan was adamant. "I need to keep busy. Keep my mind off things. Thanks anyway, Sam."

When they reached the Castle, Zita and Rachel sat together making arrangements for the interview that Zita was planning to do with Rachel the following Wednesday. It meant her 'Pamper Rachel Day' would be cancelled but Rachel reckoned being interviewed for a TV show could be considered pampering of a sort. After the interview in the morning, they would have lunch in the canteen and then Zita would show her around the studios and let her see behind the scenes of some programmes in action. It was all so exciting.

31

Dermot was in the shop when Ronan arrived on Tuesday morning.

"Listen, Ronan, Sam told me you weren't feeling too good last night so if you'd like to take the day off, that's no problem. I can manage on my own. It won't be a busy day."

"No, I'll be fine, thanks anyway, Dermot."

"Well, if you do need a break, just tell me."

Ronan was very grateful but working was the only thing that would keep him sane. He wondered what Louise would do next and whether she'd want him to sell the house. There would be no point as it was in negative equity anyway. Any money they'd get for it would all go to the building society, that's presuming they could sell in this terrible economic climate. She'd said she wanted nothing from him. He hoped she meant it. His main priority now was to keep paying the mortgage and to clear her debts. At least she couldn't spend any more of his hard-earned money. He wondered if this new guy knew just what he was letting himself in for.

A new delivery had arrived from Burgundy and Ronan was happy to be kept busy unloading it and placing it on the shelves.

Sam had lent him Hugh Johnson's *Wine Atlas* and he often stayed reading it into the small hours of the morning. As a result his knowledge of wine was growing daily and he felt quite confident now advising customers. The regulars were getting to know him and found him very pleasant.

Fiona came down as usual for tea that afternoon and knew instantly that things were wrong.

"What is it," she asked after Ronan had poured the tea.

"Louise has left me."

"What?" Her cup clattered back down in her saucer.

Ronan told her the whole story from start to finish and was surprised to see tears in her eyes when he'd finished.

"Sorry, my hormones are all over the place at the moment," she said, wiping her eyes. "How awful for you – but, you know, as the song says – Judy Garland, wasn't it? – when a cloud appears you must look for the silver lining. You weren't very happy together, were you?"

"No, in fact – but I'm just thinking of something Judy Garland said once." He gave a half-smile. "She said that behind every cloud was another cloud."

Fiona laughed. "Well, you've had your two clouds – first losing your job and now your marriage. It can only get better. There must be a silver lining coming up."

"I hope you're right," he smiled, pouring another cup of tea for her.

Ellie had bought two bottles of that lovely Amarone wine from Sam for the girls although it was more expensive than what she usually bought. Still, she had to show them that she was learning something on the wine course. Indeed, her taste in wine had changed. Jacob's Creek no longer seemed like the best wine in the world to her. Yes, Italy was where it was at. She hoped her friends would be impressed by her choice. You never knew with Sandrine!

She prepared some olives which she dressed with olive oil and herbs and some Italian pecorino cheese and water biscuits. It all looked very elegant and she was very pleased with the result. It was a far cry from the Tayto and popcorn and usual plonk she served. Her mother was surprised and pleased with this new sophisticated streak her daughter was developing.

Sandrine was the first to arrive and was impressed with the nibbles Ellie had set out. Then she tasted the wine. "Wow, this wine is lovely. What is it?"

"It's an Amarone, from Italy."

Sandrine raised one perfectly threaded eyebrow. "Amarone? I've never heard of that before." She was quite put out. *She* had always been the sophisticated one in the family and here was her kid sister showing her up.

"Ellie has some fantastic news, haven't you, darling?" their mother said, turning to her youngest daughter.

"Yes. David and I found *the* cutest house at the weekend."

She was smiling broadly, her dimples annoying her sister as they always did. How come Ellie got all the pretty genes from their mother?

"Really," she asked coolly, raising her arched eyebrows enquiringly. "And where, pray do tell me? Killester? Marino?" She'd mentioned the nearest areas to Clontarf possible.

"No, actually. It's in Sandymount." Ellie was a little

hurt by her sister's sarcasm. She wished that just for once Sandrine would be happy for her.

"*Sandymount*?" Sandrine practically screeched. "But that's on the south side!"

"I know but it only took us eight minutes forty seconds to get from there to here. We even timed it," Ellie announced, unaware of the jealousy her sister was feeling.

"Well, I must say you're a dark horse. In my wildest dreams I never thought you'd go south of the Liffey," Sandrine sniffed, greatly put out by this piece of news. "I daresay David finally got you to see sense." She opened up her laptop. "I've been doing some research for your wedding."

"Research?" Ellie looked at her enquiringly.

"Yes, I've sussed out a beautiful dress for you and for us bridesmaids, and also flowers. I've also made out a menu that I think would be perfect for the reception and –"

"Hang on just a minute," Ellie cried, looking at the file Sandrine had just opened up. It was titled 'ELLIE'S WEDDING'.

She looked at her sister disbelievingly. "Sandrine, this is *my* wedding and *I* want to choose my own dress – in fact, I've already found it, haven't I, Mum?" She turned to her mother for confirmation.

"Yes, and it's beautiful, really beautiful," Marie-Noelle confirmed.

"You can't buy a wedding dress in Dublin!" Sandrine cried. "They're far too expensive. You have to take a photo of the one you like and then send it to these people in China who make it up for you at about a twentieth of the price."

Ellie was horrified. "It can't possibly be the same. The quality and material can't be as good at that price. And what about the fit? How can it be perfect if they can't fit it on you?"

"It's only for one day."

Ellie felt close to tears. Yes, it was only for one day but it would be the most important day of her life.

"The dress was perfect on Ellie," Marie-Noelle interjected, seeing how upset her younger daughter had become. "And she has the money for it, thanks to Uncle Matt's inheritance." Sandrine had used hers to buy her Kia car.

"That's not the point –" Sandrine started but thankfully was interrupted by the ringing of the doorbell.

Marie-Noelle breathed a sigh of relief to see that Keisha and Chloe had arrived. She hoped they would diffuse this conflict that seemed inevitable every time her two daughters got together. Ellie poured wine for them and, when they were all seated, she showed them the photo she'd taken on her phone of the wedding dress she'd found.

The girls exclaimed loudly at how beautiful it was.

"Yeah, I've definitely decided on it. They're holding it for me till next Saturday," she told them ignoring the disapproving face of her sister.

"Now for our dresses," Sandrine said, turning her laptop around so they could all see the screen. "I think it would be nice if we all wore white, like at Kim Kardashian's wedding."

Her mother and the two other girls all looked at Ellie who obviously didn't like the idea.

"That marriage didn't exactly last very long, did it?" Ellie commented.

"Seventy-two days," Keisha, who was a huge Kardashian fan, confirmed.

"I think there's a tradition that only the bride wears white at a wedding," Marie-Noelle observed.

"Yeah, absolutely," Keisha agreed.

"Anyway, I look crap in white. My skin's too fair," Chloe added.

"But the Kardashians –"

"To hell with the Kardashians," Ellie said through gritted teeth. "This is *my* wedding and I'd appreciate if you'd butt out. Okay?"

"I was only trying to help," Sandrine replied sulkily.

"Well, I was thinking of having a white and pale-gold theme for the whole wedding. What do you all think of pale gold for the bridesmaids' dresses?"

"Sounds great! Cool!" Chloe and Keisha chorused together.

"Isn't it a bit insipid?" Sandrine pronounced tartly. "I think a dark burgundy or black would be nice."

"Not black!" the others, including Marie-Noelle, chorused in horror.

"It's not a funeral," Ellie remarked. "I think the best thing is to have a look on Saturday at what they have in Bridal Heaven before we make a final decision.

"*Mmmm,* this cheese is yummy," Chloe said, as she speared another cube. "What is it?"

"Pecorino," Ellie informed her. "It's Italian."

Sandrine looked at her sister in surprise. My, my, she thought, Ellie has certainly changed a lot since she met David. He has obviously been introducing her to the finer things in life. Poor David! He really is making a huge mistake. He has no idea what he's letting himself in for. My little sister has always been thoroughly spoilt by everybody and no doubt will expect him to do the same. She looked on disapprovingly as Ellie and her two friends chatted and talked about girly things. They really were too silly for words.

Ellie declined to look at Sandrine's suggestions for the flowers and menu for the wedding.

"I have a fair idea of what I want," Ellie put her down subtly.

Sandrine left shortly afterwards, her tail between her legs, mumbling about the ingratitude of some people.

32

Rachel was up bright and early on Wednesday for her big day in the TV studio. She dropped the children to school and whizzed into the hair salon in Sutton. Keisha had done such a nice job on her hair for the night of the party that she was now popping in frequently for a wash and blow-dry.

Next she went into Ellie's beauty salon where she'd made an appointment for a manicure. She had considered having her make-up done there but Zita had assured her that the make-up department at the station would take care of that.

"Best of luck! Have a great day," Ellie wished her as she left in a state of high excitement.

"God, some women have all the luck," Chloe sighed as Rachel waved goodbye.

Zita came to meet Rachel when Reception called to say she had arrived. She took her up to the office where she explained to her how the interview would go and told her the kind of questions she could expect.

"Don't worry about anything because we are pre-recording it. If there's anything you're not happy about, we can always re-shoot it."

Rachel heaved a sigh of relief. "Thank God. I don't know how people do live interviews. I'd be a nervous wreck."

"You'll be fine," Zita assured her before taking her down to meet the producer, Jason.

Rachel disliked him instantly.

"We've decided to let Zita do the interview as she's a friend of yours."

Rachel could feel the tension between Zita and the producer.

After that, Zita took her down to make-up and introduced her to the women there who were very friendly and did a fabulous job on her face.

At last they were ready to start the interview.

Initially Rachel was nervous, but Zita quickly put her at her ease and she relaxed. She answered all the questions as best she could and Zita seemed happy.

"It's a wrap!" Zita said at last as she heard the message from the producer coming through her earpiece. "Well done!"

"Whew, that wasn't so bad," Rachel smiled. "I felt like I was talking just to you alone."

"That's why you were so good. It's a really good interview. You were great!"

To Zita's surprise, she meant it. Rachel had been a very good interviewee. At lunch Zita produced a bottle of white wine and they toasted each other.

"I think you've earned this," Zita smiled as she clinked her glass against Rachel's.

"You've got such an interesting job. Every day is different." Rachel's voice was admiring.

"I do love working in television but you wouldn't believe how chauvinist it is. Jason is really not that good a producer but he had political pull – so, although I've a lot more experience, he got the job. It infuriates me sometimes."

"I can imagine," Rachel said sympathetically.

"Now there's another producer job going but no doubt I'll be by-passed yet again for some stupid guy."

She sounded bitter and Rachel couldn't blame her. She'd heard this happened often.

"Could Carl help you, do you think?"

"Probably. Jason was promoted just before the previous government left office. Now that Carl's party is in, who knows?"

"I'll talk to him about it," Rachel said, indignant on her friend's behalf.

"It's a man's world out there unfortunately, even in this day and age," Zita observed bitterly.

"Oh believe me, I know it. Especially in politics."

"Yes, indeed. In the television world too. We women need to stick together," Zita stated vehemently.

"Absolutely! I'll definitely have a word with Carl about it."

"That's very good of you, Rachel. It would be great if he could help. Now, let's get back to work! As I explained, we would like to have some footage of you going about your daily life. We'll follow you around with the cameras as you do your normal duties. I'll ring you to arrange a suitable date, preferably when you have a full-diary day."

"Great. I'll think about what might be the best day."

The rest of the day went swimmingly as Rachel watched the most popular soap on Irish TV being filmed. She could not believe how fake it all was. On the small screen it all seemed so real.

"I've had a fantastic day. Thank you so much," she said as she hugged Zita. "And I really will talk to Carl tonight about your promotion."

"You're very kind. I appreciate it." Zita wanted to punch the air. "See you next Monday." God, Rachel was nice but so naïve, she thought as she went back to her office to view the day's work.

Rachel was well into her customary nightly bottle of wine when Carl arrived home that night.

"Well, how did it go at the TV studios?" he asked, pouring himself a generous whiskey.

"Fabulous! Zita wants to follow me around for a day and to film me with you, meeting constituents and such like. Is that okay with you?"

"Of course. Any publicity is good publicity." He took a long slug of his drink. "When does she want to do this?"

"I'll choose a date when I have a lunch and some charity meetings – one that suits you too of course." Her eyes were shining and Carl could see that she was thrilled with the whole thing. "I even thought that a Monday would be good and they could film a little of the wine course. That would be fun."

"Well, you'd have to square it with Sam and the other students, of course. Sam probably wouldn't mind – it would be good publicity for him – but some of the other students might not like it."

"Oh, I'm sure they won't mind," Rachel said confidently.

"Just check with them in advance," he warned her.

"And make sure you don't choose a Wednesday and have the whole country think you do nothing but pamper yourself all day."

"Of course not." She looked at him frowning, hurt by his words.

"How did you find Zita?" he asked casually.

"Fantastic! She's so professional and good at her job." She then proceeded to tell him how Zita had been passed over for promotion as a producer because of political pull.

"That kind of corruption has been rife for so long in this country. And now you say poor Zita was one of the casualties." He poured another whiskey for himself as Rachel poured the last of her wine.

"Well, she's up for promotion to producer again. I thought maybe you could do something to help her." She looked at him appealingly.

"I'll see what I can do. I'll need to talk to her first though."

"Oh, that's great, darling. She'll be delighted. I'll give you her number." She fished in her bag and took out Zita's card. "Here," she said handing it over. "She'll be ever so grateful."

I certainly hope so, Carl thought wryly as he pocketed the card.

Sandrine was still feeling miffed when she rang David on Wednesday evening.

"We really should get a life," she joked when she realised that he was working late too.

"So how are you?" he asked his future sister-in-law.

"A bit pissed off to tell you the truth, David. Ellie is really most ungrateful. I went to loads of trouble, Googling sites for dresses and other stuff to save her the trouble but she didn't want to know any of it."

David could hear the annoyance in her voice. "Well, you know Ellie," he said, trying to pour oil on troubled waters. "She's been dreaming of this wedding since she was ten years old."

Yes, and any man would slot in as the groom, Sandrine wanted to say, but she held her tongue. "Well, it's your wedding too," she told him. "Don't you have any say in it?"

"Oh, you know me. Anything for a quiet life. Anyway, it's Ellie's wedding, I'm just getting married," he joked.

"I honestly think you spoil her too much, David. You really should put your foot down sometimes."

"Ah, don't worry. She just wants everything to be perfect. She agreed to us buying this house I found in Sandymount. Did she tell you?"

"Yes. I don't know how you managed it. At least you've prevailed there, thank God for that!"

"Don't be too hard on her, Sandrine. You know what a romantic she is. You and I are different. We're realists. We have our feet on the ground."

Sandrine's only reply was a snort.

33

Carl had been waiting twenty minutes in the Merrion Inn when Zita sailed in, looking cool and collected and ten minutes late.

"Hi," she said, proffering her hand.

He took it but what he wanted more than anything was to kiss those tempting lips. However, he followed her cue and kept it formal. He'd already met quite a few people he knew. That was the damn problem with being in the public eye. One couldn't be too careful. He'd have no problem explaining why he was with Zita. He would say that he was discussing the TV show she was doing on his wife. But kissing her in public was another matter.

"You look great," he said, admiring the nonchalant way she shrugged off her brown-leather aviator jacket. Dressed in a man's pinstripe shirt with pale denim jeans ripped at the knees, her face void of make-up, she somehow was more alluring than any of the glamorous, model-type birds seated all around. Zita was an original and he liked that.

She asked for a pint of Guinness which amused him and he ordered one for himself too. She continued coolly to behave as if this was a business meeting, ignoring the fact that he had been pestering her for two weeks. She was something else, he thought, impressed by her composure.

"Rachel did a very good interview yesterday. She's quite a natural in front of the camera," she began.

He watched her lips as she spoke, not really hearing what she was saying. She occasionally licked the froth of the Guinness from her upper lip which he thought was the most erotic gesture he'd ever seen. He tried to concentrate on her words.

"Of course, I will only be the assistant producer," she sighed, "and the producer, Jason, is a total incompetent. God knows what ideas he'll come up with."

"How did he get to be producer then?" Carl asked although he knew already. He wanted to hear it from her.

"Well, we were both up for the job but he, unfortunately, used political influence and landed the position."

"How come?"

She explained then about the chauvinist hierarchy that existed in the TV world and how Jason had been promoted unfairly.

Carl was sympathetic. "I know that kind of thing happened a lot under the last government. Happily the voters recognised this and voted them out." He grinned. "Luckily for me and my party."

He really is very sexy when he smiles, Zita thought.

"Could I do anything to help you with this?" he asked her, apparently oblivious to the irony of making such an offer. "I may have some influence at the station."

Zita drew in her breath. She could hardly believe it. This was her reason for targeting him but she hadn't thought it would be quite so easy.

"That would be wonderful." She smiled up at him from under her long black lashes and squeezed his hand. Her touch was electric on his skin.

"Leave it with me. I'll see what I can do," he assured her, wanting to take her to bed right there and then.

"I would really appreciate that. I'd be ever so grateful."

He smiled, thinking of how she had parroted his wife. She looked at him boldly then lowered her lashes so that her seductive cat-like eyes were half closed. He was in no doubt what she meant. If this was what it took to have her then he was willing to move heaven and earth to get it for her. She was the most exciting woman he'd ever met. He had to have her.

They ordered two more pints and made small talk but both were aware of the chemistry between them.

He's surprisingly naïve, Zita thought – for a politician, that is. His boyish charm was seductive and she found herself relaxing and laughing at his anecdotes. He really was the best company. She was surprised to be enjoying herself so much and underneath the surface was the promise of a sexual encounter in the future.

With a shock she saw that it was after eight o'clock. "Oh my goodness!" She jumped up. "I'm supposed to be meeting Marcus at eight for dinner. Sorry, I have to run." She extended her hand again but Carl ignored it and, reaching forward, kissed her on the cheek. He wanted to inhale her scent and keep it with him. It was reckless but he didn't care. He hadn't felt this alive in a long, long time.

"I'll be in touch," he whispered in her ear. "I hope to see you again very soon and next time we'll have dinner together."

Pulling away from him, she gave him a mysterious smile. "We'll see."

With that she was gone. Carl felt empty after she'd left. It was as if a light had gone out inside him. He'd never felt like that about a woman before. She was quite remarkable.

34

Ellie was chatting to David on Thursday evening when he mentioned Sandrine.

"I think maybe you were a bit hard on her. She really only wants to help, you know."

"*What*?" Ellie shrieked. "What do you know about it?"

"She rang me yesterday. She was upset that you wouldn't listen to her suggestions."

"How dare she keep going to you behind my back! I can't believe it! And I did listen to her ridiculous suggestions. She wanted the bridesmaids to wear black. Black! It's not a goddamn funeral – it's a wedding."

"Well, black might not be such a bad –"

"*I* will decide what my bridesmaids wear and if Miss Smartypants doesn't like it, well, she needn't be a bridesmaid at all." Ellie was near to tears. "And now you can call her back and repeat everything I've said."

"Ah, Ellie –" he started but she'd hung up on him.

She was incensed. What a little sneak Sandrine was, appealing to David indeed. Did she think he'd get Ellie to agree to her wearing black? Well, I'll let her know in no uncertain terms that she'd better not try and bully me. She sighed. Sisters! Who'd have them? All of a sudden she felt sorry for Kim Kardashian. She'd had to suffer at the hands of her sister too but at least *her* sister had some kindness in her and a sense of humour. She thought of Rachel who said she'd always longed for a sister. Well, she didn't know how damn lucky she was! She'd donate Sandrine to her any day!

Rachel had spent the evening at a lingerie party organised by the wife of one of Carl's constituency workers and was obviously the worse for wear when she arrived home at eleven.

"Hello, dahling," she said as she weaved her way into the room, her words slurring. "Look what I got," she giggled, stumbling a little as she held up the racy black bra and thong she'd bought. He looked at her, disgusted, as she poured herself a gin and tonic before joining him, tripping over the mat and almost falling as she located the sofa. "*Oops-a-daisy*!" she giggled again.

"Don't you think you've had enough to drink?" Carl asked.

"Don't be such a sport spoil – ohhh – I mean sporl . . . oh, what the hell, you know what I mean." She pealed with laughter.

Carl had never seen her so bad. "Just what have you been drinking?" he demanded to know, his voice cold.

"Cock . . . tails, an . . . tequila . . . an canna rememmmber."

She had trouble getting this last word out and Carl realised that she was totally pissed. What a lethal cocktail of drinks she'd consumed. Had she no cop-on?

"I think you should quit now and go to bed," he suggested, taking her glass from her.

She grabbed it back, so forcibly that half the contents spilled all over her. She giggled again.

Carl sighed. There was no point in trying to talk sense to her now. He waited till she drained the glass and then gently he took it from her. Then he half carried her up the stairs where she fell on the bed, fully clothed. He covered her up and then left to sleep in the guest room, looking in on Jacob and Becky on the way.

Tomorrow he would have to talk to her. Her drinking was getting totally out of control. He was worried.

The following morning she was still sleeping when he left for work. When he got home there was a message to say that she'd taken the children to a school-friend's birthday party. That evening Carl had to attend the removal of an old friend and by the time he got home Rachel was in bed. The empty bottle of wine on the kitchen counter told him all that he needed to know.

Come what may, he would have to have a serious talk with her about her drinking.

35

Ronan was expecting to hear from Louise every day but he received not a word. She might just as well have vanished off the face of the earth. It was a weird feeling. They'd lived together for fifteen years and then in the flash of an eye she was gone. In one way, his life had become more peaceful without the constant arguing and the uncertainty of never knowing what she was going to do, not to mention her spending sprees.

He had a lot of support, of course. Conor and Betty were being rock solid and there wasn't a day that went by that he didn't thank Sam for his kindness. Without the job in the wine shop he would have gone crazy, pure crazy. Keeping busy was the best thing for him and the shop certainly took care of that. Dermot was on holiday so he was doubly busy and grateful for it.

Jim rang him every day and he met him for a pint the nights he wasn't working or at Conor's or at his wine course.

He'd been very surprised when Rachel had popped into the shop to ask how he was doing.

"I'm sorry I didn't get a chance to talk to you on Monday night but I was talking to Zita and when I looked around you were gone. Is everything okay? You didn't seem like yourself. I've been worried about you all week."

He was touched by her concern.

"That's very kind of you. I was pretty shell-shocked last Monday night because Louise left me over the weekend."

"Left you?" Rachel sounded shocked.

"Yes. She's met someone else apparently," he told her, trying to sound upbeat about it.

"Oh God, I'm so sorry. How awful for you!" She reached over and gave him a hug just as a customer came into the shop.

"Sorry, I'll have to go," he explained, slightly embarrassed yet touched by her concern.

"Look, why don't you come to supper next week? We'll arrange a date when we meet next Monday. Then we can have a good chat."

"That would be lovely. Thanks, Rachel. I really appreciate your dropping in."

"See you then," she smiled, waving as she left.

Fiona was, as always, a soothing influence. Nothing seemed to faze her and Ronan figured that if with all her problems she could cope alone and still keep smiling then he could surely do the same.

She came down to the shop on Friday afternoon, walking slower than usual.

"You okay?" he asked.

She grimaced. "I had an awful night. I was having contractions and I thought for a while that I was in labour but they stopped early this morning."

"That must have been scary." Ronan was very concerned

about her. "I really think it's time you went and stayed with your mother."

"Yeah, she's saying pretty much the same thing. I suppose you're right. Much as I love my independence, last night gave me a right fright."

"I can imagine. When will you go?"

"I was going to ask you if you could help me move my things. I don't have much but Mam's car is tiny and she suffers with a bad back." She patted her stomach. "And I'm not exactly in any condition to lug stuff around."

"Don't you even think about it! Where does your mam live?"

"In Blessington. It's not too far for you, is it?" she asked anxiously.

"Course not. Would Sunday morning be okay?"

"Perfect," she grinned. "Mam will be relieved."

They high-fived each other. He was happy to be able to help her out. She had become a good friend and he'd miss their daily chats, but it was better that she should go.

Carl never did get a chance to have that chat with Rachel. It had been a crazy week. He'd been going hard at it from early morning till late at night every single day and had hardly seen anything of her or the kids. She was right – they had become like ships that pass in the night. Well, he'd make it up to her in France. A whole month with nothing whatsoever to worry about.

On Friday morning he had arranged to meet up with the Director of Programmes at the TV station. They knew each other quite well as he was a supporter of the party. Carl suggested, ever so subtly, that Zita was the best person for promotion to the job in question. The director, knowing which side his bread was buttered on, readily agreed with him. It would be very handy to have an influential member of the government owing *him* one.

He called Zita into his office that very afternoon and informed her that she was being promoted. She would now be a fully-fledged producer.

"You certainly have friends in high places," he remarked, smirking.

She didn't reply but smiled knowingly, letting him know she wasn't to be trifled with.

"*Yes, yes, yes!*" Zita pumped the air with her fist after she left his office. Carl had come through after all. Now she owed him. Well, that would be no hardship. She would certainly show her gratitude. She rang him later that day. "I believe I owe you a debt of gratitude," she stated.

He roared laughing. "Well, if you like to put it like that. I take it I'm talking to the latest producer at TV2."

"You are indeed and I'd like to invite you to dinner to say thank you."

"I'll be delighted to accept but only if you'll cook it for me."

Now it was her turn to laugh. "*Touché!* Next Friday night?"

"I can't wait!"

He was an incorrigible flirt. "I'll text you the address. Seven thirty okay?"

"Perfect. I'll bring the champagne."

She smiled to herself as she closed her phone. *Mmmm . . .* now what should she give him to eat? Oysters to start, that's for sure – not that he'd need an aphrodisiac!

Zita knocked on Marcus's door, brandishing a bottle of champagne.

"Ooh, champers," he grinned. "What's the celebration this time?"

"You, sir, are looking at the newest producer at TV2!"

'You're joking," he shrieked, swinging her off her feet.

"Would I joke about anything so important?" she demanded, disentangling herself.

"Tell, tell!" he cried, taking down the John Rocha champagne glasses.

"Well, Carl Dunne was the catalyst seemingly. He persuaded the Director that I was the right person for the job."

"Wow, he's a fast worker. He sure has clout." Marcus raised his eyebrows as he poured the champagne.

"He sure has."

"You owe him now, big time, you know that?" Marcus said, grinning wickedly.

"I know, but I don't think that will be too much of a hardship." She grinned back, her eyes half-closed in that sexy way she had perfected.

"You are wicked," he laughed, shaking his finger at her.

"You have no idea just how wicked I can be!" she purred.

They both pealed with laughter.

36

Ellie and her mother picked up Chloe and Keisha on Saturday morning to go to Swords to choose their bridesmaids' dresses. Sandrine was to meet them there.

The three friends were in high spirits as they made their way up the Malahide Road. Marie-Noelle laughed at their enthusiasm. It was so exciting planning her daughter's wedding. She guessed this might be the only time she'd get to do it as the chances of Sandrine doing anything as foolish as getting married seemed remote!

They arrived at the bridal shop at three minutes past ten to find Sandrine standing outside, looking at her watch pointedly.

"I thought you said ten o'clock," she remarked archly.

Ellie threw her eyes to heaven but said nothing. She was still annoyed with her sister but was determined not to let her spoil the occasion.

"Good morning, ladies," the charming Liz said as she opened the shop door for them. "And how are you, Ellie? Looking forward to showing your friends your wedding dress?"

"Oh yes," Ellie said breathlessly, almost dancing with excitement.

Liz invited them to take a seat, pointing to the plush sofas in the centre of the room. "Coffee everyone, or would you prefer tea?" she asked, smiling at them.

"Coffee is fine," Marie-Noelle replied and Chloe and Keisha nodded their agreement.

"I'd prefer tea, if that's okay, otherwise coffee is fine," Ellie said.

"No problem." Liz smiled sweetly at the pretty young bride-to-be.

"Do you have any herbal tea?" Sandrine asked, much to Ellie's annoyance.

"Certainly. We have ginseng and rosehip and . . ."

"Any chamomile?"

Ellie threw her a filthy look. Even Marie-Noelle thought her oldest daughter was being overly difficult.

"I do believe we have. Annette," she called to a pretty young girl who was hovering nearby, "could you bring three coffees and a tea and a chamomile tea for the ladies, please?"

"Certainly." Annette smiled before disappearing into the next room.

"Now come, Ellie," Liz smiled, taking her by the hand. "Let's get you into your dress so your friends can see it."

She led Ellie to the fitting-room where her dress was hanging on a rail. Liz helped her into it and laced up the bodice. Ellie had done her hair in the style that she thought she would like on her wedding day. Much like Kate Middleton's, she had pulled back the side sections into a high ponytail and then curled the long sections with a tongs. She wanted the veil to sit high on the back of her head and cascade down in layers. Liz knew exactly what she was aiming for and arrived back with a tiny tiara and the perfect veil. She also had a pair of the most beautiful satin shoes studded with seed pearls. Ellie gasped as she saw her reflection in the mirror. It was perfect, just perfect.

Coming out of the fitting-room she saw from the reaction on her friends' faces that they thought so too.

"Oh my God, Ellie, it's just beautiful!" Keisha exclaimed, her mouth opening in a wide O.

"It's perfect, simply perfect," Chloe gasped. "You're like a fairytale princess, Ellie. Oh my God, I think I'm going to cry." She rushed forward to hug her best friend, tears in her eyes.

"Careful!" Ellie cried, half laughing, half crying. This was exactly the reaction she'd hoped for.

"You absolutely have to have this dress," Keisha said. "Nothing else will do."

"I do love that veil, Ellie," her mother observed, feeling emotional all over again.

"Me too," Ellie replied, turning to look at it from every angle in the mirror.

"And Sandrine," Marie-Noelle turned to her, giving her a sharp look, "what do you think of your sister's choice?"

"It's . . . lovely . . . quite lovely." She sounded flustered. In fact, she was completely spellbound by how beautiful Ellie looked and all the old insecurities and jealousies assailed her once again. Ellie had always been the beautiful, charmed child – their parents' pet and adored by everyone, even the nuns at school. Sandrine had always been second-best with them all, even though she was far more clever. It wasn't fair! All Ellie had to do was flash her violet eyes, smile and show her dimples and she had everyone eating out of her hand. Now here she was, looking like a beautiful princess and about to marry her handsome prince. It just wasn't fair! Sandrine felt tears of rage start to fill her eyes. Embarrassed and afraid she'd lose control, she went to hug her sister, who thought the tears were of happiness for her.

"Thank you, Sandrine," she whispered, all former annoyance forgotten.

"Now then, girls! Time to think about the bridesmaids' dresses," Liz pronounced. "Any ideas anyone?"

"I think black would be fabulous – very dramatic," Sandrine suggested, ignoring the dirty looks Ellie and the others were throwing in her direction. "What do you think, Liz?"

"God, no! Ellie is all about sweetness and light. Black would not match her personality at all. Something summery and pastel, I would suggest." Liz wasn't fooled. She dealt with brides all the time and she'd seen this type of sibling jealousy before. She'd noticed Sandrine's reaction to Ellie's appearance in her dress. And of course Sandrine would like black. It would suit her dark colouring, unlike that of the other two bridesmaids who were blonde and fair-skinned.

"I don't know. Vera Wang has even started doing black wedding dresses," Sandrine persisted. "I think it's very sophisticated."

"*Yeuch*!" Ellie grimaced.

Liz stared Sandrine down. "That might be all well and good for the Hollywood set who crave being different but I don't think that's what Ellie wants, is it, Ellie? And at the end of the day it's *her* wedding." She fixed Sandrine with a steely glare.

"Definitely not!" Ellie agreed. "I was thinking pale gold or something like that."

"I have just the thing. It's a pale buttery yellow –

226

almost gold." Liz went to the rail and took down a beautiful sleek dress in that colour.

"Oh, that's gorgeous!" Ellie cried as the others crowded around her.

"You can have this material and colour made up in three slightly different styles if you wish – one-shouldered, strapless, whatever. What do you think?"

"It's perfect, isn't it, girls?" Ellie turned to the others excitedly.

"I love it," said Chloe.

"Me too!" said Keisha.

"It's perfect," Marie-Noelle concurred. "And you could have the freesia and pale yellow roses you like so much for the flowers."

"Yes, definitely. This is the colour," Ellie decided.

Sandrine, sitting with a glum face, said nothing but nobody noticed or, if they did, they didn't care. It was decided.

They spent the next hour trying on various dress styles until they decided on what looked best on everyone. These would then be made up in the pale yellow/gold material. There was no problem with Chloe and Keisha who were as thin as whippets but to find a style that suited them while also flattering Sandrine's ample frame took a little longer. Eventually it was decided that an Empress-line style was the best option for all.

The bridesmaids' dresses wouldn't be made up until the last moment.

"You have no idea how many times dresses have had to be cancelled because bridesmaids have either gained or lost weight or become pregnant, or even in a couple of cases fallen out with the bride," Liz explained, laughing. "So we've learnt our lesson the hard way. We'll fit the girls again about six weeks before the big day and have their dresses made up then."

"That won't happen with us," Keisha and Chloe chorused.

Sandrine said nothing.

"I think that's very sensible," Marie-Noelle observed.

After much laughter and giggling the girls got dressed again and left, kissing Liz, who was now like an old friend. To Ellie's surprise and delight, her mother insisted on paying for her wedding dress and Ellie put down a deposit on the bridesmaids' dresses. They left to go for lunch in The Old Schoolhouse and to the relief of all Sandrine cried off, saying she had work to do in the office.

They had a great time and, two bottles of wine later, when the bill was presented, Chloe and Keisha insisted on treating Ellie and her mother.

"I just can't wait for your wedding day," Chloe said as she kissed Ellie goodbye.

"It will be brill," Keisha agreed as they left to get the bus into Dublin, to go shopping.

37

Ronan drove around to pick up Fiona as arranged on Sunday morning. Although the off-licence would not open until half past twelve, he saw that Sam's car was outside. He rang Fiona's doorbell and she buzzed him up. To his surprise, Sam was there.

"Just thought I'd pop in to give you a hand," he said to Ronan, after greeting him. "For a woman, she has surprisingly little 'stuff' – like shoes and bags, I mean."

"Tell me about it!" Ronan replied, grinning.

They were in sympathy with each other, having both experienced women's 'stuff'.

"I love it here and I'll miss it," Fiona said sadly, looking around the living room.

"But you'll be back after the baby is born, won't you?" Ronan asked.

"Yes, but I'll definitely take all my maternity leave. Now that Sam has you, I don't feel as if I'm leaving him in the lurch. We'll see."

"You know you can come back any time," Sam told her affectionately. "Now, let's get a move on."

They spent the next hour carrying boxes up and down the stairs, refusing to let Fiona lift as much as a feather.

At last she stood and took a long look around the room.

"Just think, the next time I see this place I'll have my son with me," she said, a lump in her throat. Running her hand over the back of the leather sofa, she blew a kiss to the place and left.

"You're going into Holles Street to have Buster, aren't you?" Ronan asked her as they drove down to Blessington.

She laughed, rubbing her tummy. "Don't let him hear you calling him that. Yes, Holles Street."

"Will I be able to come and visit?"

"Well, I'd love if you could but they have very strict visiting. Grandparents are allowed in every evening so Mam will come in then. I'm allowed one green card for my partner or whoever I nominate. Obviously, as my partner has flown the coop, it won't be needed for him," she said, looking forlorn, "and unfortunately with Mam coming up every evening, my sister-in-law Frances won't be able to come. She'll have no one to look after the five kids while Mam is away. My two brothers are farmers and it's a really busy time for them, but I could nominate you, if you'd like to visit that is," she said shyly.

"I'd be delighted. Could I masquerade as your partner, do you think?"

Fiona looked at him to see if he was serious. "Would you, really?" she asked, her face breaking into a huge smile. "I'd love that, if you wouldn't mind."

"I'd be honoured." He made a mock bow, as much as the steering wheel would allow.

"I don't mind being a single mother but I would feel strange if all the other mothers have partners visiting."

"I'll be a perfect partner, I promise," he stated, pleased that he could do this for her.

"You're the best friend ever," she said, throwing her arms around his neck.

"Whoa there!" he cried. "We'll crash and you might be in Holles Street sooner than you think."

"Sorry," she said, but her smile told him that he'd made her day.

"Gosh, it's lovely here. It's like another world," Ronan remarked as he got out of the car at her mother's bungalow, which overlooked the lake in Blessington. He could almost feel the peace descend upon him.

Fiona's mother, Doris, was a homely, plump woman who hugged him on being introduced.

"Fiona's told me what a good friend you've been to her and what a nice man you are," she said, her smile lighting up her face.

"Well, she's been a good friend to me too," he replied, warming to this lovely lady instantly.

"Come on inside. John and Brendan, Fiona's two brothers, will be here shortly to unload the car. Come in, come in!" She linked her arm through his and led him inside.

The delicious smell of beef roasting assailed him. He closed his eyes and inhaled. "*Aaahhh . . .* this reminds me of my mother's wonderful Sunday dinners when I was a kid."

"Is she still alive?" Doris asked.

"Sadly not. She died ten years ago, just a year after my father."

"Well then, I hope my dinner doesn't disappoint."

"Oh, I couldn't stay for dinner," he protested.

"Of course you can!" Fiona, who was now sitting on the couch with her legs up, cried. "It's the least we can do, after all you've done for me."

Seduced by the wonderful aroma coming from the oven, he didn't protest any more.

"I'm really happy she's here under my roof now so that if anything happens, she won't be alone," Doris said. "You can't be too careful with first babies."

"Yes, I think it's best for her." He smiled at Fiona. "We were all getting a little nervous lately."

"Well, she's in good hands now."

After lunch, he stayed much longer than he'd intended, chatting to Doris and John while Fiona went for a lie-down. Brendan had gone home for lunch with his family.

Later, driving back to Dublin, he felt warm and happy.

Doris had insisted that he come down again for lunch the following Sunday.

"I'll do roast Wicklow lamb for you. You won't get better," she'd declared.

He didn't doubt it!

He realised as he got ready for bed that night that he hadn't thought about Louise all day. For some reason that made him feel good.

38

Ellie was bubbling as she arrived at the wine course on Monday night.

"They've accepted our offer on the house," she told Rachel excitedly as they waited for the others to arrive. "And I found the perfect bridesmaids' dresses too!"

"That's great. I'm so glad things are going well for you. It's a very stressful time, isn't it?"

"You can say that again. My sister Sandrine is being a pain. She wants to run the whole show." Ellie grimaced.

"Thank God I didn't have that problem, but I'm sure you'll cope with it. By the way, did you know that Ronan's wife left him last weekend?"

"Oh, no! The poor guy! I noticed that he was very quiet last Monday. That's terrible." Ellie was shocked. "I didn't like her very much, did you?"

"Not at all," Rachel replied with distaste. "I don't think they were happy together but, still, it must be tough on him." She stopped as Zita arrived followed by the four young ones.

Finally, Ronan came in accompanied by Sam.

Rachel had no chance to talk to him until after the

class which was, as usual, fascinating. The subject of the night was Spain and Portugal and they all agreed that the Spanish wines were a pleasant surprise.

"I didn't think there was any more to Spain than Rioja," Ronan remarked, "but this Priorat is fantastic."

The others agreed and Sam noticed that, as usual, whenever the wine was exceptional, nobody bothered to use the spittoons. Yes, his little group were coming on in leaps and bounds. As he'd suspected initially, Ellie and Ronan had the best palates and were spot-on in their evaluation of the wine.

Ellie found herself walking with Ronan to the pub. "I'm really sorry about your wife, Ronan. Rachel told me about it. I hope you don't mind."

"No, of course not. It's not a secret."

"Are you okay?"

"I'm doing fine. We didn't have a great marriage to be honest but it was still a shock when she walked out."

"I can imagine," Ellie said, linking her arm through his. "Rachel is very concerned about you."

"That's sweet of her but, honestly, I'm okay. Luckily Sam is keeping me busy. Otherwise, I don't know what I'd do. And how about you? How are the wedding plans coming along?"

She told him excitedly about the house and her wedding dress, he smiling all the while at her enthusiasm. He hoped Ellie's dreams would not turn sour. He hadn't been very impressed with her fiancé the night of Rachel's party but he sincerely hoped that he would make Ellie happy. She deserved it. She was a sweet girl.

Rachel invited all of them to come to supper the following Friday night. Ronan was grateful for her kindness. He needed friends right now. It was strange how quickly they'd all become friends and it seemed to him that it was Rachel who was the ringleader in this. This was odd as he'd assumed that she must have loads of friends but he was beginning to think, from the little things she said, that this wasn't the case.

"Sorry, I can't come. I'm going to a stag party on Friday night," Sam said, rolling his eyes to heaven.

"And I'm afraid I'm working late next Friday," Ellie said.

"Oh, dear, what time do you finish?"

"Nine."

"Well, come along after work. You're only five minutes away," Rachel suggested.

"Thanks, I will," Ellie agreed happily.

Zita said she'd come too. She was brimming with good humour and insisted on buying everyone a drink to celebrate her new promotion.

"Congratulations! I'm so happy for you," Rachel cried, hugging her. "Carl will be pleased. He said he was going to ring you to see if he could intervene with the powers that be, but it looks like you made it on your own without his help."

"Yes, thank you." Zita didn't blink an eye as she told the lie. It was obvious that Carl hadn't mentioned to Rachel that he had contacted her and she wasn't about to let the cat out of the bag. After all, she'd got what she wanted.

They all raised their glasses to her in congratulation.

"And to Ellie who has secured her new house *and* the perfect wedding dress!" Ronan added, raising his glass to her.

"To Ellie too!" they chorused, all laughing happily.

They stayed later than usual due to the happy atmosphere that pervaded and Rachel and Ellie were both a little tipsy by the time they left. As always, the alcohol had had no effect on Zita. She had quite an amazing capacity to hold her liquor, both Sam and Ronan were thinking privately. As they made their way home each one of them was thinking that it was a good day when they decided to join the wine club.

Carl was in bed when Rachel got home. She went straight to the bedroom where he was almost asleep.

"Hi, honey!" she called out, turning on the main light.

"Please, Rachel, turn off the light, I'm almost asleep."

"Excuse *me*," she grumbled, turning out the light.

"I'm sorry but I've had a heavy day and I'm shattered."

"Well, I just wanted to tell you the good news. Zita has been promoted to producer."

Carl was instantly awake. "That's good," he mumbled, waiting to hear if she'd heard that he'd had a say in it.

"So you don't have to do anything about it now," she added.

Carl let out a sigh of relief. Obviously Zita had had the cop-on to stay mum about his involvement in it. He had big plans for Zita and the less Rachel knew that they were in touch, the better. He figured this was one liaison that she was better off not knowing about.

"Thank you anyway, darling, for offering to help her," Rachel said as she bent down to kiss him goodnight. "You go back to sleep. I'm just going down for a nightcap."

She tiptoed out as Carl pretended to go back to sleep. He could tell that she'd had more than enough to drink already but he didn't say anything. Thoughts of Zita now filled his mind. He felt himself getting aroused and when his erection wouldn't subside he had to take care of it.

It was over an hour later when Rachel came to bed. He heard her stumbling about the room but feigned sleep, knowing better than to get into an argument with her when she was in that state.

39

Much to Zita's delight, Jason, the idiot, was dropped as producer of the programme *The Women Behind Our Successful Men* and she was chosen to replace him. She was now in full control and knew she could make a top-class documentary – one that could even win an Irish Film and TV Award. That would make people sit up and notice her! She wondered idly if Carl had had anything to do with this latest development. She must remember to ask him when she met him on Friday night.

She rang Rachel on Thursday afternoon to say that she wouldn't be able to attend her supper party the next evening.

"I'm really disappointed you can't come," Rachel said. "It's a shame."

"I know. I'm very disappointed too but all hell has broken loose here since my promotion. You can't imagine!"

"I understand. Don't worry about it. See you Monday."

She wasn't as understanding with Carl when he rang on Friday afternoon to say that something had come up and he would be tied up all night.

"Carl, I've asked these people to supper. You have to be here." She was furious with him.

"Rachel, there are other important things in life besides your social life. This is a crisis. You know how things are in politics. I have no choice in the matter."

"Very well," she replied, sighing.

"You'll be fine without me. They are *your* friends after all."

This supper was turning into a disaster. It would be only Ronan and herself until Ellie arrived later.

To Zita's surprise, she was looking forward to the evening with Carl a lot. She took days deciding what she would cook for him and poor Marcus had to listen to her endless ponderings of oysters versus goat's cheese tartlets or salmon versus lobster. Eventually everything was done and she was ready.

He arrived on the dot of seven thirty, brandishing a bottle of Krug champagne which he'd obviously had chilled somewhere and a bottle of the wonderful white Burgundy wine, Puligny-Montrachet, which he'd also had chilled. He also produced a bottle of the famous Premier Cru red Bordeaux wine, Haut-Brion. Had he offered her these wines two months ago she would not have appreciated them but thanks to Sam and his wine course she was suitably impressed.

"*Mmmm* . . . you certainly know your wines," she observed.

"Well, actually, the guy in Mitchells chose them," he admitted, slightly embarrassed. "I didn't know what you would be cooking, so I tried to cover all eventualities."

To her surprise she saw that he was nervous. It gave her a sense of power over him.

"That's perfect. You couldn't have done better," she observed as she went into the kitchen and placed the white wine in the fridge.

He had followed her and, as she took down two champagne glasses, he opened the champagne.

They moved into the living-room which to his surprise was decorated in a very classical Georgian style. In fact, the whole apartment surprised him. He had thought that she would be living in an ultra-modern place, decorated likewise. But this reminded him of his in-laws' Georgian mansion in Kinsealy, all high ceilings and large sash windows.

"To a very beautiful woman!" he toasted her.

"To the future!" she replied. She didn't know what had made her say that. It had somehow slipped out.

Slightly embarrassed, she went and brought out the oysters, which she'd placed on a bed of ice and seaweed, and placed them on the table.

"*Mmmm . . .* oysters . . . my favourite," he said smiling at her. "I hope you don't have an ulterior motive, serving me an aphrodisiac food."

"I'm sure you have no need of it," she replied seductively, looking up at him with her cat-like eyes.

He laughed. He enjoyed sparring with her. He was enjoying himself enormously.

When they'd finished the champagne and oysters, she led him to the dining area where she lit the candles. The table was set with a white linen tablecloth and napkins, silver cutlery, crystal glass and there was a low bowl of white roses in the centre. It was charming and elegant. She surprised him constantly.

She opened the white wine he'd brought and then served the lobster salad that she'd finally decided on. It was divine. They flirted back and forth as the delicious wine made them ever more relaxed. By the time she served the tender rare rib-eye beef they were laughing and joking as if they'd known each other forever, but underlying this was a sense of excitement, a sexual chemistry which both of them knew would ultimately lead to the bedroom. It was as if they were playing a mating game.

She served the tiramisu which he tasted and declared to be the best he'd ever had. He took a spoonful and fed it to her and, closing her eyes sensually, she licked the cream and chocolate from the spoon, leaving a trail on her upper lip. He reached over and ran his tongue slowly over her lip.

It was the most erotic caress she'd ever experienced and, sitting transfixed, she parted her lips, feeling the desire rising inside her. He probed his tongue into her mouth, tasting the sweetness there. With a passion that surprised them both, she kissed him back and then they were frantically pulling their clothes off as she propelled him into the bedroom where they collapsed on the big four-poster bed.

Afterwards, Zita marvelled at the tenderness he'd shown as he'd slowly made love to her. It was something she'd never experienced before and it opened up a world of pleasure to her. He was an expert lover, knowing where to touch and caress her, driving her crazy with desire and making her cry out for him. She lost count of the times she came with him and, when they finally lay exhausted, he told her that he'd never felt like that in his life before either.

They drifted off to sleep, wrapped around each other, and it was some time later that he woke with a start.

"Holy shit!" he cried, looking at his watch. "My God,

how did I fall asleep like that? Sorry, my darling, I have to rush off and leave you. Even Rachel will not believe I've been at a meeting till this hour."

It was the first time he'd mentioned his wife's name all night. It was as if any mention of her would have spoilt the magic. Zita felt a surge of jealousy towards the other woman.

"It's been a wonderful, wonderful evening. I hope we can repeat it soon." He kissed her gently and then he was gone.

Zita felt somehow deflated after he'd left. The apartment felt big and empty. She tried to go back to sleep but it was useless. Finally, she got up and made herself hot chocolate. Pacing the room, she felt a loneliness engulf her. Damn him! It wasn't meant to be like this. It was meant to be just sex but somehow he'd made it into something else. He was different from any man she'd ever met. Very different! It unnerved her.

Ronan was looking forward to the evening at Rachel's. For somebody with such a high public profile and such wealth, she was amazingly down to earth. He was surprised to see that Carl wasn't there.

"He sends his apologies but has a crisis at work. The life of a politician!" Rachel laughed but it had a hollow sound to it. He could tell she was upset.

"I'm afraid Zita cried off too. So it's just you and me till Ellie arrives later."

"I can't think of a nicer companion," he said, bowing from the waist.

She made a little curtsy, smiling at his gallantry.

She served a starter of scallops and black pudding, which was very unusual but delicious. The main course was a lovely dish of sole stuffed with prawns. Of course, living in Howth meant there was always wonderful fresh fish to be had, though he suspected that she hadn't prepared it herself. She opened a bottle of Chablis to go with it but he had only two small glasses as he was driving.

Rachel was very sweet and he found himself telling her all about his life and his disastrous marriage to Louise. It was a relief to be able to talk about it and Rachel was a good listener, which surprised him, as she was usually so chatty.

"Maybe it's for the best," she commented. "Sometimes we don't understand at the time why things happen but later we see that they'd happened for a reason."

Somehow, he felt comforted by her words. "Maybe you're right. To be honest, if I'd stayed with her, she'd have bankrupted me. Now, at least, I don't have that worry."

"Things will work out for you, I'm sure," Rachel said sympathetically, reaching across the table and patting his hand. "You're still young enough to meet someone new."

He laughed. "I can't see that happening somehow. Once bitten . . ."

"Well, you never know," Rachel stated as she opened a second bottle of wine.

"No more for me thanks, I'm driving," Ronan said, putting his hand over the top of his glass.

Rachel refilled her glass with alacrity. He was surprised at the speed with which she drank.

"Well, at least *you* seem to have a charmed life," he observed as he relished the last of the sole and prawns dish.

"Oh, how I wish that were true," she said wistfully. "Everything is not always as it seems. I was so happy when Carl was elected and the first few weeks were wonderful but I quickly learnt that most of the people I meet are insincere and hypocritical. Besides that, I hardly ever see Carl any more. It's as if his political life has replaced me. It consumes him and I feel like a nagging wife when I ask him to spend more time at home."

Ronan saw the tears well up in her eyes and now it was his turn to reach across and pat her hand.

"I'm sorry," she blubbered as he handed her a white handkerchief. She dabbed her eyes with it, thinking what an old-fashioned gesture it was. This made her smile and he smiled with her. "I know it's stupid but I feel like my life is getting out of control. I seem to spend every night alone, with a bottle of wine. It's the only thing that helps. I feel so lonely and isolated."

"But drinking isn't the answer, you know. You really need to be careful, Rachel. I've seen too many people ruin their lives with alcohol."

She nodded numbly again. "You're right," she whispered. "I must try and cut down."

"There is help out there, you know," he said gently.

"Oh, I don't think I'm that bad," she laughed. "It's just that I'm lonely."

"Well, you've got the support of all of us now. We're your friends – Sam and Ellie, Zita and me – we really like you for yourself. We're not two-faced like those other people you meet."

"I know, I know," she agreed with him, smiling through her tears. "I really appreciate all of you. I'm sorry, I don't know what's wrong with me. I seem to cry at the drop of a hat these days."

Just then the bell rang. Rachel looked at her watch. "That must be Ellie!" She stood up, then paused and said, "Thank you so much, Ronan. You're a real friend and I'm sorry for off-loading on you when I'm the one supposed to be comforting you tonight."

"You're welcome, Rachel."

The bell rang again and she hurried into the hall to answer the intercom.

"Hi, Rachel, it's me!" came Ellie's sing-song voice as she leaned out the window of the taxi she'd come in. She gave a little wave at the camera.

Rachel smiled. "Come on in, Ellie," she replied, pressing the button which opened the electric gates, then going to open the front door for Ellie.

A minute later, Ronan was amused to see Ellie bounce into the room and halt in surprise.

"Where's everyone?" she asked.

"It's just us, I'm afraid," said Rachel. "Carl and Zita are both working and couldn't make it."

"That's fine," Ellie replied, a little relieved that Zita wasn't there.

Rachel reheated the main course for her and was pleased to see Ellie eating it up with gusto.

Ellie lightened the mood of the evening and by the time Rachel served up the chocolate terrine dessert they were all laughing and in good spirits. The time sped by and suddenly it was almost midnight.

"Oh my gosh, look at the time!" Ronan exclaimed, looking at his watch. "We'd better get a move on. I'm working tomorrow." He had offered to drop Ellie home.

"I've had a wonderful night, thank you, Rachel. You've certainly cheered me up," Ronan said, kissing her goodnight.

"I'm glad and I appreciate your advice. I have taken it on board," she assured him.

Ellie hugged her and thanked her for the fabulous food.

"I hope you'll both come and visit more often," Rachel said as they left.

They promised they would.

Ronan was wondering where the hell Carl was, working at midnight on a Friday night. Very strange, very strange indeed!

As he drove home after dropping Ellie off, Ronan thought how lucky he was to have met these lovely people. Strangely, the people most supportive during this bloody awful time – besides Conor and Jim, that is – were these new friends he'd met through his wine course. Sam, Fiona, Dermot and now Ellie and Rachel – they were making life much more bearable for him at the moment. Maybe Rachel was right. Things happen for a reason. He felt almost light-hearted as he let himself into his lonely house.

Luckily, when Carl got home Rachel was in bed. Obviously, she'd had quite a lot to drink earlier. Of course, Ronan and Ellie had been for supper though he doubted that they'd drunk very much of the two empty bottles that stood on the kitchen counter.

When he'd told Rachel that he had an important meeting and couldn't be there for supper she'd been furious with him. Now, as he slipped into bed beside her he was grateful for the wine she'd drunk. She never stirred and so he didn't have to give her the elaborate excuse he'd prepared on his way home. She'd never know that he'd arrived home after 3 a.m. Thank God for small mercies! It was his lucky night.

40

Ellie had made an appointment to meet with Gabriella, the wedding co-ordinator at Clontarf Castle, on Saturday at noon. She'd told David about it the week before so when he rang on Friday to say he couldn't make it she was very upset.

"David!" she cried, dismayed. "You have to be there. It's a really important meeting!"

"You don't really need me there, do you? Can't you manage it alone?"

"How can you say that? Of course I need you there." She burst into tears.

"Okay, okay," he acquiesced, not wanting another scene. They'd been having too many of them lately. "I'll try and make it but it will be closer to one o'clock, I'm afraid."

She reluctantly accepted this.

He felt that she didn't understand how very busy he was at work, not to mention buying the new house and putting his apartment on the market. Dresses and flowers were the last thing on his mind. To be honest, he was sorry now they hadn't eloped or at least gone abroad to get married. Ellie had been pressurising him for a list of the people he wanted to invite. He promised he'd have it for her by the following day. He sighed deeply. Women and weddings – Lord preserve us!

Ellie had already made out her list. She hoped to keep the numbers to one hundred – fifty invited by David and fifty by her. Then another eighty of their mutual friends would be coming along to join in the evening celebrations. Her father had always said he would pay for the reception but when he saw that it would cost almost €100 per head, he set a limit of €10,000 on it. She thought this was more than generous. She'd spent ages deciding what fifty people she wanted there and now she was waiting for David's list. He'd promised he'd bring it with him to the venue on Saturday.

She and her mother were welcomed by Gabriella who offered them coffee and biscuits before sitting down to discuss the reception. With the brochures and photos spread out before her, it really hit home to Ellie that this was her wedding they were planning and she fairly bubbled over with excitement. Gabriella liked her instantly and decided that she would do everything in her power to give Ellie the wedding of her dreams.

"I'm afraid my fiancé will be a little late," Ellie explained. "Business, you know," she added lamely.

"Trust me," said Gabriella, "I've discovered that most grooms are reluctant to get involved in all the nitty-gritty details of the wedding. They don't have a clue how much organisation goes into it so that everything runs smoothly on the day." She gave a little laugh.

Ellie smiled gratefully at her. So David wasn't the only reluctant groom. That was something.

"How many guests are you planning to have?" Gabriella asked.

"Well, we're having one hundred at the reception and dinner and then another eighty who will join us afterwards. So one hundred and eighty for the evening buffet."

"That's a nice number. Have you decided on a colour scheme?"

"Well, I'll be wearing white, naturally," Ellie smiled, "and I've decided on a pale yellow/gold for the bridesmaids and flowers."

"Perfect!" Gabriella clapped her hands. "The Great Hall will be just right for you. Come on and let me show you. It's all set out for a wedding later today."

She led Ellie and Marie-Noelle there and they gasped as they saw the magnificent chandeliers and gold velvet chairs. The tables were beautifully set with white and pink linen, sparkling crystal and silver and the flowers were pink and white.

"It's beautiful," Ellie exclaimed, taking it all in.

"*Magnifique*!" Marie-Noelle agreed.

"The wedding today has a pink theme, hence the pink linen and flowers," said Gabriella, "but as you can imagine, your yellow/gold theme will be even more effective."

Ellie was so happy that she'd dug her heels in and insisted on having the reception here. After all, it had been the scene of many family celebrations in the past. All their Communion and Confirmation lunches had been held here, not to mention other birthdays and also their parents' twenty-fifth anniversary which had been a resounding success. Now, looking around the Great Hall, Ellie knew she'd made the right decision.

"It's not too big for just a hundred guests?" Marie-Noelle asked with concern.

"Well, a hundred is really the minimum or they'd be lost in here. Any less and I'd suggest The Viking Suite."

"Oh no, I want it in here and we've planned for a hundred," Ellie butted in quickly. She hoped David would have fifty guests to invite.

They made their way back to the Indigo Lounge to discuss menus and Ellie was beginning to despair about David turning up when she got a text from him to say he'd arrived. She breathed a sigh of relief. She so wanted him to see the Great Hall and how beautiful it all was and secretly hoped he'd agree that it was the perfect venue for their nuptials. She texted him back, telling him to come to the Indigo Lounge.

A minute later he arrived and she introduced him to Gabriella.

"I think the Fairytale Wedding Package is the best one for us and the menu is lovely. What do you think, David?"

He glanced briefly at it. "Fine, that looks fine to me. Whatever you decide, darling."

"Just wait till you see the Great Hall where we'll hold the reception. It's wonderful." Ellie's eyes were glowing as she turned to Gabriella. "May I show him?"

"Of course," Gabriella smiled, pointing the way.

Ellie took David's hand and eagerly led him down the corridor. They entered the Great Hall.

"Wow!" said David. "That is something else!"

"Isn't it fabulous? Can't you just see it?" Ellie's eyes were shining.

He loved her when she was excited like this.

"As long as you're happy, my love," he said, kissing the tip of her nose.

They went back to the others where Marie-Noelle asked him if he had decided on his list of invitees.

"More or less," he replied, taking a sheet of paper from his pocket. "There may be a few more."

Ellie took the paper from him and looked down

through the list, blanching as she did so. "But David, there's over a hundred names here. I said fifty each."

She continued reading, dismayed that there were so many strange names on it. David had a small family and she'd met them all at his father's sixtieth birthday, earlier in the year. She knew all of his friends and some of the people from Buckley Steadman, but there were dozens of names here that she didn't recognise at all.

"Who are all these people?" she asked, pointing to the bottom forty or so people on the list.

"Oh, they're people from work."

"But David, this is not a business thing, it's our wedding!" she wailed.

"I know but I can't ask one and not another. It's very difficult." He looked glum as he saw her downcast face and Marie-Noelle frowning.

"Look, why don't you two discuss this later and let me know the number when you've decided," Gabriella suggested helpfully.

"That's a good idea," Marie-Noelle agreed, as she stood up to take her leave.

Ellie thanked Gabriella and said goodbye, promising to let her know the final figure once they'd decided.

Once they were safe in his car Ellie spoke, her voice trembling.

"David, how could you? I asked for fifty names. That's all I have. How could you do this?"

"I have forty from my family and friends alone," he tried to explain. "The other sixty are my colleagues from Buckley Steadman and their partners."

"But I don't even know most of these people," she cried. "They're not friends, they're just work people that you've only met in the past two months!"

"These people might be our friends in the future," he insisted.

Ellie was close to tears. "My father is paying for the reception. He can only afford to pay for one hundred. I can't ask him to pay for all these extra people."

"Money isn't a problem. I'll pay for it. After all, it *is* our wedding day and hopefully it's the only one we'll ever have. Why don't you invite another fifty and your dad can pay for your hundred guests and I'll pay for mine. Let's do it in style and have a *big* wedding."

Somewhat mollified, she thought about it. She'd had a problem keeping it to fifty herself and she knew there would be friends and relations miffed at not being invited – and she supposed, if David was willing to pay for it, why not? It would also mean that the Great Hall would be filled with people. It wasn't what she'd planned but there didn't seem to be anything else she could do.

"Okay, if that's what you want. As long as you can pick up the tab for your guests, then Dad can pay for mine."

All in all it was a good solution and, both happy, they went for lunch in the Bay restaurant on the Clontarf Road.

Ronan drove down to Blessington on Sunday to visit Fiona and her mother Doris, as he'd promised. He was certainly being well fed these days – much better than when he'd been married to Louise. He'd enjoyed a lovely meal with Rachel on Friday, another at Conor's last night where Betty had cooked a wonderful Indian curry and now here he was en route for a delicious Wicklow lamb Sunday roast. He'd better watch it or his weight would balloon. He planned on going back to the gym the following week, so that should help.

He hadn't heard a word from Louise since she'd left

and he wondered how things were working out for her. He was sure, if she needed money, she'd have been in touch. Long may it last, he thought.

He received a very warm welcome in Blessington. Fiona's brothers John and Brendan, along with Brendan's wife Frances and their five children, were also at the lunch and it was a big happy family that laughed and loved around the table.

Ronan agreed with Doris that Fiona was looking much more content and relaxed as she awaited the birth of her baby.

"'Tis the good Wickla air," Doris announced in her flat Wicklow accent.

They all laughed at this.

"Gosh, I don't know how you could want to live in Dublin when you have a beautiful place like this at your disposal," Ronan said to Fiona as they sat having tea later that afternoon.

"I know," she sighed.

"Sure, I want her to stay here with me when the little fella's born," Doris told him. "'Tis a much healthier place to bring up a child than the big city."

Ronan was inclined to agree with her and he could see that Fiona was not averse to the idea.

"Yes, and it's important to have family support around you when you have a baby," he agreed. He left unsaid the fact that the baby's father was nowhere in sight to support her at this time.

"Yeah, I guess you're right," Fiona replied. "We'll see. I've plenty of time to decide."

He hugged them both goodbye, making sure that Doris had his phone number so that she could notify him when the baby arrived.

41

Zita had been oddly unsettled all weekend. Carl was on her mind and she couldn't get him out of it. Even Marcus had got annoyed with her when he realised that she wasn't listening to a word he'd been saying.

"What is the matter with you? Don't tell me that Carl Dunne has bewitched you?"

"Of course not," she snapped at him, confirming what he'd suspected, that Carl had indeed got under her skin.

She'd spent Sunday evening working on her *The Women Behind Our Successful Men* programme but she found it hard to concentrate. She checked her phone every ten minutes expecting that Carl might text her, but he didn't. She felt strangely disappointed. She had made an arrangement to film Rachel doing her thing on Thursday week which meant she would get to see Carl then as she would be filming them in their home. However, she hoped she'd see him before that. She felt a flutter in her stomach at the thought.

The long-awaited text finally arrived on Monday: **Really enjoyed Friday night and not just the fab meal. How about a replay? Carl xx**

Zita wanted to play it cool but before the day had ended she had replied: **Sure. When do you suggest?** He texted her back immediately. **Tomorrow night?** She badly wanted to say 'No, sorry, I can't make it then' but instead found herself texting back: **Great, look forward to it.**

She was annoyed at herself for being so easy but she couldn't help it. Damn him!

At the wine course everyone seemed in good form. It was obvious that the two youngsters, Keith and Karen, were by now madly in love and Sam found it difficult to capture their attention as they gazed into each other's eyes. Dave, his other young employee, was turning out to be a very bright student, genuinely interested in wine. Sam felt that he had great potential and saw him as someone who could certainly manage a wine shop in the future. The biggest surprise of all was Hayley who, rather than spending her time texting her friends, was now hanging on Sam's every word. He was impressed.

During one of the breaks, Ellie found herself standing beside Hayley.

"Hi! How are you enjoying the course?"

"Oh, I love it. Isn't Sam just fantastic?" Hayley enthused.

"Eh, yes," Ellie responded, seeing the adoration in the teenager's eyes.

"I think he's just divine," Hayley continued, "and so cool. He's like a film star."

Ellie tried not to smile. Poor Hayley! It was obvious she had a major crush on Sam. Well, if it means she learns a lot about wine, she thought, I suppose that's not a bad thing. She felt like giggling, thinking how embarrassed Sam would be if he knew how Hayley felt.

"Well, I'm sure he's very impressed with how you're doing," she said.

"I hope so. I study every night and I want to go on and do my Higher Certificate Course too," Hayley beamed.

"Good on you. I'm sure Sam will be pleased."

"Oh, I hope so," the young girl said dreamily. "He's so fabulous."

Luckily Sam had called the class back for the tasting session just then or Ellie would not have known how to continue. Poor little Hayley! Ellie didn't think she had a hope in hell of attracting Sam's attention in that way. Still, you never knew with men. They were the strangest creatures with the weirdest tastes.

They decided to go to The Yacht that night for a change and as they walked there Ellie fell into step with Ronan.

"How are you, Ronan?" she asked, her voice full of concern.

"I'm just fine, sweetie. I had a lovely weekend." He smiled brightly at her to assure her that this was the case and she had to admit he was looking back to his normal self.

"Oh. I am glad," she smiled back, linking her arm through his.

To his surprise she was up way past his shoulder. He'd always thought of her as a tiny wee thing. Looking down, he saw the reason why.

"Holy God, how do you walk in those vertiginous heels?" He couldn't believe the height of them.

"They're very comfortable really," she explained, stopping and lifting up one foot to show him.

"Dear Lord, those heels must be at least five inches high," he exclaimed, bending down for a better look.

Ellie giggled at his expression. "Six actually. But they're very clever. See this platform here?" She pointed to the sole of the shoe. "Well, that's two inches high so the heels are actually only four inches high."

He roared with laughter. The logic of women! He'd never understand it. They had an answer for everything! As they continued walking he was surprised to see that she was actually walking along quite briskly in them. Being on stilts didn't seem to impede her progress at all.

"Well, how are the wedding plans coming along?" he asked.

Ellie launched into the whole story of Saturday and the now-extended guest list. Ronan smiled at her enthusiasm. Ah, the innocence of youth, believing in a golden future with all their dreams fulfilled. Life wasn't like that, as he'd discovered. It was full of disappointment and heartache – but no doubt that was something Ellie would find out in due course. He certainly didn't think much of her fiancé David and had disliked the way he'd treated her the night of Rachel's party.

"I hope all your dreams come true and that you have a wonderful wedding," he wished her as they arrived at The Yacht.

To his surprise she reached up and kissed him on the cheek.

"Thank you, Ronan," she smiled, her dimples making her look about fourteen years old, not a woman on the cusp of marriage. He patted her arm as they entered and took their seats.

Zita and Rachel had walked down together, discussing what would happen at the shoot the following Thursday week. It was all so exciting, Rachel thought, and she'd arranged a very full day to show people exactly what a politician's wife had to go through. They needed to know it wasn't all cocktails and lunches! She'd also had a brilliant idea for the evening. She waited until Sam arrived – he'd had to stay back to make some calls – to make her announcement.

"Listen, everybody," she said. "I'm doing a film shoot with Zita on Thursday week and she thought it would be nice if I were to host a dinner party that night for some friends and, I thought, what better people to have there than my wine group? Will you all come? Just yourselves, no spouses this time."

Ronan was relieved to hear that. "I'd love to, but I work Thursdays, unless I could get Dermot to change nights with me." He looked at Sam expectantly.

"That shouldn't be a problem. You can ask him tomorrow," Sam replied. "Count me in too, Rachel," he added.

"Great! And you, Ellie?" Rachel turned to her.

"Well, I work late every second Thursday but I'm sure I can get someone to change with me too."

"That's settled then. Thursday week, seven thirty. And I'm sure the TV station will arrange for taxis, won't they, Zita?"

Zita grinned. "If it means you'll all get drunk and make for entertaining television then I'm sure it could be arranged."

"A bit like *Come Dine With Me*," Ellie giggled.

"Oh Lord, I certainly hope not." Rachel put her hands to her face, horrified at the thought.

They all erupted with laughter.

42

Zita was in a tizzy waiting for Carl to arrive on Tuesday evening. She'd prepared an osso bucco earlier and it was now cooking away gently in the oven. She'd found a recipe on Yahoo which used lamb shank instead of veal and could be cooked in the oven, which meant she could entertain her lover and not have to stand over the cooker all night. She'd cooked this before for Marcus and it had been a great success. She hoped Carl would be impressed. She'd also called into Susan Hunter and bought some sexy lingerie which was something she'd never done before in her life. She didn't dare tell Marcus or he'd never let up on her. As it was he was teasing her unmercifully about becoming a boring housewife. To be honest, she was annoyed with herself. This was so out of character for her, yet she had this need to please Carl like a silly teenager in love.

He arrived as before, brandishing champagne and wine, but this time they had barely time to put the champagne in the ice-bucket before they were heading for the bedroom, unable to wait a moment longer.

"*Mmmm* . . . very nice," Carl murmured huskily, excited by the sexy lingerie. "Come here, you sexy vixen!" He pulled her to him and slowly opened the laces of the basque she was wearing while kissing her neck and the top of her breasts as he did so. She longed for him to take her nipples in his mouth but he was teasing her, kissing and caressing her breasts but avoiding the most sensitive area of all. She was crazy with desire by the time he slipped the basque from her shoulders and laid her on the bed. Finally he gave her what she wanted and she moaned with pleasure as his lips closed around one nipple and his fingers caressed the other.

Their lovemaking was even better than before and she marvelled at his stamina. She couldn't get enough of him and yet he was able to pleasure her again and again. Finally, exhausted and satiated, she lay back on the pillows, smiling lazily at him.

"You are one hell of a sexy woman," he said, tracing her lips with his finger.

All she could do was sigh with pleasure. Now she knew why people made such a fuss about sex. She'd never understood it before and had ridiculed those who did. She stretched, thinking of what she'd been missing for all those years.

"Now, I thought you were going to feed me, woman," Carl said, smacking her bare bottom as she got up out of the bed.

She put on a robe and went into the kitchen where she put the dauphinoise potatoes she'd left ready into the top oven. Then she ran a bath and brought the champagne into the bathroom.

After a lovely bubble bath together, where they sipped the glorious fizz and laughed and joked like an old married couple, they got dressed again and she checked on the lamb and potatoes. They were both perfect and shortly afterwards they sat down to the delicious meal.

"*Mmmm* . . . I could get very fond of being here with you," Carl said, stroking her hand. "You make me feel so relaxed. You're a very special woman."

She looked into his eyes and saw that he meant what he was saying. There was something vulnerable about him that was extremely attractive.

"Can I see you Friday night and this time I'd like to take *you* out to dinner?" he asked. "I guess I owe you one by now."

"You don't owe me anything but, yes, I'd love that." Her heart soared at the fact that he wanted to see her again in three days.

"I wish I could stay the night with you," he admitted as he kissed her goodnight, holding her head in his hands. "Maybe I could stay on Friday night?"

"Oh, yes," she whispered, kissing him back. "I'd like that more than anything. But how would you manage it?"

"Leave that to me. I'll think of something."

After he'd gone, she lay in bed hugging the pillow that held the scent of him still. She was acting crazy, she knew, but she didn't care. She'd never felt so whole and complete as she did with this man. Could this be love? The very thought scared her but she realised that, if it was, she was powerless to do anything about it.

43

On Thursday night Ronan was just coming back from his tea break when Louise's friend, Melissa, came into the shop.

"Can I have a word, Ronan?" she asked.

His heart sank. He'd pretty much put Louise out of his mind but he had a feeling that she was about to barge in again.

"Of course." He turned to Dermot who had been standing in for him. "Could you hold the fort for a few minutes longer, Dermot?"

"No problem."

Ronan showed Melissa into the small staff-room behind the counter and pulled up a chair for her. "Tea? Coffee?"

"No, thanks. I just heard that you were working here. I'm so sorry, Ronan – about Louise and everything." She was obviously feeling very uncomfortable.

"Have you come with a message from her?" His heart plummeted at the thought.

"No, no. I just wanted to see you and say how sorry I am."

"Oh!" Ronan was at a loss for words.

"How are you doing?" she asked, her voice full of concern and sympathy.

"I'm fine, really I'm fine. Getting by, day by day."

"I was sorry to hear you lost your job too. What an awful time it's been for you!"

He was touched by her concern. "That's life. No one said it would be easy." He grimaced. "What about Louise? How is she doing? I haven't heard from her since she left."

"I haven't heard much from her either. She seems to spend all her time shopping and she doesn't bother with me any more." Melissa's voice was bitter.

"Yeah, well, that's Louise for you."

She got up to go, giving him her hand. "Anyway, I just wanted to say that I'm sorry and I know you didn't deserve that treatment."

"Thanks, Melissa, I appreciate that," he said as he showed her out.

That was nice, he thought. It was obvious that Melissa was miffed that Louise had dropped her. It didn't surprise Ronan in the least.

Marcus couldn't believe what he was hearing. "Are you crazy, Zita?" This guy's married *and* a politician. You can't be serious?"

"I know, I know," she said grumpily, annoyed with him for raining on her parade. "Nobody need know about it. We'll be very discreet."

"Are you mad? Get real. This is Dublin you're talking about, where everybody knows everybody else. *And* he's a public figure to boot."

Zita said nothing. She didn't care what Marcus said. Carl didn't appear to be worried about being seen in public with her, so why should she be? She was secretly delighted that he wanted to do this. It meant that their relationship was moving to another level.

She and Marcus went out for an Indian meal together but things between them were strained. He couldn't believe how foolishly she was behaving. Could she not see that Carl Dunne was only using her? This was so unlike Zita that he was seriously worried. He wanted to help her but she was being stubborn. Damn that man anyway. Marcus wanted to throttle him.

Ellie had great fun making out a new list of wedding guests. She'd decided to ask the group from the wine course – Rachel, Ronan, Sam and Zita. She wasn't too wild about the latter but she couldn't very well invite the others and leave her out. Pretty much how David felt about his colleagues, she supposed.

She arrived into work on Friday morning and knew instantly that something awful had happened. Chloe was crying and Susan, the boss, looked devastated, her eyes red and swollen from crying too.

"What's wrong?" Ellie asked, terrified that someone had died or something.

"I have to close the business for good this evening," Susan said. "I'm sorry."

"But why?" Ellie cried.

"Well, you know business is down and now that the lease is up, the landlord has put up the rent to an unacceptable level. I just can't continue."

"But what will you do?" Ellie knew that Susan's husband was unemployed and that she had five kids to support.

"I'll continue from my own home but unfortunately I can't take you or Chloe with me."

Ellie went over to Chloe and put her arm around her. "Don't worry, you'll get something else. You're a great beautician *and* qualified. You'll find something."

"No, I won't," Chloe replied, wiping her eyes which made her mascara smudge all over her face. "Beauty salons are closing left, right and centre. There are not enough jobs out there for us all." She sniffed and blew her nose.

"Well, maybe this is your chance to open up on your own," Ellie said. "You always said there was a need for a salon in Baldoyle and you have the space in your dad's house." She desperately wanted to lift her friend's spirits. "We have a lot of customers here and Susan will not be able to handle them all on her own. Isn't that right, Susan?"

"You're right," Susan replied, brightening up. She felt really bad for the girls, making them unemployed at such a time. If Chloe could start from home, that would make her feel a lot better. "I won't need all my equipment so I'm sure we could come to a good arrangement."

As for Ellie, Susan knew that it was an awful time to be pulling the rug from under her, what with her wedding just around the corner, but she had no choice. There was nothing she could do. At least Ellie's fiancé was pretty well off.

Chloe had brightened up considerably. She rang her dad straight away to ask him if what they suggested was possible. To her relief he thought it was a great idea and agreed to finance the equipment.

The rest of the day was a flurry of activity. They made out little cards with Susan and Chloe's new locations on them and handed them out to the clients who were all very sympathetic. The champagne that Susan had sent Ellie to buy from Superquinn helped to placate them and they assured the two girls that they would continue to give them their business and spread the word. As Ellie observed at the close of business while the three of them sat sipping the remnants of the champagne, "They don't actually have much choice. There's no other beauty salon in the area. I think you'll do great, girls."

"Let's drink to that!" They raised their glasses to each other.

Ellie had tried to put on a brave face all day but on her way home in the DART that evening, she wondered what the hell she was going to do. She wasn't a qualified beautician so there was no possibility of her going out on her own. She wasn't really qualified for anything and there were no jobs available anyway. It was utterly hopeless. Luckily her dad and David were paying for the wedding reception and the money Uncle Matt had left her would take care of everything else. Otherwise she would have had to downsize the wedding, big-time.

Carl rang Rachel at five thirty. "Honey, we have an emergency here. I have to go down to Wexford tonight to represent the Minister for the Environment at a dinner as he can't get away. I'm sorry, sweetheart. It will probably be very late so I'll stay the night there. I hope you don't mind."

"Well, I don't suppose it matters whether I do or not," she said resignedly.

"Love you, sweetie," he said as he hung up.

Carl arrived at Zita's apartment at six thirty brandishing, not champagne this time, but a huge bouquet of red roses.

"Oh, they're lovely," she exclaimed, burying her nose in their wonderful scent.

He watched her as she put them in a vase of water,

noticing that she was wearing a fitted dress that hugged her body like a second skin. She was also wearing very high black heels and black fishnet stockings – or at least, he hoped they were stockings. He felt his erection starting but tried to calm down. If they went into bed now they'd never get to the restaurant. He'd booked them into a very upmarket, expensive restaurant in Dalkey. He'd been there before and he knew that the clients who frequented it were not the type to go running to the paparazzi. It was very discreet and exclusive. If they did bump into anyone he knew, he could always use the excuse that they were discussing a TV programme she was producing.

As it turned out, they met no one they knew, which was a relief. They had a wonderful meal and he was his usual charming, seductive self so that by the end of it Zita had to admit to herself she was falling in love with him.

Rachel meanwhile, depressed after Carl rang to say he'd be away for the night, opened a bottle of wine. She put the steaks back in the fridge. No point in cooking just for herself. She'd fed the children already so she'd just have some cheese with her wine later.

Settling down with her wine she watched the news on TV but her thoughts were miles away. She was quite drunk by the time Carl rang at eleven to say goodnight. Even so, she could tell he was angry with her. To hell with him! She wouldn't be drinking so much if he was home with her. She dragged herself up to bed, wondering if this was how her life was going to be in the future.

Meanwhile, back in Zita's apartment, Carl made fantastic love to her and it was wonderful to feel his body next to hers all through the night.

The next morning she cooked him a proper Irish breakfast which he ate with gusto. She smiled at his appetite. It was as healthy as his appetite for sex and life. He was wonderful. She felt a deep sense of disappointment when he said he had to leave. She knew he had to get home to Rachel and the thought of him there filled her with envy. How fantastic it would be to be living with him and have him in her bed every night!

Marcus had gone away for the weekend and she missed him as he was the only one she could talk to about Carl. It was going to be a lonely weekend.

When Carl eventually got home, Rachel was in very bad form.

"I'm getting sick of it," she cried. "You're out every evening and now you're even missing at weekends. It's not fair, Carl. Not on me and not on the kids." She looked at him accusingly and he had the grace to look guilty.

"I'm sorry sweetheart. Look, why don't we go out tonight, just the two of us. I'll call and book The Brass Monkey." He took the phone and dialled. "Then tomorrow we'll take the kids somewhere for the day – maybe the zoo."

She looked at him to see if he was joking. Carl hated the zoo with a vengeance. Even though they had an annual family membership for it, he could never bring himself to join them there.

"What about your golf game?"

"I'll cancel it."

She was disbelieving. This was a first. Somewhat appeased, she wondered if he was feeling guilty about something. "Well, Jacob and Becky will be delighted. I'll go and tell them."

As he booked the restaurant, she went to the playroom to break the good news to the kids and to tell Paloma that she could have the following day off. The nanny was delighted as, since the children were now on school holidays, she had them much more than usual.

"Daddy! Daddy!" The kids came flying into the kitchen. "You're coming to the zoo with us!" they yelled, jumping up on him.

Rachel came in behind them, smiling at their exuberance. Smothering them with kisses, Carl felt another pang of guilt. They were growing up so fast. He really would have to make more time for them in the future.

Winking at Rachel, he swung Jacob on his back and took Becky by the hand. "Come on, kids, let's go out to play."

Whooping and yelling, the three of them made their way to the state-of-the-art playground. Rachel poured a glass of white wine and stood by the kitchen window, sipping it and smiling at her family. This was how she wanted it. This was how life was meant to be. Family was the most important thing in the world. She wished Carl felt the same way.

As Carl was pushing Becky on the swing he thought about his situation. He *was* feeling guilty. He really would have to be more careful. Rachel wasn't stupid. He dreaded to think what would happen if she ever found out about Zita. *Phew!* Not only would she kick him out but his political career would be in ruins. The Irish electorate wanted their politicians to be squeaky clean. Greater men than he had fallen foul of their high expectations.

He also suspected that Zita was falling for him and this was making him uneasy. Still, she was wildly exciting and a powerhouse in bed and he was getting excited just thinking about her. He'd have to be very careful now. He wasn't willing to put his life on the line for her but he couldn't give her up quite yet. She was coming to the house to film them the following Thursday and he'd need to play it very cool and keep his wits about him. He had much too much to lose.

44

Ellie was a little down in the dumps at the wine course on Monday.

"Are you okay, Ellie?" young Hayley asked. She really admired Ellie and wished she could be like her.

"The beauty salon where I work closed on Friday, just like that!" She clicked her fingers. "So now I'm unemployed, just like half the country."

"Maybe Sam will give you a job. He rang me on Saturday and asked if I'd be interested in working in his new Marino shop." Hayley was grinning broadly. "I said yes, of course." She looked overjoyed.

"Is he looking for other staff?" Ellie wanted to know.

"I don't know. Why don't you ask him? He has two new shops opening, one in Marino and one in Howth."

"When are you starting?"

"In six weeks. I'm very excited about it."

Ellie mulled over what she'd said as the others filed in. She had no experience of working in a wine shop but then neither had Ronan and by all accounts he was doing very well.

They couldn't believe that there was only one more week of the wine course left. Where had the time gone? Sam sprang quite a surprise on them then.

"Actually, there will be a little exam next week. It's a simple, multiple-choice test and, for those of you who wish to continue on to the Higher Certificate Course in September, it's essential to have passed this Lower Cert Exam."

"An exam!" Ellie wailed. "I'm useless at exams."

"You'll pass it with your eyes closed, Ellie," Sam assured her.

"Lordy me, it's over eighteen years since I sat an exam," Rachel lamented, not feeling too happy about it. "I don't think I'd pass."

"Nonsense, you're all more than capable of passing it," Sam said matter of factly. Afterwards we'll have a really good tasting and then I suggest we have a right knees-up to celebrate."

This was greeted with whoops and clapping. They really had all gelled together very well.

"What do you say we organise some food from the local deli. If we collect ten euro from each of us for the food then I'll be happy to supply the wine for free."

They all thought this was a great idea. It somehow made the exam seem not that scary if there was to be a party after it.

They went to the Castle for a drink but Ellie didn't get a chance to speak to Sam alone. She called him the next day.

"Hi, Sam, it's Ellie. Do you have a minute?"

"Of course, Ellie. What can I do for you?"

"Well, Hayley was telling me that you're opening two new wine shops and I was wondering if there was any chance that you might need a salesgirl?"

Sam was taken aback. "What about your job in the beauty salon?"

"It closed down on Friday," she told him glumly.

"Oh, I'm sorry to hear that. Gosh, businesses are closing left, right and centre. Yeah, I'm sure I can find something for you but it won't be for six weeks."

"That's okay. It's better than nothing – especially with the wedding coming up."

"Of course. That must be stressful enough without this landing on top of you. Leave it with me, Ellie. I'll get back to you."

"Thanks, Sam," she said gratefully, relief flowing through her.

Sam rang back an hour later. "Ellie, can you work a computer?"

"Sure. I did computers at school and I took an advanced night course last year. I'm quite good on it actually," she said proudly.

"Fantastic! And you speak fluent French, I remember you telling me? You and your mother often speak French together, don't you?"

"Yeah, all the time."

"Brilliant!" Sam sounded really excited now. "Well, I've been thinking. My PA is setting up my new online business at the moment and she's completely overstretched. She could do with some help while she gets the online business up and running, but I need someone with fluent French and computer skills. How about it? Would you be interested, until the new shop opens up?"

Ellie held her breath. She could hardly believe it. Her mother looked up from the book she was reading to see the big smile on her daughter's face. Ellie gave her the thumbs-up.

"Would I be interested? You bet I would!" She covered the mouthpiece with her hand and whispered to Marie-Noelle, "*Sam's looking for a temporary PA!*"

"Great. You could start right away, I take it?"

"Tomorrow, if you like."

Sam laughed at her enthusiasm. "Can you meet me here Thursday morning? Is nine thirty okay?"

"Sure, see you then!"

Ellie hung up, grabbed her mother and waltzed her around the kitchen.

"Tell me, tell me!" Marie-Noelle demanded, dying to know what had transpired.

Ellie explained and her mother hugged her tightly. This was fantastic! Maybe this was Ellie's niche after all. "Thank you, God, thank you, Sam!" she prayed. Right now they seemed like one and the same person!

Ellie couldn't believe her luck. She went to meet Sam on Thursday morning feeling apprehensive in case it didn't work out. She needn't have worried. Sam wanted her to start right away and to top it all he was offering her much more than she'd been earning in the salon. She would be working from the office in his house which was just around the corner from where she lived. It was all working out great.

He introduced her to Sylvia, his PA, who was overjoyed to have her on board.

"You've no idea how delighted I am to have you here," she exclaimed, pumping Ellie's hand enthusiastically. "I was afraid my husband would divorce me if I kept up working these hours. He's starting to suggest that I should pack it in as he never sees me, but I love my job and Sam is a great boss." She smiled happily at Ellie. "Sam says you're a computer expert and fluent in French. Probably much better than I am." She made a face.

"I wouldn't exactly say I'm an expert on computers but I have done an advanced course, and I am fluent in French."

"Thank God for that," Sylvia sighed. "I dread having to try to understand the French producers when they call. I did French at Uni but my accent is crap."

Ellie liked Sylvia enormously. She was very open and friendly and Ellie knew that they'd get on well. Sylvia called a spade a spade and she liked that. Yes, she'd have no trouble working alongside this woman.

"Sam says you're his top student on the wine course," Sylvia continued.

"Oh, I wouldn't say that," Ellie blushed at the compliment, "but I do love it. Sam makes it all so interesting."

"Do I detect a mutual-admiration society here?" Sylvia commented bluntly. "I've been dying for Sam to meet the right girl. Maybe you're the one." She cocked her head to one side, looking Ellie over.

"Oh, definitely not," Ellie giggled. "I'm getting married next January."

"What a pity! You and Sam would be perfect together." Sylvia shook her head in disgust as Ellie blushed a deep red.

"He has a girlfriend – Orla – hasn't he?"

Sylvia pealed with laughter. "God, no! Orla's his cousin. She sometimes helps out here. Anyway, let me show you how the company system is set up."

They spent the next hour going over everything that Ellie would be responsible for. It seemed straightforward enough.

"It's great that you've done the wine course. It all makes more sense then. Okay, time for coffee and chocolate biccies," Sylvia said, leading the way to the small kitchen behind the office. "I'm really pleased that you're joining us," she told Ellie, her voice serious, "and I know Sam is too."

"Yeah, well, it's a lifesaver for me, you know. I lost my job last Friday."

"So Sam said."

Sylvia then went on to talk with pride of her baby daughter Isolde who was eighteen months old. "Thank God I'll get to see more of her, now that you're here."

Ellie was happy to be helping out. It was great. She felt she was really needed here. She couldn't wait to start. Somehow she felt it was the start of a whole new life. The song was right – behind every cloud was a silver lining. Who would have thought it?

45

Rachel did her usual pampering on Wednesday and then went to the TV studios to discuss the following day's filming with Zita and her production assistant. It was all so exciting and she'd bought a beautiful new Louise Kennedy suit for the day and a fabulous Richard Lewis silk jersey dress for the evening. Everything was ready to go.

The following morning the crew arrived at the house at seven thirty and Rachel invited them all in for coffee. The children were looking adorable and had been warned to be on their best behaviour. Carl greeted Zita with a handshake and although she held it for a fraction too long she was cool and professional towards him, thank God. He breathed a sigh of relief. Having his wife and lover in the same room made him uncomfortable.

Zita saw how great he came across on film. He was one of those rare people that the camera loved. She really must seriously consider doing a programme on him in the future. That would give them a great excuse to be seen together without raising eyebrows. Yes, she must definitely look into it.

After filming the family breakfasting together, they followed Rachel to the care home in Baldoyle where she talked to the elderly residents there. From there it was on to the local day-care centre where she chatted with the staff and even joined in the karaoke session that was taking place. She then went to a charity luncheon being held for the hospice and worked the room like an old pro. She had a natural charm which came across on camera and Zita knew they'd have some great footage for the programme.

After lunch it was on to the summer school where she presented prizes to the children taking part. From there she went to the local Brownie camp-out and presented certificates to the little girls, delighted that Becky was one of them.

It all made for terrific filming and Zita had to admire the gracious way Rachel dealt with everyone she met. She appeared to have boundless energy and never flagged for a second.

In fact Rachel was in her element, feeling like an actress playing the part of a politician's wife. So what if people thought she did this every day? They wanted action and she'd given it to them.

On the way home she stopped off in Superquinn to pick up some last-minute things and then home to cook dinner for her wine group. She had considered getting caterers but it would look so much better if she did it herself and besides, she *did* love cooking. All the time the cameras rolled and Rachel almost felt like a contestant on *Come Dine With Me*. Thank God the guests wouldn't be marking her efforts though. That would have been too much! By the time Carl arrived home Rachel was all glammed up in her new Richard Lewis dress and looking forward to the evening ahead.

Carl presented his wife with a big bouquet of flowers and, as he kissed her and whispered something in her ear that made her smile, Zita felt the pangs of jealousy stir. Seeing them together with the children was heart wrenching. They were the picture of the perfect family, all blonde and beautiful. The children were adorable and were allowed to stay up to greet the guests.

Sam and Ellie arrived first and Zita lifted an eyebrow at the fact that they'd arrived together. Was she missing something here? Ellie straight away bent down to chat to Jacob and Becky and it was obvious that she loved kids. Sam seemed a little uncomfortable with the cameras on him. He looked stupendous with those gorgeous dark eyes gazing moodily into the camera. God, he was sexier than most film stars!

Ronan was next to arrive and he also had brought a bouquet of flowers for Rachel. He seemed shy in front of the cameras which didn't surprise Zita. He was a lovely bloke.

They filmed everyone having a glass of champagne and then Zita called for attention.

"Okay, everyone, we're not going to spoil your evening by filming every bite you put in your mouth. We'll just restart when you sit down to table and after the first course has been presented, we'll wrap up. Alright?"

Sam and Ronan both heaved a sigh of relief and even Ellie was not too happy to be in the spotlight. Rachel was pleased. She'd had enough for one day.

She served the starter and Zita called, "Okay, it's a wrap!" as the stifling hot lights were turned off and everyone relaxed.

The camera crew clapped spontaneously and Rachel blushed sweetly. She left the table to offer them some drinks and snacks she'd prepared for them.

"That's one right lady," Zita overheard one of the soundmen say to another.

"Class act," the other man agreed.

And it was true, Zita had to admit. Rachel had been the perfect subject all day long, gracious and kind.

"Zita you are staying for dinner, aren't you?" Rachel enquired.

"I'm not exactly dressed for a smart dinner party," Zita replied, looking down at her jeans.

"Nonsense, you look lovely."

Carl joined in. "We'd love you to stay."

She looked into his sexy blue eyes and was lost. More than anything she wanted to spend the evening in his company, even though his wife would be there too.

"Okay, if you insist," she consented feebly, unable to resist him.

"That's my girl," he whispered, when Rachel had gone into the kitchen, winking at her.

She felt like a fly caught in a spider's web.

"Tomorrow night?" he whispered.

"Sure," she whispered back, her heart soaring. The pain of watching him with Rachel was almost unbearable. Now she felt she was having her revenge.

Rachel had had to be very careful not to be seen to be having a drink while the cameras were on her. While having her shower and dressing, she'd sneaked a large vodka and orange. She couldn't have risked a gin – the smell would have been a giveaway – hence the vodka. Once the cameras were turned off she let rip however and

279

sneaked a gin and tonic in the kitchen before dishing up the main course. Once or twice she saw Carl frowning at her but she ignored him. God damn it! She'd had a rough day, she deserved it. And she'd done it mainly to promote Carl's career. You'd think he'd have been grateful.

After they'd all left, she'd kicked off her shoes and poured herself a cognac. Then she sank down on the couch with a sigh. "Wow! What an exciting but utterly exhausting day."

"Don't you think you should go to bed?" Carl asked.

"Don't you think I deserve a drink? I have to relax," she said, rubbing her feet which were aching. "I think Zita was very pleased with the result though," she observed happily.

"She's certainly good at her job," he remarked, deciding to pour himself a whiskey. If you can't beat 'em, join 'em, he thought to himself. His wife was certainly knocking back the booze big-time. He'd have to do something about it.

"Do you know that's the first night you've had dinner here this week." Rachel looked at him, trying not to sound as if she was criticising.

"Oh Rach, give over," he sighed. "I've had a tough day too. And by the way, I won't be home for dinner tomorrow night either. I have a previous engagement."

She shook her head helplessly. This was obviously the way their life was going to be in the future.

He then opened his laptop and she flicked through a magazine, neither of them speaking. When she'd drained her glass, she poured herself another one, ignoring her husband's disapproving look.

46

Ronan was busy stacking shelves in the shop on Friday afternoon when his mobile rang.

"Hi, Ronan, it's Doris here, Fiona's mother."

He tensed himself, waiting for the news. He'd spoken to Fiona yesterday and she hadn't been feeling too good. He'd tried ringing her that morning but it had gone to voicemail and she hadn't rung back, which was most unusual.

"Just want to let you know that Fiona started labour during the night and as of twenty minutes ago is the mother of a beautiful baby boy!"

"That's wonderful!" he exclaimed. "How is she?"

"Tired, but deliriously happy. She asked me to call you straight away."

"Thanks, Doris. I'm so glad you did. When can I come visit her – er, them?" he laughed.

"Well, you can visit any time except mealtimes. I've just left her and I know she'd be very happy to see you . . . and Ronan, thank you for doing this. I can't tell you how much it means to Fiona." Her voice was very emotional.

"I'm happy to be able to do it. She's a wonderful girl."

"Yes, she is and she'll make a wonderful mother."

"I've no doubt. I'll call in after work tonight, probably around seven."

"She'll be delighted to see you." Doris had grown exceedingly fond of him in the short time she'd known him.

Ronan gave the news to Sam and Dermot who were delighted that all had gone well and then he dashed out during his tea-break to buy a large bouquet of yellow roses for Fiona and a cool little suit for the baby.

Fiona's face lit up when she saw Ronan enter the ward. She looked tired but extremely happy. In her arms she was cuddling the cutest little baby Ronan had ever seen. He'd seen Conor's sons when they were newborn and they'd been scrunched up and ugly but this baby was not at all like that.

"Isn't he beautiful?" Fiona asked him, stroking the baby's smooth cheek.

"He really is," Ronan agreed. "Not at all wrinkled, like I expected." He bent in over the little bundle, putting his finger in the baby's hand. The tiny baby grasped it with a strength that surprised him. "Wow, he's strong for such a little fellow!"

Fiona laughed. "I've named him Oisín," she smiled, "and I'd like you to be his godfather, if you'd like that."

Ronan felt tears come to his eyes. "I'd love that," he told her. "Hello, Oisín!" To his amazement the tiny baby gave a little smile. "Well, look at that," he said, love for the child welling up in his chest. This little guy needed him and he'd make sure he was a great godfather.

Fiona didn't inform him that the smile was probably wind!

He sat happily, looking at the baby and chatting to Fiona, until he saw she was getting tired. He took the baby from her and put him back in the crib.

"Congratulations again," he said, kissing her on the forehead as he saw her eyes close.

Well, what do you know, I'm a godfather, he thought to himself as he walked jauntily back to the car.

Marcus dropped into Zita's flat that evening. He was on a high because he'd just won a big contract and wanted to celebrate.

"Come on, let's go out on the town," he suggested.

"Sorry, I can't. I'm busy."

"Don't tell me it's that asshole Dunne again." He looked at her with disgust.

"Don't call him that!" she yelled, furious with him.

"God, you're pathetic. Can't you see he's only using you?"

"How do you know that? You don't know how he feels."

"Oh *puhleeese*, you are delusional!" He saw her blushing and realised with horror that she really was serious.

"I don't believe it. You're in love with him! Oh, Zita, Zita, honey, how could you let that happen?" He just couldn't believe it. What had happened to her? Where had her common sense gone? She was behaving like a lovestruck teenager, for God's sake! He was wasting his time. There was no getting through to her. This guy had bewitched her.

"Well, sweetie, I'll leave you in his clutches." He got up and headed for the door. "No doubt I'll be around to pick up the pieces," he threw at her laconically as he exited the apartment.

"You know nothing!" she yelled after him. "You have

no idea what I've been through in my life! You couldn't begin to imagine the things I've done!"

But he had gone.

Zita felt sad that Marcus couldn't be happy for her. He was her best friend but he didn't understand how she was feeling. She was thinking of Carl every minute of every day and now, as she waited for him to call, she was filled with excitement and anticipation.

He didn't disappoint. Their lovemaking had reached new heights. She'd prepared a lasagne earlier but neither of them had wanted to waste precious time eating, so they stayed in bed for the whole evening.

"I'll treat *you* to dinner next week," he told her as he stroked her hair. "We'll go back to that nice restaurant in Dalkey that you liked so much."

She smiled happily. It wasn't the restaurant that was important – it was the fact that he was happy to be seen in public with her. That had to mean something, she told herself after he'd left.

Finally, she understood why people over the centuries had been moved to write love poems. She felt like writing one herself!

Yet another Friday night in alone, Rachel thought as she opened a second bottle of wine. She couldn't understand what had happened to the wonderful life she thought she'd had just a few short weeks ago. The gloss had worn off very quickly. Carl was so busy that they spent hardly any quality time together any more. When he was home he was distracted and spent the time alone in his study. At the back of her mind lay the suspicion that he was seeing someone again. She tried to push it away but with every sip of wine she became more convinced that this was the case.

When he finally arrived home at midnight, her courage fuelled by the wine she'd drunk, she tackled him about it.

"Oh for God's sake Rachel, you're paranoid. I'm off to bed."

"That's right," she screamed. "Ignore me! That's all you do nowadays."

"Maybe, if you weren't always drunk, I'd come home earlier," he snapped.

"I drink because I'm alone every night. I never see you any more."

"I'm tired. I'll sleep in the guest room tonight," he said in a resigned voice as he started to leave the room.

"You bastard!" she screamed, hurling her glass of wine after him.

He looked at her, disgusted, and kept going.

She looked in horror at what she'd done. Watching the red wine streaming down the wall, she sobered up pretty quickly.

"Oh my God, what have I done?" she whispered, putting her head in her hands.

She sobbed for at least ten minutes before going to clean up the mess. When that was done she made herself a cup of coffee and thought about what he'd said. She was drinking too much, she knew that, but she didn't know how she would cope without it. It kept her sane.

47

Ellie was in brilliant form on Saturday morning. She absolutely loved her new job and it was fascinating learning more about different wines every day.

As for the wedding preparations, she now had the final number of guests – two hundred and twenty. Yes, David had gone over even the hundred allotted. She didn't know half the people on his list but . . . he who pays the piper . . . as her mother reminded her. If this was what David wanted – well, it was his wedding too. Hopefully, some of his invitees would not be able to make it. She had wanted him to come and choose the menus with her but he'd said he had to work and was quite happy to leave it all up to her. Did all men about to be married behave like this, she wondered.

Sandrine was another story altogether. Annoyed at not being included the previous week, she insisted on accompanying them to the Castle to choose the menus. Marie-Noelle was afraid that her older daughter would make waves but she needn't have worried. Gabriella supported Ellie in all her choices and poor Sandrine could only grin and bear it.

"It is, after all, Ellie's wedding," Gabriella had told her

firmly, "and at the end of the day, what she wants is what's important."

Sandrine had met her match so she shut up and went along with it, wondering why she'd bothered to come at all. Two hundred and twenty guests! It was incredible. It was going to be a huge wedding. When she saw the Great Hall she felt even more jealous. She grudgingly agreed with her mother that the yellow/gold theme Ellie had chosen would go perfectly with the décor in the room.

It galled her to hear Ellie raving about Sam and her new job during lunch, which they took in the bar there. The fact that their mother was so proud of her younger sister rubbed salt into her wounds. How did Ellie do it? She could fall in the gutter and come up smelling of roses! Sandrine felt very bitter at how life was treating them both.

They invited her to go with them to the florist to check out the flowers but she cried off, pleading a headache. She'd had enough of happy families and big weddings for one day! Ellie and Marie-Noelle were secretly pleased. Somehow, Sandrine put a damper on everything. They headed to Clontarf Florist and a meeting with the owner, Bernie, who was exceptionally helpful. They looked through her brochure and the moment they saw the bouquet with the white and pale-yellow roses interspersed with pale-gold freesia, they knew this was the one. They ordered the full package: bouquets, corsages, flowers for the church and reception.

"That's a great day's work done," Marie-Noelle smiled at her daughter. "I think it's all going to be beautiful."

Ellie felt the same. Everything was going beautifully. The following Saturday they would decide on the wedding cake. Ellie had been to a wedding the previous year where the cake had been absolutely fabulous. She'd discovered it had been made by Killinure Cakes, a small one-woman operation in Glasson outside Athlone, and she and her mother had arranged to go down there the following Saturday. She'd looked it up on the internet and loved the cakes displayed there.

When they got home that evening they brought Ellie's father Tom up to date on all the arrangements.

"We're going down to Athlone next Saturday to check out the wedding cake," Ellie informed him.

"Oh, can I come too?" he asked. "It's been years since I've been down that way."

"Wonders will never cease!" Marie-Noelle laughed, rolling her eyes to heaven.

"Why not? It's my daughter's wedding. I want to be involved too." He looked so forlorn that Ellie rushed to give him a hug.

"Great! I'd love you to come, Dad, and I'll treat you both to lunch there. I hear there are smashing restaurants in Glasson!" Ellie said, clapping her hands.

"It's a date," her father replied, grinning and giving her a high-five.

She was thrilled that he wanted to help out and, blowing him a kiss, she went up to dress for the evening.

She and David had been invited to Frank and Judith Buckley's house again. Seemingly it would be the final dinner as Judith was off to Marbella for eight weeks. She remembered what Anna had said at the last dinner there: "The women decamp to Marbella and leave the men to have their little flings in Dublin." Rumour had it that the Dublin matrons had quite a few flings of their own in the Spanish sunshine. Ellie didn't doubt it.

Ronan had Saturday off and played golf in the morning – his first Saturday playing in a long time. His friends were delighted to see him back and in such good form. He played extremely well and was thrilled to be the winner of the jackpot, amidst much teasing about secretly practising when they weren't around. He had lunch and a few beers with the lads in the clubhouse afterwards.

He felt exhilarated as he made his way in to visit Fiona again that afternoon. This time he brought her chocolates and a little teddy bear for baby Oisín.

"Oh, you're so sweet, Ronan," Fiona said, tears coming to her eyes. "You don't *have* to come in every day."

"I want to. I wouldn't be much of a 'partner' or godfather, if I didn't!" He smiled at her, peeking into the crib at the peacefully sleeping baby.

Fiona was crying. "Sorry," she said, wiping her eyes. "Hormones, I'm afraid. I'm so happy it makes me cry."

"Well, that's allowed. I was worried it was me making you cry."

"Yes, well, your kindness does it too." She smiled through her tears. "He's such a good baby," she told him. "He hardly ever cries."

"Of course not – he's my godchild after all."

This had her laughing.

"When will they let you out?" he asked.

"Monday, I think."

"Oh, that's very early. I'm off Monday. Would you like me to take you home?"

"Could you?" she asked hopefully. "Mam's back is giving her hell and I hate asking her to drive all the way up from Blessington when she's in such pain. It would be great if you could."

"I'd be delighted."

It was all arranged.

48

Ellie felt much more confident going to the dinner that evening, knowing what was expected of her. She'd been so nervous the first time she'd visited but now she was well able for Judith – and Frank for that matter.

Frank greeted them, giving Ellie his usual lascivious glance which she ignored.

"Hello . . . sorry, I've forgotten your name," Judith said bitchily.

"Ellie, and sorry, I've forgotten your name too," Ellie replied, smiling sweetly.

Judith frowned. Behind her back, Frank made a down-stroke sign, meaning: round one to Ellie.

She grinned at him, pleased.

"Yes, well, what would you like to drink?" Judith asked, ignoring the put-down.

"Do you have any Alsace white wine?" Ellie asked. "Preferably Riesling, but Pinot Gris is okay too." She smiled innocently at Judith, her dimples making her, as always, look like a teenager.

"I'll check," Judith replied archly, furious with this young whipper-snapper. She went off to check with the waiters.

David was furious with his fiancée. What was she playing at?

Ellie was pleased to see that some of the younger crowd from Kitty's were there this time and they greeted her warmly. Frank pulled David away to the side to discuss something with him, leaving Ellie chatting to the women.

"How are the wedding plans coming along?" Joanne asked her.

"Just great, though you were right, maybe we should have eloped."

The others laughed, nodding their heads in agreement as Judith returned.

"I'm afraid we don't have any Alsace wine but we do have some Italian Pinot Grigio or German Riesling," she informed Ellie through tight lips.

"The Pinot Grigio will be fine." Ellie smiled innocently at her as Frank and David rejoined them.

"You *do* know your wine, don't you?" Joanne remarked.

"Oh, I remember now Sam told us you were on his wine course." Frank winked at Ellie. "Is he any good?"

"He's brilliant."

"I'll never understand how my son has become so successful," Judith sniffed. "He was useless at school."

"He has a great business head and of course he's passionate about wine," Ellie told them. "I'm actually standing in as his PA at the moment and it's a fascinating business."

"Really? Pretty *and* bright," Frank said, winking at her again.

Judith gave him a dirty look.

Ellie was relieved when another couple arrived and Judith and Frank had to go and greet them.

The evening passed pleasantly enough. The boring

James was not in evidence this time and Ellie was sitting beside Anna's husband Mike who was very interesting and had a great store of jokes. Yes, it was certainly a more successful evening than the previous time she'd been here.

49

Rachel had had a real scare and felt very bad about having flung the wine at Carl. She hadn't seen him since and guessed that he was avoiding her. She felt lonelier than ever and was trying desperately to cut back on her drinking, but she was finding it terribly difficult.

Carl was playing golf on Sunday morning and then joining her and the kids for lunch at her parents' later.

Her father came to pick them up. He looked at her, a worried frown on his face. He noticed that she didn't look as polished as usual.

"Is everything okay, honey?" he asked.

"Fine, Dad," she lied. She didn't want to say anything in front of the children. She was afraid she'd break down crying.

When they arrived at Kinsealy, after greeting Alison her mother, she asked him for a brandy.

"Rachel, it's only midday."

"I know, but I could do with a drink."

He poured it and handed it to her, disapproval showing in his every movement. He'd been worried for some time about her drinking. He saw how her hands were shaking as she held the glass.

"Is something troubling you, Rachel? I can see you're not yourself." His voice was gentle.

"No, I'm fine," she gulped.

Carl arrived just in time for lunch. He behaved as cheerfully and naturally as possible but Rachel didn't respond to his efforts. He wondered if her parents noticed the strain between them. If so they never let on. Thank God for Jacob and Becky who chattered on all through the meal.

Then a text arrived for him. His father-in-law frowned at him, mobile phones being forbidden at the table. Carl excused himself and went outside to take it. It was from Zita: Missing you like crazy. Feeling very hot. Wish you were in my bed right now. Zxx He smiled to himself and texted back: Hot for you too. Let me see what I can do. Cxx

Coming back into the dining-room he announced, "Sorry about that. Bit of a crisis, I'm afraid. I'll have to go into the office after lunch."

"Oh, no, Carl!" Rachel cried, exasperated with him. Could he not even spend one afternoon with his family?

"Must be some crisis," Alison said bitingly, "to drag you from your family on a Sunday."

Rachel could discern the dislike in her mother's tone. She'd never been a big fan of Carl.

"I must say I've never known a politician who's had to go into the office on a Sunday afternoon," her father commented grumpily.

"Sorry, but we go into summer recess on Wednesday and there are a lot of loose ends to be tied up."

"Daddy, you said you'd take us to the beach," Jacob whined, beginning to understand what was going on.

"Sorry, kids. We'll have lots of time on the beach in France soon." He ruffled his son's hair.

He left even before dessert. "See you at home later," he said, kissing Rachel's cheek, and then he was gone.

Zita had been feeling miserable all morning. She missed Carl terribly. He was so much larger than life that when he wasn't there she had a great big empty hole in hers.

Marcus was keeping his distance. All they did these days was fight – about her obsession with The Prick Dunne – as he called Carl. The fun had gone out of their relationship and she missed his friendship too.

Feeling bored that morning, she had decided to go in to work. She was watching the film they'd taken at Rachel's dinner party on Thursday night and seeing Carl there on the screen she'd become overwhelmed with longing for him. She'd texted him, never dreaming that he could come to her and yet here was his reply: **Be with you in thirty minutes. Can't wait Cxx** Her stomach did a somersault and she rang a taxi and quickly cleared up before dashing home to meet her lover.

There was no champagne, no wine, no lovely dinner, but it was the best afternoon she'd ever spent. The sex was wild and they couldn't get enough of each other. They were discovering new things about each other's bodies every time they met.

"That was sensational," he whispered in her ear when at last they were both satiated. He stroked her hair gently. "You make me so hot. I want you every single day."

"You can have me any time you want," she whispered back, kissing him gently.

"I wish," he sighed.

Leave your wife and come to me! she wanted to scream at him, but she held her tongue.

"What will I do without you for the whole month of August?" he sighed again.

She hadn't wanted to think about him going away. The thought of him playing happy families with Rachel made her feel ill. She would die without him.

"Oh God, look at the time!" Carl yelled, hours later, jumping out of the bed.

She watched him get dressed hurriedly and, feeling miserable, kissed him goodbye.

"I can see you on Tuesday night for a while, if you want," he suggested.

"Of course I want," she replied, reluctant to let go of his hand.

He took her hand to his lips. "Till then, *chérie*." He kissed it and then he was gone.

Rachel had felt the rest of the afternoon fall flat after Carl had left. She was aware of her parents' disapproval at Carl's defection. Her father drove her home and she was surprised when he said he'd like to come in. She handed the kids over to Paloma, who took them off to the playroom, and joined her father in the living room.

"Would you like a drink?" she asked him.

"Of course not, I'm driving," he replied, watching as she poured a gin and tonic for herself and curled up on the sofa.

"Something's troubling you and things are not right between you and Carl. Do you want to tell me about it?" He stood with his back to the fireplace as he'd always done at home.

She sighed. "Well, besides the fact that he's never here, you mean?" Her voice was bitter. She stared into her glass glumly. She'd always run to her father with her problems but this was one problem he couldn't fix. "We had a terrible row the other night," she told him, her voice almost a whisper.

"Do you want to tell me what it was about?"

"I did a terrible thing," she admitted, feeling ashamed and embarrassed. "Carl was very late coming home and I was angry with him. I'd had quite a lot to drink and . . ." Now that she'd started the words were coming out in a torrent. "Anyway, I attacked him and threw a glass of wine at him. It splashed all down the wall of the den." She stopped to take a sip of her drink.

"Oh my God, Rach!" her father cried, shocked at what she was telling him.

"He accused me of drinking too much," she said in a small voice.

"You *are* drinking too much," her father stated sternly. "I've been worried about it for some time."

She looked at him in dismay. It shocked her to hear him say this. "But I only drink because I'm alone here every night. Carl is so consumed by his work that he has no time for me any more." She heard her voice wobble and was afraid she'd start crying. She took a deep breath. "And, besides . . . I think he's having an affair . . ."

"What makes you think that?"

"I don't know. It's just a feeling I have."

"Well, you may be wrong so let's not jump the gun, but you really do need to sort this out between you. You have to sit down and talk with Carl as soon as possible."

She knew he was right.

"And, Rachel, honey, you just have to cut out this

drinking alone. That is not helping matters one bit. Think of the children. You must stop it at once."

She looked at him forlornly, knowing that what he was saying was true. With a sigh she put her drink down and got up and gave him a hug.

"You're right, Dad, I know. I will try and cut it out. Honestly! What I did the other night really scared me."

"Promise me you'll have a talk with Carl tonight, darling, and no more drowning your sorrows in booze."

"I promise. I suppose I'm feeling a bit adrift at the moment," she said through her tears, nodding her head.

He held her close, rubbing her head as he'd always done when she was upset as a child.

"I love you, Pops," she said.

"And I love you, Princess."

She smiled at the use of their pet names for each other.

"Now, I'm off," he said. "Go ring that husband of yours and sort things out."

"I will. Thanks, Dad."

He went in to hug his grandchildren goodbye before leaving, giving Rachel the thumbs-up as he drove away.

He was right. She made coffee and rang Carl's mobile to tell him that she wanted to have a serious talk with him that evening. It was on voicemail – how strange. She then rang his office. As she dialled, she laughed bitterly to think that she had to ring for an appointment to talk to her own husband. His answering machine picked up.

"Hi, Carl, I know you're there. Can you pick up?" No response. "Ring me as soon as you get this, please."

She kept busy the rest of the afternoon, studying her wine manual. She wanted to do well at the exam tomorrow night.

Carl sauntered in just after seven o'clock. "Hi, honey. How was the rest of the lunch?"

He leant forward to kiss her but she avoided his lips.

"What's the matter?"

"I'd like to know where you were till now?"

"I was in the office."

"I rang there. Your answering machine picked up."

"I was in John's office. We were working together on something," he lied glibly.

"I also tried your mobile."

"We didn't want to be disturbed." He was getting angry now at her questioning.

She knew he was lying but she couldn't prove it. She felt certain now that there was another woman involved. But there was no point in challenging him. He would lie his way out of it, like he had last time.

"Would you like a glass of wine?" he asked.

"No, thanks."

He raised his eyebrows in surprise and poured himself a whiskey.

It took her all her self-control not to change her mind but thinking of what her father had said, she resisted.

He went into the television room to watch the golf while she curled up on the sofa in the den, studying for her wine exam.

There was no point trying to discuss things with him now. It would only end in a big row. They had a whole month in France ahead of them. Time enough to have it out then.

Ronan had to work on Sunday and afterwards went in to the hospital to see Fiona, who was falling more in love with baby Oisín every hour. Doris was there, cuddling her little grandson as Fiona looked on happily.

"You're very good to offer to take them home," Doris

told him. "I'm not much use to her with this old back. John had to drive me up this evening."

"It's no problem. You'll be a great help over the next few weeks. That's when Fiona will need you most," he assured her.

"I don't know what I'd have done without Ronan," Fiona said, tears springing to her eyes.

They made arrangements for the journey home the following morning.

"I'll have a nice roast ready for you," Doris beamed.

"Why do you think I offered to take her home?" Ronan teased.

They all laughed aloud as baby Oisín slept peacefully on.

Ronan spent the rest of the evening studying his wine manual. He wanted to do well in this exam as he wanted to continue on and do the Higher Certificate Course. He was becoming utterly fascinated with this whole wine thing. If he was offered a job now with an architect, he knew he would miss the wine business terribly. The chances of that happening were very slim, however.

At around nine thirty Rachel took a break from studying to make herself a hot chocolate. She decided to give Ronan a call.

"Hi, there. It's me, Rachel. I hope you're not studying too hard."

"I have grape varieties coming out my ears."

She laughed. "Me too. I'm just having some hot chocolate for sustenance. I've been studying all evening. I'm really nervous about the exam."

He sensed her apprehension. "Don't be. You'll fly through it. You've done the work."

They chatted on, enjoying the sense of camaraderie, until Ronan said, "Now I'd better get back to the Rhône Valley, which is where I was when you rang."

She laughed. "See you tomorrow night."

He was such a pet, she thought to herself as she poured the hot chocolate. Taking it back to the den she contemplated how different her life would be if she'd married someone like Ronan. With a sigh she immersed herself in her manual once again.

50

Fiona was ready and waiting for Ronan when he arrived to pick them up the following morning. He carried Oisín in his little carry-chair as Fiona thanked the nurses and said goodbye to the other patients. She was a little tearful as they walked out to the waiting world.

"Don't mind me, it's these bloody hormones. Nobody told me I'd be crying at the drop off a hat," she said, wiping away the tears. "It's just that I'm so happy."

"I understand," he replied gently. "My sister-in-law Betty was like a waterfall after her babies were born and she never cries normally. She's very down-to-earth."

He saw people smile at him carrying what they obviously thought was his new son and he smiled back at them, almost feeling that Oisín *was* his son. Strapping the chair into the back seat beside Fiona, he said, "Well, little fellow, welcome to the big wide world."

Fiona smiled, thinking what a shame it was that Ronan had no children of his own. It was obvious that he'd make a great father. They headed off on the journey down to Blessington and Fiona saw everything through new eyes – the eyes of a mother, she thought happily.

Doris was there to greet them and couldn't wait to take her grandson into his new home. As always there was the delicious smell of food roasting. After Fiona had fed and changed Oisín, they sat down to a lunch of roast pork with the best crackling and roast potatoes Ronan had ever tasted.

"We're thinking of having the christening next Sunday," Fiona said. "I'd really like to have him christened as soon as possible. Do you think you can make it down for then?" She looked at Ronan hopefully.

"Try and keep me away," he teased. "Of course I can make it. I'm off next Sunday."

"It'll be a wonderful day," Doris predicted, "and you can stay overnight if you wish. We wouldn't want you driving back to Dublin after all the champagne, would we, Fiona?"

"Definitly not."

"That's settled then," Doris announced.

"That's very kind of you." Ronan was touched by their thoughtfulness. "I look forward to it."

After lunch he told them he had to get back as he wanted to study for his wine exam that night. Fiona was going for a lie-down anyway as she was exhausted. He kissed both the baby and Doris goodbye and Fiona walked out to the car with him.

"Ronan," she began shyly, "I can't tell you how much this has meant to me – you coming to visit in the hospital and bringing us home. I'll never forget you for it. You're the kindest man I've ever met." She started to cry again.

"Oh, no! Waterworks again," he teased as she tried to brush away the tears.

"Come here," he commanded, putting his arms around her. He held her close and rocked her gently. "You're so brave," he whispered, "and I know you're going to be a wonderful mother." He kissed her gently on the cheek and released her.

Doris, who had been watching all this from the front window, said a little prayer. "Please Lord, let them fall in love. They'd be so good together."

She decided there and then that she would make a novena to St Jude. He never let her down.

51

Ronan was the first to arrive at the wine course. Sam had asked him to come early and help him arrange tables so that nobody would be sitting too close to anyone else. Just as they finished doing this, Rachel arrived. Ronan could see that she was a bag of nerves.

"Hi, Rachel, are you all set?" Sam greeted her before going to his office to collect the exam papers.

"Are you okay?" Ronan asked her gently, worried at how pale she was.

"I'm terrified. I was tempted to stop off for a drink on the way to calm my nerves but I resisted the urge. Now I'm sorry I didn't!" She laughed but in fact she was deadly serious.

"You'll be fine," he assured her with a smile.

"I spent the day cramming but now I can't remember a thing." She twisted her hands nervously.

"Don't worry. It will all come back once you get the paper. Anyway it's multiple-choice questions so you have a one in three chance of getting it right."

"I suppose that's one way of putting it," she laughed,

relaxing a little. "I suppose you were studying all day," She looked at him enquiringly, her eyebrows raised.

He laughed. "I wish. Actually, I collected my friend Fiona and her new baby from Holles Street today and dropped her down to her mother's in Blessington. I didn't get a chance to do as much last-minute cramming as I'd have liked."

"Oh!" Rachel was a bit taken aback. "How nice. Is it her first?"

"Yes, I'm going to be godfather. His name is Oisín and he's the most beautiful baby." He took out his phone and showed her the photo he'd taken in the hospital.

Rachel admired the baby and looked at Ronan strangely. Was he trying to tell her something? Was the baby his? Surely not! "Who is Fiona? Is she a girlfriend?" For some reason she felt a little jealous and that bothered her.

Ronan laughed. "Of course not – she's the girl I'm filling in for in the wine shop. She's a wonderful girl and I'm very fond of her."

"Oh, I see," she replied, surprised at her feelings. She was being stupid. Ronan was just a good friend and there was absolutely nothing between them.

They had no more time to talk as the others filed in one by one and Sam returned with the dreaded exam papers.

They were all quiet, some of them reading through their manuals one last time. The usual chatter was missing and there was a sombre air in the room. They sat where Sam directed them. He was surprised to see how nervous they all were, with the exception of Zita, who seemed totally unconcerned.

Sam handed out an exam paper to each of them and then explained how to fill it out. Then he set the timer he'd brought with him for one hour, the time allotted for the exam. And with that they were off.

He sat at a table at the front of the room, his laptop in front of him. He watched them as they read all the questions first, as he'd directed, and smiled at their intent faces poring over the pages. There were fifty multiple-choice questions and as he read down through them he had no fears for his students. He had covered all of the subjects asked, although there were a couple of tricky questions included. Otherwise it was quite straightforward, for those who had studied the manual.

Hayley looked as if she might chew her pencil to bits as she pondered some of her answers.

Ellie was finished first and one by one the others finished too, till finally Sam called time-up. He collected their papers and put them into the official envelope, sealing it and putting it in his briefcase. It would be on its way to London the following morning where the papers would be marked.

"Okay, everybody, that wasn't so bad, was it?" he asked, grinning as he looked around at them.

They all started gabbling at once, relieving the tension that had built up and asking each other the answers to the trickiest questions.

"It was much easier than I expected," Rachel acknowledged, "but I'm still glad it's over."

The others agreed with her.

"Great!" said Sam. "But let me warn you, the Higher Cert exam is a lot more difficult, for those of you thinking of going on. Okay, take five, everyone, while I set up the tasting wines!"

Sam started opening bottles while Keith helped Ronan move the extra tables to the side.

The wines they tasted that night were superb and much too good to spit out so, by the time the party started, they were all in great form.

Ellie and Rachel set the food out on the side tables as Sam and Ronan opened some more bottles. Hayley had her manual out and was checking the answers to the questions that the others had been unsure of. By now most of them knew what questions they'd messed up and which ones they'd been lucky enough to guess correctly. They all seemed happy with how they'd done and so the party began.

"How did you do in the exam, do you think?" Sam asked Ronan, as they were opening bottles.

"I'm just worried about one question that I wasn't sure about."

"Only one? What one was that?" Sam was curious.

"At what temperature should you serve sparkling wines?"

"What did you answer?"

"Between 7 and 8 degrees." Ronan look at him anxiously.

Sam grinned wickedly and said nothing.

"Oh, damn, I got it wrong, didn't I? It's 8 to10, isn't it?"

Sam roared laughing. "No need to worry. You got it right." He clapped him on the back as Ronan sighed with relief.

"When will the results be back?" Ronan wanted to know.

"A month to six weeks. I thought we might organise a meal out somewhere and I'll present the certificates then."

"Great idea!"

As the party got under way, Rachel came over to Ronan to ask how he'd done in the exam. He noticed that she was drinking water.

"You're not drinking," he observed. "Are you driving?"

"No. I came in a taxi. I'm just trying to pace myself." She kept her voice low, not wanting anyone else to hear. "I'm trying to cut down on my alcohol intake." She smiled wanly.

"I'm really pleased to hear that. Drinking can spiral out of control very easily. I've seen it happen to some friends of mine. It's a killer."

"I know. I've started to realise that."

Everyone was in great form and the decibels in the room rose with every glass of wine that was poured. They were all relieved that the exam was over but a little sad that it was the last night of the course.

Shortly after the party started Zita came over to Rachel. "I've been working on the footage of what we shot last Thursday, and it's excellent, really good. You come across great on camera and as for Carl – what can I say? I think we may do a programme on him alone in the autumn."

"That's wonderful. He will be pleased. When can I see myself?" Rachel asked.

"I should be finished it by Friday. Can you call out to the station then?"

"Well, we're off to France on Sunday so I'll be up to my eyes, but I'll make time."

Ronan, who was listening to this exchange, thought he saw a strange look flit across Zita's face but was sure he must have imagined it.

"Right, I'll be in touch before Friday. I'm off now. Goodnight, Ronan. See you Friday, Rachel."

"But it's still early . . ." Rachel started to say but Zita had gone.

"Weird!" Ronan observed.

"Yeah, she's been acting strange tonight," Rachel agreed, worried that there was something the matter with her new friend. "I'll call her tomorrow and make sure she's okay."

The party continued on until after midnight but Rachel and Ronan left just after eleven. She insisted that her taxi drive through Raheny and drop him off. He was so tired that he didn't object.

As the taxi pulled up at his house, Rachel leaned over and kissed him on the cheek. "You truly are a gentleman, one of the kindest people I've ever met," she said, her voice sincere and gentle.

Gosh, twice in one day I've been told that! He smiled to himself, as he waved her goodnight and let himself into the house. Pity my wife never thought it, was his last thought as he fell into a deep sleep.

52

Sam was sending off the exam papers to be marked and he hoped they'd all done well. He'd chatted to all of them the previous night at the party and, from what Ronan had said, Sam thought that it was a possibility that he might even have scored 100%. That would be amazing. None of his previous students had ever scored that. 98% had been the previous best. He figured Ellie had done well too. She'd checked out the answers to some of the questions after the exam and she knew she had got two of them wrong for sure. He smiled to himself. For all her giggling and madcap ways she was really extremely bright and intelligent. Rachel and the young ones seemed very happy with what they'd done too. The only one who hadn't discussed the exam with him was Zita. He'd often thought that her mind was a million miles away and wondered why she was on the course in the first place. She was an enigma. She'd been acting strangely after the exam. She was weird. He couldn't figure her out at all. He didn't give her another thought as he sent the papers off. It was highly unlikely that she would want to go on any further whereas all of the others had expressed a wish to join the Higher Cert Course which would start in the autumn.

Carl and Zita passed another sex-fuelled night together on Tuesday and it was midnight before he could drag himself away. She tried not to think that she would have to live without him for the whole month of August but every time she mentioned it he shushed her. She was terrified that he would forget her, or rejuvenate his marriage – which she suspected had cracks in it – or her worst fear of all, that he would meet someone new. He tried to brush her fears away but they were very real to her.

Thankfully, Rachel was in bed when he got home and he tip-toed into bed beside her, careful not to wake her. In fact, Rachel was wide awake and got the faint scent of perfume from him. She knew now without a doubt that he was seeing another woman. Her instinct had been right. Well, this would be sorted out in Cannes. She wasn't going through that scenario again! She was no fool, as Carl would find out to his cost. She would not 'stand by her man' a second time. He'd used up that chance.

53

Ronan was in exuberant form as his redundancy cheque had arrived and was already safely lodged in the bank. It was such a relief to be able to clear off all his bills (well, Louise's bills actually) and his overdraft. It was a burden lifted from his shoulders.

He still couldn't believe that Louise had not been in touch. He assumed that no news was good news and wasn't about to tempt fate by calling her. If she wanted anything he had no doubt that she'd get in touch. He had settled into his new life without her and, if truth be told, he was much happier than when they'd been together. He had peace now and he also had two new female friends, Fiona and Rachel, and Sam was turning into a great mate. Oisín was thriving and every minute thing he did was recounted in Fiona's daily phone calls. The baby was seemingly the best baby ever born. Ronan was delighted that she was so happy.

On Friday afternoon Rachel went to the TV station to view the footage that Zita had taken. To her surprise, Carl wanted to accompany her.

"I'd like to see it. I can work late tonight finishing up things in the office," he'd said.

She shrugged her shoulders. "If you want."

They agreed to meet there.

It was obvious that Zita was thrilled that Carl had come too. She was being very charming and attentive.

"I'm really glad you're happy with it," Zita purred. "I definitely think we should do a programme on you, Carl. The camera just loves you."

He grinned.

Rachel looked from one to the other of them. Zita was being unusually coquettish. God, he can even charm and seduce her, Rachel thought disgustedly. From talking to Zita, she'd concluded that she was anti-men – but not where Carl was concerned apparently. She and Carl parted ways, she to go home and finish packing, he to the office to finish up, or so he said.

"I'll probably be late tonight," he told her, kissing her goodbye.

Zita grinned at him as he winked at her over Rachel's shoulder.

Carl went straight to the Merrion Inn after Rachel left and Zita joined him shortly afterwards. They drove back to her apartment where they made non-stop love for two hours, the last time in the shower. Zita would have been happy to stay there all night but Carl had made a reservation for the restaurant in Dalkey and he was starving. He hadn't eaten all day. Reluctantly, she got dressed for their outing.

Arriving at the restaurant, he scanned the clientele to make sure he knew nobody. All good, the coast was clear! He had requested a secluded table and they were shown to a quiet one in the corner. He ordered a bottle of champagne and they both chose scallops for starters and black sole meunière for mains. When the waiter had poured the champagne Carl handed her the glass and, lifting his glass, wrapped his hand around hers which brought their faces very close together. They sipped it and she giggled as the fizz went up her nose.

Louise was looking over the wooden rail of the mezzanine floor. They had just ordered their food and Alan had excused himself to go to the "little boys' room". Louise was scanning the ground floor to see if there were any celebrities there. She almost fell off her chair when she saw Carl Dunne sitting below, his hand wrapped around a woman's, as they sipped champagne. Louise couldn't see the woman's face because her back was to her but one thing she was sure of, it wasn't his namby-pamby wife, the stuck-up Rachel. This woman had a short straight black bob, not Rachel's long silky blonde hair.

Taking her phone, Louise focused on them and took a photo. Carl then stroked the woman's cheek and she reached forward and kissed him fully on the lips. Louise snapped again. She couldn't believe her eyes. The adoring husband caught in the act.

Just then, the waiter approached the couple's table and the woman turned. Louise gasped in shock. She recognised Zita instantly. She snapped again. Wow! Who would believe it? She sniggered with glee. My, oh my, so Ronan's friends weren't all he made them out to be. Holier than thou indeed! She remembered the disgust on his face the last time she'd seen him. Well, she'd show him that his poncy friends weren't any better than she was. Hah! What a stroke of luck. She laughed aloud at the thought.

When Alan came back to the table he saw that she was in high spirits.

"What's happened?" he asked.

"Nothing at all," she lied, hugging the secret to herself. Alan would never understand.

Ronan rang Rachel to wish her bon voyage and was surprised that she was not in better spirits.

"Is everything okay?" he asked. "You don't sound very excited for someone about to spend a whole glorious month in the south of France."

"I know. I'm sorry, but I'm really not looking forward to it. Carl and I have some issues that we have to sort out and I'm not looking forward to that."

"I guessed something of the kind. You haven't been your usual happy self lately."

"Oh boy, do I know! It's because I hardly see Carl any more and when I do I hardly recognise the man I married."

"That happens," Ronan said sadly, thinking of the disintegration of his own marriage.

"So, I'm going to take this time in France to see if we can get back on track and if not . . . ? Well, I don't want to think about that possibility." She sounded very determined.

"That's a good idea," he agreed. "I do hope you can work things out. Maybe that was why you were drinking."

"It was. Some people comfort-eat, I was comfort-drinking." She laughed a hollow laugh.

"The main thing is you found that out and you've stopped. Listen, I really hope that you can work things out with Carl."

"Thanks, Ronan, you're a star." She felt tears prick her eyes. "Well, I'd better go finish packing. Take care, Ronan."

"You too and you have my number if you ever need me. Remember, I'm only a phone call away, even from France. Have a great holiday!"

"I will, thanks."

She hung up, a lump in her throat. He was a good friend indeed.

54

The following day Ellie drove with her parents down to Athlone to choose the wedding cake. Killinure Cakes was based outside the small village of Glasson which was so pretty, overlooking Lough Rea and choc-a-bloc with cute little restaurants. They decided to make a day of it and, as luck would have it, it was a glorious sunny day.

They dropped Ellie's father in the golf club which was only a stone's throw from where they had to go. It was a small cottage industry that the young woman, Katie, ran in her own kitchen which had a gorgeous aroma of baking coming from it. They sat in her living room where she showed them photographs of wedding cakes she had made. They were spectacular and, when they heard how reasonable the prices were compared to those they had checked in Dublin, they almost passed out with disbelief.

While Katie was making coffee for them, her two adorable children chatted shyly to Ellie and her mother.

Sipping the coffee along with some homemade cake, they agreed that if the wedding cake tasted anything like what they were eating, it would indeed be a great success.

Katie asked Ellie what ideas she had for the centrepiece of her special day and after an hour discussing various options they finally came up with the perfect cake. Delighted with the outcome they waved goodbye, thrilled that they'd made the journey down from Dublin. It had been well worth it.

They picked her father up from the golf club where he was deep in conversation with some other golfers. Ellie then took them to The Wineport for lunch. She'd seen it on television on the Celebrity Chef programme and wanted to treat her parents to a special meal. It didn't disappoint and after a trip into Athlone they headed for home, content that another piece of the jigsaw that was her wedding reception was in place.

"You know, I'm really glad the salon closed down. Chloe's doing great out on her own and I realise now that I wasn't really happy there at all. Working for Sam is so much more interesting and the wine business is fascinating. I just love it!"

Her eyes were shining as she spoke and her mother crossed her fingers and hoped that Sam would keep her on in this job. It was obvious that she was perfect for it and she hoped Sam saw that too.

Sam had indeed seen it. Ellie had been a revelation to him. She was brilliant on the computer and had a great way with all the customers. They were constantly singing her praises. And as for the French producers – she seemed to have them under her spell. Her personality and her grasp of the French language had them all eating out of her hand.

"*Ooh la la, cette Ellie, elle est magnifique!*" he heard more than once. Yes, she is wonderful, he agreed with them.

Not that poor Sylvia hadn't been a good PA, but her people skills left a lot to be desired and her grasp of French – well, he didn't want to go there! She was much happier taking over the online business and God knows he needed someone to do that for him. He just didn't have the time any more. Added to that, she and Ellie were getting on like a house on fire and the atmosphere in the office was positively light-hearted and fun.

Yes, he had some big decisions to make. Well, actually, no, he had made them. He was going to ask Ellie to stay on as his PA. He hoped she'd accept.

55

All was chaos in the Dunne household as they prepared for their month's holiday in the South of France. Rachel's father was taking them to the airport and was tapping his feet impatiently as Rachel scurried around like a lunatic, doing last-minute chores. Paloma was coming with them and she followed them in a taxi with the luggage. The children wanted to go in the taxi too, of course, but Rachel put her foot down. They were hyper with excitement and she was terrified one of them might go missing at the airport – far safer to keep them in her sights. Finally she'd got them settled in the car as Carl set the alarm and locked the door. At last they were on their way. One whole month of bliss! They couldn't wait to get there.

Zita stayed in bed until midday that morning. All she could think of was Carl swanning off with his happy little family to the Côte d'Azur, not giving her a second thought. She could just imagine Rachel with her fabulous body, lying on a sun lounger, her olive skin turning a deep mahogany while her two perfect blonde children splashed in the pool. She tried to cut Carl out of this idyllic picture but she couldn't. He was very much a part of it, his blond hair becoming blonder and his blue eyes bluer against his golden tan. She pictured him bringing Rachel a cocktail and then them making love in the balmy night air. She felt she would go crazy but she couldn't get that picture out of her mind.

She couldn't resist sending him a text: **Missing u dreadfully. Hope ur missing me Zxx.** He didn't text her back.

Ronan and Sam arrived in Blessington at noon on Sunday to find a wonderful lunch awaiting them. Sam had met Doris before when she came to visit Fiona in the apartment but this was the first time he had visited her home.

"Congratulations, sweetie! You look marvellous," he said as he hugged Fiona "Where's this little fellow of yours then?"

She pointed to the pram where Oisín was sleeping peacefully.

Sam looked in at him and was amazed to see how tiny he was. "Gosh, were we all that small once?" he asked, his voice full of awe.

"I guess so," Ronan said, laughing as he hugged Fiona and Doris.

Sam had brought Oisín a silver money-box into which he'd placed a large euro note. Ronan's gift was a silver frame which he'd had engraved with Oisín's name, date of birth and birth weight. Also, thanks to his redundancy money, he could now afford to give Fiona a substantial cheque for Oisín, to buy whatever she wanted with it. He knew that supplying a small baby with everything it needed could be very expensive and Fiona had limited means now and no support from the father.

"Thank you, Sam," she said, kissing him as she saw

the money-box with the €100 note sticking up out of it. "I'll be able to borrow off him now."

They all laughed. She read his card and put it on the mantelpiece with all the other cards.

Then she opened Ronan's present. "Oh, that's lovely, Ronan! How sweet of you to have it engraved." She showed it to her mother who added her appreciation. She then opened his card and gasped in shock at the cheque for €500. "Oh, Ronan, I couldn't possibly accept this," she cried. "It's far too much."

"Of course you can. As his godfather I would like to have bought his bedroom furniture or pram or something but I wouldn't have a clue what to get, so I'll leave it up to you to get whatever you need for him."

Fiona reached up and kissed him on the cheek. "You're far too good."

"Come along, boys," called Doris, seeing that her daughter was getting emotional. "Lunch is ready."

They sat down and surveyed the wonderful spread.

"You shouldn't have gone to so much trouble," Ronan protested.

"Nonsense! It could be well nigh on five before we get to eat this afternoon and I know how hungry young men can get," Doris proclaimed.

"It's been a while since anyone called me a young man," Ronan laughed and Sam and Fiona joined in.

"It's all relative," Doris declared, cutting some of her delicious homemade soda bread for them. They devoured everything with gusto.

When lunch was over Fiona lifted the baby for a feed before dressing him up for the grand occasion.

"Can I hold him?" Sam asked to Fiona's surprise. He took him very gently from her and rocked him in his arms as he talked to him. Oisín stared up at him, eyes unblinking.

"You'll make some girl a great husband someday," Ronan teased him.

"Not on your life!" Sam answered with a snort as he handed the baby to Fiona. "I'm not the marrying kind."

The christening went off without a hitch. Oisín never made a sound, not even when the water was poured on his head. Ronan was very proud of him, as was Fiona.

After the church ceremony they moved on to Tulfarris House, a lovely hotel overlooking the lakes where they gathered for a wonderful meal and a fun evening.

They took numerous photographs outside and when Ronan held Oisín in his arms he felt a lump come into his throat. His biggest regret in life was that he and Louise had never had a child. He guessed there wasn't much chance of it happening for him now. He couldn't ever see himself getting married again. Once bitten, twice shy, he figured.

Fiona searched Sam out and drew him into a quiet corner.

"I'm a little tiddly," Fiona laughed. "After nine months without alcohol, even one glass now goes to my head. I wanted to talk to you, Sam." She was looking very serious. "Having Oisín has changed my life completely."

"I can imagine," he remarked. "In more ways than one."

"That's it. Nothing prepared me for how I would feel about him. I can't bear to be away from him for two seconds."

"I have a feeling you're trying to tell me something." He raised his eyebrows enquiringly.

"I hope you don't mind, but I've decided I won't be returning to work, not in the foreseeable future anyway. He's too little to leave him in a crèche with strangers and

I wouldn't expect you to keep the job open for me. I hope you understand." She looked at him worriedly.

"Don't worry," he patted her hand. "Having met Oisín I can understand how you feel."

"If you didn't have Ronan, I wouldn't let you down, you know."

"I know that," he smiled at her. "He is working out really well. I'm actually doing an overhaul of the shops at the moment so I'm glad you told me now rather than later when I'd have to maybe change things again. But if you ever do feel like coming back, you know I'll always find a place for you somewhere."

"I'm so glad you understand. Thank you, Sam. You and Ronan are two fantastic guys."

"You enjoy that little man," Sam said, giving her a hug before returning to the party.

Ronan returned to Dublin with Sam that evening having decided that, as he had a lift, he didn't need to stay overnight. It had been a fabulous day.

"Fiona is so happy with the baby. She'll make a wonderful mother," Sam observed.

"Yes, indeed," Ronan agreed. "I realise now what I'm missing." He sighed.

"I'm thinking of renting out my house and looking for something smaller. It holds too many memories for me. It's hard to move on when Louise has been such a large part of my life there."

"Good idea," his friend advised.

That night Sam sat deep in thought as he considered how Fiona's decision would affect his own. He had some serious thinking to do. *Mmmm* . . . things might work out well for everybody. Behind every cloud . . .

56

The second night that Rachel and Carl were in Cannes, they went out for dinner alone together. She chose a bottle of Burgundy Meurseult white wine to go with the starter of scallops and the main course of bass they'd ordered. It was delicious and he had to admit that she certainly had learnt a lot about wine since she'd started that course.

They walked along the promenade, La Croisette, afterwards and Carl suggested that they go into the Carlton Hotel for a drink.

"A Perrier, please," Rachel ordered from the handsome young waiter.

"A Perrier," Carl asked her, shocked. "Wouldn't you like a glass of champagne?"

"No, thanks." She looked at him levelly. "A Perrier is fine."

For some reason it made him uncomfortable. He'd intended tackling her about her drinking while they were here in France but it looked like he'd nothing to criticise any more.

"I think it's time you and I had a serious talk," Rachel began.

"About what?" he asked, sipping the Jack Daniels that he'd ordered.

"About us, our marriage, where it's going," she replied coolly.

"I think we're fine."

"Well, no, actually, we're not."

He watched her sipping her Perrier, cool as a cucumber, and felt a fear grip his insides.

"I strongly suspect that you're having an affair back home. If you are, then I think you should at least be honourable enough to admit it."

Carl saw his whole world crumble before his eyes. What did she know? How should he proceed? He did as he always did when cornered – he acted like the wronged one.

"How can you even think that?" he cried. "It's not worthy of you – of us!"

"Are you denying it?"

"Of course! I love you. You're my life. I couldn't do it without you." He looked at her in anguish.

"Oh, really? It doesn't look like that from where I'm standing. Politics is your life. You love *you*. Being admired and worshipped by people who don't really know you and who don't care a shit about you, that's your life, but it's not mine." She paused, then continued, her voice calm and collected, "I've supported you in everything you've done because I love you, but if I'd known that it was going to change you so much then I'd never have gone along with it."

"Please, Rachel," he begged, taking her hand, "don't be so hard on me. I love you! Come on, have a glass of champagne or a glass of wine at least." He beckoned to the waiter.

327

"Sorry, I don't want anything," Rachel smilingly told the young man.

"I'll have another Jack Daniels, please," Carl said.

The waiter hurried off.

"Why aren't you drinking, Rachel," he asked, perplexed.

"Because I realise I've been drinking as a substitute for having you in my life. I'm not doing that any more."

Although he wasn't quite sober Carl heard what she was saying. In that moment he admired her greatly. She was one classy broad, his wife. In an instant he realised how much he would miss her if she should desert him. But he knew Rachel would never do that. She treasured the family too much. Still, she'd given him quite a scare. Life without Rachel – and the kids? Unthinkable! He knew, with his politician's instinct, that it was time to eat humble pie. He'd make it up to her. He had a whole month in Cannes to woo her back. He felt confident that he could do it. Yes, siree. He could and he would!

Zita was miserable. She missed Carl desperately. She'd texted him almost every day but he hadn't replied once. She was beginning to fear that he might have forgotten about her altogether as he sunned himself on the French Riviera. Her jealousy of Rachel knew no bounds and she found herself thinking of ways that she could wipe the smile off her smug face.

On top of that, the dreadful nightmares had returned and, as a result, fearful of sleeping, she was constantly tired during the day. More and more she found herself thinking of the past, the past she'd worked so hard to blot out. She had also lost her best friend as she and Marcus could not meet without rowing over Carl. The only positive in her life was her work and she threw herself into it with fervour.

While Rachel was sunning herself on the Côte d'Azur, Ellie was talking about taking a holiday with her mother in Bordeaux. They would have preferred not to go in high season but, as Ellie was hoping to start in Sam's wine shop in September, they felt they had no choice. She decided to talk to Sam about it.

"My mum and I were thinking about spending a few days in Bordeaux and I was wondering if I could finish up here a little early before I start in the wine shop."

"Well, there's a bit of a problem there," he said slowly. "I'm restructuring the whole company and I'm not sure that the wine shop is quite right for you."

Ellie's heart almost stopped. She felt as if he'd punched her in the stomach. Was she going to be out of a job again, so soon after the last one? Her face fell and she looked at him dejectedly.

"Why not?" she asked, wondering how she could change his mind.

Sam grinned mischievously. Ellie was starting to feel angry with him. It was no laughing matter.

"Because I think you're doing such a fantastic job here," he said, "that you should stay on as my PA."

Relief flooded through her. "Are you serious?" she squealed.

"Deadly," he said, deadpan.

"Oh Sam, Sam, I love you!" she shrieked, jumping up and down before running to hug him.

"Put me down, woman!" he cried, laughing.

"Sorry," she said, releasing him. "Oh my God, this is

just the most fantastic news. Oh my God!" She twirled around the floor.

"I take it you're pleased," he remarked drily.

"Pleased? I'm ecstatic! This is just the best news ever. I love the job."

He laughed at her enthusiasm. "Well, I really need you here and Sylvia has her hands full with the online business which is just about ready to roll. If you could postpone your trip to Bordeaux for a month or so, then I can see no problem with your taking some days off."

"That suits us even better!" she cried. "We don't really want to go in August anyway as it's high season there."

"I agree. It will be much nicer in September. I have to go myself then to meet with some producers. Maybe you could meet up with me there and I'll introduce you to some of the producers you've been dealing with on the phone."

"That would be brilliant! It's always nice to have a face to put with the voice. Gosh, Mum will be delighted."

Marie-Noelle was indeed delighted and set about checking flights for mid-September.

Ellie rang David with the good news that Sam was keeping her on as his PA.

"Well, thank goodness for that," he said. "I didn't like the idea of you being a shop girl at all."

"Shop girl?"

"You know what I mean. A sales girl in an off-licence isn't exactly the most prestigious of jobs. Most of the guys' wives here are either lawyers or accountants too – professionals at least –"

Ellie stopped him dead. "I see nothing wrong with being a sales girl if it means I'm earning my own living."

"Oh, Ellie, you know what I mean. I have a status to keep up here. Having a PA for a wife is much more impressive. Even you can see that!"

Ellie was seething. How dare he! He was becoming a pompous prick. This new job of his had truly gone to his head. She finished the call because she knew if she stayed on the line they would have another horrendous row. She sighed. That's all they seemed to do nowadays. It seemed like David had turned into a different person since they'd become engaged. Maybe it was the stress of the wedding. She'd heard that it affected some people like that and that once they were married everything went back to normal. She certainly hoped that this would be the case.

57

Ronan was looking in the newspaper at 'apartments to let' when his phone rang. Looking at the caller ID, his stomach did a somersault. It was the phone call he'd been expecting since Louise had left. He'd known she'd be in touch sooner or later. His heart was in his mouth as he answered.

"Louise!"

"Hello, Ronan, how are you?"

"Fine, and you?"

"I'm great, just great."

"To what do I owe the honour?"

"Well, I have some juicy gossip for you."

He took the phone away from his ear and looked at it. Was he hallucinating? She was calling to give him some gossip?

"Louise, my life is too busy to be listening to gossip," he retorted angrily.

"Oh, you'll have time for this," she said gleefully. "Guess who's having an affair?"

"Louise," he said coldly, "I have no time for this or for playing games."

"Not even when your very dear friends are involved?"

"What do you mean?"

"It concerns your friend, Mrs Perfect Politician's Wife, Rachel Dunne. Her husband is cheating on her."

Ronan was rocked back on his heels. "What do you mean?"

"I mean," she said, obviously enjoying herself, "that Mr Carl Dunne is screwing around."

Ronan winced at her coarseness. "How do you know this?"

"I saw him with the lady in question."

"Anyone we know?" he asked sarcastically.

"Well, yes, actually." Louise couldn't keep the delight out of her voice. "Your other friend, the pseudo-lesbian, Zita Williams."

"That means nothing. They were probably discussing business or perhaps a TV show."

"No, they were most definitely discussing sex."

"I don't believe you!"

"No? Well, I have the photos to prove it!" she crowed triumphantly.

Ronan was speechless. "I'd like to see that evidence with my own eyes before believing it," he finally said.

"Certainly, I'll text the photos to you. Maybe you'll believe me then. Bye!"

Ronan was incensed after he put the phone down. It couldn't be true, could it? He hoped not, for Rachel's sake. Still, at the back of his mind was the niggling feeling that maybe it was. He remembered Rachel saying how alone she felt and that she hardly ever saw Carl. Could it be possible? But with Zita of all people! That was the hard thing to believe. With a shock he remembered how Carl couldn't be at the supper and that Zita had cried off too. Oh, God. Ronan had a horrible sinking feeling in his stomach.

Ronan looked at the first two photos that Louise had sent him and felt a shiver run down his spine. It was most definitely Carl who was with a woman who was most definitely not Rachel. The woman had her back to the camera as Carl firstly stroked her cheek, and in the second photo she reached across and kissed him on the lips.

Then another photo came though. Now the woman's face was clearly visible and with a shock Ronan saw that it was clearly Zita who was looking at Carl adoringly.

"Oh my God!" Ronan moaned aloud. Poor Rachel, he thought. That bastard has been cheating on her and with Zita of all people.

The final photo was a bit blurred but there was no mistaking that it was Carl and Zita. It had been taken outside the restaurant and they'd been caught in a passionate embrace.

He stared at the photos for a long time, wondering what to do. If Rachel ever saw these, it would kill her. God, what a dilemma! What should he do?

58

Rachel could see that Carl was making a huge effort. He brought her breakfast in bed, spent a lot of time with the kids during the day and bombarded her with gorgeous gifts: orchids, jewellery, a beautiful white Versace evening gown and, what really touched her, a pair of Manolo Blahnik shoes which fit her perfectly and were absolutely divine.

For her birthday, he hired a yacht and took her over to Monte Carlo for lunch at Alain Ducasse's three-Michelin-star restaurant in the Hôtel de Paris. It was simply wonderful. Then on the trip home he presented her with a stunning diamond bracelet.

But at the end of the day it wasn't about the presents. How he was behaving towards her was the most important thing and how he would continue to behave when they got back to Dublin. In the meantime she was enjoying the holiday and willing to give him the benefit of the doubt.

Zita was distraught. She had not had a single word from Carl and she didn't know what to do. She'd even called his mobile and left messages on his voicemail, with no response. For a crazy moment she considered hopping on a plane to Nice and confronting him but realised that no good could come of that. She didn't know which way to turn.

Carl, meanwhile, was terrified that Rachel would intercept Zita's texts or calls. He blanched at the thought of that happening. How could he possibly explain it away? Rachel was no fool but he was slowly gaining ground with her. They were almost back to their old intimacy. He had to find a way to stop Zita. She was becoming a bit of a bunny-boiler. He'd thought that ignoring her was the best plan of action but now he saw that it was making her even more insistent.

At his wit's end, he finally texted her: I'm sorry but I can't go on with our relationship. Please stop texting and calling. Carl

Zita read his message with disbelief. Was he serious? Did he think she was like an old sock that could be discarded just like that? If so, he had another think coming. Nobody messed with Zita Williams like that and, if they did, they paid for it dearly, as someone else had found to his cost. She closed her eyes and gave a shiver as she thought of the gory scene she'd left behind all those years ago in Australia.

Two things happened that evening that almost sent Zita into orbit. The first was a newspaper photograph of Carl and Rachel at a party on a yacht in Cannes. They both looked tanned and glamorous. On either side of them were a famous actor and his equally famous wife, who were seemingly the hosts. The thing that riled her most was the way Carl was gazing adoringly at his wife who was laughing up at him. Zita banged her fist into her other open palm, seething with fury. '*Still Madly In Love*' was the caption. Well, that was a lie for starters. She knew otherwise.

She was still furious with him when she received the call from Ronan.

Ronan had been at his wit's end, wondering what to do with the information he'd received from Louise. His main priority was to protect Rachel. The best course of action would be to tackle Carl about it man to man but that was obviously out of the question. The next best solution was to appeal to Zita. Surely she wouldn't want word of their affair to reach the media? It could destroy not only Carl's marriage but also his career.

He gathered his courage and rang her.

"Hi, Zita, it's Ronan from the wine course here."

"Ronan, hello. What can I do for you?"

"I know it's none of my business, but certain information has come to my attention with regard to you and Rachel's husband and I'm very concerned about what it might do to her, were she to find out." He heard her gasp.

"What kind of information?"

"That you're having an affair with Carl Dunne."

There was silence on the line.

"Zita, are you still there?"

"I'm still here," she replied, her voice cold and hostile. "You're right, it *is* none of your business, and may I ask how you came by this information?"

"I was sent some photographs of the two of you together and it's pretty obvious –"

She cut him off. "I'd like to see these photographs for myself before I comment – if you don't mind."

Ronan saw that he was wasting his time. He would get no satisfaction from this quarter. "I'll text them to you."

She hung up without saying goodbye. Ronan was troubled. He realised that Zita hadn't denied the affair.

Zita sat transfixed, looking at the photographs Ronan had sent. There was no mistaking Carl – he was as recognisable as could be – and in the full-face photo, so was she. Nor was there any possibility that Carl could pretend it was a business dinner. He was stroking her and kissing her and there was one grainy photo of them just outside the restaurant, embracing passionately. Zita felt a pang remembering how good it had been. It couldn't be over. They were soul-mates. They were meant to be together, forever. He said he wanted nothing more to do with her but she didn't believe it. She had no doubt that it was that witch Rachel's fault. She'd obviously spent the holiday wooing him back. Zita felt the hatred well up inside her against the other woman. She sat for a long time thinking of how she could get her revenge. Eventually it came to her and she grinned evilly as she planned how she would do it.

59

Ronan had just finished his shift and was poring over the 'apartments to let' section of the evening paper, circling suitable properties, when Sam came into the shop.

"What are you doing there, mate?" he asked.

"Looking for a place to rent. The problem is that by the time I get there they're usually gone – the good ones, that is. They're snapped up immediately."

"Actually, I want to talk to you about that. Can you come for a pint now?"

They went into the pub on the corner where Sam ordered two pints of Guinness.

"I've decided to restructure the business," Sam said. "Firstly, you should know that Fiona has told me she's not coming back to work anytime soon."

"I figured she wouldn't want to leave Oisín till he's much older."

"No, and she's damn right. Kids grow up so quickly. Besides, I think it would break Doris's heart if she were to take him back to Dublin."

"You can say that again. Doris intimated as much to me."

"Yes, well, here's what I've been thinking . . ." Sam stroked his chin as he chose his words. "I've decided to open a new shop in Naas and I was wondering if you would be interested in going down there as manager. What do you think?" He looked at Ronan eagerly, waiting for his reaction.

Ronan was speechless for a moment. "Me? Manager?"

"Yes, how about it?"

"Gosh, thanks, Sam! I'd be delighted to do it – if you think I'm up to it, that is."

"I wouldn't ask you if I didn't think you could do it. I run a business, not a charity. You've learnt all aspects of the business amazingly quickly. Dermot was even saying the other day how you've streamlined the stock control. I think you're more than capable. Would you like to think about it?"

"I don't need to. I'll take it. It will be great to get away from Raheny. It holds too many memories." His eyes were shining at the prospect.

"The property I have my eye on has an apartment overhead, so hold your horses till the deal is finalised. You may be able to live there."

Ronan grinned at him. "That would be fantastic. I quite like the idea of getting out of the city and it will be much easier to visit Fiona and Oisín from Naas than brave the awful traffic going out of Dublin to Blessington."

Sam knew that Fiona and her baby had become very important in Ronan's life. "You can say that again. You don't miss working as a draughtsman, do you?"

"Not in the least. I find the wine business fascinating and anyway the prospect of getting a job as a draughtsman any time soon is zilch."

"Okay so. Let's shake on it."

"Thank you, Sam. I'm beginning to think you're my guardian angel. How can I ever thank you?"

Sam roared with laughter. "Well, you can start by ordering me another pint!"

Ronan ordered another two pints and thought about his good luck. Everything seemed to be falling into place for him all of a sudden. The only fly in the ointment was what he'd learnt about Carl and Zita's affair. He considered confiding in Sam about it but decided not to. The fewer people that knew about it, the better. If the tabloids got hold of it they'd have a field-day. No – better to say nothing and confront Carl when he got back from France.

60

Ellie and David had just had another huge row on the phone. After he'd hung up, she sat thinking about their relationship and how it had changed lately. Her parents were out and she was sitting in front of the TV alone, looking at it but not really seeing it. She felt miserable. This was not how things were meant to be. She and David seemed to be drawing further away from each other instead of closer together.

It was three weeks since they'd made love because David had claimed to be too tired the last couple of times they'd spent the night together. If this was how it was now, what would it be like when they were married for a couple of years? Suddenly, she became very afraid. Were they making a huge mistake? Was David having second thoughts? He seemed to be constantly in bad form whenever they were together. He was not the same man he'd been when she had agreed to marry him. She blamed his job at Buckley Steadman for this. He had started to change from the time he went to work for them. He idolised Frank Buckley and seemed to be modelling himself on him. Lord forbid that he would turn out like him! For the first time Ellie wondered if they were really suited to each other at all.

Everything was pretty much set for the wedding now and Ellie had been looking forward to relaxing and enjoying the weekends with David, now that she wasn't rushing around organising everything.

"Why don't we go away for the weekend?" she'd suggested when he rang her the previous week.

"Sorry, Ellie, I can't. I have to work this weekend."

"Well, maybe we could just go down to Wicklow on Saturday night and stay over."

"Ellie, you're not listening. I have to work. I've been given an important new client and this is my chance to prove myself."

She flinched at the irritation in his voice.

She'd let it go, disappointed as the forecast for the weekend was for glorious weather and Wicklow was beautiful at this time of year. So instead they'd stayed in Dublin, and what a disaster the weekend had turned out to be! David had gone out with the guys as usual on Friday night. She wondered why work hadn't interfered with that weekly outing. He'd had to work all day Saturday and claimed he would have been too tired to see her that night. The only time she'd seen him was when he took her to brunch in Kitty's, on Sunday, with all the gang from his work. Even then, they'd hardly spent five minutes in each other's company. She watched him laughing and joking with the guys and wished that they could have been somewhere alone together. Directly afterwards, David put her in a taxi, saying he was going back to the office to work.

"Will I see you tonight?" she'd asked him as he'd kissed her goodbye.

"Ellie, for God's sake, give me a break!"

His words had stung her and she'd felt very hurt. She'd had to steel herself to hold back the tears and not let him see her cry.

And now on the phone when she'd suggested that they go somewhere, just the two of them, for the following weekend he'd replied, "Oh, sorry Ellie, I meant to tell you, I've promised to join Will and the guys for a golfing weekend in Wexford. Maybe the weekend after?"

She didn't think it unreasonable to be annoyed that he hadn't remembered to tell her, but he seemingly did, and so they'd had another blazing row. Now, as she thought about their relationship, she began to feel very afraid. She didn't know how to make things better. David had become a stranger and suddenly she was fearful of what the future held. She was glad now that she had agreed to go to Bordeaux with her mother. Maybe the time away from each other would improve things between her and David.

61

Kathleen O'Sullivan was scrolling down her Twitter messages when one in particular caught her eye. It was from @politicalscandals and it had a link to a blog *Trouble in Paradise*. Curious, she opened it and what she read made her very uneasy indeed.

Kathleen had spent forty years working as a cook for Rachel's mother, Mrs Stewart. Now in her eighties, she was more or less confined to the house due to ill-health. Her main contact with the outside world, besides her television, was the computer that her son, Donal, had given her one Christmas. Every single day she blessed him as she surfed the internet, emailed her friends, skyped her children and grandchildren and tweeted. She'd made lots of friends on Twitter and was gaining new followers every day. It was wonderful! She was following all kinds of interesting people, even famous ones. She lived alone but Twitter made her feel like she had company all the time.

It had taken her a little while to get the hang of it but, though her body was frail, her brain was as sharp as ever. She'd had help, of course, from the local convent school.

Their students had taken part in a scheme to help the elderly master computers, and the lovely youngster who came to Kathleen once a week had been a great teacher. That had been a godsend! She still popped in from time to time to see how Kathleen was getting on and followed her on Twitter too.

Now as she read the blog she had a suspicion that the politician in question was Rachel's husband Carl. All the other newly elected politicians in North Dublin were older and certainly couldn't be called handsome. Besides, Mrs Stewart had visited Kathleen last week and mentioned that Rachel and Carl were holidaying in the south of France.

Kathleen hoped she was wrong and sat for a time, pondering what she should do. She decided to wait until Donal came in and ask him for his advice. He was home on holiday from Australia where he was a detective in the police force in Adelaide. He would know what she should do. When he arrived back that evening she showed him the blog and told him of her suspicions. His advice was to call Rachel's mother and mention it to her.

"Whether it is lies or not, I think Rachel should be made aware of it."

"I fervently hope it is lies," his mother said vehemently. She shook her head sadly. "Carl seems such a genuine bloke. Just goes to show, it's true what they say, you can never trust a politician!"

It was obvious to Donal that she believed the story to be true.

"You remember Rachel, don't you?" she asked him as she picked up the phone to call Mrs Stewart.

"I remember a beautiful little girl with white blonde hair and dark-brown eyes who always wanted to chat with me whenever I went to collect you. I remember thinking that she was very lonely."

"Yes, well, you should see what a beauty she is now –" Kathleen broke off as Rachel's mother answered the phone.

Meanwhile, on the Côte d'Azur, Carl was oblivious of the events unfolding in Dublin. It had been a wonderful holiday and he felt that he and Rachel were in a much better place than when they'd arrived.

Rachel, for her part, had had a wonderful holiday and she couldn't fault his behaviour, but at the back of her mind was the thought that he was trying too hard. He was so attentive to her every need that she feared it only confirmed that he was guilty of wrongdoing. However, they'd had a long talk and Carl had promised her sincerely that things would change when they got back home.

They were enjoying their second-last day in this idyllic place when Rachel got a call from her father.

"Rachel, honey, I don't know whether I should tell you this or not but I've heard something and I think you should know about it. Maybe it's all a load of rubbish. I hope so but anyway . . ." He paused, trying to find the right words.

Rachel knew that something really bad was about to happen.

"Well, Kathleen rang your mother this morning . . ."

Rachel could sense her father's distress. "Go on, Dad!"

"Well, she said there is some kind of message on Twitter about a blog – *Trouble in Paradise*, she said it's called. Anyway, Kathleen seems concerned that it may be associated with you and Carl. Maybe she's wrong – I don't understand all this Twitter and blog stuff – but maybe you can check it out."

Rachel felt fear clutch her heart. Her blood felt like it was running cold through her body.

"Okay, Dad, I will."

"Listen, Princess, even if it is about Carl, you'll survive it. Maybe it's all lies. Let me know what happens and I'll fly out there tonight if you want."

"Thanks, Dad. I will. I'll check it out this minute."

She hung up and Googled the blogsite *Trouble in Paradise*. Her eyes blurred as she read down through it and her heart raced uncontrollably.

'One of our newly elected politicians from north Dublin, who is holidaying in the South of France with his beautiful wife at the moment, also has a mistress tucked away back home. Does his wife know? No prizes for guessing who the handsome young politician in question might be!'

There it was in black and white. The thing she'd suspected and feared. There was no question that it was Carl the blog alluded to. There was no other 'young, handsome' politician in North Dublin. No wonder Kathleen had immediately jumped to the conclusion that the blog concerned Carl. Rachel closed her eyes and grabbed the table to steady herself, afraid she might faint. She took a deep breath and sat down. She wondered who the woman in question was. No doubt that information would come out over the next few days. That was the way these things worked – teasing and tantalising until the whole country was agog to know the gory details.

Her instinct had been right, as always. She rang her father back. In a weary voice she told him that she'd read the article.

"It's about Carl alright. As I suspected, he's been having an affair which is why he's never been home lately. It's no surprise really."

"Oh, honey, I'm sorry. Do you want me to come down there?"

"No, Dad, we'll be home the day after tomorrow. There's no point. I'll be fine."

"Are you sure? I'll collect you from the airport."

"No, Dad, I'd prefer if you didn't. Carl can book two limos to meet us. I'll call when I get home."

"Okay, if that's what you want, honey. "Are you sure you're alright, Rach?"

"I'm fine, Dad. I'll discuss what I want to do when I see you. One thing's for sure. My marriage is over."

Unbeknownst to her, a couple of Carl's friends had contacted him to tell him of the blog article. He logged on to the website and knew instantly that he was the subject of the blog. This could destroy all the good that he'd achieved with Rachel over the past month. This could wreck not only his marriage but also his fledgling career. Who was doing this to him? Who knew about him and Zita? Could it even be Zita herself?

He texted her, the first time since he'd told her it was over: 'Do you know anything about this blog? C.'

The reply came through straight away: Fuck off! Z.

He wondered if it was she who was writing the blog. If it was, he swore he'd throttle her.

Rachel went to bed early that night, pleading a headache. She was not about to let him know that she knew. There was no point in discussing it anyway. He would just deny it. She didn't want to spoil the last day of the holiday for the children. Time enough to let him know their marriage was over when they got back home.

The following day, their last in Cannes, both Rachel

and Carl logged on to *Trouble in Paradise* separately. Sure enough there were some more salacious titbits: **'Which NEP (newly elected politician) showers his mistress with Krug Champagne and the best Burgundy and Bordeaux wines?'**

"Damn her," Carl said aloud, reading this. He was pretty sure now that it was Zita. She was clever, very clever. He had to stop her. He'd contact her the minute he got home and stop this craziness once and for all.

Rachel blanched when she read this latest blog. The reference to fine wine made her uneasy. Somehow she felt that whoever was writing this was trying to get to her. She couldn't wait to get home to discuss this whole thing with her father. He would know what to do. She could always trust him.

They spent a last tense night on the Côte d'Azur, both lost in their own thoughts and anxious to get back to Dublin to sort things out.

62

Carl and his family arrived at Dublin airport on Sunday afternoon to find a photographer snapping them as they came out of the terminal building to the waiting limos. Carl wondered how he'd known that they were due in. Rachel tried to shield the children from the snapper as Carl ushered them into the first car. Carl wondered if he was being paranoid. Maybe this guy just happened to be there for some celebrity or other and happened to spot him and his family. He hoped this was the case. He detested the paparazzi. They were like vultures! Bloodhounds seeking blood! He hoped to God that they wouldn't get wind of this latest mess he'd got himself into. He knew he would have to work hard and fast to end this blog and curtail the damage. He'd have to hope and pray that Rachel didn't get to hear of it.

When they arrived home, Carl went immediately into his bathroom to open up the blog in private, dreading what he might read next. 'So who is this attractive NEP who has been cheating on his wife? Watch this space and all will be revealed.' Christ! She wouldn't, would she? He felt sick.

He rang Zita immediately but got her voicemail. He left a message. "Please call me asap. We need to talk."

She texted him back: **We have nothing to talk about.**

We bloody well do! was his reply.

You ain't seen nothing yet! she answered him, sending him into a spin.

Rachel rang her father. "We're home, Dad."

"I'm on my way," he said. "Keep that husband of yours out of my sight or I won't be responsible for my actions."

"He's not here, Dad. He left immediately we got home. Probably to visit his mistress," she added bitterly.

"Don't worry, Princess. I'll be with you soon."

Her father arrived and was surprised when she told him that she hadn't let Carl know that she'd seen the blog.

"I'm waiting for him to make the first move. If I accuse him he'll only deny the whole thing. Let's wait and see if they name him and then I can act."

"That's a wise move."

"You know, Dad, when this happened I just wanted to get blotto. I wanted to drink myself senseless, but I didn't. I kept my cool and resisted the urge and I'm really proud of myself for that."

"That's my girl! I'm proud of you too, Princess. You'll get through this and come out stronger. Just you wait and see."

She smiled at him feebly as she hugged him. He stayed for dinner and, as always, she felt that she could survive this with him on her side.

Zita was nowhere to be found. Carl banged on her door and kept his finger pressed on her bell but got no response. He rang Marcus's bell too but got no response from him either. They could very well have been in there together, laughing their heads off at him. He had no way of knowing. There were no other tenants in the building, only offices which were closed up for the weekend.

He tried her cell phone every five minutes but she had it turned off. He visited all the places that he knew she frequented but there was no sign of her anywhere. Eventually, defeated, he returned home. Rachel was sleeping and he slipped into the guest bedroom so as not to disturb her.

63

Fiona had been thrilled to hear about Ronan being offered the manager's position in Naas when he phoned her with the news.

"Gosh, that's great. It will be good for Oisín to have you close by." She didn't add 'and me too'.

"Are you absolutely certain that you won't want to go back to Dublin?" he asked.

"Don't worry, Ronan, my decision is made. This is the best place to bring up Oisín and I have all the support of my family and friends here." She paused. "I'm delighted that you're going to be nearer too. And my mother will be pleased!"

On his last visit, at Doris's insistence they had gone for a drive up to the King's River, leaving Oisín with her. By this time, Ronan had realised that Doris was hoping he and Fiona would get together but he had no such intention. In any case, the hurt from his marriage break-up was too raw.

Ellie and Marie-Noelle had booked their holiday to Bordeaux for the last week in September. Her mother had insisted on asking Sandrine to join them but thankfully she said she couldn't come due to work pressure. Sam would be in the city at the same time and would take Ellie to meet some of the producers of the Haut-Medoc.

When David heard the dates they'd planned he was quite upset.

"You can't go then, Ellie. I've got the Chartered Accountants' annual dinner dance on the twenty-seventh. I need you there with me."

"I'm sorry, David, but I just can't change it now. We've already booked and paid for it. You never told me about the dinner dance."

"I can't go unaccompanied," he informed her. "I'd be the odd man out." There was nothing David hated more than being odd man out.

"Why don't you ask Sandrine? She can't come to Bordeaux with us. I'm sure she'd love to go."

"That's an idea. I'll give her a call."

Sandrine rang Ellie that evening. "What's this I hear that you can't go to the Chartered Accountants' Ball?"

It was elevated to a ball now, Ellie noted! "You know I can't, Sandrine. Mum and I have already booked our trip."

"Well, I think you're being extremely selfish, Ellie. You always only think of yourself. Poor David is quite distraught. It is quite the most important event of the year."

"To you and David, maybe, seeing as how you're both accountants but going on holiday with Mum to Bordeaux is much more important to me."

"Selfish," Ellie heard her sister grumble.

"Anyway, hasn't David asked you to go with him?"

"Well, yes."

"What's your problem so?"

"I just think you're being awfully selfish, leaving poor David on his own."

Ellie snorted. "You'll both have a great time."

"Huh, no thanks to you," was the reply.

Ellie could tell from her sister's voice that she was delighted with the outcome.

"Have you ordered the wedding invitations yet?" Sandrine enquired.

"No. I have to show the samples to David. He's been too busy to look at them this past week."

"Honestly, you're so disorganised," her older sister complained. "It's almost September already. You'll really have to stop dragging your heels."

Ellie threw her eyes up to heaven.

"And what about the hen weekend?" asked Sandrine. "I was thinking West Cork would be lovely."

Ellie sighed. Stuck with Sandrine in West Cork for a weekend in December was not her idea of fun. She was thinking more of maybe a long weekend in Tenerife, brushing up the tan.

"We'll think about that after Bordeaux. We still have plenty of time. I need to discuss it with all the girls."

Now it was Sandrine's turn to sigh.

64

Ronan had seen the blog too – it had gone viral and was quite a topic of conversation in the pub. He guessed it was Carl they were talking about. He realised that it was too late to have a talk with him now. Somebody was spilling the beans and he wondered if it was Louise who was the culprit. He would put nothing past her. Anyway, it was obviously out in the open now and he hoped to God it didn't have a disastrous effect on Rachel. He was wondering whether she was home yet and whether she'd heard about the blog when he saw the photograph of her and Carl arriving at Dublin Airport. She was trying to shield the children from a photographer. He looked closely at the photograph and saw the strain on Rachel's face. Carl looked pretty frazzled too. What a change from the happy smiling photo in the newspapers just two weeks ago! He hoped Rachel would call him.

Rachel checked the blog every five minutes the following day, waiting to see what juicy details they would leak to the world about her husband and his mistress.

And then the photo appeared. She gasped when she saw it. No one would be left in any doubt now but that Carl was the NEP in question.

The photo was crystal clear. He was staring lovingly into the eyes of a woman, leaning across a table and stroking her face. It was the desire on his face that shocked Rachel most. The woman had her head turned at an angle away from the camera and she had short black hair. The whole of Dublin would recognise that it was not Rachel in the photo.

She sat there like a zombie, unable to move. She had no doubt Carl would see the photo fairly soon. One thing was for sure – this couldn't be brushed under the carpet any longer. So this woman was the reason for his thoughtfulness and consideration while in France. She felt disgusted. And all those expensive presents he'd given her. Guilt gifts, she realised now. The bastard! She started to get angry. Why should she wait for him to make the first move? Attack is the best method of defence, her father had always said. She wouldn't give Carl the chance to attack – she'd do it first. She texted him: **Come home. We need to talk.**

Carl knew the minute he got the text that the game was up. He had just seen the latest blog with his photo in it. He had been trying to contact Zita to stop her, but now he knew that it couldn't be her behind the blog. She couldn't have taken that photo. Whoever had taken it was the culprit. But who could it be? Who hated him so much that they wanted to destroy him?

He rang his friend Stan, who was a whizz kid on computers, and asked him if he could find out who was behind it.

"Yeah, shouldn't be too difficult though some of these

geezers are very clever. Hard luck, mate, getting caught like that."

"I've got to stop any more photos appearing. I don't want my wife to find out who the lady in question is. Please get back to me asap."

Whoever it was, Carl would make sure that he, or she, paid for what they'd done. With a heavy heart he drove home to Howth.

Rachel had sent Paloma out with the children and told Olga to take the day off so they wouldn't witness the confrontation to come. She was calm and collected when she faced her husband but he could hear the steel in her voice.

"Well, Carl, so you've been at it again," she began, looking at him coldly.

"It was nothing – meaningless, please believe me, Rachel." He ran his fingers through his hair, his eyes distraught.

"Well, it wasn't meaningless to me. Would you mind telling me who the lady in question is?"

"A nobody, honestly, just somebody I met at a function and we went on to dinner and you know how it is . . ." he finished lamely.

"No, actually, I don't know how it is. And that's an even bigger insult to me – a nobody is all you could manage."

Carl looked at her to see if she was serious. Would she have been happier if it had been someone famous or a beautiful model? Women! He'd never understand them!

"Do you want to tell me her name and what exactly happened?"

"I don't even remember and it was only the one night, I swear."

"I see," she said, feeling disgusted. A one-night stand! "Okay. Now I'd like you to go and stay somewhere else for a few days while I think this out."

"Please, Rachel, let me explain . . ."

"Go now!" she shouted at him, "before I change my mind and throw you out straight away."

He went sheepishly and collected his night things and some changes of clothes. With a last look at the house to see if she was watching, he drove his BMW down the drive.

He rang Stan to see if he had come up with anything.

"Well, whoever it is, they're damn clever. They're using a foreign proxy server so there's no way of finding their IP address. It could take weeks and court orders and that's still no guarantee that you'll find out who's behind this."

Carl was sweating profusely. What else did this person know? Somebody must hate him very much.

That night, he received a call from Bill, a reporter he knew on one of the tabloids.

"Carl, just thought I'd let you know that we're running the story of the *Trouble in Paradise* blog. Sorry, but once they get wind of a politician doing something wrong, they're on him like a pack of dogs."

"Can you not do anything to stop it?" Carl asked, perspiration breaking out on his forehead.

"'Fraid not. All the tabloids are running with the story. Bad luck for you that it happens to be a bad news day. Just thought I'd let you know, to prepare you for the onslaught."

"Thanks, Bill, I appreciate it."

Prepare for the onslaught? His photo splashed across those rags and paparazzi camped outside their front door! He was in a panic at the thought.

The following morning, he bought the three daily tabloids. There in black and white on the front page, he read: **Trouble in Paradise – Mystery blogger threatens to reveal all!**

Rachel woke to find the paparazzi camped outside the front gate. Luckily the children hadn't yet started back at school as she would not have been able to get past those hounds unscathed. She rang her father to tell him.

"Would you like me to come and collect you and the kids?" he asked.

"No, I think it's better to sit tight. I don't want to disrupt Jacob and Becky's routine."

"Then just stay indoors. Those vermin will get tired of waiting when they see you're not coming out or when another bigger story breaks," he advised.

Her phone was hopping but she kept it on voicemail, unable to face talking to anyone. She suspected that they would be mostly media hounds looking for a comment. As a result she missed the concerned calls from both Ronan and Ellie.

Sitting looking out across Dublin Bay that evening she was very tempted to open a bottle of wine but she resisted the urge. Instead, she went for a long soak in the hot tub and wondered what tomorrow would bring.

65

Nothing could have prepared Rachel for what she saw when she opened the blog the following morning: **Mystery Woman Revealed**. And there in full view was a photo of Carl kissing a woman passionately on the mouth and in a second photo the woman was smiling sexily at him, her face revealed for all to see. Rachel gasped and her hand flew to her face. There, smiling seductively, her eyes half-closed, was Zita.

Her head was spinning and her heart palpitating as she realised this was the 'nobody' Carl had said was just a one-night stand. Rachel's fury knew no bounds. Jumping up she went into the bedroom and, grabbing his suits, she opened the window and flung them out into the garden. She followed them by his shirts, sweaters, trousers, shoes – everything that he possessed. By the time she'd finished there was not a trace of him left in the bedroom.

She then went down to the garage and threw his golf clubs out on top of the pile. That would do for starters!

Then she rang her father and told him what she'd done and asked him to get his locksmith to come immediately and change all the locks. This he did before driving straight to his daughter's house. When he saw the photographers camped outside her gate, he was grateful for the gate-zapper to her house that he kept in case of emergency. As he drove through the gate he knew they knew better than to follow him. It was private property and to do so would have landed them in trouble.

By the time Carl had seen the blog and driven out to Howth, he was not so lucky. The flash of the cameras almost blinded him as he drove in the gate. "Bloody bastards!" he spat out.

He knew at once when he saw the huge pile of his clothes and golf clubs on the driveway that nothing he could say would make any difference. He tried his key in the door and realised that she'd already changed the locks. His father-in-law came out to meet him.

"Please remove your things from Rachel's driveway and give me your zapper for the gate," he instructed him frostily.

"I'd like to speak to Rachel," Carl said.

"She told me to tell you that she doesn't want to talk to you. Please remove your things and go. You'll be hearing from her solicitor."

He held his hand out for the zapper and Carl was too intimidated to refuse to give it to him.

As Rachel's father turned and went back in the house, Carl started throwing his things into his car, tears coming to his eyes. He'd lost her. She'd never forgive him for this betrayal. He'd gone too far this time and he knew it. Slowly he drove out the gate for the last time, tears blinding him.

66

Rachel rang Ronan later that morning.

"Rachel, I've been trying to contact you. How are you?" he asked, concern in his voice.

"Surviving, just about! I suppose you've seen the photos?"

"Yes. It must be a nightmare for you!" He felt very guilty knowing that it was his wife who had taken them.

"Oh, Ronan, I'm just devastated. I'm so hurt. I thought Zita was my friend. I can't believe they've done this to me."

"I can only imagine how you're feeling. I felt pretty much the same when Louise left me but at least she didn't run off with my friend. Can I do anything for you?"

"Not at the moment but I do appreciate knowing you're there. And, by the way, you'll be glad to hear I haven't turned to alcohol to drown my sorrows." She gave a little laugh.

"Well, I'm delighted to hear that. Remember what *you* told me . . . every cloud has a silver lining."

She laughed again. "I know but right now I feel like behind every cloud there's another one!"

"Well, at least you can still laugh. That's something!"

Ellie had heard about the blog from Chloe and when she logged on that morning she was shocked to see the photo of Zita on there. "Oh no!" she cried, recoiling in horror.

"What's wrong?" Sam asked, alarmed at the anguish in her voice. He came over to her desk.

"Look!" she cried, her face white and her eyes wide like saucers. She turned the screen around to face him. The photo of Zita looked out at him.

"Zita! It's Zita!" she exclaimed.

"What's Zita?" he asked, puzzled.

"Zita is the mystery woman. Carl and Zita were having an affair."

"You can't be serious – not Zita!" The shock was evident in his voice.

"I'm afraid so. There's a photo of them kissing too, look! There's no doubt about it, Zita and Carl were having an affair."

"What a bitch! Pretending to be Rachel's friend and getting invited to their house while all the time she was planning to screw her husband. She makes me sick!"

Ellie had never seen Sam so angry.

"Poor Rachel," she said. "She must be devastated. What a bastard! I never liked that Zita – didn't trust her for some reason. Now it seems I was right."

"Yeah. I often wondered why she came on the course in the first place. She wasn't all that interested in wine," Sam mused. "In fact, she's the only one not interested in going on to the Higher Cert Course."

"I rang Rachel yesterday and left a message but she hasn't got back to me."

"Anyway, I think you should call her again and offer our support," Sam suggested.

"Bang on. I'll try her again now," Ellie said, reaching for the phone.

When Rachel saw it was Ellie calling, she answered immediately. She was very grateful to her for ringing and thanked Sam who also assured her of his support. It was amazing how few of their old cronies had bothered to contact her. She guessed they were hedging their bets to see how Carl would survive.

"Maybe you could come out and visit some evening," Rachel suggested to Ellie, sounding very forlorn. "I don't go out much in the evening. I'd love to see you, and Sam and Ronan too if they can make it. It would cheer me up no end."

"Of course and I'm sure Sam and Ronan would love to be there too. Leave it to me. What night suits you?"

"Any night at all," Rachel replied. "Tomorrow night?"

"Great. I'll check with Ronan and see if he can make it."

"Oh thank you, Ellie. You're a star. I feel so alone. I really appreciate this."

"You're not alone, Rachel, and if you need anything, anything at all, you know where to call."

Rachel thanked her, tears in her eyes. They were the best friends she'd ever had.

David had a field-day with the *Trouble in Paradise* blog.

"We're all putting bets on who the lady in question might be," he'd told Ellie before it had been revealed to be Zita.

"Don't be so cruel," she'd retorted.

"It's hilarious!" he said now. "Come on, Ellie, these people get what they deserve. And you thought they were your friends!" He hooted with laughter.

She slammed the phone down.

"Insensitive moron!" she said aloud.

"David?" asked Sylvia who had overheard the conversation and stopped typing. Ellie nodded her head. Sylvia shook hers sadly. How many times had she witnessed Ellie rowing with David in the few weeks since they'd been sharing an office? She'd lost count. God help them, she thought.

67

Kathleen O'Sullivan was sitting at her computer in Malahide when she gasped aloud. "So that's the floosie! Would you look at her!" she cried, peering intently at the computer screen.

Donal, who was having his breakfast, laughed at his mother and her obsession with the internet. He was delighted that he'd thought to give her a computer for Christmas. He'd never imagined that she'd take to it so well. She said it had changed her life and he was happy about that. He found it hilarious that his mother, in her eighties, should be following a blog on the internet though he supposed she had a vested interest, seeing as how she knew the people involved.

"What floosie?" he now asked, coming to peer over her shoulder.

A photo of Zita filled the screen. He stared at her. He knew this woman. Her face was etched in his brain. He felt the excitement rise in his chest. My God, was it possible? After all this time? He checked the name – Zita Williams – it meant nothing to him but he'd know that face anywhere. He and his colleagues back in Adelaide had spent fifteen years looking for this woman and now here, out of the blue, she'd landed in his lap.

He looked at his watch. It was six o'clock in the evening back home now. Phil might still be in the office. He ran to the phone. His mother looked at him, thinking he'd taken leave of his senses.

"Phil? Thank God I got you!" Donal said breathlessly.

"Gudday, mate! How's Ireland treatin' you? Are you missin' us so much that you had to call?"

"Phil," Donal said excitedly, "can you do something for me? Can you fish out the file on the Lee Simmons case and email it to me?"

"The Lee Simmons case? From fifteen years ago?"

Donal could hardly contain his excitement. "Yes. Phil, I think I've found her. I've found Dolores Wright."

"Jesus, mate, are you serious?" Phil's voice was equally excited now.

"Yeah. Send that to me immediately, will you? We need to act quickly. We don't want to lose her again."

"Will do, mate. I sure hope you're right. Good luck!" He hung up to do as his friend asked.

Donal waited impatiently for the email and when it arrived he whooped with joy when he saw that this Zita Williams was without doubt the woman they'd been searching for. She hadn't changed her appearance all that much, which showed how confident she was that she'd escaped detection.

He emailed back to Phil to say that he was certain they had their lady. Then he asked him to notify the chief and set about getting a warrant for her extradition. They both knew the chief would be ecstatic. He hated having unsolved crimes in his department. They'd have no trouble getting the warrant. Donal emailed Zita's photo to the chief to assure him that they'd found their woman. Her demise was set in motion.

He then contacted a friend of his in the Criminal Investigation Unit who told him to come straight into his office. Interpol would have to be alerted. Donal stressed that there was no time to lose.

68

The scurrilous comments about Carl continued in the *Trouble in Paradise* blog. Carl was no closer to finding out who was writing it than he had been before. It was driving him crazy. People were avoiding him and he was not receiving invitations to functions he knew were taking place. This blog was damaging him. Now, whoever was writing it, not content with destroying his marriage, was out to wreck his career too. There were hints about payments received and deals done which were blatantly untrue. But try as he might he couldn't discover who was behind it.

He had moved in with his friend, Steve, but it was far from ideal. He missed his beautiful home in Howth and his two wonderful children. Most of all, he missed Rachel. Only now was he beginning to realise what an idiot he'd been but she wouldn't talk to him – not on the phone and most definitely not in person. He felt lost.

The accusations of corruption measured against him were becoming more intense daily yet he was helpless to refute them. He was becoming a nervous wreck. He wished with all his heart that Rachel was by his side to help him through, but she wasn't.

The following day the photo of Zita was splashed all over the tabloids and they were asking 'Who is this woman – the other woman in NEP case?'

It didn't take them long to find out. They were inundated with calls from people pointing the finger at Zita. She'd even rung them herself, giving a false name, to be sure they identified her.

She was quite enjoying the notoriety. Her colleagues were looking at her with renewed interest. She knew they were seeing her in a different light. She even overheard herself being referred to as a femme fatale. It was quite exciting. The whole of Dublin was following her blog avidly. She was loving it!

There was also a photograph in the newspaper of Carl's clothes strewn on his driveway with the caption 'Hell hath no fury'. Zita laughed gleefully. Now he'd come crawling back to her and she'd be waiting with open arms. She didn't give a thought as to how Rachel might feel.

That night, Marcus returned from a blissful two weeks in Ibiza where he'd fallen madly in love. He couldn't wait to tell Zita all about it. He was hoping he'd find that she'd finally got over this obsession she had with Carl Dunne. He knocked on her door, bottle of Cava in hand. Eventually the door opened.

"Hello, sweetie! Welcome back," she drawled, slurring her words. "How was Ibiza?"

"Ibiza was great," he replied, realising that she was drunk. He couldn't believe it! Zita *never* got drunk. It took the wind out of his sails. There was no point in telling her about his new lover while she was in this state.

"Come in, come in," she cried, flinging the door back and practically falling over.

He grabbed her to stop her falling down.

"I have the most wonderful . . . bloody great . . . news! Carl has left . . . what's her name . . . his wife. Amn't I clever?" She grinned at him.

"What had you to do with it?" he asked her, lowering her on to the armchair.

"*I* did it with my blog!" she giggled.

"What are you talking about?" he asked puzzled. "What blog?"

"*Trouble in Paradise* blog. Don't tell me you haven't read it?" Her eyes were wide with disbelief. "Everyone's read it. I'm famous!"

She threw the tabloids with her photo splashed all over them at him.

Reading them, he paled. "Zita, are you crazy?" he shrieked. "You can't do this! You'll never get away with it! You could be arrested for this."

"I'm much too clever for that," she laughed. "They'll never catch me. And he's left her, hasn't he?"

Marcus looked at her and realised that she really believed it. She thought she would get away with it. She was nuts!

"I've got away with much, much worse than this," she drawled. "You have no idea what I've got away with." She wagged her finger at him. "I have a verrrry dark past. And it's dangerous to mess with me."

Something about the way she said it sent a shiver down his spine. Her eyes glittered with malice. She scared him.

He quickly said goodnight and hot-tailed it back to his

own apartment, locking the door carefully behind him. He Googled her blog. God, she was nuts! She had totally lost her grip and he didn't like it.

The only fly in the ointment in Ronan's life at the moment was Rachel's unhappiness. Still, she was coping wonderfully, all things considered. He wondered if she might change her mind and give Carl another chance but she was adamant. She was finished with him and was going to seek a divorce. She was proving to be a remarkably strong woman, as was Fiona who kept in touch with him daily and who had been very sympathetic about Rachel's predicament.

The deal for the premises in Naas was concluded and Sam was busy getting it up and running. Ronan had always thought Naas was a great town and when Sam had taken him down to see the premises he'd been charmed with both the shop and the cosy, yet spacious apartment above. It was bang in the centre of town and he knew he'd be very happy there.

He'd received a letter from Louise's solicitor to say she was filing for divorce. She wanted it as quickly as possible so was going to do it through the English courts. Alan had seemingly found a way to do this. She wanted nothing from Ronan which was a relief. He replied, saying he would not contest it. Yes, indeed life was good. He'd found the silver lining behind his cloud!

If only this awful thing wasn't happening to Rachel.

Zita knew that she would have to close the blog when Carl came back to her. She would miss it. It had given her a sense of power but, let's face it, when she and Carl became a couple, it would be like cutting her nose to spite her face. No, the blog would have to end.

She rang Carl that afternoon. "Hi, it's me." When he didn't respond she said, "Zita."

"Zita? What the hell do you want? Haven't you done enough damage?"

She was taken aback. She'd thought he'd be pleased to hear from her.

"What do you mean?" she snivelled. "It's not my fault that somebody is out to get you."

"If I'd never met you none of this would have happened. You obviously blabbed about our relationship to people. Have you any idea who might be writing this rubbish?"

She was shocked. This wasn't what she had expected. "I've no idea who it could be," she protested. "I've been wronged here too, Carl, but we can cope with it as long as we're together."

"Zita, get real, there's no 'together' for us," he snapped, his voice bitter.

"But now that you've left Rachel, I thought that we –"

"Don't be ridiculous. You were never more than a diversion to me." He heard Zita gasp. "And I didn't leave Rachel, she threw me out, and I plan to do everything in my power to get her back. Now don't contact me again. We're through!" He slammed the phone shut.

Zita was in shock. This wasn't panning out the way she'd planned it at all. What had he called her – 'a diversion'? She seethed with anger. He'd been using her, the prick! And to think of all the trouble she'd taken to destroy his marriage. He had no intention of coming back to her, ever. He'd made that clear. She closed her eyes and heard again the way he'd spat out "We're through."

The bastard! She'd get him for this. She recalled the saying from the film *The First Wives Club*: Don't get mad – get even. She'd get even alright! She'd planned to close the blog but now she decided to redouble her efforts.

Sam, Ellie and Ronan headed out to Rachel's house that evening. She hugged them all and was very happy to see them. Ellie was shocked at how much weight she'd lost and, although she'd made up her face very carefully, the strain was showing on it.

Sam had brought wine, Ellie chocolates and Ronan flowers. "Oh, you're so kind, all of you," she cried, tears coming to her eyes.

She'd prepared a Thai curry for them and as they sat around the table eating it Rachel felt some form of normality return. By the end of the evening she was laughing again, something she hadn't done for what seemed like ages.

Ronan was happy to see that although she had a couple of glasses of wine she wasn't throwing it back like she used to. She was really quite a remarkable woman.

"Well, your exam results are due in early next week," Sam announced, "so I suggest we all go out for a slap-up meal next Friday, what do you say?"

"Oh yes, that would be fabulous," Rachel cried, her eyes shining.

"Cool," Ellie remarked.

"I'll contact the four young ones and let them know," Sam said. "I take it we're all in agreement that Zita is not to be invited?"

Rachel grimaced. "I couldn't come if she were there. Maybe I shouldn't?" A shadow crossed her face as she spoke.

"Don't even think about it," Ellie warned. "She can't come. I would possibly throttle her."

"No, you wouldn't because I'd get to her before you," announced Ronan.

Rachel smiled at them gratefully. They were great friends to have. "I hope we have all passed," she said tremulously to Sam.

"You'd better have," he pronounced, "or I'm in trouble."

69

Zita was drunk again. Very drunk! She'd arrived home that evening, planning her revenge, and opened a bottle of wine as she thought about it. When that one was finished she'd opened a second one.

When she heard Marcus coming in she waylaid him in the hall, waving the bottle of wine. He saw that she was in a bad way. He had been avoiding her since the previous evening.

"Christ, Zita! What are you doing?"

"My life is over," she blubbered. "Carl says we're through."

"For God's sake, woman, get a grip! You knew it wasn't going to come to anything," he commented irritably, still standing in the hallway. He didn't want to invite her into his apartment.

"I thought if I ruined his marriage he'd come back to me," she whimpered.

Marcus shook his head. How could she be so naïve? He didn't understand her.

Suddenly, she changed tack. "I'll get my own back,"

she hinted slyly. "He won't know what's hit him. I have plans – big plans." She laughed gleefully.

Marcus didn't know whether he preferred her maudlin or hostile. She was an enigma. She could change like quicksilver.

"I think you should quit this wine-drinking and go to bed," he told her gently.

"You don't believe me?" she said sharply. "I can tell you things I've done to people who've wronged me that would make your toes curl."

He believed her. He'd believed her the other night too. She'd obviously done something really bad in her past and he didn't want to know about it. He was anxious to escape her presence.

"Aren't you going to invite me in?" she asked, lounging against his doorframe.

"Zita, I'm really exhausted. Let's do it another night." He quickly said goodnight and slipped into his flat. God, she really was a psycho! He'd seen what she was capable of with that blog she'd written which had destroyed Carl's marriage. How much further had she gone or would she go to destroy him? Marcus shivered, glad he wasn't the one in her sights.

Zita went into her own apartment, put out that he hadn't invited her in. Angry, she switched on her laptop and started her blog: **NEP not satisfied with a womanly woman. No, he's into little children too!** She pressed send and laughed wickedly at the thought of what Carl would think of this latest ploy of hers.

He'd learn that he'd trifled with the wrong woman!

The following morning, Carl read the blog and a terrible fear clutched him. This was slander of the worst kind.

Although it was blatantly untrue, mud sticks, and unless he could take this evil writer to task and prove himself innocent, people would remember this and probably believe it.

His phone rang and he saw with relief that it was Rachel.

"Oh, Rach," he cried, tears coming to his eyes. "I'm so happy you've called."

"Carl, I'm just calling to say that I read the blog this morning and whatever else you've done I know that this is not true."

"Oh Rach, please come back. I love you and miss –"

"No, Carl. We're through. I've applied for a separation. I just wanted to tell you that I know you're not a paedophile. Goodbye, Carl."

Click. She hung up.

Carl let the tears flow. She'd sounded so cool yet he'd loved the sound of her voice. It was so noble of her to ring to tell him that. He was grateful for that at least.

His phone rang again. He answered, hoping it was Rachel and that she'd changed her mind. It was Stan and he sounded excited.

"We've got her, Carl, we've found the blogger. She made a big mistake last night, blogging from her own computer. Up to now she's used internet cafés but she slipped up last night." He couldn't conceal his exhilaration.

"Who is it?" Carl asked hoarsely.

"Zita Williams – your mystery lady."

Carl felt his legs go weak. "I don't believe it. What can I do?"

"I suggest you get your lawyer to deal with it. He will report it to the Computer Crime Investigation Unit and they'll take it from there. They're very efficient."

Carl felt relieved. "What I want to do is go round and throttle her," he said.

"That's the worst thing you could do. You mustn't let her know you've found out it's her. You can't give her the chance to destroy the evidence. Trust me, they'll catch her."

"Whew! I can't believe she could be so evil."

"Well, she'll pay for it, never you fear."

The results of the wine exam were on Sam's desk. He read them with a smile. He could almost have predicted them. The only surprises were that Hayley had done so well and that Zita had done so badly. He supposed he'd better call her.

"Hello, Zita, Sam here, from the wine course."

"Oh hello, Sam." She held her head which was throbbing unmercifully with her hangover.

"The results of the exam are in and I thought I'd let you know that unfortunately you didn't pass." His voice was cold.

"Oh!" She wasn't terribly surprised and right now she didn't care. She didn't give a shit about anything! "Oh, I see. Well, thanks, Sam," she said, thinking 'Fuck you, I bet you enjoyed that!' in her own mind.

She had stayed home that morning as her hangover was the worst she'd ever had so she was surprised when she heard a knock on the door. Bloody Marcus, she thought, opening it angrily. Two plainclothes detectives stood there flashing their IDs at her.

"Miss Zita Williams?"

"Yes."

"We have a warrant to detain you for questioning under Section Four of the Criminal Justice Act."

She tried to close the door but they were too quick for her. She lashed out at the first man but within two seconds his partner had her in handcuffs.

"Let us warn you that anything you say may be taken down and used against you in evidence."

"*Fuck off!*" she shrieked. "What are you accusing me of?"

"Incitement to hatred."

She struggled with them all the way down the stairs but she was no match for them. They bundled her into the car.

In the station they fingerprinted her and took her photograph and then she was led to a room to be questioned.

She quickly realised that they somehow knew that she was behind the blog. She'd slipped up somewhere. She demanded to see her lawyer.

The police in both Ireland and Australia had moved with great speed and during the twenty-four hours that Zita was being held for questioning, Interpol confirmed that her fingerprints matched those of Dolores Wright, the woman wanted for murder in Australia. An extradition warrant was sought and granted against her. Murder was murder in any country.

As Donal had read through the file he received from Phil, he recalled the gruesome details of the horrific murder of Lee Simmons. The fact that the victim was a pimp who had mistreated and brutalised his 'girls' didn't make his death any more acceptable.

He'd been killed in the most horrible manner. His hands and feet had been tied to his bed with four sets of handcuffs. His genitals had been cut off, his body mutilated and his throat slit. It was one of the most horrific murders any of them had seen.

They'd interviewed numerous prostitutes who admitted that they were happy he was dead but all of them had been ruled out as the killer. The only 'girl' in his stable that they couldn't trace was a woman called Dolores Wright. They'd been given a photo of her from one of the other prostitutes but, try as they might, they couldn't locate her. They heard from many of the other girls that Dolores had hated Lee with a vengeance and had been heard threatening to kill him. Many of the girls said they'd been afraid of her – that she was a 'psycho'.

There was damning evidence that she was the culprit. She was the only person caught on video camera entering his apartment that day. She'd stayed for only half an hour and it was within the timeframe that the coroner had said was the time of death. They'd taken fresh fingerprints from the handcuffs and from a glass that was found beside his bed. They couldn't find a match for them anywhere but had retained them on file. They set about searching for her but she seemed to have vanished off the face of the earth. And now Donal had found her. He couldn't believe his luck.

Zita was being very uncooperative and hostile but the evidence stacked against her as the blogger was incontrovertible and the following morning she was charged with incitement to hatred and remanded on her own bail. She smirked as she prepared to leave the court, knowing that she would never have to stand trial. She was way cleverer than they were. She would simply disappear again.

Then, as she was leaving the court, her worst nightmare

came true. She heard the Australian accent and knew what was coming.

"Miss Zita Williams aka Dolores Wright, we have a warrant for your extradition to Adelaide, Australia, to stand trial for the murder of Lee Simmons."

Zita almost fainted. She was thrust back into her nightmares of Lee's body rising up to stab her and then the awful feeling of not being able to run to get away from him. That's how she felt now. She couldn't move.

It was all over in a flash.

Because of the extradition warrant, the case against her for incitement to hatred was rushed through the courts. She was found guilty of slandering Carl in the blogs. She was ordered to make an unequivocal apology to him and retract everything she'd said, admitting they were lies. She was also ordered to compensate him to the tune of €30,000. This was the least of her troubles. There were much worse things to come.

Eight hours later she was on a flight to Australia, wondering where and how it had all gone so terribly wrong.

Zita's face flashed out from every TV network that evening. She was big news. The author of the scurrilous blog was also wanted for a gruesome murder back in Australia. Rachel was flabbergasted. How could she have misjudged someone so badly? She felt such a fool. But she didn't feel half as bad as Carl felt. He realised what an error of judgement he'd made. In fact he was beginning to realise how lightly he'd got off. When he read the awful things she'd done to that poor guy in Australia he broke into a sweat thinking what she could have done to him. She was evil through and through. Thank God she was out of his life forever.

He hoped Rachel would contact him but she didn't. The following day he received notice that she was applying for a legal separation. She had allowed him to visit the children but only under the supervision of Paloma. She herself had kept out of sight. He would have to wait for the court to decide on custody but that was a foregone conclusion. Rachel was the injured party in their relationship.

With sadness he recognised that his marriage was well and truly over. He would have a tough time repairing his reputation but if they say a week is a long time in politics then three years is an eternity. Hopefully by the next election he would have reinstated himself in the public eye. It was time to start rebuilding and move on. The Zita episode in his life was now closed.

The wine group were all mesmerised by the details that had emerged about Zita. To think they'd been friends with a murderess! It was like something out of a movie.

They had their celebratory dinner in Wong's Chinese Restaurant in Dollymount that Friday. Although they had all been in touch with each other when the Zita story broke, out of deference to Rachel, nobody mentioned it that night. In a strange way it was as if she was present with them. Sam gave out the results and they were all delighted with them. Everyone clapped Ronan on the back when Sam announced he'd scored 100%. Sam presented him with a copy of Hugh Johnson's *Wine Atlas* which delighted him. They cheered Ellie who had scored an excellent 94% and Rachel 92%. Hayley had also scored 92% which surprised everyone but Ellie, who knew she'd studied very hard in an effort to please Sam. The young girl blushed madly when Sam kissed her on the cheek as he presented her with her certificate. They were all looking forward to starting the

Higher Certificate course which would run from September to Christmas.

"As a matter of interest how did Zita do?" Rachel asked. It was the first mention of her name all night.

Sam grinned. "She failed."

As one they all raised their glasses and then burst out laughing. Zita's presence was gone from the gathering. They had a great night and all of them looked forward to getting back together for the Higher Cert Course.

Ronan went down to Fiona's in Blessington the following Sunday. He was looking forward to seeing Oisín again. It was amazing how quickly the baby was changing. He was still a very placid baby and growing at a great rate.

"I'm thinking of applying for a part-time job in the Lakeside Inn," Fiona told him. "Mam is willing to baby-sit for me."

"Will you like bar work?"

"Well, not as much as working in a wine shop but beggars can't be choosers. I just think it might be good to get out of the house and meet people for a couple of hours a week." She smiled wanly.

"How about coming to work part-time in the new Naas shop?"

"Are you serious?" She looked at him hopefully.

"Deadly! We can always do with experienced staff and you know I'd love to have you working alongside me."

She hugged him, her eyes dancing with delight. "That would be fabulous! Thank you so much, Ronan!"

"To be honest, it was Sam's idea but I would have asked you anyway," he grinned.

She punched him playfully. "I should hope so!"

He took her down to Naas to see the shop that

afternoon, strapping Oisín into his chair in the back seat. Fiona smiled to see how gentle he was with her son. On the drive down he told her all about Zita. She'd read all about it in the newspaper but Ronan filled her in on all the gory details.

"My God, what a horrible woman! You're lucky you didn't get involved with her!"

"In a way I feel a bit sorry for Carl, although he was an idiot. Anyway, he's lost Rachel for good now."

"She's very beautiful from what I can see in her photos."

"Yes, she is," Ronan agreed, "and it's not just her looks. She's a really lovely person too."

"You're very fond of her, aren't you?" Fiona asked, cocking her head to one side.

"Yes, I am. Anyway you'll certainly meet her soon. I plan to invite some friends down at some stage, after I get the shop up and running."

"That's great! I'm looking forward to meeting them."

"You'll like them," he told her, "and I know they'll like you and love baby Oisín."

70

Ellie was very excited about her visit to Bordeaux but not as excited as Marie-Noelle. They were booked into the Grand Hotel and neither was expecting the sheer luxury of the hotel. It was very central and Marie-Noelle felt it was like a homecoming, which in a way it was.

"Just imagine it, my parents walked these streets as children," she said to Ellie as they explored the beautiful city the first afternoon.

They had a wonderful time and on Saturday took a tour up to St Emilion where Ellie's mother was amazed at her daughter's knowledge of the wines they tasted. On Sunday they were going to lunch with Marie-Noelle's cousins whom she had contacted. Sam was flying in on Sunday morning and Marie-Noelle asked her cousin, Josette, if she could bring Sam along to the lunch.

"But of course, we would love to meet him," Josette declared.

Meanwhile, back in Dublin, David was calling for Ellie's sister, Sandrine, to take her to the Chartered Accountants' Ball.

"You look nice," he said, as she slipped into the passenger seat of his BMW.

She should have, as she had spent all day getting ready and had bought a new very expensive Marchesa gown for the occasion. For the first time in her life she'd had a spray tan and hair extensions. This was the kind of behaviour that she ridiculed when Ellie indulged in it, but she had to admit that she felt a million dollars and she knew she looked better than ever. She was so excited about the coming evening. She thought Ellie was an idiot not to have postponed the Bordeaux trip to be with David tonight. But Ellie's loss was her gain. Halleluiah!

They entered the Four Seasons' ballroom and David introduced her to everyone. She saw a few raised eyebrows but when they heard that she was Ellie's sister and that Ellie was away, they made her feel very welcome.

She had a wonderful evening and got on famously with everyone. These were her kind of people, mature and intelligent, and the jealousy that she'd always felt towards Ellie intensified as the night went on.

David was a pet and it was obvious that he was very much at home in this environment. She could see how much he enjoyed and admired these new friends. They would all be invited to the wedding, he told her. Towards the end of the night one particular guy who had been flirting with her all night and was now a little the worse for wear, stumbled up to David and said, "I think you're marrying the wrong sister, Davy boy. This one's a corker."

David laughed, embarrassed, and Sandrine blushed prettily. In fact, David was delighted with the way Sandrine had fitted in with his crowd. He wished Ellie was as compatible with them. He sighed, wishing that his fiancée would take a leaf out of her sister's book.

When David dropped her off at her apartment, Sandrine leaned over and gave him a kiss. He held her for a minute.

"I've had the best night of my life," she told him, her eyes glowing. "I can't ever thank you enough."

"I'm the one who should be thanking you," he said, slightly embarrassed. "You were brilliant and all my friends loved you. And I really enjoyed your company too."

Driving home, he thought that what he'd said was true. Sandrine was very good company. He really had been more relaxed tonight, knowing that she was happy to be there among his friends. With Ellie, he was always on edge knowing that she wasn't enjoying herself. Maybe Daniel was right. Maybe he had chosen the wrong sister. Sandrine would certainly make a more suitable wife and he felt a strong connection with her. Oh God, too late to do anything about it now!

Sandrine was unable to sleep. She hadn't been able to resist sending Ellie a text when she'd come in: **You missed a simply fabulous night. Really great! S.** She was on a high and flushed with success. She felt like she'd belonged there by David's side. He was so wonderful. And as for his friends – it was obvious they'd all liked her. More than a few of them had said they thought she'd be much more suitable for David than Ellie was – and she agreed with them.

"I don't think she likes David's friends very much," one girl had commented.

"I can't imagine why not?" Sandrine replied demurely. "I think they're wonderful."

"Men are bowled over by that innocent blue-eyed look," another girl – whose husband was constantly remarking how pretty Ellie was – sniffed. "They don't look further than looks in a woman which is not exactly the perfect recipe for a happy marriage."

She sounded bitter but Sandrine agreed with her. It was so unfair that Ellie would have this wonderful life when she didn't even appreciate it. Life was cruel!

The following morning Sandrine rang David to thank him for the wonderful evening.

"Yes, it was splendid," he agreed, "and my friends really took to you."

"I took to them too. They're so nice and such good company."

"I wish Ellie felt that way about them," he remarked bitterly. Before he could stop himself, he found himself saying; "Listen, we're all meeting in Kitty's for brunch. Hair of the dog, don't you know!" He laughed and so did she. "Why don't you come too?"

"Oh, David, I'd love that. Are you sure?"

"Of course. My friends will be delighted to see you again. I'll pick you up at twelve. Okay?"

"Perfect," she said. "I'll be ready."

Gleefully, she ran to her wardrobe to choose a dress that she thought David would like. "Yesssss!" she cried, as she pumped the air.

She had a wonderful time yet again and the brunch went on late into the afternoon. Sandrine had never been happier and for the first time in her life felt like she belonged. She was reluctant to end the afternoon and, when David suggested that she go with him to see the house in Sandymount, she jumped at the chance. He'd just received the keys the day before and was excited to show it to her.

"Oh, it's gorgeous, just gorgeous," she exclaimed,

loving the cool chic neutral colours. "I can't imagine Ellie living here though. She hates neutral colours. She'll want red and yellow walls, I'm sure."

David grimaced. "I know, that's what she said when she saw it for the first time, I'm afraid."

"No, David, you can't allow her to do that. It's so classy and it will just end up tacky, if I know Ellie."

"*Mmmm . . .*" David said thoughtfully. "Ellie and I are not really well suited, are we?"

"I'm afraid not. I think you deserve someone very special," she said softly, placing her hands on his arms.

It seemed the most natural thing in the world for him to reach down and kiss her. Sandrine responded passionately and then, realising with a shock what he was doing, he pulled away.

"I'm so sorry, Sandrine, that was unforgivable," he said, embarrassed.

"No, it's what I wanted too, David," she whispered, looking up at him. "I've wanted it for a very long time."

"Oh, Sandrine!" he cried, anguished. "What can we do?"

"Don't worry. We'll work it out," she replied, moving back into his arms. She was jubilant as he kissed her once again.

71

Sam arrived at Ellie's hotel just after noon on Sunday. Ellie and Marie-Noelle greeted him warmly. He had hired a car and drove them to Josette's house which was just outside the city. To their surprise she had gathered all the relations together and there were about thirty various cousins waiting to welcome Marie-Noelle and her daughter into the family fold. Sam got a warm welcome also.

It was a beautiful sunny day and the tables were set out in the garden, under the pergola of overhanging vines. Ellie felt so at home and was delighted to see her mother so happy. She was enjoying herself enormously with all these new cousins and Sam had all the females from five to ninety eating out of his hand. He was so easy-going and charming and of course his sultry good looks didn't hurt either.

Marie-Noelle watched him as he chatted to her ninety-year-old grandaunt who was actually flirting with him. He was extremely good-looking but seemed to be totally unaware of it. He had a way of looking at you intently with his laughing eyes that women of all ages found irresistible. When he was speaking to you he made you feel like you were the only person in the world. What woman didn't love that? Marie-Noelle thought, smiling.

"He's really got a way with women, hasn't he?" she remarked to Ellie who had come and plonked down beside her.

"Yeah, he's a dote but he gets on really well with men too. He's great fun." Ellie looked over to where Sam was laughing at something her great-grandaunt had said. He caught her eye and winked at her.

Marie-Noelle caught the glance between them. She noticed too that Ellie was positively glowing. She had never seen her daughter as happy as she'd been today. She wondered if it was Sam that was the cause of it. There was obviously a lot of affection between them.

Later a couple of relatives brought out a guitar and an accordion and started playing and all the young ones got up to dance. Ellie's granduncle pulled her up and as she tried to waltz with him Marie-Noelle saw Sam's eyes following her daughter.

"You're very fond of her, aren't you?" she asked him as he came to sit beside her.

"Yes, she's terrific. I love her joie de vivre. It's infectious."

"She's always been like that, ever since she was a little girl. I do hope she'll be happy with David." A frown creased her forehead.

"Do you not think she will be?" he asked, alarmed.

"I don't know. Lately I've been thinking that perhaps David is not the right man for Ellie." She blushed, surprised that she'd voiced her fears to Sam, whom she barely knew.

"Funny you should say that. Sylvia who works in the office with Ellie has said the same thing to me."

Marie-Noelle looked at him, eyebrows raised. "Really?

God, I hope we're both wrong or, at least, if we're not, that Ellie discovers it in time."

Sam patted her hand. "Don't worry! I'll have a chat with her if you like."

"Would you, Sam? I don't want to be seen to be interfering. Ellie can be very stubborn, you know."

"Who are you telling!" They both laughed aloud.

It had been a fabulous day and they finally took their leave at ten o'clock that evening.

"Some lunch!" Ellie laughed exhilarated.

"That's lunch French-style," Sam assured her.

Sam and Ellie left early the next morning to drive to the Haut Medoc where they would meet with his producers. Marie-Noelle waved them off, looking forward to pampering herself in the hotel spa for the next few hours.

Ellie was fascinated with what she saw in the wineries they visited and bowled over by the passion for their wines that each producer displayed. They in turn – true Gallic gentlemen – were charmed by the pretty young Irish girl who spoke fluent French and who was so very interested in everything. One after another she had them eating out of her hand.

Ellie had never had such a good time. Sam was a wonderful companion and they laughed a lot together. He was very impressed with how she handled the producers. He was pleased that he'd suggested she stay on with him as his PA. She was certainly an asset to the business.

Their last stop was at the famous winery, Château Lynch-Bages which Sam informed her was his favourite Bordeaux wine. When she tasted it, she was not in the least surprised. It felt like silk and velvet on her palate. The owner, Jean-Michel, gave them a tasting of vintages from as far back as 1982. It was the most magical afternoon Ellie had ever spent. He was as charmed by her as the other producers and invited them to dinner at the château that night.

"We'd love to stay but unfortunately I am driving back to the city tonight and I know if I start drinking your wonderful wine, I will not be able to resist it," Sam declined graciously.

"This has been a fantastic day," Ellie said, as they drove back to Bordeaux. "Honestly, I don't think I've ever been happier."

"There's a lovely bistro I know, quite close to the city. Do you fancy stopping off for a bite to eat there?"

"You had me at 'bistro'," she grinned.

He'd noticed that Ellie hadn't called David all day. This was surprising. Most girls he knew seemed to have their phones practically glued to their ear or otherwise were constantly texting, which infuriated him. Not Ellie.

"I'll go on ahead if you want to call your fiancé," Sam suggested as they arrived at the restaurant. "They don't allow mobile phones in here, I'm afraid."

"Oh no, I don't have to ring him," she replied.

A cloud had passed over her face as she spoke and Sam noticed it. He had no time to question her further as the patron of the bistro came to greet Sam like an old friend. He showed them to a table and brought them the blackboard menu and a bottle of wine which he told them came from his brother's winery.

"With my compliments," he said as he opened it. He poured the wine for them and Sam told him that they would eat whatever he recommended.

"Excellent!" the owner replied, rubbing his hands

together. He hurried off to prepare something special for them.

"*Santé*," Sam toasted her.

"Thank you for *the* most fabulous day ever," she smiled at him, raising her glass too. "I feel like I'm in a dream and I don't want to wake up."

He heard the emotion in her voice. "Is everything okay between you and David?" he asked, looking at her with raised eyebrows as he waited for a reply.

She hesitated and took a sip from her glass. "Well, I don't know. Things have not been very good between us lately. I feel very disloyal saying this but honestly, I seem to be much happier when I'm not with him than when I am. Does that sound awful?"

"Well, it doesn't exactly sound like a recipe for a happy marriage," he said, his voice gentle.

"It's just that David has changed so much since I met him, even just since we got engaged."

"Yes, well, relationships are never easy," Sam observed.

"I feel like we've become . . . disconnected. Do you know what I mean?"

Sam was worried now. "Don't you think you should sort this out with him before you walk down the aisle?"

"That's the problem! Everything is organised for the wedding. I can't back out now. It's too late."

Sam put his glass down and took hers from her and put it on the table. Leaning towards her, he took her hands in his. "Ellie, listen to me. It's never too late. This is the most important decision you'll ever make in your life and it has to be the right one. If not, you'll be miserable for the rest of it."

She looked at him, tears in her eyes, not wanting to hear what he was saying.

She was aware of the urgency in his voice. She took her hands from his and reached for her drink, spluttering as she took too large a mouthful.

He sat back in his chair and took his glass up, taking a good sip from it.

His voice was quieter as he continued. "I've seen my parents live in an unhappy marriage and I wouldn't wish it on anyone."

"Why didn't they divorce?"

"Because my mother is too concerned with appearances. All she cares about is what other people think. I've told her many times that it's not important but she won't listen." His voice was bitter as he spoke.

"You don't get on with her, do you?"

"Not at all! We've always had a problem relating to one another. We're too different, I suppose. I don't give a damn what people think. She thinks I'm a social misfit and I think she's shallow. I'm more like my father, minus the bottom-pinching and womanising, of course."

Ellie laughed. "Thank God for that."

"Seriously, Ellie, please say you won't go ahead with this wedding until you've sorted things out with David."

"I'll talk to him, I promise."

The waiter arrived with their first course, much to her relief. She didn't want to think of David right now. They enjoyed the fabulous food with no more mention of her fiancé. Sam drove her back to the hotel and was sad to see her go. He invited Ellie and her mother out to lunch the following day, which was to be their last.

Tired and happy, Ellie gathered up her bag and shrug as she opened the car door. "Goodnight, Sam."

"'Night, Ellie. Sleep well!"

"Thanks for a brilliant day," she said, as she leaned forward and kissed his cheek. Then she was gone.

The following day, Sam collected them and took them out to Arcachon, on the coast, where Ellie tasted oysters for the first time. To her surprise they were delicious. They were lunching at a beachside restaurant.

"I wish I could stay here forever," Ellie sighed.

"What about David? Aren't you longing to get home to him?" her mother asked.

Ellie didn't reply but Marie-Noelle caught the glance that passed between her and Sam. Oh, God, she thought, I wonder if anything has happened between them.

When Ellie left the table to go to the restrooms, she pounced on Sam.

"Has anything happened that I should know about?" she asked nervously.

"Not at all," Sam assured her, his eyes twinkling with merriment that she should have thought that. "But I did have a chat with Ellie."

"And?"

"Well, it seems that she and David have lately become . . . disconnected, was the word she used. I did advise her to sit down and sort things out with him before it's too late." He rubbed his chin thoughtfully. "I do think it's hitting her that there will be a life with David after the wedding and she may be having doubts about that."

Marie-Noelle sighed. "Well, we'll have to wait and see. I'll have a long chat with her when we get home. Thanks, Sam." She patted his hand as Ellie came back to the table.

72

Ellie thought David was acting strangely. He hadn't called her since Sunday which was unusual in itself and his texts were very brief and strange. Was he still annoyed with her that she'd chosen Bordeaux over his ball? She wondered if perhaps he'd had a miserable night as he hadn't mentioned it once. But then she realised that it couldn't have been that because Sandrine had texted her at 3 a.m. on Sunday to say they'd had a fabulous time. Ah well, no doubt she'd find out soon enough.

She sighed as the plane came in to land at Dublin airport. She half expected David to be there to meet her but he wasn't.

He rang her shortly afterwards.

"Hi, you're home," he said tersely. "Did you have a good time?"

"Wonderful," she replied, trying not to be too enthusiastic.

"Ellie, we need to talk. Can you meet me in The Yacht in twenty minutes?"

She was taken aback. "Yeah, sure," she agreed, wondering what was going on. He usually called for her at home. This was weird.

He was sitting in a corner waiting for her. The minute she saw his face she knew something was wrong. Fear gripped her. She hoped nothing had happened to either of his parents.

"What is it, David? What's wrong?" she asked, sitting down opposite him.

"Ellie, I don't know how to tell you this." He avoided her eyes as he spoke.

"Oh God, what is it, David? Just tell me!" she cried, fearing the worst.

"I'm afraid I can't marry you!" he blurted out.

"What?" she asked, confused. "What are you talking about?" She knew her voice had risen a couple of notches and that the couple at a neighbouring table had stopped their own conversation and were eavesdropping on them.

"I'm so sorry, so sorry," he said, still avoiding her eyes.

"*David, what are you talking about? What's happened?*" she said, not caring that she was almost shrieking.

"Well, you'll have to agree that things have been terrible between us lately," he said, looking at her finally. "And I now realise that I love someone else. I'm sorry."

She looked at him stupefied. "Who?" she asked, wondering how and when this could have happened.

"This is so difficult for me," he replied, wringing his hands. "It's Sandrine," he whispered, so low that she could hardly hear him.

"Sandrine? My sister Sandrine?" She stared at him disbelievingly, her mouth open.

"Yes. I'm so sorry. I feel terrible about it but that's how it is and it wouldn't be right to marry you when I feel like that. It would have been a terrible mistake. I hope you can forgive me."

"What does Sandrine have to say about this?" she asked, starting to feel angry.

"Well, she says she's loved me for quite a while," he mumbled sheepishly.

"My own sister! How could you?" she cried. "And how could she do this to me?"

"I know it's terrible but these things happen."

"I can't believe it. So, I take it our wedding is off?"

The neighbouring couple were goggle-eyed and not even trying to hide their interest in the conversation any more. Ellie didn't care about them but David was very uncomfortable and shifting in his seat.

"I'm sorry," he repeated yet again. "You have to admit that it's as much your fault as mine."

"Don't give me that shit!" She had raised her voice again and now other people nearby were looking on. "That's because you've changed so much since you started working for that bloody company. In fact, I'm beginning to think that you didn't really want to get married in the first place. Well, I hope my bloody sister makes you happy. You deserve each other." And with as much dignity as she could muster, she got up and, with her head held high, marched out of the pub leaving David embarrassed and the other customers open-mouthed.

She couldn't believe it! What had just happened? All her future plans had been blown sky-high. No wedding, no David. And to think it was her own sister who had betrayed her. She felt utterly deceived but somewhere in the back of her mind she remembered that she hadn't wanted to come home to him but would happily have stayed on in Bordeaux.

Confused and upset, she walked along the seafront trying to make sense of it all. She realised that what upset her most was the fact that it was Sandrine he was leaving her for. But that wasn't right. She should have been devastated that the man she was about to marry had left her, regardless of who he was leaving her for.

Her mind was a muddle. She needed to think clearly. She couldn't go home as her mother would know something was wrong and she didn't feel like she could discuss it with her quite yet. Somehow she found herself on Sam's doorstep.

"Ellie, what a surprise . . ." He broke off, seeing the look on her face. "What's wrong? Come in." He ushered her inside. "You look like you could do with a drink." He poured her a glass of wine from a bottle that was open on the coffee table.

"What's happened?" he asked again, concern in his eyes.

She gulped the wine. "David's broken it off with me."

"He's what?"

"Yes, he's in love with someone else." She took another large swig out of the glass. "My sister, Sandrine."

"Is he crazy?" Sam cried, jumping up and pacing the room. "Are you serious?"

"Deadly," she replied, nodding her head. "Still, I suppose it's better that I found out now than after the wedding." Suddenly the reality hit her and she started to cry.

"Don't cry. He isn't worth it," Sam said, sitting down beside her on the sofa. "He's a right little shit!"

"I know!" she bawled. "I could have taken it if he'd said that he was having doubts about it, like I am, but to be leaving me for my sister!"

He handed her a pristine white handkerchief and she wiped her eyes and blew her nose loudly in it. "Oh, sorry. I'll wash it and bring it back to you," she said apologetically.

"Never mind! You know, Ellie, after what you told me in Bordeaux I was beginning to think that David was not the right man for you anyway and I think you would have come to that conclusion too, sooner or later. I think you've had a lucky escape."

"Do you really think so?" she asked, as he refilled their glasses.

"Absolutely!"

"I suppose if I'm honest it's the fact that it's my sister that hurts more than anything. She's always wanted everything I had."

"Well, they deserve one another."

"That's what I told him as I got up and left." Ellie giggled at the thought.

"Think about it this way. Now that he's the one to break it off, you won't have to."

Ellie was feeling much better. Sam was right, she thought, as she threw back her wine. She would not have been happy living the life David wanted. In a way it *was* a relief.

"This calls for a celebration," Sam exclaimed, leaving the room.

He returned brandishing a bottle of champagne in an ice bucket and two glasses. "Only the best," he said, showing her the label. "Krug!" He poured two glasses and handed her one.

"To my lucky escape!" she said, smiling as she raised her glass to him.

"I'll drink to that." Sam smiled at her.

"Oh Sam, what would I do without you? Here was I thinking it was the end of the world but now I realise it's the start of a new one. You're right, he's an asshole and I'm better off without him."

"You're worth much more than that, Ellie, and never forget it!"

"It's true what you're always saying," she smiled at him. "There *is* a silver lining behind every cloud."

When Marie-Noelle heard that David had called off the wedding because of Sandrine she almost had a fit.

"I don't believe it," she cried, appalled at what Ellie was saying. "I'll kill her!"

"No, Mum, don't be angry. In fact she did me a favour. David was wrong for me – I know that now. Sam helped me to see it."

"Sam?" her mother asked, surprised. "What has Sam got to do with it?"

Ellie blushed. "Well, I called around to him after David gave me the news."

"You called around to Sam?"

"Yes." She felt embarrassed now. "Yeah, well, I didn't really want to face you straight away and Sam and I had a long chat in Bordeaux about my relationship with David. Then tonight, after David's announcement, I found myself on Sam's doorstep without realising it. Sorry."

"That's okay."

"Anyway, he's made me see that I've had a lucky escape. David and I were not right for each other."

"You're certain about that?"

"Absolutely! So no wedding, I'm afraid. I guess you'd better call Bridal Heaven and see if you can get your money back for my wedding dress."

Ellie was feeling pretty rotten about that.

Marie-Noelle was relieved but hated to think of all the work Ellie had put into organising the wedding, now gone to waste. It was a shame but without doubt it was all for the best. Much better that than ending up married to the wrong man.

73

Ronan went down to Blessington the following Sunday to find Fiona in exuberant form. He was amazed at how much Oisín had grown. He was almost three months old now and was smiling and gurgling at everyone he met. He was sleeping through the night now too, Fiona explained, which meant she was much less tired than before. She had also lost weight and Ronan could see that she had a terrific figure. He'd only ever known her pregnant.

As they ate lunch Fiona's phone rang three times and each time she cut it off.

"Simon again, I suppose," her mother commented, rolling her eyes to heaven.

"Who is this Simon fellow?" Ronan wanted to know. "Do you have a new beau?"

Fiona blushed prettily. "Oh, just someone I met in the pub."

"Oh, I see."

"He rings her fifty times a day," Doris exclaimed. "He's obviously very keen."

"Mum, stop!" Fiona cried. "You're embarrassing me."

Her phone rang again. Excusing herself she went outside to take the call.

"Who is this guy? Does she fancy him?" Ronan asked Doris.

"I don't think so. He's just some young fella she met in the Lakeside and he's been calling her ever since. I'd really like her to meet someone nice." She leaned forward to whisper. "I had high hopes that you and Fiona would get together. She's very fond of you, you know."

"Oh, I'm too old for her and besides I have much too much baggage. My divorce is not even through yet. No, Fiona is much better off with a young fellow, like this Simon."

"Is there any chance that you might get back with your wife?"

"Not a chance in hell!" Ronan laughed. "I'm very much enjoying single life at the moment."

He was more than enjoying life. He loved his job and Sam was turning into a good friend. The Higher Cert wine course would be starting the following week and he was really looking forward to it. Life was much better than he could ever have hoped.

Sandrine had been expecting to get an irate call from either Ellie or her mother but after a week . . . nothing. She realised that they were waiting for her to make the first move and she was dreading it. She had no doubt that her mother would give her a bollocking and she was not looking forward to it. She was quite miffed when she heard that Ellie had said she and David deserved each other. She felt sure it wasn't meant in a nice way. Well, tough shit! He's mine now, Ellie!

She had hoped that David would ask her to marry him

but he'd said it was much too soon to think about that. She knew he was feeling guilty about Ellie, which annoyed her. Her bloody younger sister seemed to spoil everything for her. However, she knew that once David got over his guilt everything would be okay. She had dropped hints about them both moving into the Sandymount house together but David had said, "Easy on there, let's take things slowly. Let's get to know each other better first." David could never be accused of being impetuous, she thought to herself as she screwed up the courage to call her mother.

Ellie was sitting watching *Downton Abbey* with her mother when her sister walked defiantly through the door. To Sandrine's annoyance they told her to sit down and be quiet while they watched the final minutes of their favourite programme.

As soon as it finished, Marie-Noelle turned to Sandrine.

"Well, Miss, what do you have to say for yourself?" she demanded archly, glaring at her older daughter. "You took your time coming to face the music."

Sandrine jutted her chin out. "It's not me Ellie should be annoyed at, it's David. *He's* the one who left her." She glared at them both.

"I'm not annoyed at anyone," Ellie said sweetly, smiling.

This completely took the wind out of Sandrine's sails. "You're not?" She was flabbergasted to hear this.

"No. In fact, I'm grateful to you. I've had a lucky escape."

"You wh . . . what?" her sister gabbled, not believing what she was hearing.

"Yes. It made me realise that I didn't love David either."

"You do-do-don't love David?" Sandrine was now blabbering.

"No, not at all. So thank you, dear sister, for your help." This Ellie said with a malicious grin.

"Well, I never!" Sandrine cried, trying to regain her composure. "And here was I thinking I was the guilty one."

"And so you were, Miss!" Marie-Noelle was unable to stay quiet any longer. "What you did to your sister was despicable but then you've always wanted whatever Ellie had. *She* may not be angry with you any more but I certainly won't forget your betrayal."

Sandrine quivered under her mother's gaze and was even more upset when her usually quiet, gentle father cut her dead. She left the house in tears, feeling that somehow she'd lost again.

74

Carl was still reeling from the fallout of the Zita affair and was struggling to get his life back on track. He accepted now that Rachel was not going to have him back. In fact, she seemed to be almost enjoying life without him. He called to take the children out every Sunday and at least now she was talking civilly to him. She was doing it for the sake of the children, of course. Last Sunday she had actually told him that she had become much closer to them, now that she didn't have to run around doing all that 'political wife' stuff. She was even considering letting Paloma go and taking care of them full-time herself. Whatever next!

He, meantime, was having to arse-lick everyone to try and make up for the ground he'd lost over the Zita affair. Not surprisingly, married women in particular were cool to him and they accounted for a large part of the voting public. Yes, he had a lot of humble pie to eat if he was to regain his position in the party. He still attracted the wild young ones who hoped they'd gain some media attention by going out with him. He wasn't interested in them. He could not afford another scandal and besides he knew now that Rachel was the woman he loved.

He logged on daily to the *Advertiser* and the *Australian* and was up to date on what was happening in Adelaide. Zita had been charged and the judge had refused bail. She was now in prison awaiting trial. Carl hoped she'd rot in there. What an evil person she was and he had been unlucky enough to fall foul of her – though not as unlucky as the poor guy she'd murdered! He wondered how she was coping.

Zita was coping admirably well. She'd been allotted free legal aid but she didn't think much of the lawyer who was handling her case. He was an idiot. She knew she didn't stand a chance with him defending her. There was too much evidence stacked against her.

She had become very good friends with another murderer, Martina, on her cell block. She was a woman who had also been abused by men all her life and she and Zita started a relationship. She convinced Zita to keep a diary.

"Who knows, one day you could write a book," Martina had said, so Zita did as she suggested. She wondered what they'd done with the documentary they'd made on Rachel. Probably binned it by now, she guessed.

TV2 had done nothing of the sort. They realised the pulling power the programme would have due to the notoriety of Zita. They were waiting for her trial to start to spring it on an unsuspecting public and an even more unsuspecting Carl. The Director of Programmes had contacted Rachel to see if she was okay with the programme going out. Why not? Rachel thought. It showed her in a good light. It was the truth of what her life had been. Too bad that Carl had seen fit to blow it all apart! This might be her last small revenge against him. Then it would be over.

At last all was set for the opening of the shop in Naas. Sam and Ronan had been working day and night to get it ready and Ellie had been a great help, setting up the computer and getting the stock file up and running. Fiona had rowed in too and they all agreed they couldn't have done it without her help. Ronan had found tenants for his house in Dublin and they wanted to rent it furnished. In a way he was pleased as it removed all the last vestiges of Louise from his life.

Sam had also found tenants for Fiona's old apartment in Dublin and asked her if she could take her furniture away. She offered it to Ronan for his apartment in Naas.

"Oh, I couldn't possibly accept. I'll just buy some new stuff," he assured her.

"Please take it, you'll be doing me a favour," Fiona said firmly. "I have nowhere to store it."

"Well, if you insist," Ronan accepted graciously and arranged to have it brought down that very week. He was finishing work in Raheny on Saturday in order to set up the Naas shop with Sam.

He moved into the Naas apartment the following Monday and Rachel came down to help him. He introduced her to Fiona who had also offered to help. The two women hit it off instantly.

"I've heard a lot about you and Oisín," Rachel told her. "I hear he's real cute."

"I think so, but then I'm prejudiced," Fiona laughed. "Ronan's told me a lot about you too. He's very fond of you."

"I love him. He's a great friend."

Fiona nodded in agreement as they both looked fondly at the object of their conversation who was unaware that he was being discussed.

"Hey, Ronan!" Rachel called. "I think you should throw a house-warming party."

"I don't have time to organise a party," Ronan said, laughing.

"Don't worry, we'll do it all, won't we, Fiona?" Rachel looked to the younger girl for confirmation.

"Oh, yes! That's a brilliant idea!" Fiona exclaimed, nodding her head.

"Okay, okay," Ronan laughed, feeling outnumbered. "I'll pay for it but don't expect anything more from me."

"Fine, just give us a guest list and we'll take care of the rest."

The two women high-fived each other, excited at the prospect. They planned it for the following Sunday afternoon.

Things were not going as Sandrine had planned. She couldn't believe her ears when she heard that Ellie was seemingly having a ball. She'd expected to find her moping because she'd lost David.

"She's really enjoying herself," Marie-Noelle had reported with satisfaction. "Sam has taken her under his wing and is introducing her to all his friends, who love her, naturally. She's having a great time."

"She didn't exactly waste any time, did she?" was Sandrine's bitter retort to this news.

She recounted this later to David and had expected him to be as furious as she was that Ellie had so blithely gone from being his fiancée to being flavour of the month on the Dublin social scene. Instead, he was visibly upset and hardly said a word all night.

When she mentioned moving in with him again, he snapped at her.

Seeing that she was hurt, he apologised. "I'm sorry, Sandrine, but I'm just upset about Ellie. I obviously didn't mean very much to her at all. Let's not talk of moving in together for the moment. I just need a little space right now."

She said nothing but she was annoyed with him. She had hoped to be out of her poky flat by now and happily cohabitating with him. It looked like it wasn't going to happen any time soon. David could be very stubborn when he wanted to be.

75

Rachel was first to arrive in Naas the Sunday of the party, laden down with boxes. Carl had taken Jacob and Becky for the day. She got down to business decorating the apartment, placing candles on every available surface. Next she set the table with the red tablecloth and napkins that she'd brought and placed the beautiful flower arrangements she'd made on it. With the silver and crystal that she'd taken from home, it all looked very festive. She had brought plates of perfect little *amuse-bouches* and tiny canapés that looked almost too good to eat. She also produced some marvellous salads and a whole baked salmon from a cooler box she'd brought with her.

Fiona arrived to help out shortly after with Oisín in tow. He gurgled with delight when he saw Ronan and held out his chubby little arms to him. Ronan picked him up and threw him up in the air, making the baby peal with laughter. The two women looked on, smiling.

Fiona then unloaded numerous Tupperware boxes stuffed with sausage rolls, Cornish pasties and quiches that Doris had baked for the party. They could be reheated in the oven later, and there was also a coffee cake and chocolate brownies.

Conor's wife, Betty, had said they would bring something as well. There would be more than enough to go round.

Ronan couldn't believe his eyes when he finally came up from the shop to get ready for the party. He thanked them both profusely as they stood grinning, happy that they could do this for him.

"It's all Rachel's doing," Fiona insisted. "She did most of it."

"You really have a gift for this sort of thing," Ronan observed, smiling at Rachel while admiring how lovely the apartment looked.

"I love doing it," she told him, happy that he was pleased.

"Have you ever thought of doing it professionally?" he asked her. "I'm sure there are people who would appreciate having someone like you to take the hassle out of their parties."

"I have, actually. It's something I think I'd really enjoy."

She was looking radiant, Ronan thought. It was good to see her back to her bubbly self.

"Well, I think you should look into it seriously. With all your contacts and your flair, I'm sure you'd be a huge success."

She blushed, embarrassed by his words, and Fiona, looking on, wondered if perhaps Rachel wasn't a little in love with Ronan. Maybe Ronan was in love with her, without realising it. She hoped not!

While Fiona fed Oisín, Rachel went to change and when she came from the bathroom, looking beautiful in a slinky red silk dress and very high black-patent Louboutin shoes, Fiona was more than a little envious. She saw the admiration in Ronan's eyes and felt a pang of jealousy. She couldn't blame Ronan one bit if he was in love with Rachel. How on earth did she keep that figure when she'd had two children? Fiona patted her own tummy bulge, determined to start a diet the following day.

The champagne was chilling and all was ready when the first guests, his brother Conor and Betty, arrived. She was carrying a big saucepan of chicken curry and Conor one of rice. Doris arrived next, then Ronan's friend Jim and his wife, Sheila, and lastly came Sam with Ellie. She immediately made a beeline for the baby, asking Fiona if she could take him in her arms. He was so cute that she was reluctant to give him back to Fiona when she said it was time for his nap.

It was a wonderful party and everyone was delighted to see Ronan in such high spirits. The party lasted well into the evening when everyone enjoyed a bowl of Betty's delicious curry.

"That was wonderful!" Fiona, who was the last to leave, laughed as she helped Ronan clear away. "I really like your friends."

"Yeah, they're a great bunch," he agreed.

When they'd finished, he helped her on with her jacket, kissing her on the cheek before she left. She knew she was falling for him but she couldn't stop herself. What a mess!

The shop in Naas opened the following week and was an instant success. Sam was delighted and Ronan was in his element. There seemed to be no shortage of money in this wealthy town and he quickly established a loyal clientele. He got to know his customers and their preferences and they came to appreciate and trust his advice. He was happier than he'd ever been. Keith, who was continuing on to the Higher Cert course, moved from the Malahide shop and worked full-time along with Ronan. He took on two students to help out part-time evenings and weekends. It was all going very smoothly.

76

The second Monday in October, Fiona took over in the shop while Ronan and Keith left for Clontarf and the first night of the Higher Cert course.

Sam hadn't been joking! It was way more difficult than the Lower Cert course but all of them were committed to learning more about wine and were eager students. It was also a chance to meet up together again.

Rachel had invited Ronan to stay over on Monday nights but, as they were both in delicate marital negotiations prior to their divorces, he didn't think it was appropriate. Instead he stayed with Sam. They were becoming great friends, as were Ellie and Rachel.

Occasionally the four of them met up for a meal in a restaurant or in Rachel's house. That was better than any restaurant, they all agreed! She had started her party-planning business and was slowly but surely getting it off the ground. She'd let Paloma go and was taking care of the children herself with the help of Tiffany, the new baby-sitter, who was turning into a treasure. She was a Trinity student who lived two doors away and she had a great way with the children. They adored her and so everyone was happy.

David had found out very quickly that Sandrine was not the girl he'd thought her to be. To his dismay, she kept pushing for him to make a commitment. After the mess with Ellie, he was very loath to rush things. Sandrine wanted to move in with him almost immediately and it had taken all of his talents to avoid this. When she started insisting that he take back Ellie's engagement ring – well, that was a step too far. He felt quite guilty about Ellie. All the planning she'd done for the wedding – she'd even bought her wedding dress! He felt quite ashamed of how he'd treated her and was more than happy for her to keep his ring. She could sell it or do whatever she wanted with it.

What Sandrine didn't know was that Ellie had offered to give the engagement ring back to David but that he had refused to take it. When she did find out, she was furious. She berated David loudly about it but he wouldn't budge.

"No, I gave it to Ellie and I'm not going to take it back," he insisted angrily, to her disappointment.

She would have loved that ring.

Shortly after that, David had told her he couldn't live with himself and that she was a daily reminder of what he'd done. What a cop-out!

Sandrine was disgusted. All in all, David had turned out to be a big disappointment. She'd been so jealous of Ellie when she'd arrived home with him and had been green with envy when they'd got engaged. Well, that had been misplaced because she knew now that David was not at all what he had seemed to be.

So now she was alone once more while Ellie got everything she wanted, as usual.

To Sandrine's amazement Ellie had forgiven her and had even tried to pour oil on the troubled waters between her and her parents. They at least spoke to her now, thanks to Ellie's insistence, but it was an uneasy relationship. She knew that Marie-Noelle would never forgive her betrayal.

Fiona loved working with Ronan and, more than that, she was now deeply in love with him. She knew it was hopeless. He was seeing Rachel regularly and she often heard him on the phone with her, laughing, his voice warm. She guessed that they were waiting for their respective divorces to come through before they went public with their relationship. She knew she shouldn't complain. She was lucky – she had Oisín, who was the light of her life. He was such a happy baby and becoming more of a little personality every week. He brought her great joy. No one had said life would be perfect, she sighed. She guessed she was happier than most.

Ellie was happy and enjoying her new single status. Every day she thanked her lucky stars for her 'lucky escape'. She realised now that she had been so focused on the wedding that she hadn't honestly thought much further than that. That was stupid and she'd never think like that again. She had thought she was mature enough to decide with whom she should spend the rest of her life but it was patently obvious to her now that she wasn't. She knew now that there was much more to marriage than a fabulous wedding. However, that was all a long way off in her future and she was happy living in the moment, enjoying the now.

She loved her job and the new circle of friends she'd met through Sam. Despite their age difference, she and Rachel had become very close. Yes, life was good!

77

Rachel was planning to head off to her parents' house in Marbella with the kids, despite Carl's objections. He'd hoped that they might all spend Christmas together. She couldn't risk that. Christmas was such an emotional time and she was afraid that she would succumb and be sucked back into Carl's web. Her parents were on an extended tour of Australia so she had invited Ellie, Sam and Ronan to join her at their villa.

Ellie delightedly agreed to go as her mother and father were travelling to Bordeaux to stay with Josette, and she did not fancy Christmas alone with Sandrine.

Ronan would have liked to go but the shop would be much too busy over the Christmas and New Year period for him to take time off. Likewise Sam, who said he couldn't possibly leave the business at this, the busiest time of the year.

Rachel was dreading this Christmas, her first one without Carl. How would she survive it?

The Monday before Christmas was the final night of the course and the night of the Higher Cert exam. They all agreed that the course was much more difficult than the first one and the exam had been more difficult too but they were all reasonably sure that they'd passed.

Sam held a party in his house afterwards to celebrate. Ellie acted as hostess and when Rachel suggested to Sam that they were maybe more than just friends, he'd laughed.

"Don't be daft! Ellie's the marrying kind and I most definitely am not, but she's a bloody great PA. I don't know how I ever survived without her."

"What will you do for Christmas Day?" she asked Ronan.

"Probably sleep," he replied, to much laughter. He wasn't joking. Signs were that he would be run off his feet by Christmas Day.

Doris had invited him for Christmas dinner but, as she already had all her family there, he felt she had enough on her plate. He decided that he'd probably visit there on Christmas morning with the presents and then go on for dinner with his brother Conor and his family. That was if he didn't decide to stay in bed all day!

The party was a blast and Ronan was sad to say goodbye to them all.

"We'll see you in the New Year," Ellie said as she kissed him.

"Let's hope it's a better one than this year has been," he replied.

"It can't be any worse!" Rachel and Ellie cried in unison.

"You've all survived, haven't you? And the future is looking very bright!"

They had to agree with him.

"As I always say . . . behind –"

"– every cloud there's a silver lining!" the others chorused together, laughing.

It was the best Christmas Ellie had ever had. Lying by the pool on Christmas Day sipping Pina Coladas was as close to heaven as she thought she'd ever get.

Rachel was amazed to see how good Ellie was with the children. They adored her and were constantly calling to her to come and play with them, which she did without complaint.

Having Ellie around helped ease some of the pain of being without Carl. Rachel tried not to think about him but it wasn't easy. He rang twice a day, on the pretext of talking to the kids but she knew that he was hurting too, remembering past Christmases.

They spent their days in the sun, lying by the pool chatting and playing with the children. Sometimes they took Becky and Jacob to the beach which they loved. They ate simply and got a baby-sitter for the kids on the evenings they went out to eat.

On their last night Ellie invited Rachel for dinner in their favourite restaurant. They both agreed that it had been a wonderful holiday and they were sad to be leaving. She and Rachel had become very close – BFFs, Ellie said. Seeing Rachel's puzzled look she then had to explain that it meant 'Best Friends Forever'.

Ellie ordered a bottle of champagne and Rachel toasted her. "To my BFF!" she said, laughing.

Ellie raised her glass, smiling. "AAF!"

"Now what does that mean?" Rachel asked frowning, thinking that she was definitely getting old.

"Always And Forever," Ellie explained laughing.

They both enjoyed the superb food. Then, as the waiter placed their desserts in front of them, Ellie had a feeling that someone was staring at her. Looking around she saw that it was a young man who had just arrived at another table with a big group of friends. His eyes were a very vibrant blue and, as she met his glance, he held her in his intense gaze. Throughout the rest of the meal she was aware of him and, every time she looked over, he was staring at her. His friends were laughing and talking loudly in Spanish but he didn't seem to be taking part in the conversation. She felt her stomach flutter as she caught his gaze once more. He was very good-looking with dark curly hair and a square jaw-line but it was his eyes that were mesmerising. She felt as if they were the only two people in the room. *Va-va-voom!*

Rachel noticed her discomfiture and looked around to see what was causing it.

"Oh, goodness, he's very handsome and he seems interested in you," she said, grinning at Ellie who was blushing madly.

"Yeah, well, what's the point? I'm leaving tomorrow."

Soon afterwards, Rachel got up to ask for a taxi.

Ellie stood up and slipped on her jacket. She looked over at the young man and saw a distraught look on his face. Next moment he was standing beside her. As she gazed at him, her heart almost stopping, he said something to her in Spanish.

She shook her head. "Sorry, I don't speak Spanish," she said breathlessly.

"Oh my God, you're Irish!" he exclaimed, his blue eyes lighting up.

From his accent she guessed that he was English.

"I'm Robin," he said. "Can't you stay a little longer?"

"Ellie, our taxi's here!" Rachel called, beckoning to her.

"Sorry, I have to go," Ellie said.

"So you're Ellie. I have to meet you again. Please?"

She felt like she was drowning in those blue eyes as she sadly shook her head.

"Sorry, I have to go," she told him, leaving quickly.

She couldn't get him out of her mind all that night and hardly slept at all. Looking out of the plane as it took off from Malaga the next day, she wondered where he was now and what he was doing. She closed her eyes and thought about those intense blue eyes that seemed to see into her soul. She sighed. If only she'd had one more day in Spain. Who knows what would have happened? Life was cruel!

78

David had given women a wide berth for a few months after his encounter with Sandrine. No matter what he said or did, Ellie was adamant that she would not return to him. Then, just when he finally accepted that he would not be able to win her back, he discovered online-dating. It was wonderful. You could have a long online courtship with a girl and then when you met her, if you didn't like her, you could dump her. Definitely the way to go!

Carl, meanwhile, was brooding on *his* situation. He had been slowly making up lost ground in his career but his life was empty. The only joy in his life was seeing his kids every Sunday. He'd lain very low where women were concerned after getting his fingers burned with Zita. You couldn't be too careful! He wondered if he was getting paranoid.

What bothered him most was that Rachel seemed to be blooming without him. She was looking more beautiful than ever and seemed to have found an inner contentment that eluded him. Her party-plan business was doing very well, he'd heard. She was a remarkable woman and he knew he'd been a stupid idiot to lose her. He realised that he still loved her but much good that would do him. Of course she was joined at the hip to that bloody wine crowd. Damn them! That was what had started all his problems in the first place. They had all seemingly passed their Higher Cert exam and Rachel was talking of going on to study for her Diploma of Wine. Whatever next? She was full of surprises.

He read in the *Australian* that Zita's case was going to trial the following week. He hoped that there would be no fallout for him from it. The media were like vultures. They picked up on every titbit of gossip they could find. He'd keep his fingers crossed.

Now he should go for a run but he hadn't got the energy. He had gained over a stone since Rachel had kicked him out. Comfort eating and drinking! He really would have to do something about it. All of his clothes were tight. It depressed him. Going to the fridge he took out the two doughnuts and tucked in.

Rachel had worked hard to stay positive since that awful time when her whole world had been blown apart. It had been very difficult for her but, thanks to the support she'd received from her wine group, she was doing fine, all things considered.

Jacob and Becky were fantastic and seemed not to have suffered too much as a result of the break-up. The fact that she spent much more time with them these days meant she had become much more involved with them on a day-to-day basis. Her party-plan business had taken off in leaps and bounds. She was now *the* 'in' party-planner and she was enjoying it enormously.

She had also decided to pursue her wine studies and study along with Ronan and Ellie for her diploma. Sam had let them all know that it would be a big leap forward and that they would have to put in quite a few hours' study every week but she loved it and this knowledge of wine was very useful for her party business.

She still wasn't able to meet Carl without her stomach clenching, but time is a great healer and it was getting easier. Now when he called for the children on a Sunday she could be quite civil, even friendly with him. He looked wretched and uncared for and it upset her to see him like that. After all, she couldn't just erase all the happy years they'd had together as easily as that. She still cared for him despite everything he'd done. His swagger was gone now and he was quite humble. She much preferred him like this. Gone was the arrogant, cocky man she'd been married to.

Once, he had started to suggest that they might try and give it another shot but she didn't think that was an option. She would never go back to being a political wife. She wondered if he knew that Zita's trial was due to start the next week. She'd been Googling the *Australian*. Well, *she* wasn't about to tell him. Nor did she tell him that TV2 had been on to her to say they were going to run the documentary Zita had done on her the following Sunday. She couldn't have stopped them anyway so she told them it was fine with her.

The newspapers were full of the Zita story the following weekend and the whole story was dragged up once more. She wondered how Carl felt seeing his stupidity splashed all over the headlines again. He wasn't able to take the children on Sunday so she and Ronan took them to the zoo.

After they were fed and safely in bed, she and Ronan sat down to some wine and cheese before watching the programme. She'd put the answering machine on and turned off her mobile so the outside world could stay that way.

As the titles rolled she found herself clenching her fists and Ronan reached over and took her hand in his.

"It will be fine," he reassured her. "It's all in the past now."

At the start of the programme a presenter explained the circumstances and how Zita Williams, who had made the programme, would be standing trial for murder, in a couple of hours in Adelaide, Australia. It was meaty stuff and Ronan could feel the tension in Rachel's body.

The presenter continued: "*It was an anonymous blog that Miss Williams was putting online which led to her discovery as the suspect in the gruesome murder, fifteen years previously. This blog was aimed at discrediting the TD for Dublin North East, Mr Carl Dunne.*"

Rachel sucked in her breath and wondered if Carl was watching. She heard the phone ringing and thought it might be him.

"*Since this programme was made, Mr Dunne and his wife Rachel have separated. However, we feel that at this time of Miss Williams' trial it will be of interest to our viewers.*" She concluded by saying that the station had a reporter covering the trial in Adelaide and would be reporting each day's events there in their news bulletins.

Rachel sat mesmerised, watching herself on screen, and it seemed like a lifetime ago. She remembered how excited she'd been, not realising that Zita, who was smiling and friendly with her, was cheating on her with her husband. She cringed when she saw the footage of Carl with herself

429

and the children playing 'happy families'. At that moment she hated him for ruining it all. When the programme finally ended, she felt drained. It was then she started to weep, softly at first and then it became a torrent. Ronan held her and rocked her, stroking her hair all the while. When she'd finally finished she was like a rag-doll and he helped her up the stairs to her bedroom. Fully clothed, she slipped between the sheets.

"Stay with me for a while, Ronan," she whispered.

He lay down beside her on top of the covers. Stroking her face and brushing away her tears, he thought that she'd never looked more beautiful. She was deeply upset and in need of comfort and he knew that she would have made love to him if he had made a move. But he would never take advantage of her in her vulnerable state. Besides, it would surely change their relationship and he valued that too much.

So he lay beside her and stroked her silky hair until he heard her steady breathing and knew she was asleep. Then he settled down on her sofa for the night, in case she would need him again.

Ellie watched the programme on Rachel in Sam's house and she'd cried, seeing what a great wife Rachel had been. She'd offered to be with Rachel for the screening but Ronan was going to be there so she wouldn't be alone. During the commercial break, they'd tried calling her but couldn't reach her, so Sam called Ronan. Ronan had been very quiet but had assured him that Rachel was okay.

"She can't talk to you right now but don't worry. I'll stay with her, if she wants me to," he'd said.

"Well, give her our love and, if we can do anything, anything at all, tell her we're here for her."

"She knows that, Sam, thanks. I'll take care of her."

Sam and Ellie were relieved that she wasn't alone.

Zita was found guilty and sentenced to life imprisonment. Luckily for her there was no death penalty in Australia. The trial had been on the news every single night. Maybe now the furore would die down. Next week it would be old news.

Since coming home from Marbella, Ellie hadn't been able to get the young Englishman in Spain out of her mind. She had little interest in going out to parties although she was invited to many. She knew this was crazy but he had somehow got under her skin. Now it was Valentine's night and Ellie couldn't decide whether to stay in and watch *Mama Mia* again, or go to the party that one of Sam's friends had invited her to. In the end Sam pressurised her to go as it was being held in the local rugby club and was close enough to walk to. He had said he'd call for her and they would walk together.

She had just entered the packed hall and was calling out greetings to all the people she knew when she saw him. She gasped. Was it possible? Was that really Robin standing just twenty feet away from her? She'd given up all hope of ever meeting him again and for a moment she wondered if she'd conjured him up in her imagination. But no, he was here, talking to some friends, and she stood transfixed, unable to tear her eyes away. He must have felt her gaze on him because he looked up and those intense blue eyes that she remembered so well opened wide in shock. He said something to his friends who all looked towards her and then, within seconds, he was by her side.

"Ellie!" he said breathlessly, taking her hand.

"Robin!" she whispered, gazing into his eyes.

"You two know each other?" Sam asked, amazed.

They didn't answer. They hadn't even heard him as Robin took her hand and led her away.

She soon discovered that he'd been as smitten with her as she'd been with him and that he'd thought of her constantly too. He told her that he was the manager of a big British wine chain which had opened in Ireland the previous year. He knew Sam well and was surprised to hear that she was working for him. The coincidence of finding each other again seemed incredible and was fate, he assured her. As he took her on to the dance floor for a slow number and pulled her close, Ellie felt an excitement that she'd never felt before. *Va-va-voom!*

"I believe in love at first sight, do you?" he whispered in her ear.

"I think I do now," she whispered back.

It certainly felt like it.

"What did you say to your friends when you first saw me tonight?" she asked, curious.

"I told them that the angel who had just walked in was the girl I was going to marry," he admitted shyly.

"Oh, Robin," she said, kissing him right there on the dance floor.

"Well, I never!" was Sam's reaction as he watched them.

79

Conor rang Ronan with some amazing news the following week.

"Ronan, you won't believe this. I met a guy I play golf with who is friendly with Louise's new bloke and he told me that their relationship is going down the Swanee." Conor's voice was gleeful. "Seemingly, even though he's fabulously wealthy, he'd like to stay that way and Louise is making serious inroads into his fortune. My friend says that they are constantly fighting, even in public. What do you think of that?" He could barely conceal his merriment.

"Well, she's made her bed," Ronan said sadly. "We're no longer a couple so it's nothing to do with me." He didn't wish Louise any ill-will. She was just a selfish, spoilt woman.

A couple of days later Louise rang him.

"Hi, Ronan, how are you?" Her voice was sugary sweet. "I've been thinking a lot about you lately. I'd really like to see you again. I think maybe we've made a mistake, separating so quickly like that."

433

"No, Louise, and I didn't make any mistake. I really don't want to see you again."

"You bastard!" she yelled into the phone.

Ronan hung up. He didn't want to hear any more.

It was Becky who started it. She had started waking in the night and calling for her daddy. Rachel was worried. The following Sunday Carl took the kids to the zoo even though it was a fiercely cold day. How ironic that he was taking them there regularly now whereas he had always refused to go before.

"I want Daddy to come in for tea," Becky had cried as Carl dropped them off. "Please, Mummy? He's awfully cold from the zoo." She grabbed Carl's hand and tried to pull him into the house.

"Yes, Mummy, that would be nice," Jacob said solemnly, his big brown eyes looking at her hopefully.

"Did you put them up to this?" Rachel demanded, looking accusingly at Carl.

"I swear, Rach, I didn't say a word."

She believed him.

She looked at her children's pleading eyes and gave in. She realised he must have been frozen, dragging around the zoo on such a freezing cold day.

"Okay, come in and warm up, just this once."

"Thank you, Rach." He looked at her gratefully.

Of course, it wasn't 'just this once'. The children insisted that he come in every Sunday evening and it had very quickly become a ritual. She had to admit it was very pleasant, all four of them together, chatting and laughing just like – she was afraid to say it – any normal family.

Then the children started asking when was Daddy

coming back? It was hard, trying to explain to them that he wasn't coming back. That was when Becky started having nightmares.

Rachel had thought that the separation had not affected the children but now she saw that she was wrong. They were suffering, just as she and Carl were suffering. One Sunday evening, she decided to share her fears with Carl.

She set up a DVD for the kids to watch and joined Carl in the den.

"I'm very worried about Becky," she told him. "I think this whole business is affecting her badly."

"Yes, it is. I've noticed that she's got much more introverted lately and Jacob has changed too. He's not the happy little boy he once was."

"What can we do about it?" she asked, a worried frown creasing her brow.

"We could be happy again, Rachel, I know we could, if you would give me another chance." He moved over from his chair on to the sofa where she was sitting, his face earnest as he continued. "I know I screwed up, Rach, but I'm a different man now. I swear to you. I realise now just how much I love you and what I've lost."

He started to cry then and Rachel had to steel herself not to reach out to him.

"Please, Rach, please, let's try again. I promise you I'll never do anything to hurt you again," he said, through his tears. "I've learnt my lesson, believe me. For the sake of the children, if not for me, please let's give it a try."

She sighed as she took his hand. "I don't know, Carl. I could never go back to that life – being a politician's wife, never seeing you, living in the public eye all the time. I hated it." She shook her head.

He took a deep breath. "Rach, I'll give up politics if that's what it takes to get you back."

She looked into his eyes and saw that he meant it.

"You'd give up politics?"

"Yes! I'll resign tomorrow if I could have you and the kids back."

She couldn't believe what she was hearing. "But what would you do?"

"Well, I have enough money never to have to work again but maybe we could do something together." His eyes brightened as he spoke. "Why not start an online party-planning business, like Kate Middleton's family. There's an opening for that here in Ireland."

She looked at him amazed. The idea was exciting. "Are you really serious about resigning?"

"I swear. You do still love me, Rach, don't you?" He took her hands in his, fear in his eyes as he waited for her reply.

"Yes, Carl, I still love you," she said, in a small voice, and then she was in his arms. She wanted desperately for him to take her to bed and make love to her but she knew they had to take things slowly. It would not be easy to put the past behind her but she knew she had to give it a try, if only for the children's sake.

"Why don't we go away together next weekend?" he suggested, "and see how it goes?"

"Do you want to do that?"

"Oh, darling, I'd love that more than anything. And I meant what I said. I'll resign my seat, if that's what it takes to get you back."

Becky and Jacob came in just then, whooping as they saw their parents kiss and jumping on them for a group hug. Rachel smiled at Carl over the little blonde heads, hopeful that everything was going to work out alright. One could only wait and see and hope for the best.

Ronan was happy for Rachel when he heard that they were thinking of getting back together again. He'd always known that she'd never stopped loving Carl. He was happy now that he hadn't made love to her that night when she was so distraught. What a mistake that would have been! She'd have regretted it and it probably would have ruined their friendship.

Business had quietened down in the shop after the New Year but they were still doing a steady business. He and Fiona were a great team and he had grown more and more fond of her as the weeks passed. She now worked every weeknight and he found himself with a spring in his step as he waited for her to come on duty.

He adored Oisín, who had inherited his mother's sunny personality and, like her, was always smiling. Most Sundays he took them both out for the day, either up the Wicklow Mountains or to Brittas Bay if the weather was fine.

The weather was particularly horrendous one night as he and Fiona were closing up the shop. Thunder crashed and as the lightning flashed, Ronan could see that Fiona had gone terribly pale and was shaking.

"I'm terrified of lightning," she said, moving closer to him as the rain lashed against the windows.

"Well, you can't go anywhere in that storm," Ronan said as he locked the door and switched off the lights. "Come on upstairs and wait it out."

Gratefully, she followed him and, just as they got into his apartment, the lights went out and they were plunged into darkness.

"Damn!" he said and fumbled for the torch he kept on top of the bookshelf. Grateful now for the candles that Rachel had brought for his party, he moved around lighting them, one after the other.

Fiona was huddled on the sofa, her arms wrapped around her body. He poured each of them a whiskey and sat down beside her. She took hers in her shaking hands and took a big slug, almost spilling it all as another crash of thunder echoed around the room.

"Oh my God!" she cried, edging closer to him.

He put his arm around her and she snuggled into his body. It felt good. Before he knew what was happening, he was kissing her and to his surprise, she was kissing him back. As the storm raged, unabated, they sat in the candlelight, holding each other.

"I don't know how this happened," Ronan told her, his voice gentle. He took her face in his hands.

"Oh, Ronan, you ninny! Don't you know I've been waiting for it to happen? I've loved you for ages," she admitted, shyly.

Ronan was thunderstruck. She was right, he was a ninny not to have seen that or to realise that he had fallen in love with her too.

"Could you ring your mother and say that the storm is too bad for you to travel home tonight and that you have to stay here?"

"I already did. When you went to the loo a while ago," she laughed.

"Oh, you seductress!" he cried, pulling her down on the sofa.

She quieted him with her lips. He was lost!

80

Four Months Later

Rachel was busy preparing for her Midsummer's Eve party but this was a very much smaller affair than the one the previous year. She had invited only eighteen people, but they were eighteen good friends. Charlotte was coming from Italy with her new boyfriend and Naomi would also be there with her husband, all the way from New York. Carl's two brothers and their wives would be there along with his old friends, Mark and Steve and their partners, She had also invited her wine friends and was looking forward to meeting them all again. In comparison to last year's party it was small fry, but much more select, as she'd said laughingly to Ellie.

So much had happened to them all in the past twelve months. "If you put it in a book, nobody would believe it," she'd remarked to Ronan, when she'd called to invite him to the party (no specially printed invitations this time), and it was true!

Firstly, there had been the awful Zita affair. Rachel still shuddered every time she thought of that woman and the narrow escape they'd had. She had tried very hard to put

439

it all behind her but it hadn't been easy. However, time is a great healer and she could now go days at a time without even thinking of the whole awful episode. It had certainly changed their lives and now it looked as though it was for the better. As her friends were so fond of saying, "Behind every cloud, there's a silver lining" and it appeared that this was the case. She and Carl were in a much better place now than they had been when the whole Zita thing had imploded their lives.

Carl had been true to his word. He'd resigned from the Dáil, as he'd promised, which was something she still found hard to believe. He had loved politics so much that, when he gave them up for her, she realised that he did truly love her. They were closer now than they had ever been and the children were in a much happier, healthier environment than before.

Working together had helped. They had started the online party-planning company Carl had envisaged and to everyone's surprise, it was taking off at a great rate. That was mainly thanks to Carl's entrepreneurial skills. He was a brilliant marketing man and, as always, everything he touched seemed to turn to gold. It was not easy learning to trust him again and it was an ongoing work-in-progress but she felt she was getting there. He did seem to have changed and was much more relaxed and happy than before. Rachel felt hopeful for the future.

Carl was a terrific father and spent lots of time with Becky and Jacob who were growing up fast. So when Carl suggested having another baby, Rachel was not altogether against the idea. She was really quite excited about the possibility and hoped it would happen soon as neither of them was getting any younger.

She and Ellie had kept up their friendship and tried to

meet up at least once a week, if only for a coffee. Ellie could talk of little else but Robin.

Ellie was still working for Sam although Robin had tried to entice her away to work for him. But Ellie and Sam were still bosom buddies and she stayed loyal to him. She and Robin had moved in together and were head over heels in love. Robin had hinted at marriage but Ellie wanted to take it slowly. She hadn't forgotten how close she'd come to marrying the wrong man before. This time she wanted to be absolutely sure and was enjoying living with Robin and getting to know him.

She'd never have believed it possible to be so happy. Robin was a wonderful partner and lover and was always touching and caressing her, unable to be away from her for a moment. She still talked of her 'lucky escape' but now she could laugh about it. It gave her some satisfaction to know that things hadn't worked out for David and Sandrine although she felt no bitterness towards David. Her relationship with her sister was still very strained and Sandrine was more jealous of her than ever after she'd been introduced to Robin.

Sam had a new girlfriend, a glamorous TV presenter, but it didn't look like it was going anywhere. Everyone had thought that Sam and Ellie might have ended up together but that was before Robin appeared on the scene. It seemed that Sam would be another George Clooney – a perennial bachelor! They were all looking forward to the Diploma Course which was due to start in September. By all accounts it was very rigorous and Rachel hoped she'd find the time for all that study but Carl assured her that he'd take over the business to allow her to do it.

Ronan and she still had a very close bond. They'd been a great support to each other through the troubled times and neither of them would ever forget it. They still kept in touch regularly but they were both busy with their new careers and both had moved on in their personal lives too. She was very happy that he'd found love with Fiona. Rachel hadn't been at all surprised when he'd told her. She'd known that Fiona was in love with him but like all men, Ronan had been a bit slow on the uptake. He was mad about Oisín who was now a darling bundle of energy, walking already, although he wasn't quite a year old. Becky and Jacob adored him. Fiona was having a big party for his first birthday and Rachel suspected that there might be another announcement made at that time. She hoped so. Ronan deserved to be happy. He was such a wonderful guy.

As she waited for the first of her friends to arrive, she surveyed the beautifully set table. Just then Carl came up behind her and wrapped his arms around her waist. She leaned back into him.

"What a difference this is from last year," he said, nuzzling her neck. "But you know something? I like this much better."

"Me too," she agreed, her voice gentle.

"I guess it took all that heartache for us to realise what really matters. Family and friends," he remarked, turning her around in his arms.

"I guess behind every cloud, there *is* a silver lining," she said softly, as she reached up to kiss him.

If you enjoyed
Behind Every Cloud by Pauline Lawless
why not try
A Year Like No Other also published
by Poolbeg?
Here's a sneak preview of Chapter One

A Year Like No Other

Pauline Lawless

POOLBEG

1

"Paris? You can't be serious!" Felicity cried, the shock registering on her face. "Please tell me you're joking, Maxwell?" Her voice wobbled as her eyes searched her husband's.

"I'm afraid not, dear," he replied gently, looking away uncomfortably. "It's Paris, I'm afraid – for a year." He shifted from foot to foot, not knowing what to say to make it more acceptable. He wondered if he were tall, dark and muscular instead of small, blond and rotund – cuddly, his daughters called him – might he be able to handle this situation better. He was easy-going and jovial and hated confrontations and rows.

"Oh God, not Paris," Felicity continued, her plummy well-modulated voice rising uncharacteristically. "You know I detest France. Nobody speaks English there and the French are so rude. Do we *have* to go?"

Max sighed, at a loss for words to calm her.

"Well, I suppose you could stay here in London and I could commute every weekend," he suggested hopefully, thinking of what bliss it would be to have a Felicity-free working week.

"Oh, no, that's out of the question," she replied, panic flitting across her face. "You couldn't possibly manage without me."

The reality was that he could manage perfectly well without her but he knew Felicity would never manage without him to take care of her.

Max sighed again as he watched her pacing up and down, her pencil-thin body taut with anxiety as she struggled to cope with the news. Felicity, always a lady, in her cashmere twinset and pearls with not a hair out of place, was doing her best to retain her composure but failing miserably.

In fairness, the fact that he was being sent to Paris had come as a complete surprise to him too. He'd been hotly tipped to be taking over in either Dubai or Hong Kong, so when the president of the bank informed him that he'd be joining the new finance group in Paris, it had come as quite a shock. It was a fantastic opportunity for him and a great step up in the banking hierarchy and he was already very excited at the prospect. He'd known, of course, that Felicity would be less than happy with the news and so her reaction to it came as no surprise.

"How can I possibly face my friends? They're all madly jealous at the prospect of my moving to Dubai or Hong Kong and now I have to tell them that I'm just popping across the Channel," she sniffed.

"Seriously, dear," Max tried another strike for his freedom, "I would of course find it very difficult to cope without you but I couldn't bear for you to be unhappy. Perhaps the best solution is for you to stay here in London and I'll come home at weekends. What do you think?"

"No, I wouldn't hear of it," she reiterated. "I've never shirked from doing my wifely duty, so if I have to come to Paris with you, I will. But I really don't know how I'll survive there," she shuddered, clasping her arms even tighter around her flat bosom.

Max sighed. "This is a big promotion for me, Felicity," he explained gently, putting his arms around her. "If I make a success of this – then who knows – the sky's the limit."

"I need a drink," she said, breaking away and going to the cocktail cabinet where she poured herself a gin and tonic. She sat down carefully in the leather armchair, back ramrod straight and legs crossed in a ladylike manner as she took a very unladylike gulp from her glass.

"What will I do for friends in Paris? At least I would have known Gloria in Dubai and Diane and Myrtle in Hong Kong," she said, dangerously close to tears. "And of course, everyone speaks English there."

"Well, you'll have the other wives in Paris. There are four others on this project with me and no doubt they'll be bringing their wives too, so you'll surely make friends with them."

"Are any of them English?" she asked hopefully.

"I'm afraid not." He moved over to pour himself a large whisky, throwing his eyes up to heaven. He eased himself into his favourite armchair, willing this conversation to be over.

Felicity was English to her very backbone, he thought. She hated foreigners with a vengeance and truly believed that every other country was uncivilised. She wore her Englishness like a mantle and without it she was lost. Once out of England, she was out of her comfort zone. Would she survive in France? He sighed. One thing he knew, Felicity or not he was heading to Paris. This job was too good to pass up. If she insisted on coming with him, then she would just have to adapt.

He loved his wife dearly but she was a product of her very conservative, upper-class background. She'd barely had any contact with her parents as a child and had been packed off to boarding school at eight. Her mother, Georgina, was a veritable dragon, domineering and controlling and as a result Felicity was crippled with insecurity and low self-esteem and was generally a bundle of nerves. From time to time her genes showed through and she could be haughty and arrogant, like her mother, but only ever with Max and their two daughters, never with outsiders.

He'd been christened Maxwell, after his grandfather, but had been known as Max all his life. He liked the name Max – it suited him – but Felicity insisted on calling him Maxwell.

"Max is so common, darling," she'd said.

'Common' was the biggest sin in Felicity's book. So it was that, like so many other men, his wife was the only one to call him by his full name.

Their two daughters Alexandra and Philippa suffered the same fate. From a young age they had called each other Alex and Pippa as had he, but despite this Felicity still insisted on using their formal names, which made them squirm with embarrassment in front of their friends. Now aged sixteen and eighteen and quite the little rebels, they frequently protested. But still Felicity persisted, causing many an unholy row.

Alex was in her first year at Cambridge and wanted to be a journalist. Pippa was a boarder at Benenden School and one week wanted to be an artist, the next a model.

Felicity was a wonderful mother but, when the girls

reached their teens, she couldn't understand how it had happened that her two charming little daughters had turned into these argumentative, rebellious teenagers. Max had tried to explain that they were simply growing up but poor Felicity just didn't get it. She was in a time warp and could be heard sighing regularly, at their hairstyles, clothes, music and just about everything else.

Both girls were thrilled when Max broke the news that they were only moving to Paris and not the Middle or Far East.

"Cool, Pops," Pippa had squealed, hugging him. "Now I'll be able to pop over with my friends at half term."

"That's great, Pops. Paris is much closer." Alex smiled. "Harry and I will be able to visit often." Harry was the latest squeeze.

Max tried to envisage Felicity's reaction to all these teenagers invading her space. She could barely cope with her own two, never mind all their high-spirited friends.

Felicity called her younger sister, Penelope (Penny to everyone else).

"Penelope, you won't believe where we're going. Not Dubai or Hong Kong – but Paris," she said, stifling a sob.

"Oh you lucky duck!" was her sister's reply, much to Felicity's surprise. "You always land on your feet. Imagine it! Afternoon tea in the Ritz every day and the fabulous designer shops of the Rue du Faubourg Saint-Honoré on your doorstep – not to mention all the chic parties that you're sure to be invited to." She sighed dramatically. "I'm green with envy."

This stopped Felicity somewhat in her tracks. "What about Dubai or Hong Kong? I was really looking forward to one of those."

"Can you imagine the toll the Dubai sun would take on your face, Felicity?" Penny took great care of her own face and body. "Seriously! Have you even considered that? And Hong Kong is very over now, you know, definitely old-hat. Consider yourself lucky, girl." She sighed again. "I wish Jeremy would whisk *me* off to Paris for a year. You wouldn't hear *me* complaining!"

Somewhat mollified, Felicity had to agree that she hadn't thought about the skin damage she'd incur in the hot desert sun. At thirty-nine, that was the last thing she needed. She had a typical English rose complexion and inspected her face regularly for signs of aging. So far, so good – she had great genes and had taken reasonable care of herself over the years – but she wasn't getting any younger and one could never be too careful.

"And just think, it means you'll be escaping from Georgina's clutches for a whole year, you lucky thing. God, I've just realised that means I'll have to cope with her on my own while you're away," Penny groaned.

"I know, I'm sorry, but you're much more able to deal with Mummy than I am. She still terrifies me. And we're just across the Channel, if you need me."

Felicity hadn't thought about the bonus of escaping from her mother's demands for a year. That put a new light on things.

Next she rang her cousin Gloria in Dubai, who burst into tears at the news that Felicity would not, after all, be joining her there.

"Oh, dear, how shall I ever stick this place without you, Felicity?" she'd cried. "It's so damn hot. I can't put my nose outside the door. As for our fellow-Brits – all nouveau-riche, my dear, not at all the class of people we're used to."

Well, Felicity thought, patting her mousy-blonde hair, so much for the fantastic life she raved about last time I spoke to her!

Next, she rang her old school-friend, Myrtle. Things were equally bad in Hong-Kong.

"I'm terribly disappointed that you're not coming out," she told Felicity, "but, honestly, you've had a lucky escape. Things have changed dreadfully here. Not the same at all. And Diane has turned out to be a prize bitch. We had a dreadful row and now we don't talk at all which, I needn't tell you, is very embarrassing when we meet at functions."

Phew! Felicity thought. I have had a lucky escape. Imagine being caught between those two! The more she heard, the more she was beginning to think that Paris wasn't so bad after all. It was at least within driving distance of London. She brightened up at the thought that they could quite easily pop back to London – every weekend if they wanted to.

If you enjoyed this chapter from
A Year Like No Other by Pauline Lawless
why not order the full book online
@ www.poolbeg.com